PARK AVENUE
PLAYER

PENELOPE WARD
VI KEELAND

This book is a work of fiction. All names, characters, locations, and incidents are products of the authors' imaginations. Any resemblance to actual persons, things, living or dead, locales, or events is entirely coincidental.

PARK AVENUE PLAYER
Editor: Jessica Royer Ocken
Proofreading by: Eda Price and Julie Deaton
Photographer: Hudson Taylor
Cover designer: Letitia Hasser, RBA designs
www.rbadesigns.com
Formatter: Elaine York, Allusion Graphics, LLC
www.allusiongraphics.com

PARK AVENUE
PLAYER

CHAPTER ONE

Elodie

Sometimes, I wished I was ugly. Maybe not giant-wart-on-your-nose, three-of-my-teeth-turned-black-and-those-are-the-only-ones-I-have, scar-running-down-my-cheek, thinning-haired-woman-comb-over ugly—because I do have to look at my own reflection every once in a while—but it would be nice to walk into a room and not get eye-fucked by every shiny-suit-wearing, stockbroker asshole in the bar.

Do I sound bitter? I'm sorry. But downtown stockbroker bars always get to me. Aren't brokers just used car salesmen in fancier suits? If they're so great about picking stocks, why aren't they home counting their thousand dollar bills earned from gold-laden investments, rather than selling advice to others?

I was minimally grateful that tonight's catch wasn't a stockbroker.

Speaking of which… My target had just noticed me. It took the leering pig a solid minute to work his way up to my face. At least this cheater looked exactly like the picture we'd been given: tall, fit, inky black hair slicked back, square jaw, imperious nose. *Squinty eyes.* One look, and I knew I'd walk the other way if this weren't a job.

My unsuspecting opponent for tonight was an attorney from the Upper West Side—an entertainment lawyer with a penchant for fucking starlets who hadn't yet learned to look beneath the three-thousand-dollar wool suit and check for a wolf.

Our non-refundable retainer was forty hours for this job. I'd bet money I could be done in a fraction of that time. *Hmmm...maybe I will bet.* Soren was always up for a little wager. Of course, it was a win-win for him since it motivated me to finish the job quickly, which, in turn, meant I was free to start another one sooner.

Only, I hoped there wouldn't be any more jobs like this one. I had an interview for a *real* job tomorrow night—one that didn't involve getting pawed on a daily basis—and with any luck, this crap would soon be over.

Sensing Larry the lawyer ogling me across the bar again, I fluttered my lashes as I looked up and shot him my best you're-a-big-rich-tough-guy-and-I'm-just-a-little-old-stupid-girl smile. Just for fun, I added a twirl of my naturally platinum hair as I hoisted my D cups in his direction. His flat-chested brunette wife had mentioned he favored blondes with big boobs.

You're in luck, Larry. Ring-a-ding-ding. Come and get it, you dog.

By the time I finished texting Soren about a wager, the courthouse conniver was already at my side.

"You look like you could use a drink," he said.

I bit my lip and cast my eyes down, feigning shyness for a few seconds, then raised my big baby blues to him. "I don't usually drink with strangers."

He offered me his hand. "Garrett Lopresti."

And so it begins. Lie number one, *Larry Mercer.*

Putting my hand in his, we shook. "Sienna Bancroft."

He didn't let go. "Now we're not strangers, are we, Sienna?"

I smiled, as if flattered by his attention. As if men being attracted to long legs and a great rack wasn't the bane of my existence. When my phone buzzed, I knew it was Soren. "Excuse me just a moment."

Soren: Leo just parked. He should be inside any minute.

Elodie: I'm feeling lucky. Or should I say *Larry* is feeling he might get lucky tonight with Sienna. What do you say to my wager?

Soren responded seconds later.

Soren: Pull this job off in four hours or less, and I'll double your fee.
Sorry, Larry/Garrett. You won't even be copping a cheap feel tonight. But what you will be getting...is exactly what you deserve.

I tossed my phone into my purse and tilted my head coyly. "Did you mention a drink?"

Sometimes I felt badly about what I did. There were two sides to every story, and we only got to hear one of them. On occasion, the women who hired us were nasty bitches. Although that still didn't give any man the right to cheat. Walk away, Prospective Mr. Cheater. There was always that option.

But then sometimes we got a bitchy wife coupled with a husband that took weeks to secure even the slightest hint of infidelity on camera. I might have felt a touch of guilt with those jobs. But *tonight* was definitely not one of those nights.

Thirty minutes after Garrett suggested we sit in a booth so we could have privacy, his wedding-ring-indented hand was on my knee under the table. *Such a slimeball.* Yet I still had to play along, knowing Leo wouldn't be able to catch the hand with his video camera on the other side of the bar.

I wanted his hand off my knee.

I wanted him away from me.

So I played dirty. The camera wouldn't be able to capture what I said.

He'd been staring at my lips the last few minutes like he was about to devour them. I hated when any of my jobs kissed me on the mouth—or kissed me at all, for that matter. So a little push in the right direction was definitely in order. The bastard opened the door, enabling me to kick him right through.

"So whatta you say we get out of here?" he suggested. "Go back to your place?"

I leaned in and lowered my voice. "Don't I get to sample the goods before I take them home?"

"Gorgeous, you can have anything you want. What do you have on your mind?"

"Well…" I pushed my arms tight against my sides, causing my breasts to pop up and out of my already low-cut blouse, showcasing a ridiculous amount of cleavage. His eyes followed. "My neck is very sensitive. I like the skin under my ear sucked."

"I can do that. But what are you going to *suck* for me in return?"

I swallowed the bile in my throat and forced a smile. "Whatever you want."

I didn't even have a chance to brace myself before he was on me. His mouth went straight for my neck. I let him get in a few disgusting kisses and sucks before I glanced over to where I knew Leo was positioned. He gave me a curt nod, and I shoved Larry back and lied through my teeth.

"That feels so good. Let's just go to my place. I'm *dying* to give you a good suck, too."

"Lead the way."

"Give me two minutes to go to the powder room so I can freshen up."

He took my hand and cupped it around his hard-on through his pants. "We'll be right here waiting for you. Hurry."

"Oh, I will."

My departure was always well planned in advance. A few days ago, I'd stopped by the bar and found an emergency exit at the end of the hallway that led to the bathroom. Since it was at the back of the building, I'd parked my car on the street behind the bar.

Pushing open the door, I strutted through and took a deep breath of fresh air. I was going to have to go home and shower after having that guy's lips on me. But for now, I was done. I texted as I walked to my car.

Elodie: Done. There's a sucker born every minute.

Soren responded quickly.

Soren: Are you referring to me because of our bet or Larry the lawyer?

Elodie: Both. Thanks for the extra cash. See you payday.

Bang!

Shit.

I closed my eyes. This was the last thing I needed. I was forty-five minutes early for my interview, but that wasn't enough time to deal with an accident. I put the car into park, being careful to leave it exactly in the position the accident had occurred, and got out. The front fender of my old Jeep Wrangler had a small dent and a few scratches, but the other car definitely bore the brunt of the damage. Its back tire was hissing and already halfway to flat. The rear wheel well had crumpled inward and pressed against the tire. The fancy-looking new Mercedes seemed to almost implode on impact.

"What the hell? You've got to be kidding me." The driver of the Mercedes got out of his car and joined me to look at the damage. He raked his hand through his hair. "Didn't you see me? I was backing into the spot."

Of course. I not only hit what was probably a hundred-thousand-dollar car, but the driver had to have the jawline of a Greek god. Figures he'd be gorgeous to match his ostentatious car. I disliked him instantly.

"I was there first. You started backing up *after* I'd already started pulling in."

"Already pulling in? I don't think so. You tried to slip in while I was already backing up to parallel park. No one was behind me when I started."

My hands flew to my hips. "Oh, yes, I was. You just didn't see me. I pulled up behind you and waited. When you didn't move after a minute, I even honked my horn. So I figured you were just double-parked, and I was clear to take the open spot. If you wouldn't have nailed the gas, you would've had time to see me and stop before you hit me."

His brows jumped up. "Hit *you*?" He pointed to his car. "I think it's pretty obvious who hit who by the damage."

I ignored him. "What, were you on the phone or something?"

He scowled. "I hope you have insurance."

"No. I drive around without insurance." I rolled my eyes. "Just because I don't drive a fancy car like you doesn't mean I'm a criminal."

Mr. Mercedes huffed. "I have an appointment to get to. Can we just exchange information and be on our way?"

I took out my phone and started to take pictures of the damage. "No. We need a police report."

"That'll take an hour or two, at least. We don't need a police report for such an obvious accident."

"Are you going to admit it was your fault to your insurance company? Because while *you* may be able to afford a rate hike, I can't."

"I'm not going to admit it was my fault, because it *wasn't* my fault."

"That's why we need a police report."

Mr. Mercedes grumbled something I couldn't make out and pulled his phone from his pocket. I assumed he was calling the police. But apparently, he wasn't. I listened as he barked at whomever was on the other end of the phone.

"Tell Addison I'm running late and to start without me."

No *hi* or *hello*. The man might be handsome and drive a nice car, but he was rude. He swiped to hang up without a goodbye, too.

My face apparently didn't hide my disdain.

The jerk looked at me. "What?"

"I hope that wasn't your wife. You weren't very polite."

He squinted at me. "I need to make another call. Why don't you make yourself useful and call the police in the meantime?"

What a dick. I walked around to the other side of my car to grab my registration and insurance information from the glove compartment. When I walked back to where Mr. *Rude* Mercedes stood barking into his phone again, his eyes were glued to my legs. I shook my head and dialed 9-1-1.

The operator answered. "9-1-1. What's the nature of your emergency?"

"Hi. I just had an accident on the corner of Park and 24th."

"Okay. Is anyone hurt and in need of medical treatment?"

I covered the phone and asked the other driver, "Are you hurt in any way? They're asking if we need medical treatment."

His response was curt. "*I'm fine.* Just tell them to hurry it up."

I returned to the operator. "No, thank you. We're both okay. Apparently the only things damaged are our cars and the other driver's *manners.*"

Mr. Mercedes scowled at me.

I scowled right back.

After I hung up, I held out my paperwork to him. "Why don't we exchange insurance information before the police come? I *also* have an important appointment to get to."

He grabbed papers from his own car and pulled his license from his wallet. I took a photo of Hollis LaCroix's ID. Naturally, he actually lived on Park Avenue—that went with the whole package. After snapping a shot of his insurance and registration, I noticed he was still examining my license when I finished.

"I can assure you it's real, if that's what you're thinking."

He took a photo of my license and held it out to me with my other paperwork. "Connecticut, huh? That explains a lot."

I snatched my stuff from Mr. Rude Hollis LaCroix. "How so?"

"You don't know how to parallel park."

My eyes narrowed. "I'll have you know, I'm a very good driver."

He tilted his head toward his car. "I have ten thousand dollars' worth of damage that says otherwise."

I shook my head. "You're an ass. You know that?"

I could've sworn I saw his lip twitch, like he enjoyed getting a rise out of me. Thankfully the police arrived so I didn't have to deal with him anymore. After talking to the officer and giving my version of the story, I went to sit in my car. The police then spoke to Hollis. My stomach growled while I watched the two men talk outside, so I grabbed the bag of junk food I'd bought to watch movies with Bree tomorrow night and munched on a box of Junior Mints. Eating the snack made it feel like I was in the audience watching a show—a show with one damn good-looking leading man.

Hollis really was handsome. Tall, broad shoulders, narrow waist, Coppertone tan, dark hair that was a little too long at the collar and didn't exactly match his immaculately tailored suit. But it was his bright green eyes and thick, dark eyelashes that were the showstoppers.

As if he felt me staring, he looked over at my car, and our eyes met. I didn't bother to turn away and pretend I hadn't been watching. *Screw him.* If he could check out my legs, I could look at his pretty-boy face. When he didn't stop staring, I flashed an overzealous and clearly phony full-tooth smile.

That time there was no mistaking the twitch, mostly because it was followed by a full smirk. Hollis looked away, turning to speak to the police officer again, and I felt like I'd won an unspoken staring contest. By the time they finished and the officer walked over to my car, I'd downed the entire box of Junior Mints.

"Alright, Ms. Atlier. This paper has your police report number on it. You can go online and get the actual report in about twenty-four to forty-eight hours, or stop down at the precinct and pick up a copy."

I took the paper. "Thank you. Did you put down that the accident wasn't my fault?"

"I listed the facts. It's up to insurance to assign the percentage of fault to each driver."

I sighed. "Okay. Thank you. Is there anything else? Because I have an appointment I really need to get to."

"No, ma'am. If your car is drivable, you're free to go. Mr. LaCroix has to wait for a tow."

"Okay. Great. Have a good day, officer."

"You, too. And be careful driving."

It felt odd to just pull away without saying anything to Hollis. So I waited a minute, until the cop got back into his car and drove off. Then I got out of my car and walked over to the Mercedes. Hollis was leaning against his trunk, playing with his phone.

"Umm...is there anything you need?" I asked. "A ride or anything?"

"I think you've done enough for the day. Thank you."

God, why did I even ask?

"Great." I offered an insincere, plastic smile. "Have a nice life."

CHAPTER
TWO

Hollis

Addison was going to kick my ass for being late. I'd asked her to sit in on the interviews as a favor, and wound up missing the entire first one. I looked at my watch. The second one was likely half over by now, too.

The elevator arrived at the fifteenth floor, and I walked through the double glass doors, tossing my briefcase on the reception desk. Everyone was gone for the day, but I heard voices coming from the conference room down the hall. I was already late, so stopping at the men's room couldn't make it any worse.

I yelled to let Addison know it was only me. "Addison, it's Hollis. I'll be there in a minute."

"Nice of you to show up!" she shouted. "Maybe you need to replace that gaudy Rolex you wear with a Timex."

I ignored her and went to the men's room. I'd had to take a piss for the better part of an hour while waiting for the damn tow truck. After washing up, I took off my jacket and headed to the interview. With the day I'd had, I really hoped the candidate was a good one. I needed help desperately.

Addison had pushed her chair back to look down the hall and saw me coming. She tapped her watch. "Had this thing for fifteen years. Paid only fifty bucks for it, if I remember correctly. Yet it miraculously manages to keep time."

"Sorry I'm late." I walked into the conference room and turned to offer an apology to the candidate sitting with her back to me. "Someone hit me while I was trying to pull into a parking spot."

The woman turned and started to speak. "That's funny... I—" She stopped mid-sentence, and I looked down to find out why.

You've gotta be freaking kidding me. I shook my head in disbelief. "You?"

Her smile fell just as quickly as mine. She closed her eyes and sighed. "Hello, Hollis."

Elodie.

No.

No fucking way.

I held my palms up. "Okay. I'm very sorry, but this is not going to work. I don't want to waste your time or mine. So, I suggest—"

"Are you serious? You're not even going to give me a chance because you think I caused an accident that was *your* fault?"

"Just the fact that you still believe you had no part in it shows you may be a bit delusional, Elodie. That's not a trait I'm looking for when it comes to this position."

Addison interrupted our squabbling. "Well, it's quite a coincidence that you two had an accident, *and* Elodie is one of your interviews today. But let's move on. Clearly, you're already too biased to make a fair decision on this, Hollis. I think you need to at least give Ms. Atlier a shot by allowing her to sit for this interview as planned and not judge her based on something that has nothing to do with the job."

I shut my eyes, letting out an exasperated breath. It had been a long day, and I didn't really have the energy to protest.

Let's just get this over with.

Rubbing my temples and feeling like a vein in my neck was about to pop, I said, "Fine." I took a seat and held out my hand toward Addison. "Show me her resume."

Addison handed me the sheet of paper, and I examined it. Elodie Atlier from Connecticut had been a nanny for two years, but that was a long time ago. After that, she had a pretty big gap in employment, and then she'd spent the last two years working for a private investigator.

"What exactly is it that you do for the private investigator?"

"Umm...a little of this and a little of that."

I huffed. "Enlightening. You sound very qualified."

She glared at me. "I was a nanny for twins for two years."

"Yes, and...what are you doing now? How does *a little of this* and *a little of that* at your current job make you qualified to take care of a child?"

18

"Well, I...multitask at work. And I have to...deal with a lot of different kinds of people. Those are both qualities of a good childcare provider."

My gut told me she was hiding something. "Give me an example of how you multitasked?"

She looked down. "Well, I...sometimes...assisted with surveillance and also helped out the photographer."

I tossed the paper aside. "So you helped *spy* on people...and what? Took selfies? Exactly how does your current job equate to relevant work experience, Ms. Atlier?" I couldn't help that I laughed a little at the end of that question.

"If you bothered to read further than my last position, you would see that my degree is actually in early childhood education, and I worked taking care of twins in high school."

"In high school. *Great.*" I let out a frustrated sigh. "I'm afraid you don't have the kind of background that would make you a suitable candidate to look after an eleven-year-old girl."

"I beg to differ. I think my most recent line of work prepares me just fine for this position."

Genuinely intrigued by her assertion, I tilted my head. "Oh, really? Tell me exactly how it relates, Ms. Atlier. Because for some reason, I feel like you're avoiding telling me *anything* you actually do at your current job."

Her face turned red. "My job has prepared me to handle almost anything. In my line of work, I've had to deal with all types of people. I've had to learn self-defense. If you want me to test that on you, I'd be happy to. And...it also has taught me how to remain calm under pressure. I think these are all attributes that would apply to the position at hand. Addison filled me in a little about Hailey. I'm also a good fit because I know a thing or two about troubled kids...because I *was* one."

My eyes bore into hers. "And that's supposed to make me feel more confident, that someone with a troubled past, who can't drive and who's spent the better part of the past few years working for a private investigator doing God knows what, is the right person for this job?"

She straightened in her seat. "I'll have you know that, yes, it takes one to know one. That's why I would absolutely be the best person to relate to a young girl who has family issues. I've dealt with my own share of those. Hailey's background sounds quite similar to mine. And do I have to remind you that my deficiency is in *parking*...not driving? I'm actually a damn good driver."

"Is this a job interview or a sparring match?" Addison interrupted. "Holy cannoli, you *both* are pieces of work."

Addison was right. This was ridiculous. I needed to put a stop to it. "With all due respect, Ms. Atlier, I think we need to end this right now."

Elodie's big eyes narrowed to slits. "You know what your problem is? You think just because you're rich and powerful you have the right to judge people."

"I absolutely think I have the right to judge people—this is an interview for a position, you know. That's what you do: *judge the candidates.*"

"That's not what I meant."

I stood. This was a waste of time from the beginning. "Thank you for coming, but you're not the best person for a nanny job, no matter how you try to spin it."

Her expression fell, the disappointment palpable. "Okay. Well, I'm not going to sit here and beg for a chance if you don't want to consider me." She turned to Addison. "The truth is, he made up his mind about me the second he saw my face."

"I'd have to agree with you," Addison said.

"Thanks for your support, Addison," I barked. "Maybe you should ask Elodie to find out if there are any openings doing *this* and *that* at her current employer."

"I think I'd quite enjoy a job somewhere else for a while. Maybe she and I can switch for a day. She'll want to blow her brains out here." Addison laughed. "Oh, come on, Hollis. In all seriousness, you're looking for Mary Poppins, and she doesn't exist. Why not give Elodie a shot?"

I was just about to consider that possibility for a millisecond when Elodie shot up from her seat and proclaimed, "Mary Poppins would poke your arrogant ass with her umbrella!"

And there goes any hope of giving her a shot.

Buh-bye, Elodie.

Nice knowing you.

I bent my head back in laughter. "And she wonders why she can't find a decent job."

"Goodbye, Hollis. It was a pleasure." Elodie marched toward the door. "I have better things to do than be mocked by someone blinded by his ego."

"Better things? Does that involve Junior Mints?" I teased.

Elodie flashed the iciest glare. Something about that made my dick twitch. Was I seriously getting aroused from fighting with this woman?

"Thank you for the opportunity, Addison," Elodie said before she took off down the hall.

My amused expression faded when I sat back down and turned to meet Addison's scowl. She threw her folder at me before storming away, leaving me alone in the conference room.

I swiveled in my chair, tapping the pen against the table. The high of that experience was wearing off. While I didn't think Elodie was right for the job, maybe I'd been too hard on her.

She'd definitely been hiding something, though, and whenever I got that feeling from a woman, it tended to put me on offense. Yet another thing I could thank damn Anna for.

CHAPTER THREE

Hollis – 14 years ago

"**Y**ou suck."

"I have cancer, dude."

I reached over and knocked the backward baseball cap off Adam's bald head. He'd buzzed his hair the other day after finding the first patch missing because of his treatments.

"Yeah. And if I found a magical pill to cure it tomorrow, you'd *still suck* at this game. So don't try to play the C card with me. You already have Anna fooled."

Adam wiggled his non-existent eyebrows. "I might pretend to pass out the next time I see her in the hallway, just so she can give me a little mouth to mouth."

I gave him a good shove. He fell over on the couch, but the game controller never left his hands.

"Keep your mitts off my girl." I pretended to be pissed, but of course I wasn't. Adam was only thirteen, and my girlfriend was almost seventeen. He had about as much chance with her as a blizzard in July in New

York. Plus, Adam and I were buds. He wouldn't do that to me, even if he'd had the strength. He just liked to bust chops.

And anyway, I couldn't blame him for noticing, Anna made little boys *and* their fathers turn their heads these days. It wasn't easy dating a hot girl.

"Let's play again. Double or nothing?"

"You already lost ten bucks I know you don't have. Not sure I want to wear out my fingers trying to win a twenty I'll never see."

"Chicken shit."

I shook my head and got up to hit the reset button. As I returned to the couch, Nurse Pam walked into the lounge.

"Hollis, your mom's nurse just called down. She's awake, and you need to get ready for school."

"Thanks, Pam. I'll head upstairs."

"Saved by your *mommy*," Adam said. "I was about to kick your ass in the rematch."

I walked toward the door. "Sure you were. I'll stop in later to show you how it's done again."

"Better yet, send your woman to show me how it's done instead."

I chuckled and went to the elevator. On the ride up to the ninth floor, I caught a glimpse of the time on the watch of the guy standing next to me. Six o'clock already. I couldn't even remember what time I'd wandered down to the pediatric wing. It had to have been about three. Adam seemed to be the only person with more trouble sleeping than I had lately, so I'd figured he'd be up playing video games in the pediatric oncology patient lounge like he usually was.

I'd found that hangout three years ago, the first time my mom was admitted overnight. She always insisted I go home, but I didn't like to leave her alone in case she needed anything—or in case anything changed with her health. On the nights I had trouble sleeping, I'd go hang out in the pediatric unit for a while—the place was stocked with snacks and video games. That's where I'd met Adam the first time. And Kyle. And Brenden. And over the years, a shitload of other teenagers that were too young for cancer. Hell, my *mother* was too young.

This was the third time I'd seen Adam back in for a long stay. I didn't like to bring up his illness because he'd once told me that us hanging out and playing video games made him feel normal. I didn't treat him differently because he was sick like most everyone else did. I'd done that to the kids I met at the beginning—letting them win at games, not arguing over who would go first, helping them do stuff they wanted to be left alone to struggle with on their own. I learned my lesson fast. Treating them like any other kid was what they wanted. Especially Adam—his mother handled him like glass, and I knew he hated it. He wasn't as fragile as she thought. But I also knew it wasn't good that he was back in the hospital again. It wasn't good for my mom either.

Some people liked to say *third time's the charm.* But in my experience, third rounds of chemo were anything but. Over the years, I'd lost two friends I'd met here to cancer—both after third rounds.

Mom was on her fourth this time.

She put down the book she'd been reading when I walked into her room. "There you are. I was beginning to get worried you fell asleep downstairs on the couch and would be late for school again."

"Nah. Just hanging out and kicking Adam's butt in Grand Theft Auto."

"Oh." Mom frowned. "Adam's back?"

"Yeah."

"I'm sorry to hear that."

I nodded and grabbed my backpack off the reclining chair that often doubled as my bed. "What do you have planned for today while I'm at school?"

Mom's frown tilted to a smile. We played this game every morning when she was in the hospital, making up stuff we were going to do that day.

"Well, I was thinking I'd cook up some fresh scones and roast some coffee to take over to Central Park and eat on a picnic blanket since it's so nice out," she said. "Then I'll go up to the Museum of Natural History for a few hours before taking in a matinee on Broadway, since it's Wednesday. After that, maybe I'll catch a flight up to Boston to have lobster for dinner. What about you?"

I leaned in and kissed my mom on the cheek. "I was thinking of acing my second-period chem test and then cutting out for the rest of the day to take Anna to the beach."

Mom's eyes narrowed. "The only made-up part of that better be about cutting classes, young man. I expect you to ace your chem test."

"Love you. I'll see you after the beach." I winked. "I mean school."

Anna didn't see me coming.

She hadn't told me she'd planned to meet me at the hospital this morning, but I knew it was her, even from behind. After the last month, I could identify that ass in a lineup. Anna Benson had been my friend since we were kids. Six months ago, things changed. I'd always loved her, but I'd never thought of her that way—until one night when we'd spent twelve hours in the ER with my mom. Anna had fallen asleep with her head on my shoulder, and when she woke up, she looked up at me and smiled. Those big brown eyes were the color of honey, and suddenly, I had a sweet tooth. It was like getting hit over the head with a two-by-four. How had I *not* thought of her that way before? I leaned in and kissed her right there in the germ-infested emergency room, and neither of us ever looked back.

I still loved her like I had when we were kids, but now I also got to see her naked. So I'd say things had changed for the better—a hell of a lot better.

Anna was busy flipping through a notebook with her back to the glass revolving door, so I tiptoed up behind her and kissed her exposed shoulder.

She slapped the book shut. "Kenny, is that you?"

I wrapped my arms around her and squeezed tight. "Cute. Very cute."

She turned to face me, hooking her arms around my neck. "I brought you breakfast and wrote the short story that's due today in English—you know, the one you completely forgot about."

English paper? "You're the best."

"How's your mom doing?"

"Better. Her white blood count has come up a little, and she got up and walked a bit last night. Her color looks better, too. She's not as gray. But the doc said it's going to take a while. This last round of chemo really kicked her immune system's ass."

Anna sighed. "Well, better is good. What can I do to help? Maybe I'll make her some cookies after school and stop by the library to pick her up some new books before I visit tonight."

"Actually, there is one thing you can do to help her."

"What?"

I pressed my forehead to hers and brushed the hair back from her face. "You can cut out after fourth period with me and go to the beach."

She laughed. "And how exactly will that help your mom?"

"Well, I've been stressed lately, and she can sense it. That, in turn, makes her stressed, and stress isn't good for her already weakened immune system. So a day at the beach, looking at you in that little bikini I like so much, would help me relax, which would make Mom relax, and help her immune system."

She narrowed her eyes. "You're so full of shit."

"No, really." My lip twitched at the corner, but somehow I managed to contain my smirk. "Basically, my mom's life depends on this."

Anna leaned in the little bit separating us and kissed my lips. "I'll cut out with you for a beach day, but only because I do think you've been stressed lately and could use a few hours of carefree time—*not* because I'm buying any of your crap."

I flashed an eager smile. "You're the best."

"But you're also going back for baseball practice after school while I go home and make Rose some cookies. After, you're going to pick me up to take me to the hospital to visit for a few hours tonight, and on the way over we *are* stopping at the library and getting her some new books."

"Deal." I brushed my lips with hers and spoke so my words vibrated against them. "By the way, I love it when you're all bossy."

"Well, that's good. You should probably get used to it."

CHAPTER FOUR

Elodie

After leaving my meeting with Hollis, my throat was parched. That had taken a lot of energy out of me— for nothing. Well, at least I'd tried. *A* for effort, Elodie. *F* for fucking up the whole thing with your temper.

I went in search of some water and ended up in a cafeteria off the lobby of the building. There was complimentary coffee in several urns, along with a couple of vending machines. Spotting a water cooler, I went to the other side of the room.

Just as I was grabbing a paper cup, I noticed a girl sitting down, the contents of her floral Jansport backpack strewn across the table. She was bouncing her legs up and down nervously.

"Hi." I smiled.

She placed her index finger over her mouth. "Shh."

I looked around. *Did she just shush me?*

"Why are we shushing?" I took a sip of water.

"I don't want anyone to notice me here."

"Why are you hiding?"

"Because I ditched my after-school program today and got myself into some trouble. And I'm not ready to get yelled at."

"Okay. Well...what did you do?"

She sighed. "After I walked out of school, I took the bus to Macy's. I got caught stealing lipstick from the MAC counter."

Ah. "You really shouldn't do that. But I'm sure you already know that. Why did you feel the need to steal it? Can't you ask someone to buy it for you?"

"It's not the money. I had the money. Had a big pile of cash in my pocket." She closed her eyes for a moment. "I don't even know why I did it, okay?"

God, it's like meeting my younger self.

"You steal for the thrill," I said matter-of-factly.

She blinked a few times. "Yeah. I...I think so."

I pulled up a seat next to her. "When I was your age, I did something similar—stole headbands and other hair accessories from Claire's at the mall. Got caught, too. I also had enough money to buy everything."

"Did you get in trouble?"

"Well, my dad had some issues of his own. I think that might have been one of the reasons I did it—acting out. But the store did call my mother. She obviously wasn't happy." I sighed. "How did things go down at Macy's? And what color did you choose?" I winked.

"It was Ruby Woo Retro Matte."

"Ah...bright red. Bold."

"Yeah." She smiled. "The lady who caught me didn't call the police. But when I told her I'd left the after-school program, she made me tell her where I went to school, and then she called the principal to tell him I was at Macy's. I took the bus back to school and then came here."

I finished off my water. "Okay, here's the thing... While sometimes it feels good to do something bad, it's only a fleeting satisfaction. You just end up wanting to do something else, and it never really satisfies the itch for very long. The next time you try something like that, you'll get into even bigger trouble. Eventually, these things will catch up with you, and the lady at the store won't be so nice. But I get it. Doesn't make it right, but I get why you did it."

"Thanks for not judging me." She stood up and wandered over to the vending machine. Wearing neon pink Chucks, she looked about ten or eleven. She tapped her foot as she thought about what to buy.

Turning to me, she asked, "You wanna share a Twix bar?"

My stomach growled. "Oh...no. Can't. I'm on a diet."

"What kind of diet? You don't look fat."

"Well, thank you. I had candy already today, and when I'm not cheating on my diet, I try to eat mostly protein. It's called Keto."

Her eyes went wide and she covered her mouth. "Oh my God. *Keto*? With a K? Nooo!"

I tilted my head in confusion. "Yes, why?"

"Do you have Keto crotch?"

"What?"

"Does your coochie smell like bacon?"

My mouth fell open. "Wha...no! What are you talking about?"

"I heard about it on the news. I didn't even know what Keto was. But I *do* know Keto crotch. My friends in school...we tease each other about it. Like, 'Haha, you have Keto crotch'."

"Well, I most definitely do *not* have Keto crotch. I think that's a myth anyway."

"Well, that's good." She giggled. "Because that would stink."

"Literally."

"Yeah." She snorted.

What has this conversation turned into?

She opened the wrapper and took a bite of her candy bar. "You're really pretty."

Taken aback by the sweet comment, I said, "Thank you. So are you."

"What's your name?"

"Elodie. And you are?"

"Hailey."

Hailey.

Hailey?

Oh shit. Hailey.

I froze. Holy crap. How had I not made the connection?

"Your uncle doesn't know you're down here?"

"No. Not yet. When there isn't someone to watch me, I sometimes come here and hang out when the after-school program gets out anyway. But he might not know I skipped today. Please don't tell him...in case the principal never called. If the principal told him, I'm toast."

"Uh...okay."

"So...you know my uncle? Do you work here?"

"No. I mean... No, I don't work here. But I *do* know him."

"Sorry to hear that," she joked. "Just kidding."

"I hadn't put two and two together. I knew he had a niece, and I knew your name was Hailey. Just didn't connect the dots until now."

"So, if you don't work here, how do you know my uncle Hollis?"

I wasn't sure whether to admit I'd interviewed to be her nanny. I didn't want to badmouth Hollis in front of her. And there was really no good way to tell that story without it reflecting negatively on him.

"Your uncle and I... We got into a little fender-bender earlier. I was here handling some business."

"You messed up his precious car?"

I cringed. "I did."

"You might be in more trouble than me. Did he yell at you?"

"Not really." *Well, that certainly isn't the truth.*

She took another bite of her bar. "I know how to get him off your case."

"How?"

"Ask him to buy you maxi pads. Shuts him right up."

I chuckled. "Okay, probably won't be doing that, but thanks for the tip." I took her in and pondered what she'd just said. "Wow...aren't you...a little young to have your..."

"I'm eleven. And I have it...so no, I'm not."

Jesus. It hit me just how much of a handful Hollis had inherited. I could only imagine how overwhelming it must have been for him to have to suddenly take on this responsibility. From what Addison told me, he was doing the best he could for his niece, but he'd had to figure things out as he went along. It had understandably been a struggle, thus the need for a nanny.

"You sure you don't want my second Twix?" she asked. "They give you two bars so you can share one."

Just as I was about to open my mouth, a deep voice from behind me answered, "If they were Junior Mints, she'd gobble them up like a Hoover."

I jumped and flipped around, my heart pounding. Hollis had entered the cafeteria. It felt like a teacher walking in on two kids gossiping, for some reason. His gorgeous eyes were piercing.

"How long were you standing there listening?" I asked.

"Since Keto crotch."

Great. Just great. "I was just getting water. I didn't know she was your—"

He cut me off, turning to Hailey. "You want to tell me why you skipped the after-school program and robbed a makeup counter today?"

"The principal called you?"

"Yes."

"Okay...I know it doesn't make sense. But I think Elodie helped me figure out why I did it."

He looked over at me and raised his brow. "Oh, she did, did she?"

"Yes. And I won't do it again. I promise."

"I'm supposed to believe that?"

"I'm not like my dad. If I say something, I mean it."

The look on Hollis's face transformed from anger to something else. Sadness? Understanding, maybe?

As much as I was curious to stay and observe their dynamic, it wasn't my place.

"I'll let you two talk." I turned to her. "Hailey, it was really nice meeting you."

"You too, KC." She winked.

It took me a moment to realize it was an acronym. *Keto Crotch.*

"Uncle Hollsy, don't be mad at Elodie for denting your car. She didn't mean it."

"Wise girl. You should listen to her, *Hollsy.*" I winked before sauntering out of there.

CHAPTER FIVE

Elodie

Soren was screwing the new secretary. He sat in his high-back leather executive chair, hands clasped behind his head with his feet propped up on his massive dark wood desk. And Bambi (yes, she claimed that was the name given to her at birth) was straddling him and giggling.

They hadn't heard me come in, too busy feeling each other up.

I plopped my butt down on the visitor chair. "Classy. Can I watch?"

Soren chuckled at the way Bambi jumped out of his lap. She apologized as she scurried back to her desk.

I dug a file from my oversized purse and attempted to save a nail that had chipped on the drive over to the office. "You know, that could have been a client instead of me."

"It's not like we run a tea shop. Women are coming in here because their husbands are fucking around. Bet some of them would like to watch me stick it to Bambi."

"You're a pig. I have no idea why I even work for you."

"Because I overpay you." He took his boots off the desk, and they clanked meeting the floor. "And I put up with you being a bitch. Now that I think about it, I'm not sure how I work with *you*."

I smiled. "You're going to miss me when I'm gone, aren't you?"

"You got the job? The one watching the kid for the big shot?"

I sighed. "No."

"Why not?"

"There was a small incident."

Soren lifted his coffee mug to his mouth. "What'd you do? Spill something on him or tell him off?"

"Neither. Well, not really."

"So then why are you sitting across from me and not in some hurdy-turdy, fancy penthouse?"

"I got into a little accident."

"Another one? What is that now? The third one in the last eighteen months? Your insurance must be a damn fortune."

"Parallel parking is impossible. Though, this time I wasn't even backing in. I just don't get why they can't make the spots bigger on the street so people can easily pull in."

"Because real estate is almost two grand a square foot here, sweetheart."

"I might have to start taking public transportation."

"Been telling you that since the day you started here. No one drives. Learn the subway system already."

I sighed.

Soren set his empty coffee mug on the desk and clasped his hands behind his head again, leaning back in his chair. "What the hell does your accident have to do with you not getting the job you wanted? Were you late or missed the appointment or something?"

"Oh. I had an accident parking down the block from where my interview was. Turns out the driver, *who wouldn't admit the accident was his fault*, was actually the guy I was supposed to interview with."

Soren threw his head back in a fit of laughter. He actually snorted from laughing so hard.

"I'm glad you find my disaster of a life so amusing."

"You're one hot mess who's lucky she's hot. You're either hitting something, spilling something, or tearing apart some schlep's life. Your brother would kick your ass for the shit you do. Hell, he'd kick both our asses for the shit I let you do. In fact, the only thing he'd approve of is that I overpay you."

Soren was an ex-marine, ex-cop, and all around badass. He'd been my older brother's sergeant in the corps. He also let me pick and choose the jobs I wanted, make my own schedule, and he actually *did* overpay me—three of my favorite qualities in a man.

After my last job with Larry the lawyer, I had hoped to be done working for Soren. Not that I didn't appreciate him giving me a job when I'd quit the last one without a dime to my name and showed up at his office—because I did. But I needed to get a job on my own. Someone else had been helping me for the better part of twenty-five years. It was time, although apparently not today after all.

"So what's on the agenda for this week?" I asked.

Soren put on a pair of reading glasses that sat at the tip of his nose. They detracted from his coolness negligibly. "Got another cheater job for you, if you're up for it. Wife will be here at five, so I need you to stick around."

"Me? Stick around?"

It was rare that I spoke to the wives. Women weren't generally fond of me to begin with. And Soren felt that a woman already scorned didn't need the woman about to seduce her husband shoved in her face.

"This one asked specifically for you. Said she was referred by a friend of a friend. Of course, she wouldn't tell me who. Not that it matters as long as her check clears."

I should have worn a less lacy bra today. Or skipped lunch.

My meatball parm hero had dripped sauce onto my white blouse. Soren had bellowed unexpectedly as I attempted to remove the stain by pouring a bit of seltzer on the spot, causing me to startle and spill the full bottle all over myself. Now I had a giant red stain, a soaked blouse, and one pert nipple visible through the sheer, damp fabric of my bra and shirt.

"Your five o'clock appointment is here," Bambi announced through the intercom.

I sat in one of the guest chairs on the other side of Soren's desk as he gave me the once-over. He shook his head and looked like he was about to *tsk*.

"What? It's your fault I look like this."

"My fault? In the two years you've worked here, you've never left this office after a meal without wearing it. It's a good thing you have great tits. Most men will overlook a stain or two for a rack like yours."

"So stop looking at me like that. Overlook the stain like all the other assholes will."

Soren grumbled and pushed the intercom button. "Show Ms. Brady in, please."

Soren's divorce-assistance private investigation services, where we gathered evidence that serial cheaters were just that—*cheaters*, was one of the more popular services he offered. But the client seldom wanted to meet the woman seducing her husband, so I was curious to see what set this one apart from the others.

They all came to tell us about their lying, cheating, asshole husbands—yet they were *always* all done up for the occasion. The women with reasons to come here had bruised egos, cracked hearts, and fissures in their faith in the male gender, but they stood tall as they told their stories. Getting all dolled up was part of the untold story they wanted to tell us.

It isn't my fault.

My husband didn't cheat because I gained an extra forty pounds, greeted him wearing stained sweatpants every day when he came home from work, and hadn't given him a blow job in ten years.

He cheated because he's an asshole with a character flaw.

The thing is...most of the wives probably *did* let themselves go a little—got comfortable, stopped spending time on themselves because they were taking care of others. But none of that should matter. These women didn't need to prove anything. Just being here, I already knew it didn't matter if they met their man at the door decked out in a lacy negligee and dropped to their knees. Because it wasn't the faithful partner's fault. No matter what. It was the cheater's.

I should fucking know.

Caroline Brady was petite. Dressed in a conservative pantsuit that covered most of her thin frame, she looked more like a banker than a scorned woman. Her mousy brown hair was thick and straight, cut in a blunt bob with heavy bangs. Oversized dark sunglasses covered half her face. She looked like she was trying to hide eyes that were more than likely swollen from countless hours of crying over her piece-of-shit husband.

Soren stood and introduced himself, then looked to me.

I softened my normally bitchy attitude and extended my hand. "I'm Elodie. It's nice to meet you, Ms. Brady."

After she shook my hand, she stared down her nose at me for a solid thirty seconds. I stood my ground and stared right back. I could see her judging me, even hidden behind her glasses.

Soren finally intervened in our stare off. "Why don't you have a seat?"

With her eyes shielded, she continued to gape at me for a few heartbeats, and then finally sat.

"What brings you here today, Ms. Brady?"

Her voice was cold. "I want *her* to sleep with my asshole husband."

Soren held up his hands. "Whoa. Hang on a minute. That's not what we do here. I'm afraid you've been misinformed."

I glared at her. "I'm not a whore."

She pursed her lips, but she didn't have to say a word. Her face said it all.

I stood. "You know what, Soren? I'm actually not going to be able to do Ms. Brady's job anyway."

The one thing I knew about Soren was that he cared about me more than any retainer.

He nodded. "No problem, babe. Why don't you head out, and we'll talk tomorrow. Got plenty of other work for you to do."

"Thanks." I smiled and didn't give Caroline Brady the satisfaction of a last glance on my way out.

I was deep in thought as I drove toward the Whitestone Bridge. There was a time when I'd actually gotten off on the work I did for Soren. My own messed-up relationship had taken such a toll on me that I needed a few years of screwing asshole men over. Every time Leo snapped the camera, I envisioned it was me getting the proof and screwing over my ex, Tobias. Oddly, setting up cheaters for their wives was cathartic for me—and a hell of a lot cheaper than a therapist.

At the last second, right before turning onto the bridge to go home, I made a rash decision. The horns blaring as I cut across two lanes of traffic to evade the entrance ramp showed just how last minute my decision had been.

I was done working for Soren, at least in the capacity that I was currently employed. When I'd first started working for him, he had wanted me to do computer work, anyway. I was certain there were enough other things that needed to be done to keep me busy. But before I took that path, before I sat down and talked to Soren, I needed to give what I really wanted one last try.

Pulling an illegal U-turn, I headed back uptown—back toward Hollis LaCroix's office. It was late; he might not be there anymore. But I also had a picture of his driver's license in my cell phone, and I wasn't above using it.

CHAPTER SIX

Elodie

Groveling wasn't my thing.

But groveling to a good-looking guy like Hollis *really* made me uncomfortable.

Though I wanted the damn job.

I *really* wanted the job. Especially after I'd met Hailey and realized we could actually relate to each other. So if crawling with my tail between my legs was what it took, then today I'd be a mouse instead of the cat.

Standing in front of the penthouse at the address I'd gotten from his license, I lifted my hand to knock, then lowered it.

God, why does he have to be so damn good looking? Tall, confident, bone structure that would make a sculptor weep—he reminded me of all the men I loved to hate. I didn't want to find him attractive.

I stood tall and gave the door a good, firm knock. From the outside, I looked like the picture of confidence, but inside I squirmed and hoped he wasn't home.

No such luck.

The door opened, and Hollis immediately frowned.

I attempted to start off on the right foot. "I should have apologized the other day. I came to rectify that. The accident was all my fault."

Silence fell between us. Hollis's face was unreadable as he stared at me. I knew having to get your car repaired was annoying, but it wasn't like I'd killed a kitten or anything. Unfortunately, the silence only gave me another opportunity to soak up the good looks of the man standing before me. And it pissed me off that he wore casual clothing even better than the expensive suit he'd had on the other day.

"Can you really even hold the fact that I'm not a great parker against me? Aren't certain classes of people protected by federal employment law or something?"

Hollis perked one brow. "Not sure bad drivers fit into the constitutionally protected classes like race, sex, and religious preference."

I waved my hand. "Whatever. And for the record, I'm not a bad driver. I'm just a bad parker."

Hollis squinted. I got the feeling he was gauging my sincerity, trying to decide what to make of my showing up. He wasn't the typical guy I ran across; batting my eyelashes didn't gain me entrance to wherever I desired to go. But I stood my ground while he assessed away, and I maintained eye contact. I'd screwed up, and I would own up to it.

Eventually he stepped aside. "Come on in."

A few steps over the threshold, a loud voice called out from somewhere within the apartment. The sound made me jump.

"Anna's home!" *Squawk!* "Anna's home!" *Squawk!* "Anna's home!"

Hollis dropped his head and looked down. "Ignore that. It's my bird."

"That was a bird?"

As if he understood what I'd asked and wanted to provide confirmation, the voice called out again. "Anna's home!" *Squawk!* "Anna's home!" *Squawk!* "Anna's home!" Only this time the bird punctuated his statement with the sound of rapidly flapping wings, which validated that he was, indeed, a bird.

Hollis nodded his head toward the inner sanctum of his apartment. "Come inside. If he doesn't get to see you, he'll never shut the hell up."

I followed Hollis through the marble foyer and into the sleek stainless steel kitchen. His apartment was incredible, with a sunken living room open to the kitchen and floor-to-ceiling, sweeping views of Central Park—though the view was partially obstructed by a large, white cage that stood next to those windows, housing the biggest, most exotic-looking bird I'd ever seen.

The thing was gorgeous. Slate-black body, dark gray beak, long black tail, a full mane of proud feathers forming a Mohawk on the top of his head, and crimson coloring on both his cheeks, which were devoid of any feathers. The thing had to be two feet tall.

I walked through the apartment and over to the cage. "Wow. I've never seen a bird like this. What kind is he?"

"The pain-in-the-ass kind."

"What's his name?"

"Huey."

"Is he named after Huey Lewis, the singer?"

"No. But that's not a bad guess. He's named after Hugh Jackman."

I chuckled. "Fan of Wolverine?"

Hollis walked over and stood beside me. "Not a chance. He belonged to my ex. He's an Australian black palm cockatoo. She rescued injured and endangered birds and thought he should be named after someone from Australia."

The bird squawked again, making me smile. "He's beautiful. I'm sorry I'm not Anna."

"I'm not," Hollis grumbled before turning around and walking back to the kitchen. He opened the refrigerator and called to me, "Can I get you something to drink?"

Hmm. His manners were a hell of a lot nicer at home. "No. I'm good. Thank you." I walked back to the kitchen to join him.

He took a water bottle from the fridge, unscrewed the cap, and leaned against the kitchen counter. Tilting it in my direction before he brought it to his lips, he said, "The accident wasn't all your fault."

"What do you mean?"

Hollis drank from his water bottle, watching me over it. "The office building has a ton of cameras inside and out. This morning I went down to security and asked them to replay the footage from the time of our accident. You did what you said. You waited a minute and then honked your horn to see if I had been waiting to take the spot."

"I told you that."

48

"Yes, but I didn't believe you. I was on the phone and didn't hear you."

My eyes widened. "So you *were* on the phone and not paying attention, yet you made me feel like it was my fault. I knew it!"

He squinted. "Why did you come here today saying it was your fault, if you knew it wasn't?"

"Truth?"

"No, lie to me."

I rolled my eyes. "Because I want the job."

"Why?"

"Because I like to eat."

"You aren't going hungry. You have a job. If I remember correctly, one where you do a lot of *this* and *that*."

I sighed. Hollis wasn't an idiot. He'd known something was fishy during the interview. I made a spur-of-the-moment decision to come clean. I had nothing to lose at this point.

"I don't do much admin work at my current job. I use my looks to assist the private investigators in surveillance."

"Go on." He folded his arms across his chest. "I can't wait to hear this."

"Well, the firm I work for provides assistance in divorce cases—tailing spouses and taking photos of incriminating situations, usually evidence of them cheating. Sometimes it's difficult to get the evidence, because once the divorce starts, the soon-to-be alimony-paying cheater becomes more discreet."

"Okay..."

"One of my jobs is to bait the cheaters. Show up in a bar, flirt a little...then once they take the bait, our photographer snaps a few photos, and I pretend I need to go to the ladies' room. Then I slip out the back door."

Hollis's eyes roamed my face. "Do they always take the bait?"

"Are you doubting my capabilities?"

His lip twitched. "How exactly does one get into such a profession?"

I sighed. "Soren, the guy that owns the agency, was in the military with my brother."

Hollis scratched his chin. Today he had a five o'clock shadow, and the look really worked for him. "Do you enjoy doing this job?"

The right answer should probably have been no—let him think I did it for a paycheck. But I'd already aired half my dirty laundry; I might as well throw it all out there.

"I did at the beginning. I took the job right after my own divorce. I was married for nine months to a professor I met in college. Long story short, I walked in on him with a student. It doesn't take a psychologist to figure out what made me enjoy the job at the beginning."

"What about now? You said you enjoyed it at the beginning. Does that mean you don't anymore?"

I shook my head. "I want to move on. It's difficult to do that when you're reminded every day of all the reasons you aren't happy to begin with."

Hollis stared at me for a long time. "Thank you for being honest with me." He set his water bottle down on the kitchen counter and put his hands on his hips. "So that's why you're here, then? A last-ditch effort to convince me to hire you for the job? Not an overwhelming need to apologize for the accident being your fault?"

"The truth?"

"Let's keep giving that a shot, yes."

"I still didn't think the accident was my fault when I decided to come today. I wouldn't be here if it weren't for the job."

Hollis's lip twitched again. "Previous occupation aside, Addison told me she'd asked you about your driving history. Ours wasn't your first fender bender. I'm sure you can imagine why I'd have concerns about you taking care of Hailey. At times, you might need to drive her places."

My shoulders slumped. He was right. I couldn't even park in front of his building. Why would he trust me to take care of his niece? And he didn't know about all my other accidents. Yet I wasn't ready to give up. Working as a nanny might not seem like a life-changing event to most people, but it was what I needed. My life needed to start going in the right direction. I wanted to *start* my life again. It had been a long time since I'd wanted something for myself that wasn't destructive. And I really felt like maybe I'd connected with Hailey.

"I'll work for two weeks for free. If you don't feel like I'm competent, or if I have another fender bender, then don't hire me after the two weeks are over."

Hollis did that staring-at-me thing again. He seemed lost in thought. I assumed he was tossing around my offer, debating whether I was worth the hassle, but apparently his mind was somewhere else.

"Have we ever met before yesterday?"

My brows drew down. "I don't think so."

He scratched his chin. After another long bout of contemplation, he pushed off the kitchen counter and extended his hand. "Let me think about it and talk to Hailey."

"Really?"

"No promises."

I'd just parked in front of my little rental house in Connecticut when my cell started to ring. I dug it out of my messy bag and checked the caller ID.

"Hello?"

"As far as I'm concerned, if you aren't five minutes early, you're late. I hate it when people keep me waiting."

Hollis. The man really needed to learn how to talk on the phone.

"Ummm... Who's this?"

"Don't screw with me. Do you want the job or not?"

I inwardly fist pumped and jumped in the air. "Yes. Yes, I think I do."

"When can you start?"

"How about Monday?"

"Monday. Seven o'clock."

I smiled. "I'll see you at five to seven."

Even though Hollis had said he'd think about it, I hadn't left his place feeling too confident. I certainly hadn't expected a call barely an hour after I walked out his door. But I was thrilled he'd changed his mind. I tapped my steering wheel in amazement.

"And I can't wait to get to know Hailey better."

A little voice inside of me, one I refused to answer, added, "*And you, Hollis LaCroix.*"

CHAPTER SEVEN

Elodie

"I got the job!" I held up a bottle of Dom Perignon when Bree opened the door, handing it off to her as I helped myself inside her house.

She studied the label. "Wow. Must pay well if you're splurging for the good stuff."

"Nah. Someone from the college sent it to Tobias as a wedding gift when we got married. I put it aside to have as something special on our one-year anniversary. When I packed his stuff, I gave him the figurines someone else had sent us. You know, since he hated shit like that. I only kept the stuff I thought he would've really enjoyed. I forgot I even had it until now."

Bree smiled. "Good call. He loves pretentious crap like this. That'll make it taste extra delicious for us."

I slipped off my shoes and plopped down on the couch, bringing my legs up under me. "I hope you can open it. Last time I tried, I wound up splitting the cork into pieces and digging them out with a fork. I had to spit out cork bits after every sip."

Her response was a loud pop a few seconds later. She held the cork up for inspection, still very much intact, between her thumb and forefinger, and coughed. "I'm not supposed to have any. But I'll make an exception for your celebration."

Bree was actually my ex-husband's stepsister. A few months before Tobias and I broke up, she'd moved back to the little town in Connecticut where we lived, to be closer to her family. Tobias hadn't had much contact with her before that, and I'd only met her once at a wake for one of their cousins. But the two of us hit it off immediately. We'd become fast friends, and when I'd caught Tobias sleeping with one of his students and kicked him out, she was my biggest supporter.

One night, after a few glasses of wine, she'd admitted she never liked her stepbrother much. The best thing I'd gotten out of my short-lived marriage and subsequent divorce was Bree.

A few months ago, when the lease to her apartment was up, the cottage next door to me happened to become available for rent. Since she'd moved, I pretty much saw her every day. She'd become the sister I never had. And it allowed me to keep an eye on her health. Bree had moved back home to be near her father because she has lymphangioleiomyomatosis, a horrible lung disease with a sickening short-term survival rate. Only fifty-five percent of those afflicted lived five years. Twenty percent made it ten years. But you'd never know it from Bree's attitude.

She untangled the tubing attached to the oxygen machine she spent her days tethered to and walked over to the couch to pass me a wine glass. "Champagne flutes are for amateurs. Wine glasses hold more." She clinked her glass to mine, and we both drank.

"So...tell me...about the job?"

"Oh my goodness...well, where do I start? I'll be taking care of an eleven-year-old girl, who I happened to meet accidentally when I was leaving his office that first day. She reminds me so much of myself when I was a kid. I really think I have a lot of insight to offer her."

"That's great. I'm excited it worked out."

I gulped some more champagne and pointed to her. "I have you to thank for that. If you hadn't read that classified ad, I'd be getting mauled by Mrs. Brady's husband tomorrow."

"Who?"

"One of Soren's clients."

"Oh. Well, I'm thrilled you'll be working in the field you went to school for. But I'm even more thrilled you won't be working that crazy job anymore."

I sighed. "You know, I feel like everything works out for a reason. That job might not have been ideal, but it paid well and gave me a place to blow off the steam I needed to after everything happened with Tobias. Although it was also a constant reminder of all the reasons there are to hate men, and it probably wouldn't be a healthy profession to stay in if I'm ever going to move on."

"I couldn't agree more." Bree smiled. "I've been telling you to quit that job for a year."

"Yeah. I guess I just needed some time."

I drank more champagne and decided to be honest with my friend about another thing that might have caused my sudden change of heart. I felt a little sheepish mentioning a man to Bree. I knew it was silly. She'd never given me reason to feel that way. Just the opposite, in fact. Bree had encouraged me to get back into the dating world, almost before the ink was dry on the divorce papers from her stepbrother.

I took a deep breath and pushed off the weird feeling I had. "So, also, the guy I'll be working for is kind of gorgeous."

Bree had been mid-sip and started to cough. Lately, she spent half the day coughing because of the progression of her disease. But this time, my admission had caught her off guard.

"Shit." I grabbed the wine glass from her and patted her back as her face reddened. "Are you okay?"

She held her hand to her chest and tried to take a few deep breaths. "I'm fine," she said, straining to get out the words.

After a few minutes of residual coughs and sputtering, the color in her face started to return to normal.

"I'm so sorry. I shouldn't have said that. I know you're not his biggest fan, but Tobias is your brother. I'm an ass."

"First of all, *step*brother. And second of all, don't be crazy. I'm…happy to hear you met someone. I just didn't expect you to say that."

"Are you sure? I understand if it might be weird for you."

She nodded. "I'm positive."

"Okay. Well, it's not like he's interested, anyway. I didn't exactly make a good first impression. And I'm not ready to start dating again either. But it felt good to feel a little spark from my blackened heart. Like maybe it isn't dead after all."

Bree got up to grab the champagne in the kitchen. Her steps were slow, but I knew she didn't like me jumping in and taking care of things for her. I stayed seated, even though it wasn't easy to watch her struggle. She walked back to the living room, winded.

Refilling my glass she said, "It takes a while after we get hurt to feel ready. And trust me, you're not a proper judge of the first impression you make on men. I'm sure his impression was *today must be my lucky day*."

"You know what's funny? I think one of the reasons I found myself attracted to him was because he *didn't* seem bowled over by my looks."

Bree smiled. "You like a challenge."

I sipped. "I like honesty. And beauty is the biggest lie of them all. People look at you, see the outside, and assume the inside is a match. But a mirror doesn't show who you are."

Bree sighed. "God. My asshole-very-handsome stepbrother really burned you badly."

"My uncle thinks you're hot."

I stopped mid-braid, with a handful of Hailey's hair in each hand. "He told you that?"

She shook her head. "I overheard him on the computer."

"What do you mean you overheard him on the computer?"

"He installed this program on my cell phone so he can listen to my phone calls. He thinks I don't know.

But I do. So one night I swiped his phone and installed the same thing on his. When I'm bored, I listen to his calls."

I had soooo many questions. *Why would you do that? Why didn't you just speak to him? Do you know that two wrongs don't make a right?* But yet, I led with...

"Who was he talking to when he said I was hot?"

"His friend Lucas. He's like...seven feet tall. He has to duck going through doorways."

Let's not get off track here. "What else did he say about me?"

"He said you were a...brasif." She shrugged. "Whatever that is."

"Abrasive?"

"Oh, maybe that's what he said. What does *abrasive* mean?"

"It's sort of someone who gets on your nerves."

She smiled. "Uncle Hollis is abrasive for me then."

I chuckled. *Yeah, he's abrasive to me, too.*

But I had to back up. Returning to braiding, I tried to set the right example. "You know, Hailey, when you found out your uncle had put something on your phone to monitor your calls, you should have sat him down and spoken to him about it."

"*Sat Hollis down*? You have met him, right?"

I guessed she had a point. "You know, your uncle comes off as sort of...difficult...at times. But he can be reasonable, too. Look at him and me—we didn't meet under the best of circumstances, and I never thought he'd give me a shot after that. Yet here I am. I came back to talk to him, and then he thought about it and changed his mind about hiring me."

I tied a rubber band around the bottom of the second French braid I'd made in Hailey's hair, and she turned to face me.

"Uncle Hollis hired you because of tampons."

"Ummm...come again?"

"After we met in the cafeteria, I asked Uncle Hollis if you were one of the people interviewing for the nanny job. He said yes, but that you weren't qualified. The next day, he had some man come to the house from a nanny agency—a *guy* nanny. I heard Uncle Hollis saying how much great experience he had, and it sounded like he was going to hire him. So he called me out from my room to meet the dweeb and asked if I had any questions for him. I asked if he could show me how to put a tampon in."

My hand flew to my mouth to cover my smile. "What did the guy from the agency say?"

"He said he would find some appropriate YouTube instructional videos that I could watch. I looked at Uncle Hollis and said, 'Elodie has an *actual* vagina'."

Oh my God. This girl was like looking in the mirror fifteen years ago. "What happened after that?"

She shrugged. "The guy left five minutes later, and my uncle sucked back that golden stuff he usually drinks from a fancy glass after a long day."

I bet he did.

"Anyway," Hailey continued, "you were hired because of tampons, not because Uncle Hollis is reasonable."

It dawned on me that she'd mentioned maxi pads the other day and now wielded a tampon like a weapon against her uncle, which meant she might actually have some feminine-product questions that were the source of her anger.

"Does your uncle buy your supplies for you when you get your period?"

She made a face and nodded.

"You're not...using tampons, are you?" She wasn't old enough for that.

"No, but can I use them? The other stuff is like wearing a diaper."

"Can you show me what he buys you?"

Hailey led me into the bathroom attached to her room and opened the cabinet beneath the sink. She pulled out a package of something more appropriate for someone who was incontinent, rather than having her period.

"You're too young for tampons. But I think we can do a lot better than these things. They must be uncomfortable. And you need wings. I'll tell you what. After school today, we'll take a trip to CVS and do a little shopping."

"Okay."

"Why don't you go get dressed so you're not late for school?"

"I don't mind being late."

I laughed. "I'm sure you don't. But your uncle doesn't like lateness, and it's your last week of school before summer break, so I think we can hack making it on time for five more days."

"Fine." She didn't sound happy, but went to get dressed, nonetheless. At her bedroom door, she turned back. "Elodie?"

"Yeah?"

"I'm glad he hired you."

Warmth spread through my chest. "Me, too, Hailey. Me, too."

CHAPTER
EIGHT

Hollis

"**A**nna's home!" *Squawk!* "Anna's home!" *Squawk!* "Anna's home!"

Just once, I wanted to come home to a different fucking greeting.

I tossed my suit jacket on the round table near the front door and walked into the kitchen. The apartment smelled damn good. "Where did you order from?"

"Hello, Hollis." Elodie flashed me an obviously fake smile. "Did anyone ever tell you it's customary to greet someone before you start barking at them?"

"Did anyone ever tell you you're a pain in the ass?"

"They have, actually."

I waited for her to answer my question about ordering in, but of course, she didn't. *Because she's a pain in my ass.* Instead, she folded her arms across her chest and perked one brow.

I sighed. "Hello, Elodie. Where did you order food from?"

"I didn't. I cooked."

Well, that was a surprise. "You can cook?"

"We *all* can cook. But *I* happen to be good at it. It's one of my many hidden talents." She winked before turning around, grabbing a potholder, and opening the oven door.

The smell of something spicy wafted through the air, and she gave me a nice view of her ass as she bent to take out whatever smelled good. I started to salivate, and I wasn't sure whether it was the aroma or the view.

My eyes were still glued to her rear end when she set the casserole dish on top of the stove, and I almost got caught when she turned back around.

Fuck. I definitely need to get laid.

I cleared my throat. "What is that?"

"Cajun shrimp and quinoa casserole. The shrimp was on sale, and Hailey said it was one of her favorites."

"I didn't even realize she ate shrimp."

She tilted her head. "Did you *ask her* what she liked to eat?"

I must've. Hadn't I? Fuck if I knew.

I cleared my throat. "You don't have to cook. I left you a credit card to order in."

"I know. I used it for the groceries. And also at the drug store. Hailey needed some feminine products. Hope you don't mind."

"No, of course not. Thank you for doing that."

"Hailey likes cooking. I don't have too many great memories of my parents, but the afternoons when my mom and I cooked together were some of my favorite days."

I wanted to be a dick to this woman, but she made it hard to be when she showed a vulnerable side. I nodded. "Where's Hailey?"

"In her room finishing up her math homework."

"Impressive. She usually does that at nine o'clock at night in front of the living room television."

"That's because you *let her* do that."

I loosened my tie. "I pick and choose my battles."

Elodie pointed to the casserole dish. "That needs to cool for ten minutes before you serve it. I'm just going to go say goodbye to Hailey."

She disappeared and came out with my niece a few minutes later. Hailey had her wild hair pulled back in two pretty braids. It made her look younger and tamed.

"Hello, Hailey. How was your day?"

My eyes darted to Elodie and back, and she smiled as I did what she'd asked—*greet* Hailey.

I guessed maybe it really wasn't something I normally did, because my niece's face wrinkled up in confusion. "Hi, Uncle Hollsy."

"How was your day today?"

"Uhhh...fine?"

"It wasn't a trick question."

"Then why are you acting so weird?"

Elodie chuckled. "Hailey, honey, why don't you go wash up? Your uncle is going to walk me out, and then you guys can have your dinner. The dish is really hot, so wait for him. Don't try to serve yourself."

"Okay. I'll see you tomorrow, right?"

Hailey sounded nervous that Elodie might not come back.

"Of course. I'll see you in the morning."

Elodie waited until Hailey went into the bathroom and then nodded her head toward the front door. "Would you mind walking me out?"

"Sure."

In the hallway, she pushed the elevator button before turning to me. "If Hailey and I are going to connect, I can't reveal the things she tells me. Unless, of course, it's something dangerous."

"Okay..."

"But maybe...sometimes I can direct you to discover things on your own."

"What is this about?"

The elevator dinged, and the doors slid open. "Borrow her laptop. Tell her yours is having an issue or something."

"Okay, but what for? What am I looking for?"

She stepped into the elevator and reached over to push a button on the panel. "By the way, I'm not always abrasive. Just when I encounter rude people." The doors started to slide closed, and Elodie flashed a last-minute playful smile. "But I am always hot."

What the fuck?

I ate half the damn casserole.

And the dinner conversation wasn't too bad either. While normally Hailey complained about everything and everyone she'd encountered during the day, tonight she couldn't stop talking about the new sitter.

"Did you know Elodie likes to paint?"

"No, I didn't. But that's great. You two have a lot in common then."

"She was married, you know."

"Yes, I did know that."

"Her husband was an art professor. They went to Paris on their honeymoon, and she went to the Louvre."

"An art professor, huh?" Now *that* I didn't know, and definitely not what I would have expected.

"She's going to take me to MOMA during summer break."

"I think that's a great idea."

The twenty-minute conversation we had over dinner might have been the best twenty minutes I'd spent with her since she showed up on my doorstep two months ago. Hailey even helped clean up and load the dishwasher, and after, we watched a little TV together.

By nine thirty, she was starting to fall asleep on the couch.

"Hey, kiddo. Why don't you go get ready for bed?"

She yawned. "Okay."

I gave her a little time to use the bathroom, and then knocked before opening her door. She was already in bed, but the light was still on.

"You want the light off?"

"Yeah."

I went to hit the light switch, and my eyes landed on the dresser along the same wall. The laptop I'd given Hailey was sitting on top, and I remembered what Elodie had said.

"Ummm... Do you mind if I borrow your laptop? I forgot mine at the office and need to write a few emails."

"Sure."

"Thanks." I took it and felt a miniscule amount of guilt for lying when she'd been so nice all night. "Goodnight, Hailey."

"Goodnight, Uncle Hollis."

I went into my home office and poured two fingers of scotch. Settling into my chair, I opened the laptop and started to poke around. Nothing looked unusual. Then again, I had no idea what the hell I was looking for. Elodie hadn't given me any direction. I opened Word and checked what documents had been recently used, and then checked the Internet search history. Nothing odd. I was just about to give up when I decided to go into the applications folder and see if anything new had been installed.

Bingo.

What the hell?

The call-monitoring software I'd installed on her cell and my laptop was also on her computer, and I sure as shit hadn't put it there. I clicked and noted the time of the latest sign in—last night at nine thirty.

Fuck me.

I shut my eyes and shook my head. I'd been on the phone with Lucas, a buddy of mine. The last thing Elodie had said before the elevator doors closed—about her being abrasive and hot—made sense now. Because that's exactly what I'd told Lucas about the new damn nanny.

Damn. I took a deep whiff. I was going to need to add some cardio to my exercise routine if this cooking shit kept up. I walked into the dining room and found Elodie and Hailey playing Scrabble.

"What did you make tonight?"

Elodie looked at me and waited.

What was her problem?

Oh. Shit. *Fine.*

I nodded. "Hello, Elodie. What did you cook for dinner tonight? It smells good in here."

She smiled. "Hello, Hollis. Thank you. We made sauce, with meatballs and sausage."

"You keep this up, and I'm going to have to spend an extra hour at the gym."

Elodie's eyes did a quick sweep down my body, but she didn't comment. Instead her eyes returned to Hailey. "Why don't you slide the game down the table, and we'll finish it up another day?"

The Scrabble board was half full, and I read one of the words spelled out with the tiles.

Youniverse? "Uhhh... Is that supposed to be universe?"

My niece smiled. "Nope. Y-O-U-niverse. It's a person who's full of themselves and thinks the world revolves around them."

My forehead wrinkled. I read another word on the board.

Carcolepsy? "What the hell is carcolepsy?"

Hailey answered again. "It's what an annoying passenger who falls asleep as soon as they get in the car with you has."

I read another. "Snoot?"

"It's the dirty, sooty looking snot that comes out of your nose after you've been playing in dirt."

"Internest?"

"The big pile of blankets you bury yourself in when you don't feel like getting out of bed and you spend the day surfing the Web."

I chuckled. "Interesting Scrabble game."

Elodie stood. "It's more fun to play with made-up words."

"If you say so."

Hailey pushed the board game down to the end of the table, and Elodie went to the kitchen. She took the lid off a pot and stirred. "It's ready when you are. There's angel hair pasta in the cabinet to have with it. You just need to boil water."

"Thank you. If it's half as good as the shrimp thing you made last night, I'll be in a food coma by eight."

Elodie smiled. "Well, I made extra since we won't have time to cook tomorrow."

"Do you guys have other plans or something?"

Her smile wilted to a frown. "Tomorrow is the year-end family picnic."

"The what?"

She walked past me and into the dining room. "Hailey? Did you forget to tell your uncle about the picnic at school?"

My niece shrugged. "I didn't think he'd want to go."

Elodie sighed. "It starts at three o'clock, right after school."

Great. *Smack in the middle of the damn day.* I had to check my calendar, but I was pretty sure I had a meeting at four. My face must've given away that the time wasn't exactly convenient.

"It's fine," Hailey said. "Elodie is going to come. You don't have to."

Well, now I felt like a dick. "No, of course I'll be there."

Elodie told Hailey to go finish her homework, and the two of them said goodbye.

"I'll walk you out," I said.

Just like yesterday, we waited until we were in the hallway and out of earshot from prying ears.

"Thank you for the heads-up about the cell phone software."

She nodded. "What are you going to do about it?"

"I closed my account, so neither of us can listen to each other's calls anymore. Since she hasn't brought it up, I think I'm going to leave it be and see if we can just move on."

Elodie pushed the button to call the elevator. "I think that might be best. Can I ask what you were hoping to hear by listening in on her conversations?"

"After I found out my brother was in prison, I told her where he was. I didn't want her thinking the worst. She asked if she could talk to him, so I put some money on a prisoner calling account so my loser brother could call his kid." I shook my head. "I don't know what I was hoping to hear when he called."

Elodie smiled. "I can understand why you'd do it, of course. But you're going to have to have a little trust in her, if you want her to have a little trust in you. We haven't talked about him yet, but I'm sure she's angry at her father for abandoning her and getting himself in trouble. I'm guessing she also feels like there's no one in this world she can depend on and trust."

I blew out a deep breath. "And her finding out I was doing shit behind her back just added to that."

She nodded and the doors slid open. "You'll get there. Look at how well you're doing with using words for greetings already."

I chuckled. "How come you can let things slide with Hailey, but you have to call me out on everything?"

She stepped into the elevator and pushed the button on the panel. "For the same reason Hailey and I get along. We both want to make all men pay for the sins of others."

The doors started to slide closed, but Elodie jabbed a button on the panel to keep them open.

"We've discussed Hailey's father, but you never mentioned why her mom is no longer in the picture. What exactly happened there?"

I frowned. "She died when Hailey was two. Hailey doesn't remember her at all. Which is for the best, considering she's the one who found her."

CHAPTER NINE

Hollis – 12 years ago

"When did your mom get this? Is it real?"

Anna picked up a necklace from the kitchen counter. The piece of crap had an obviously fake diamond dangling from a rusty-looking chain.

I frowned. "No. My half-brother showed up at our door last night to sell it to my mother. Can you believe that shit?"

"Stephen? I didn't realize you guys kept in touch with him after your parents got divorced."

"We didn't."

Stephen was my father's son with his first wife and a few years older than me. When my parents were married, he'd come visit once or twice a year. He was always trouble—smoking at eleven and sneaking out of the bedroom window in the middle of the night. And when my father walked out on my mother a week after her diagnosis, we never heard from either of them again. Good riddance to both, if you asked me.

"So he just stopped by out of the blue?"

I nodded. "And he brought his pregnant girlfriend with him. Claimed he was in the neighborhood and thought he'd stop by to see how we were doing. But then he gave my mother some sob story about how they've been living in shelters and really want to get an apartment to make a nice life for their baby. Somehow he managed to squeeze fifteen hundred bucks out of my mom. He gave her that piece of shit and told her the pawn shop appraised it for three grand, but he thought she'd like it so he gave her an opportunity to buy it first."

Anna brought the necklace up to examine it closer. "Your mom had to know it wasn't real."

"Of course, she did. But you know how she is. She'll help anyone. It's her best quality and her worst. She was hooked the minute he had her feel the baby move in his crackhead girlfriend's stomach." I shook my head. "I wouldn't be surprised if it wasn't even his kid she was carrying. He could've just rented some pregnant addict for an hour to come help con my mother out of cash."

Anna sighed. "Your mom doesn't have fifteen hundred dollars to give away anymore."

"Of course not. But my father's spawn doesn't care about that. He's selfish, just like his dear old dad. He didn't even ask how my mom is feeling. I doubt he knows she's been fighting cancer for six years or that she went back to work less than a year ago when she finally went into remission."

"I'm sorry he showed up and did that to Rose. It makes me sad that people take advantage of her good nature."

"Me too. So why don't you come over here and cheer me up?"

Anna smiled. We'd been together for a long time now, but the way her face lit up at the thought of me putting my hands on her never grew old. She walked over and wrapped her arms around my neck.

"Sorry. You'll have to take a raincheck on that cheering up. I have to babysit in fifteen minutes."

I pouted.

She laughed. "You're adorable when you sulk." Giving me a chaste kiss, she said, "Call me the second the mail comes, even if you don't get anything today."

"Okay."

Anna had gotten her acceptance to UCLA yesterday, along with almost a full academic scholarship. We'd sent in our applications the same day, but I still hadn't heard anything.

I walked her to the door and opened it, only to find the mailman approaching with a thick stack of mail in his hand. Anna grabbed it from him and ran to the table to start rifling through.

"Medical bill." She tossed an envelope to the side.

"Medical bill." She tossed a second envelope to the side.

"Medical bill." She tossed another.

"Electric bill." She tossed again.

On the fifth envelope, she froze. "UCLA! Oh my God. It's here!" She held it out to me. "Open it! Open it!"

I shook my head. "You do it."

She didn't argue. She tore into the envelope and started to read. I held my breath. Both of us had the grades to get in—that wasn't the problem. Neither of us had the money to go unless we got a lot of financial help.

Her eyes widened as she read. "Dear Mr. LaCroix, Congratulations on your acceptance to the University of California at Los Angeles. Attached please also find your National Letter of Intent, which details information on an athletic scholarship offered on behalf of the UCLA Bruins." Anna tossed that top letter into the air, and her eyes scanned the next few pages. She jumped up and down. "You got a full ride, Hollis! *A full ride for baseball!*"

I snatched the papers from her hands. There was no way UCLA was offering me that. It seemed too good to be true. But sure enough, there it was in black and white. I looked up at her, bewildered. "Holy shit. We're going to live in sunshine three hundred and sixty-five days a year."

She beamed. "And live together. They have co-ed dorms!"

Jesus Christ. Could it get any better than that? Sunshine, my girl, a free ride, and my mom would hit the one-year mark on her remission in just three days. Eighteen months ago, I never thought we'd get here. I had to swallow a few times to force back some threatening tears. Anna had seen me pussy out enough times when my mom was sick. Plus, this wasn't a time for crying. This was a time to celebrate.

"No more sneaking around to find a place to get you naked." I smiled.

"And I can get a bird!"

I chuckled. "Free tuition and my dick whenever you want it, and you're more excited about getting a bird?"

She shoved me. "Shut up. I'm excited about your dick, too."

"Oh yeah?" I hooked an arm around her waist. "Show me how excited you are about my dick."

She giggled. "I can't. I'm going to be late for babysitting. I have to go."

I groaned.

Anna kissed my lips softly. "I'll make it up to you later. Congratulations, Hollis. Things are finally looking up for you."

They are, aren't they?

"Come back right after you're done babysitting."

"Okay. And don't tell your mom without me. I want to see her face!"

"Alright."

"Actually," she said. "Why don't we wait three days? We're planning that little surprise party on her one-year remission anniversary. We can tell her then."

I smiled. "Whatever makes you happy. As long as *we* celebrate in private tonight."

Three days later, I was pretty damn anxious. I knew my mother worried about how we were going to pay for my college—even City College would be a stretch, with loans and both of us working. But she really wanted me to have the experience of going away.

I went out to the kitchen and found my mom making dinner. She had no idea we were having a bunch of people over to celebrate later.

"The mail just came. Nothing from UCLA." Mom frowned. "Sorry."

I felt a tiny bit guilty for lying to her. But I was looking forward to giving her the letter. Anna was going to bring over a box to put it in and some wrapping paper.

I shrugged. "They probably go through the applications alphabetically and Benson comes before LaCroix."

She forced a smile. "I guess. I'm just so anxious."

I watched my mom pull down some plates from the cabinet. She looked good. She'd gained some weight back, and her complexion had darkened to its naturally tanned color. She also looked happy again. Even while she cooked, she had a smile on her face. I guess after you go through everything she'd experienced with multiple rounds of chemo, you appreciate every moment.

"Why don't you set the table? Dinner will be ready in a few minutes."

She handed me the plates, and I grabbed some utensils from the drawer and a few napkins from the holder. The phone rang as I was folding the napkins into triangles like Mom liked. She had the oven door open and a hot tray in her hands.

"I got it."

"Thanks, honey."

I grabbed the phone from the wall. "Talk to me."

"Hello, may I speak to Mrs. LaCroix, please?" a man said.

"Hold on." I covered the phone and lifted my chin. "It's for you."

"Can you find out who it is and tell them I'll call them back?"

I moved my hands from the receiver. "She's kind of busy right now. Who's calling?"

"It's Dr. Edmund."

Her oncologist. My heart sank in my chest just hearing the name. I looked up at my mother. "Mom, it's your doctor."

Her smile wilted, but she tried to recover. Setting down the lasagna, she removed the oven mitts and wiped her hands on a dishtowel. "I'm sure he just wants to tell me about the checkup scans I had the other day." She took the phone.

"Hi, Dr. Edmund."

I watched her face while she listened over the next sixty seconds. The television constantly played some stupid insurance commercial that said *"A one-minute phone call could change your life,"* but that had always seemed ridiculous. Until now. Those seconds...the way her face changed...I knew. *I knew* life would never be the same. She didn't even need to repeat what the doctor said on the phone when she hung up.

I went to her and pulled her into my arms. When the first tear fell, she tried to hide it. But I hugged her tighter.

"Don't worry, Mom. We got this. You beat it before; we'll beat it again. Together."

I called the neighbors and Mom's two friends from work to tell them not to come tonight. Mom had gone to lie down, and I'd put off calling Anna. I wasn't looking forward to telling her, and she showed up early, before I could call, with a box and wrapping paper hidden in her backpack. I followed her to my room, where she took out the box. The words seemed to get stuck in my throat every time I went to speak.

Her voice was just so cheery, and I was about to ruin everything. It wasn't easy to disappoint her.

"Where's the letter? You're a terrible wrapper. I'll wrap it so it looks nice." She walked over to my desk where it had been sitting facedown the last three days. "Where'd it go?"

When I didn't answer, she looked back at me and realized something was off. "Hollis, where's the letter?"

I stared at the floor. I just couldn't get the words out.

"Hollis? Did you lose it or something?"

I shook my head.

"So then, where is it?"

My eyes lifted and met hers. Her big brown eyes were filled with excitement and happiness. Still unable to get the words out, I looked over at the wastepaper basket next to my bed. The crumpled-up letter sat all alone at the bottom.

Anna and I weren't just a couple. We'd been best friends since kindergarten; she knew me better than anyone. She followed my line of sight, and then her face fell.

"What happened?" she whispered.

I shook my head. "The doctor called with her PET scan results."

CHAPTER
TEN

Elodie

Hailey's school had reserved a section of the park for the picnic event. It was a beautiful, unseasonably cool day. With a cotton candy station, fried dough, and a full barbecue, the school had definitely gone all out. There was an inflatable bouncy house set up, along with other games.

Speaking of games, those were going to start soon, and Hollis wasn't here yet. Late wasn't his style. It was more like mine. I looked at my watch, and Hailey noticed.

"Do you think Uncle Hollsy forgot?"

I offered a sympathetic smile. "I'm not sure."

"Well, I don't want to wait for him forever to eat. They're putting out the burgers and dogs. Can I go get one? I'm hungry."

I looked around one last time. "Yeah. Why don't you go get in line?"

"You're not gonna eat?"

"No, not right now."

"Oh, I forgot about your Keto." She rolled her eyes.

"I can still have the burger. Just not the bun."

"The bun is the best part! And the ketchup."

"I'll survive."

While Hailey took off for the food table, I stretched my neck to see if by some chance Hollis had arrived and I'd missed him. Still no sign of him.

Seriously, Hollis? You couldn't ditch work for one damn afternoon?

A deep voice registered just behind my ear.

"Hi."

I turned to find a decently handsome man who looked to be in his mid-thirties standing there.

"Hi," I said.

"I don't think we've met. I'm Lawrence Higgins's dad." He held out his hand. "James Higgins."

"Oh. Nice to meet you. I'm Elodie Atlier, Hailey LaCroix's nanny."

"I thought you might be...a nanny."

I raised my brow and activated my scum-bucket detector. "Oh?"

"Well, no offense to anyone else..." He lowered his voice. "But the moms aren't usually as attractive as you."

So, that's what this exchange is all about? Can't even escape this shit at a middle school picnic.

"Thank you," I said.

"You're welcome." He sipped his water. "How long have you been a nanny?"

"Actually, not long. Only a couple of weeks."

Hailey appeared, interrupting our conversation. "You like wieners, right?"

Her question made my juvenile spirit chuckle. "Only if they're all beef, which that one probably is not."

She turned toward the man. "Who's this?"

"This is Mr. Higgins, Lawrence's dad."

Her expression dampened. "Your son is an asshole."

I cringed.

His smile faded. "I'm sorry?"

Placing my hands on her shoulders, I said, "If you'll excuse us." I then pulled her away and asked, "Why would you say that to him?"

Hailey took a bite of her hamburger and let out a deep sigh. "That kid is the worst. I thought his dad should know."

"Well, maybe next time use a more polite word to convey that?"

"He's the one who started making fun of my boobs, calling me Cyclops Tit—because he thinks one is bigger than the other."

I nodded, remembering when she told me that story. "Oh, *that* jerk?"

"Yes."

I looked back at the man briefly. "Okay. Well, screw him and his dad, then."

"That's what his dad probably wanted....to screw *you*."

"Where did you learn that term?"

"I know *a lot* of things about sex."

Shit. "Oh, you do, do you? What exactly do you think you know?"

She handed me her plate before sticking her index finger inside a hole formed by her other hand and simulating the act of intercourse.

Add to mental to-do list: speak to Hollis about a birds-and-bees talk with Hailey.

Before I could explore this subject further, my eyes landed on a very flustered-looking Hollis in the distance. He looked like he'd just run a marathon and somehow landed in the Twilight Zone. I handed Hailey back her plate and watched him for a bit.

He'd changed out of his suit and wore a navy polo that hugged his muscles. God, he looked super hot dressed casually. I mean, he was super hot no matter how you cut it, but this was a particularly good look for him. I loved everything about it—from the snug sleeves around his thick biceps to the chunky watch he wore, and the dark jeans I was dying to see molded to his ass.

He was totally oblivious to the starving moms checking him out as he made his way toward us.

Hollis finally spotted us as he weaved through the crowd.

He was out of breath. "I'm sorry I'm late. I thought I had time to go home and change—which I did—but then traffic was a bitch getting here."

"Language, Hollis," I scolded.

"Sorry."

"I'm glad you made it, Uncle Hollsy."

He cracked a slight smile. "Me, too."

Hailey had polished off her burger pretty quickly. "You want Elodie's wiener?" she asked.

His brow furrowed. "Excuse me?"

She held out the hot dog on her plate. "This. She can't eat it because of her Keto."

"Ah." He took the plate from her. "Yeah. Thanks."

Hailey looked over his shoulder. "I see my friend Jacqueline over there. I'm gonna go talk to her."

After she took off, Hollis turned to me, holding his hot dog with no bun, looking so awkward and out of place.

I couldn't help but laugh.

He wasn't amused. "What the hell is so funny?"

"You."

His lip twitched. "Me?"

"Yes."

"Might I ask *why* I'm so funny?"

I gestured to his hot dog. "You look like you don't know what to do with that thing. Like you don't know what to do with yourself here. Like you're out of your comfort zone. I take it picnics aren't your jam."

"Well, I suppose I am...a bit out of my comfort zone."

"Extra points for showing up."

"I didn't realize I was being graded."

We shared a smile. A breeze blew his musky scent toward me. It was definitely arousing. *He* was arousing. So freaking handsome.

I tilted my head. "Come on. I'll show you to the food area where you can get a bun for that lonely wiener."

We walked together to the large picnic table. I took Hollis's plate, placed the hot dog in a bun, and added a bunch of fixings. I placed a dollop of potato salad next to it and grabbed him a small bag of chips. I finished off the plate with an apple. I handed him everything with a smile.

"Thanks, Mom," he joked.

Hailey was playing horseshoes with a few of her friends, so we took a spot under a shady tree near their game. Hollis devoured his ketchup-laden hot dog and potato salad while I ate my plain burger with a fork and continued to watch him. My eyes were glued to his large hands. I loved the protruding veins that ran through them. Every time he licked ketchup off his finger, a shiver ran down my spine.

After he'd polished everything off, he licked his lips and said, "That was good. I haven't had a hot dog in ages."

"See? Sometimes it's nice to do *different*."

"Believe me, my entire life has been *different* from the moment Hailey landed at my door."

"I know it has. And I also know you're doing the best you can."

"Well, thank you for recognizing that. But I'm only as good as the help I have." He looked down at his plate a moment. "Honestly, I owe you an apology."

"It's okay."

"No, I need to say this." He paused. "I misjudged you early on, doubted your capabilities as a caretaker. But I can't imagine a better choice now. Passing you by would have been a huge mistake."

That warmed me inside and gave me a huge sense of accomplishment.

I smiled. "Wow. I don't know how to respond to that, because I'm not used to this nice version of Hollis."

"Don't get too used to it. It's probably the nitrates going to my head."

We laughed again as Hailey came over to us.

"Why did you leave your friends?" I asked.

"Lawrence started playing the horseshoe game, and I didn't want to be around him."

"Which one is he?"

"The one in the red."

No way I was going to let her be bullied by some jackass boy.

"You can't let him win like that, Hailey. You were there first. By leaving the game, you're showing him he has an effect on you. Even if he does, don't let him see that. Don't give him the satisfaction. Go back into the game, and totally ignore him if he says anything."

She let out a long breath. "Okay." She reluctantly walked back over there.

A look of concern clouded Hollis's expression as he watched her. "What's the deal with Lawrence?"

"He teases her about her boobs. Apparently, he called her Cyclops Tit, because he claims one of them is bigger than the other."

Hollis tightened his fist. "Little shit. I should wring his neck."

"The clincher? The kid's dad was hitting on me earlier. Hailey comes up to us, and when I introduced her to him, she says, 'Your son is an asshole.'"

Hollis's jaw dropped. "I don't even know whether to be upset at her for that."

"I know. That's how I felt. But I suggested she be more polite in getting her point across in the future."

Hollis and I made easy conversation over the next half hour. Then Hailey came running toward us.

"Elodie, my teacher needs your help."

"What's up?"

"The person who was supposed to do the face painting bailed. Mrs. Stein bought all these supplies, but she has no one to do the actual painting. I told her my nanny is an artist."

"Oh...I don't know. I've never painted someone's face before."

"Can you try? Please? There's no one else to do it, and we all want our faces painted like unicorns."

What the hell? How hard could it be?

I stood up from the grass and brushed the dirt off my pants.

"Who's gonna babysit Uncle Hollis if I have to do the face painting? We wouldn't want him to have to make small talk with PTO moms."

"Just go set up," she said. "Uncle Hollis is coming with me anyway."

Hollis stood up. "Oh? What am I doing?"

She pointed to the corner of the field. "Me, you, over there. Potato sack race."

CHAPTER ELEVEN

Hollis

What the hell did I get myself into?

We were in pairs—parents and their respective children.

"You have to go fast, okay? I want to win the grand prize," Hailey said.

"What's the prize?"

"A gift card from Target."

I would have happily bought her one myself if it meant getting out of this potato sack.

The announcer yelled, "On your mark...get set... go!"

At the sound of the whistle, with my legs stuck in a gray, canvas sack, I began hopping across the open field. I couldn't help but laugh at how ridiculous this was. Worse, Hailey was chiding me the whole time because I'd fallen behind the rest of the pack.

"Come on, Uncle Hollsy! You can do better than that!"

I hadn't been taking it seriously enough. She was right. I could have done better. A lot better. With that realization, I suddenly picked up my speed, hopping as fast as I could with everything I had in me. I managed to pass a few of the pairs and also get quite a bit ahead of Hailey.

I'd finally hit my stride in potato-sack racing when I passed Elodie's face-painting stand. She was still setting up. A man was standing there talking to her. I wondered if it was the same guy from earlier—the jerk's father who was trying to get in her pants.

As I hopped along, my eyes became glued to Elodie and that guy. I even turned my head to keep looking after I passed them. That's when I knocked right into the back of one of the parents.

Oof! We both fell over.

"Shit! I'm sorry. Are you okay?" I asked.

The man was *not* happy. He didn't say anything as he picked himself back up and continued the race.

I'd fallen so far behind now that Hailey had pretty much given up on us.

She caught up to me. "Are you okay? How did you fall? Did you trip?"

Yeah. I tripped over my damn dick.

"Yeah. I got distracted."

"A for effort," she said, out of breath.

"You sound like Elodie now, grading me."

She looked over toward the face-painting station. "Looks like Elodie's all set up. I'm gonna go get in line. Are you gonna be okay without me?"

"Yeah. I'll manage just fine."

I went in search of some water and came upon the guy who'd been talking to Elodie when I fell on my ass.

I took a gander at his nametag. "Are you Lawrence's father, by any chance?"

"Yes. And you are?"

"Hollis LaCroix. Hailey's uncle. Tell your son to stop disrespecting my niece."

He sighed. "Look, I just apologized to your nanny. But my son denies doing anything wrong."

"Well, Hailey's not a liar. So if she says someone is bullying her, she's telling the damn truth. Just keep your son in check. And while you're at it, keep your hands off my nanny." I walked away before he could respond.

I didn't need to add that last part. Not really sure why the idea of him trying to pick up Elodie made me crazy. Did I have a thing for her? I knew she was attractive, but I couldn't understand why this guy talking to her had irked me *that* badly.

Anyway, it didn't matter how I felt about Elodie. Now that she'd become the best thing to happen to Hailey in a long time, she was most definitely off limits. I could never fuck her, because then I'd have to not see her again, and that wouldn't work in this equation.

Hailey came running toward me. "Look! Elodie made me into a unicorn."

She beamed, proudly displaying her new pink and purple face. A horn was painted in the middle of her forehead. There were sparkles around her eyes.

"Wow. You look...great."

She grabbed me by the hand and pulled me toward Elodie's station. "Come on. It's your turn."

"Oh no. I don't want my face painted."

"Yes, you do. And look, there's no one else in line right now."

Elodie smiled wide. "Well, hello, sir. What can I do for you?"

So many potential answers came to mind.

"Apparently, I'm getting my face painted."

Hailey giggled, then whispered something in Elodie's ear.

Elodie shook her head and laughed. "No. We can't do that."

"Yes! Yes, we can."

I looked between them. "Should I be worried?"

"Sit," Elodie said.

Hailey jumped up and down. "Do it!"

Elodie sighed.

What the hell is going on here?

"Uncle Hollis, can you give me some money? I'm gonna go get a slush while Elodie paints you."

I reached into my pocket and handed her a ten.

"Bring me back one," Elodie said. "Gonna cheat on my diet a little."

"Okay." Hailey skipped away.

When Elodie's eyes landed on mine, I asked, "So what exactly are you doing to me?"

Multiple meanings there…

She cleaned her brush before opening a few bottles of paint. "Don't worry. It's all in good fun."

She leaned in and started to paint my face with small strokes. I had to say, I didn't exactly mind being this close to her. It was an innocent excuse to be near her, to breathe her in, without it seeming inappropriate.

I also couldn't help but look down into her cleavage. Fuck me. She had amazing tits. She smelled amazing, too. I'd never been *this* close to her. She smelled like a mix of flowers and candy.

"What are you looking at?" she suddenly asked.

I pried my eyes upward and didn't even try to deny it. Because it was all too clear that I'd been enjoying the view.

"Where do you *expect* me to look from this angle? I don't have many choices. I just picked the best one."

"I'm kidding, Hollis. I don't mind if you look at me."

She stopped painting for a moment and looked into my eyes. The sun brought out the highlights in her gorgeous hair. I felt myself starting to sweat, and it wasn't even that hot out. Fucking hell, she was beautiful. Okay, so maybe I did have the hots for the nanny. I needed to keep that my dirty little secret.

When she resumed painting, I closed my eyes. I quite enjoyed her hand on my chin while she worked. It was soft and dainty, and I had the urge to run my tongue along it. I wouldn't, of course.

"Can we talk about sex?" she asked.

What? My heart pounded. "Hmm?"

Did she fucking read my mind?

"Okay...so, Hailey said something to me earlier that made me wonder if it's time to have the birds-and-bees talk with her."

I breathed out a sigh of relief.

"I didn't want to do that without consulting with you first."

I cleared my throat. "Ah. Okay...well, what did she say?"

"She told me she thought the dad who was flirting with me wanted to screw me. So clearly she knows what sex is. I just wonder if maybe, given the fact that she's approaching her teen years, someone needs to talk to her about birth control and stuff."

Shit.

Fuck.

Shit.

She's too young for that, isn't she? No, it would be dangerous to assume that. Better safe than sorry.

"Okay...yeah, I think you're right."

She dabbed some more paint onto her brush. "Do you want me to do it? Have the talk with her...or would you prefer—"

"Oh, I would *not* prefer. No preferring going on here. I would *really* appreciate you handling that. I hope that's not outside of the scope of the job."

I'd give my left nut not to have to have that conversation with my niece.

"I don't think we really have a *scope*, do we?"

"Well, cooking certainly isn't a job requirement, but you do that anyway. I don't want to take you for granted. You go above and beyond. I think talking to her about sex takes the cake, though."

"I don't mind doing it. Is there anything you prefer I not discuss with her?"

"Use your judgment. I just want her to be safe when the time comes. As much as it makes me uncomfortable to even think about it, I don't want to be naïve, either. I remember kids in my middle school having sex, and I'm sure things have only gotten worse. It would be very easy to just throw it under the rug. So I appreciate your help."

She stopped painting my face for a moment. "Can I ask you a personal question?"

"Yeah..."

"Before Hailey, I assume you used to bring women back to your place. Now that she's there, where do you..."

My mouth curved into a smile at her hesitation. "Where do I fuck?"

"Yeah."

She seemed to blush. I loved it.

"Well, not in the apartment."

She resumed painting. "Right. I was curious—how you logistically make it work."

I wasn't sure about the relevance of this question, aside from her just being curious.

"Well, there are ways around it," I said.

"Like..."

"Like meeting someone at their place in the middle of the day or getting a sitter and going out at night. Having Hailey at home does limit my options, but..."

She finished my sentence. "But where there's a will, there's a way."

Thinking about sex while she had her hands on me—while I could feel her breath on my face, while her tits were practically up against me—was definitely not good. I could feel myself getting hard. I really needed to think about something else.

Hailey returned, holding two slushes. *Good. That should do it.*

"Oh my God!" She laughed. "You did it!"

"What kind of shit are you two pulling?" I asked.

"Language, Hollis," Elodie said.

I pulled out my phone to look at my face.

The red and black paint was shocking. And she'd drawn a little horn on each side of my forehead. They'd made me into the devil.

"So this is how you see me?" I asked.

"Remember, it's all in good fun, Hollsy." Elodie winked.

I wondered if she'd think it was all in good fun if I smacked her on the ass and left a handprint. Damn, I enjoyed that thought. Maybe I *was* the devil.

"Where's my slush?" I teased.

"I didn't think you wanted one."

"Did you ask me?"

"You want me to get you one?"

"I'm just kidding, Hailey."

"Here."

Before I knew it, Elodie had shoved her spoon in my mouth. Now she was feeding me slush. I had to say, she had a very motherly instinct.

I felt a lot like a horny teenager having the hots for "Stacy's Mom" right about now.

CHAPTER
TWELVE

Elodie

I set Huey's travel cage down on the floor. "Hi. I called earlier. I have an appointment at eleven."

The woman behind the reception desk typed into her computer. "You must be Mrs. LaCroix."

"Definitely not. But I am Mr. LaCroix's lackey, apparently. My name is Elodie Atlier, and I have Huey with me."

"Uhh...okay. The doctor will be with you in a few minutes." She stood and set a clipboard with papers on top of the counter. "In the meantime, you can fill these forms out, and let me know if Huey has insurance."

I looked at her like she was nuts. "Insurance? Like, health insurance?"

"Well, yes. Pet insurance."

"That's an actual thing?"

The woman pursed her lips. "You can leave that section blank when you get to it if you don't have any."

I hefted the cage over to the waiting area and took a seat. The first few questions were easy enough—name, address, telephone number. But the rest of page one and all of page two and three were questions about Huey's health history.

Great. Hollis was already annoyed that I'd had his secretary call him out of a meeting when I noticed Huey didn't look well this morning. Now I'd have to bug him again. Not to mention, I hadn't told him I was taking his bird to the vet with the credit card he gave me to use for food. I decided to text, instead of call.

Elodie: What's Huey's birthday?

A few minutes later he texted back.

Hollis: How the hell would I know? He was rescued in Australia.

God. What a jerk. And just when I'd started to think maybe I'd misjudged him.

Elodie: What about his medical history? What shots has he had in the last three years?

A minute later my phone rang.

"What are you doing?"

I rolled my eyes. Maybe you *can't* teach old dogs new tricks. "Hello, Hollis. How are you?"

"Elodie, not now. I'm in the middle of an important business meeting."

"If it's so important, why are you checking your messages?"

I heard what sounded like something covering the phone and then a muffled, "Can you gentlemen excuse me for a minute, please?" A few seconds later, a door opened and shut, and Hollis came back on the line. "Where are you?"

"So you say *excuse me* and *please* to the people in your meeting and not even a simple *hello* to me?"

"*Elodie...*"

"Fine. I'm at the vet with Huey."

He mumbled something I didn't catch. "Why?"

"I told you when I called, he looks funny."

"No one asked you to bring him to the vet."

I sat up straight. "When someone's in my care, I will make the medical decisions I deem appropriate. It's part of my job."

"This isn't Hailey we're talking about. *This is a damn bird.*"

"*A damn bird who isn't feeling well.* Are you going to answer the questions or not? I have to fill out the papers before I see the doctor."

"Where's the office?"

"Dr. Gottlieb's, a few blocks from your apartment."

The receptionist called out. "Elodie Atlier and Huey?"

"I have to go. Thanks for all the helpful information." I hung up before Mr. Grumpy could say anything more.

The receptionist directed me to an examination room, and a few minutes later an older gentleman in a white coat came in. "Wow. What a beauty."

I liked him immediately, since he didn't even seem to notice me and was actually referring to the bird.

"Thank you. This is Huey. I'm sorry I don't know that much about him, other than he's an Australian black palm cockatoo that was injured at some point and rescued. He belongs to my employer, who isn't able to be here."

"That's okay. We'll figure out what Huey's problem is." The doctor turned around, took a quarter-sized biscuit out of a jar, and opened the cage door. He offered it to Huey, who looked completely disinterested.

"That's exactly what happened this morning when the little girl I watch tried to give him a treat. Usually when anyone comes into the house, he squawks and says a few words. But he didn't say anything when I arrived this morning, and he didn't take his morning treat. So I went back to the apartment after I dropped Hailey at school, just to check on him, and I found him sitting at the bottom of his cage sort of hunched over, instead of on his perch, and his feathers seem kind of...puffy."

"Ah. Yes. Puffy feathers are often the first sign of illness. Birds tend to puff up when they're cold, but if the temperature is fine, that's often a symptom, as is irregular posture and changing positions." He nodded. "Good observations on your part."

Dr. Gottlieb stroked Huey's feathers. "He seems pretty calm right now, so I'm going to give him an examination and draw some blood, if that's alright."

"Sure. Of course. Whatever you need to do." *Make the bill nice and big for the asshole who was too busy to talk about this poor little boy.*

I watched while the doc checked Huey out and drew some blood from a vein in his wing. When he was done, he said it would take a little while for the results, and I should go take a seat in the waiting room. He kept Huey in the back, just in case there was anything wrong with him that might be transmittable to humans or pets.

I took a seat across from an older woman with a dog on her lap. I couldn't help but notice how much she and her poodle looked alike—frizzy white hair, thin faces, long noses. To keep myself from staring, I rummaged through a pile of magazines on the end table next to me and plucked out a *Cosmo*—though I couldn't help but steal glances as I flipped through the pages. Toward the middle of the magazine, I stumbled on one of those reader quizzes. This one was titled: *What type of man is most attracted to you?*

I scoffed. I knew the answer to that one without any questions. *The asshole kind.* Yet I started to take the quiz anyway.

Question one—When men compliment you on your looks, which word do they use most?

The choices were A. Gorgeous, B. Sexy, C. Beautiful, and D. Hot.

Hmmm. I'd have to say B.

Question two—What are you most complimented on by men?

The choices were A. Your face, B. Your legs, C. Your smile, and D. Your personality.

Considering rack wasn't an answer, I circled A.

Question three—How would you describe your personality?

The choices were A. Outgoing, B. Shy, C. Funny, and D. Witty.

I was just about to circle *A* when a deep voice spoke from over my shoulder. "Is there an E for bossy bitch?"

Startled, my knee-jerk reaction was to toss the magazine at the sound, which resulted in my hitting the speaker square in the face.

"What the hell?" Hollis growled.

"It's your own fault. Don't sneak up on me like that. You're lucky I didn't take you down."

Hollis's face went from angry to amused. "Take me down?"

"Yes. I know self-defense."

He chuckled. "I'm two hundred pounds. You're not going to take me down, sweetheart. Even if you do know self-defense."

"You're an ass, you know that?"

"So I've been told. Now where's my pain-in-the-ass bird?"

"Huey is in the back. I'm waiting for the lab results."

Hollis walked around and planted himself in the chair next to me. "How long is this going to take?"

"I don't know. But you didn't have to come. I could handle it on my own."

"Really? So why did you call me?"

"To let you know I thought your bird was sick, and because I needed medical information. But obviously, you didn't give a shit."

"I was in a meeting."

I narrowed my eyes at him. "You were rude to me on the phone. *Both times.*"

Hollis ran a hand through his hair and sighed. "The bird is a perpetual thorn in my side."

"What the heck did he ever do to you? I know, I know—he says your ex's name whenever you walk in. Big whoop-de-do. Get over it."

He scowled. "He cost me eighteen grand, for starters."

My brows jumped. "You paid eighteen grand for him?"

"No." His jaw flexed. "Forget it."

"Uh, no way, Hollsy. I want to know what your issue is with Huey. He's such a sweet boy."

Hollis looked away and stared out the front window for a while, then cleared his throat. "I apologize if I was rude on the phone. Some big stocks took a nosedive this morning, and I hadn't been as on top of my team as I should've been, so we took a big hit."

"What is it you do, exactly? I mean, other than bark at people?"

"I'm a wealth fund manager."

"Oh." I nodded my head like he'd cleared up some confusion. Then I smiled. "I have no idea what that means. But it sounds awful."

He chuckled. "It can be."

"Miss Atlier?" the receptionist called.

I stood. "Yes, I'm here."

Hollis followed me.

"Come on back. The doctor would like to speak to you."

It turned out Huey had an infection. He needed IV antibiotics, and in order to administer that, he needed to be sedated. The vet said it would probably be two days before he was ready to come home, so I told the doc I'd be back tomorrow to visit. Hollis looked at me funny when I said I was going to visit Huey, but he was smart enough not to comment.

Outside on the street, Hollis looked at his watch. "I need to get back to the office."

"Of course. Go ahead. I have a little while before I need to pick up Hailey, so I'm going to get some groceries."

"I might be late tonight. I need to do some damage control," he said. "Can you stay if I work a few hours later than usual?"

"Of course. I have no life."

"Is that true, or are you being sarcastic? I haven't figured out how to tell with you yet."

I smiled. "No, it's true. I wish I was being sarcastic."

He hesitated. "Why don't you have a life? I'm guessing men asking you out isn't the issue."

I arched a brow. "Are you saying you think I'm attractive, Hollis?"

"We both know you are, so cut the shit and answer my question."

I had to work at hiding my smile. "I'm on a very long, self-imposed man strike."

"How long is very long?"

I bit my bottom lip. "Going on two years now."

Hollis's eyes widened. "You haven't had..." He shook his head. "Never mind. I need to go." He started to walk away.

"Hollis!" I yelled.

He turned back and looked at me.

"*Say goodbye.*"

He shook his head. "Goodbye, pain in my ass."

CHAPTER
THIRTEEN

Hollis

I was almost midnight.

I hadn't meant to work this late. Even though Elodie had told me it wasn't a problem and to stay as late as I needed, I didn't want to take advantage. But the West Coast clients needed some schmoozing, and my staff had all stayed for damage control, too.

My apartment was quiet. It was damn pleasant to walk in and *not* hear Anna's name squawked at me. I tossed my keys on the table and went looking for Elodie. The living room TV was on, but the sound had been muted, and there were subtitles flashing on the bottom of the screen. Elodie was out cold, lying on the couch a few feet away. I grabbed the remote and went to flick off the TV, but the show caught my attention. A long-haired Fabio-looking guy was unbuttoning his shirt when a woman with a shitload of cleavage on display walked in.

What's this now?

Words popped up at the bottom of the screen as the woman marched over to the dude, saying something: "*Merhaba tatlım.*"

What the hell?

Was she watching a foreign soap opera or something? That's what this shit looked like. I once had a client from Turkey, and I could've sworn *merhaba* was hello in Turkish. The woman who'd walked in on Fabio two seconds ago already had her tits pushed up against him.

I chuckled to myself and hit the *Off* button. Elodie was definitely different. I had no idea what to expect from her one minute to the next. Turning, I watched her breathe in and out a few times as she slept. She really was gorgeous. Relaxed as she snoozed, her features were soft and feminine. Earlier, her hair had been tied back, but now a piece of her thick blond mane had come loose and rested across her cheek. I had the craziest urge to push it back off her face. Her shirt was disheveled and pulled to one side, exposing a delicate collarbone and smooth, fair skin. I swallowed. *Damn.* While a part of me wanted to fix her hair, an equally strong part of me wanted to sink my teeth into that unmarked skin—leave bite marks where people could see them. It was fucked up, and I salivated, thinking, *two years. Two years* that beautiful body hadn't been touched.

I scrubbed my hands over my face and walked over to the couch to wake her.

"Elodie," I whispered.

She didn't budge. So I tapped her shoulder. "Elodie?"

Her eyes fluttered open, and she stretched her arms up over her head. Her shirt rode up with the motion and exposed her midriff. I couldn't help myself. I hadn't been with a woman in a while, and being around Elodie made me lose my damn composure. Her stomach was just so smooth and flat, and her navel, an innie, showed off a sparkly diamond. God, I wanted to take that thing between my teeth and give it a good tug.

Shaking my head, I forced my eyes to look anywhere but at the damn nanny. I cleared my throat. "Sorry I'm so late."

"It's fine." She gave me a goofy grin and sat up, pushing that lock of hair off her face as she rose. "I love getting paid to sleep."

"I'm going to call you an Uber. I don't want you taking the trains this late."

"Okay. Thanks. I need to use the bathroom first."

Elodie walked out of the room, and I used all my strength to keep my head down and focus on calling her car, *not* look at her ass.

When she came back, I was still standing in the living room. "Your car will be here in three minutes."

"Oh wow. I better get downstairs then."

She walked around the apartment, collecting her things.

"Everything go okay tonight?"

"Yes, fine. We ate and started a series on Netflix. Pretty uneventful. Hailey went to bed at nine, but I checked in on her an hour later, and she was still awake. I think she's all pumped up about the last day of school tomorrow."

I nodded. "I'm sure."

Elodie grabbed her purse from the couch and slung it over her body so it rested diagonally across her front. I was behind her and had intended to walk her to the front door. But after a few steps she abruptly stopped, turned around, and grabbed one of my arms.

Before I knew what the fuck was going on, I was flipped into the air and laid out on my back on the floor. The wind was knocked out of me with the *umpf* of my landing.

"*What the fuck!*"

Elodie leaned over me, flaunting a gigantic smile, and offered a hand. "This afternoon you laughed when I said I could've brought you down. Now you won't doubt my abilities anymore."

"Seriously? You could have broken my neck."

"I made sure you were on the rug and went gently."

I pushed her hand away and got up by myself, dusting my pants as I stood. "*That's* gently? Where the hell did you learn to do that?"

"I told you, self-defense classes."

I rubbed the back of my neck. "I'm guessing you've used that move once or twice?"

She grinned. "That was actually the first time I did it outside of class. And I'm so *freaking glad* it worked."

She'd just knocked my manhood down a few rungs, and I'd probably be sore as shit for a week, yet I couldn't help but laugh.

"You just elevated yourself from a figurative pain in my ass to a literal one. Get out."

She opened the front door and turned back with a wink. "Night, Hollsy. Sweet dreams. And try not to dream too much about sparkly bellybuttons."

The following day, Elodie called me at work just as I was going into a meeting with an important client.

I answered, "What's up?"

She corrected me. "*Hello*, Elodie. How are you?"

"*Hello, Elodie. How are you?* What do you want?"

"Would you have any objection to Hailey and I attending an end-of-the-year party at one of her friend's houses in Connecticut after school gets out today? I guess Megan's parents have a second house in Greenwich, and since it's so warm today, they invited a few girls over for a pool party."

I scratched my head. "That shouldn't be a problem."

"We're hitching a ride with them since I took the train in again today. So you'll have to come pick us up in Connecticut tonight. Is that okay?"

I sighed. "As long as I'm not required to be there by a certain time. I don't know when I'll get out of here. Not to mention, Friday night traffic heading out of the city is going to be a nightmare."

"That should be fine. We'll just hang out until you get there."

"Okay then, text me the address."

"You sound kind of out of breath. Are you sure I didn't interrupt one of your noontime rendezvous?"

Her comment made my pulse race a little. Any implication of sex reminded me how hard up I was.

"I'm out of breath because you're making me late for a meeting."

Except now for some reason I was imagining Elodie splayed out on my desk naked. Maybe that contributed to my breathing a little, too.

A couple of hours later, my meeting was still going when Elodie called again. I almost let it go to voicemail, but then I remembered she and Hailey were traveling to Connecticut. I worried maybe something had happened.

I held my index finger up and left the room to take the call.

Speaking low, I picked up. "Everything okay?"

"Yes. We actually just arrived. But there's a problem."

"What?"

"Dr. Gottlieb's office called. Huey recovered faster than they expected. They want us to pick him up and take him home today. I'm here with Hailey, so I can't go get him."

"Can't he spend the night there? I can get him in the morning."

"I asked that, but they were insistent that we pick him up now. Something about a shortage of space."

"Crap." I ran my hand through my hair. "So, I'm supposed to go pick up Huey, bring him all the way back to my place, then jet out to Connecticut?"

"Unless you want me to leave Hailey here and go back to the city to pick him up."

I sighed and grumbled, "No. I'll get him."

"Boy, you're just loving me today, aren't you?"

If she only knew the thoughts in my head when it came to her.

"Goodbye, Elodie."

"You can't say hello properly, but you certainly have no problem saying goodbye." She laughed.

Later that afternoon, as I attempted to finish my work so I could get out in time for my chauffeuring duties, Addison walked into my office.

"What?" I snapped before she could even speak.

"What the hell has gotten into you? You're even crabbier than usual today."

I stopped typing and swiveled my chair toward her. "If you must know, Addison, I can't seem to get through the day without people interrupting me—my nanny being at the top of that list. First, she asks me to go pick them up tonight in Connecticut, which is fine, except now because she's there and I'm here, I have to go pick up the damn bird from an animal hospital he shouldn't even be in."

"What's wrong with Huey?"

"Puffy feathers and an alleged infection that probably would've gone away on its own. Elodie insisted on taking him there. She's a pain in my ass. So infuriating… So…" My words trailed off.

Addison smirked. "Oh my God."

"What?"

"You totally have a thing for her."

My jaw ticked. "What are you talking about?"

"You never let women get under your skin like this. And I've seen her—she's gorgeous. I think you're starting to fall for Elodie. And it's pissing you off. That's why you're so crabby."

"Don't be ridiculous."

"Ridiculous? I'd be willing to bet my car that you two will end up in bed in three months' time—if that long."

"You're insane. Your Bentley?"

"Yes. My precious Bentley. I have nothing to worry about, so I can safely say that if you haven't slept with her in three months, I'll give it to you."

"That's your prized possession."

"That's right."

I returned to the email I'd been working on. I banged on the keyboard and spoke at the same time. "I don't want your car, Addison."

"Well, you won't be getting it."

I stopped typing. "I'm not going to sleep with Elodie. Not only does she drive me nuts, but Hailey loves her. I would never jeopardize that relationship by inserting myself into it."

"Oh, you'll be inserting something, alright."

I laughed. "Get the fuck out of here."

I did love my relationship with my business partner. We could talk to each other like two guys hanging out at the bar.

I looked down at my phone. "Shit. I still have to call Davidson."

"I'll handle the call with Davidson. You're all wound up, and from what you told me, you have a lot of shit to do tonight. Why don't you leave early for the first time in your career?"

"Not my style, Addison. You know that."

She intentionally pushed my buttons. "Yeah, well neither is driving around birds or trekking up to Connecticut on a Friday night. This nanny sure has you wrapped around her finger."

"And you sure know how to fucking annoy me." I was sweating. "On second thought, maybe I do need a breather." I stood up. "Take the call with Davidson."

The vet's office was mobbed. There were four people in line in front of me before I could even tell them I was there to pick up my damn bird.

About the time it was going to be my turn, everyone's attention went to a man who waltzed in with a goat. *A fucking goat!*

He cut in line.

"Excuse me, gorgeous," he said to the woman at the desk. He had an Australian accent. "I have a bit of an emergency. The family and I are in the city visiting my sister who just moved here. We drove all the way from California. Anyway, we were walking down the street when a loud popping sound came from under the ground. Still don't understand what it was—an explosion of some kind. Everyone's alright. But Pixy here…well, he fainted. He does that from time to time when he's startled. But this time, he hit his head pretty badly on the pavement. Ever since, he's seemed a bit disoriented. So, I want to get his head checked."

I was pretty sure *this guy* was the one who needed his head checked.

The woman came around from behind the desk and bent down. "He's so cute."

Everyone in this damn office was now swooning over a goat. Wait. Not just a goat—a goat in a damn diaper.

"He's normally potty trained," the man added. "But when he's nervous, he gets the shits. Thus, the diaper."

Thanks a lot, Elodie. Thanks a lot for getting me into this clusterfuck.

"Excuse me," I finally interrupted. "Shits aside, I'm just here to pick up my bird. Can someone please bring him out?"

"You'll have to wait your turn, sir."

"Technically, it *is* my turn. This gentleman and his goat cut in front of me."

"I'm sorry, mate. No harm intended. Just trying to make sure my boy is okay."

"Let's take him back to see the doctor," the woman said. She then ushered the man and his goat straight through.

Baaa. I could hear from down the hall.

By the time they brought Huey out, I felt ready to kill someone. My bird looked completely normal. A little hospital tag affixed to his cage read: *Huey B. LaCroix.*

B? What the hell does that stand for?

"He's going to be just fine," the nurse said. "Thank you for coming to get him. I know it was earlier than expected."

I looked over at Huey and felt a little bad for doubting his need to come here, because he *did* look a lot better than the morning Elodie had brought him in. As much as I talked shit about him, I never actually wanted anything bad to happen. Some days I just wished he'd fly away to a happier place.

We were almost out the door when I heard it again. *Baaa.*

That damn goat was loud.

And again... *Baaa.*

Wait a minute.

It wasn't coming from down the hall. It was coming from...Huey.

He opened his beak. *Baaa.*

What. The. Fuck?

I carried him back to the desk. "Excuse me. My bird has only ever said one thing his entire life. He's hardly made another peep besides that one sentence, and now he's making goat sounds because apparently he thinks it's funny to mimic that...*animal*...back there. You want to tell me how I'm supposed to live with this?"

She shrugged. "Isn't that typical of birds like him? They mimic things? It's not really a problem."

"It's not? He comes here a bird and comes out a fucking goat, and it's not a problem?" It felt like a vein had popped in my head.

I was losing my mind. I just needed to leave.

The Australian guy emerged from down the hall. "Hey, mate. I couldn't help but overhear you yelling. Imitation is the finest form of flattery. And Pixy is *very* flattered."

The *baa* sounds drove me bonkers the entire way home.

When I dropped Huey off, I jumped in the shower and whacked one off real quick to calm myself down before getting changed into some casual clothes.

As expected, traffic was bumper to bumper almost the entire way to Greenwich. Thank goodness, I'd left work early.

By the time I pulled up to Hailey's friend's house, I was ravenous. I hadn't eaten since breakfast.

The smell of barbecue filled the air. My stomach growled.

The sun hadn't set yet. There was probably at least another hour of daylight left.

A woman spotted me approaching the property and opened a gate leading into the pool area.

"You must be Hailey's uncle?"

"Yes." I held out my hand. "Hollis LaCroix."

She took it, giving me a once-over. "Lindsey Branson, Megan's mother."

"Thank you for having Hailey."

"It's been an absolute pleasure. And your Elodie is such a hoot, too."

My Elodie?

I couldn't wait to get to Elodie and give her a piece of my mind about what happened with Huey. I still wanted to blame her for the whole thing, even though deep down I knew it wasn't her fault. I just enjoyed directing my anger toward her for some reason.

But when I got through that gate and took a look at her, I couldn't remember anything I had to say. Elodie was lying on a lounge chair wearing a bikini top that displayed her taut stomach—and cutoff denim shorts. *Fuck.* That diamond belly ring was glimmering in what sunlight was left, her supple tits pushed up somewhat. I'd never seen her so exposed. Given the environment, it wasn't even inappropriate. Just *sexy.*

When she spotted me, she hopped up from her seat and walked over.

"There you are." She smiled. "You made it. Everything work out okay?"

The entire car ride here I'd been intent on reaming her out. For what exactly? I didn't even know. Now, all I wanted to do was look at her. Well, I wanted to do more than look at her, but I knew that wouldn't be happening.

Instead of barking at her, I said, "Everything is great."

"Good." She smiled. "Hungry?"

My eyes scrolled down the length of her body. *Fucking starving.*

"I could eat."

"Let me make you a plate."

"You really don't have to do that."

"I know. I want to. You had a long day."

As I followed her toward the smell of the grill, I said, "You know, you're kind of an anomaly."

"How so?"

"Well, you hate men for the most part. You're quite independent. Yet any chance you get, you're trying to serve me or feed me. I'm not sure I understand it."

"It's simple," she said as she grabbed a burger and started making my plate.

"Yeah? Enlighten me."

"You don't expect it. You're not the type of guy who assumes a woman's role is in the kitchen or that you're superior just because you're a man. Hailey has told me what you've taught her about being a strong woman and not taking shit from people. Because you don't expect to be served, it's my pleasure to do it." She handed me the plate. "Here you go."

"Thanks."

"You're welcome."

We walked back to the lounge chairs, and Hailey finally noticed me.

"Hi, Uncle Hollsy!" she yelled from the pool.

I waved and spoke with my mouth full. "Hey, Hailey."

"Can we stay longer?" she asked.

"Yeah. A little while," I said.

I sure as hell wasn't going to push going home early when here I could gaze at Elodie's body in that getup.

Yeah, it was official. Addison was right.

I do have a thing for Elodie.

CHAPTER FOURTEEN

Elodie

Yeah. *Pretty sure he has a thing for me.* At least the way he was sneaking glances at my breasts and navel indicated that. Or maybe it was wishful thinking because I found him so attractive.

Hollis wore a gray polo shirt and khakis, his shades tucked into the opening of his shirt. I loved when he dressed down.

"I actually don't live very far from here," I said.

"That's right. I keep forgetting you're all the way out in the boonies."

"I like living outside the city. It's peaceful. My ex-husband and I had a very active social life in town. That got me nowhere. I'd much rather wake up to birds chirping than honking and yelling any day." I smiled. "And that was just in our apartment."

"Your ex seems to influence a lot of the decisions you've made."

"Yes. But the experience only made me stronger."

"Stronger or guarded?"

"What do you mean?"

"Two years, Elodie? And the only man you're spending time with is on some Turkish soap opera with subtitles?"

"How did you know about that?"

"You had YouTube on the TV when I walked in and woke you up last night."

"Oh...well, yeah... That guy is...pretty nice." I grinned sheepishly.

"And he can't hurt you."

"What are you getting at?"

"He can't hurt you, like your ex-husband did—the guy who inspired you to become a man trap. The guy behind the TV screen is safe."

"You think you have me all figured out, huh?"

His brow lifted. "Don't I?"

"I don't exactly see *you* in a healthy relationship. You can barely look at your bird because he reminds you of some broad who dumped you. I think you have a little bit of a history with heartbreak yourself."

Before he could address my comment, Hailey interrupted. She was dripping from the pool and shivering.

"Can I spend the night here?" she asked.

"No," Hollis said. "I came all the way out here to pick you up. That means you're coming home with me."

She pouted, then ran back to the pool and jumped in the water.

"I can pick her up tomorrow morning and bring her back to the city if you want," I offered.

While I'd been taking the train into the city most days to save on gas, I still used my car on my days off.

"No. She has to learn that sometimes the answer is no."

"Okay."

"Plus, you shouldn't have to work tomorrow."

"I don't have anything else going on. I actually like my job for once in my life. I look forward to Mondays."

"What do you typically do on the weekends?"

"I sleep in. Sometimes I'll go out and get breakfast and take it over to my friend Bree's house. Later in the day, I'll food shop for the week or maybe work on some of my art. I never really have plans."

"Given your two-year hiatus from men, I take it you stay in at night and curl up with Turkish Fabio?"

"He's the perfect man, right? Handsome, funny, charming, and not a cheat."

"He needs a haircut."

"Don't knock my show until you watch it, Hollsy. There's some pretty eye candy for you on there, too, considering you don't have much of a weekend nightlife, either." I winked.

During the ride to my house, Hollis told us the story of what happened to Huey at the vet. Hailey and I were cracking up. He wasn't amused.

"He says nothing but 'Anna's home' for years, and this is how he decides to branch out?" Hollis snapped.

"I think he knew just the thing to drive you over the edge," I said.

"And what the hell does the B stand for in his name? Did you give him a middle name?" he asked.

I half-laughed. "It stands for *bird*."

"Creative." He chuckled.

"Well, there was a spot for a middle name on the admission form, so..."

Hailey interrupted the conversation when she suddenly asked, "What's a DILF?"

Hollis and I looked at each other, unsure how to respond.

"Why?" I asked.

"Megan heard her mom call Uncle Hollis that. Is a DILF like a doofus?"

I bent my head back in laughter. "Nice assumption."

Hollis clearly didn't know how to answer her question.

I was quickly learning that one of my regular duties as Hailey's nanny was to save Hollis's ass when it came to addressing certain things.

"DILF stands for *Dad I'd Like to Friend*," I said.

She scrunched her nose. "Like on Facebook?"

I nodded. "Exactly."

"Oh. That's not that bad. But weird that she said that because he's not even my dad." She shrugged. "You're a nanny I'd like to friend, Elodie. Does that makes you a...NILF?"

Hollis glanced over at me, and it gave me chills when he muttered under his breath, "Elodie is definitely a NILF."

"This is me." I pointed to my little house, and Hollis pulled to the curb.

He put the car in park and looked around. "There's really not much going on out here. I wouldn't have taken you for a country girl."

"I'm not. I'm originally from Queens. I moved out here when I married Tobias. He wanted to get out of the city, and his dad had just retired and moved to a new fifty-five-and-over community nearby. He liked the area, so we rented this little bungalow to give it a shot. Except our lease lasted longer than the marriage."

"But you stayed."

I shrugged. "I like being closer to nature. Although lately I've been missing the city, and living there would certainly be more convenient."

"Why don't you move back?"

"My best friend lives next door. She's actually my ex-husband's stepsister. That's how we met. But Bree's...not well. She has a lung disease that makes it difficult for her to get around too much. So I want to stay close to help out, even though she doesn't actually let me help very much."

Hollis stared at me funny. "That's very nice of you."

"Not really. She's also my unofficial psychologist and has put up with me the last few years. I think I need her for my mental wellbeing more than she needs me for any physical assistance. In fact, if it weren't for her, we wouldn't have met."

His brows drew together. "How so?"

"Bree saw your ad for a nanny somewhere and encouraged me to apply. She hated my job with Soren."

Hailey had laid down in the back seat a few minutes after we got on the road. The last day of school and a pool party had really knocked her out. But she suddenly sat up and stretched. "I need to take a whiz."

"Hailey, don't talk like that," Hollis snapped.

"Like what?"

"Taking *a whiz*. That's about as classy as a woman saying she needs to take a piss."

"But I do need to take a piss. What would you like me to say?"

I turned and intervened. "Hailey, honey, I think your uncle prefers if you say you have to go to the bathroom...or the ladies' room. *Whiz* and *piss* are a bit crass, even for me."

"So I can't use certain words, but Uncle Hollis gets to say whatever he wants?"

Hollis said *Yes* at the exact same time I said *No*. I'd been about to explain that wasn't what he was saying, but Hollis nipped that in the bud by talking over me.

"I'm an adult," he bit back.

"So when I'm an adult, it's fine to use *whiz* and *piss*?"

"No, because when you're an adult, you'll be a lady."

"Maybe I don't want to be a lady."

"Hailey, don't push my buttons."

I almost laughed. That was exactly what she was doing. I knew what that looked like because I liked to do it, too.

"Why don't we go inside my house so you can use the bathroom, Hailey?"

"Okay!" She whipped open the back door and jumped out.

I looked over at Hollis. "Would you like to come in and take a whiz before getting on the road, too?"

He narrowed his eyes. "The two of you are going to drive me to drink."

Inside the house, I showed Hailey where the main bathroom was and then led Hollis into the bathroom off my bedroom. When I flicked on the light, I realized I had all of my underwear and bras hanging over the shower curtain. This morning I'd hand-washed things that didn't go in the washing machine.

Hollis froze.

"They're underwear. They won't bite. You'll be safe for your whiz."

He mumbled something under his breath and shut the door behind him. I went to wait for Hailey in the kitchen.

She came out of the bathroom a few minutes later, sniffing her hands. "What kind of soap is in there? It smells so good."

"It's lavender. I'll pick you up some the next time I go to Bath & Body Works."

"Thanks." She pulled out a stool that had been tucked under the kitchen counter and made herself at home. "I like the painting in the bathroom, too. It's sort of creepy, but pretty at the same time."

I smiled. "Thank you. I painted it."

Her eyes widened. "You did?"

"Yup."

"Wow. Can you teach me how to paint like that?"

124

"I could teach you some techniques. Sure." I opened the refrigerator. "Do you want something to drink before you head back to the city?"

She shook her head. "No, thanks. It'll just make me have to go to the bathroom."

I heard Hollis's voice before I saw him. "So you're capable of using the word *bathroom* for Elodie."

Hailey turned to look at her uncle, then completely ignored him and looked back at me. "Do you have more of your art anywhere?"

I nodded and pointed down the hall. "First door on the left. It's a spare bedroom, but I use it for painting."

Hailey hopped down from the stool and took off.

"Would you like something to drink, Hollis?"

"No, thank you."

He looked completely uncomfortable standing in my kitchen, so of course, I needed to make it worse. I tilted my head. "Did you touch any?"

"What?"

"My panties. Did you touch any while you were in the bathroom?"

He tugged at the collar of his polo and looked down the hall. "Where did she go? We need to get back on the road."

Oh my God!

I'd been kidding around. But...*holy shit*...he had! I covered my mouth and cracked up. "You did, didn't you! You perv!"

Hollis walked down the hall. "Hailey...let's get going."

I couldn't get the smile off my face. Something about the thought of Hollis touching my underwear amused the hell out of me. I wished Hailey wasn't around so I could ask him if he'd smelled them, too. That thought actually made me snort.

Hollis came back to the kitchen. His face was stern. "We'll see you on Monday."

I walked them to the door. Hailey surprised me with a hug. "Your stuff is awesome."

"Thank you, sweetheart."

I grinned at Hollis, who was impatiently holding the door open for his niece. "Your uncle thinks my stuff is awesome, too."

CHAPTER FIFTEEN

Elodie

I didn't notice until I started brushing my teeth the next morning. And even then, I still couldn't believe it. It *had* to be here somewhere. I pushed back the shower curtain for the second time, positive I must've overlooked my black thong the first time I'd checked. It must've fallen from where I'd hung it on the shower curtain into the tub. There was no way...

No damn way.

He would never...

Yet the tub was empty.

In denial, I searched the rest of the bathroom and all of my dirty laundry. I was positive it had been hanging in here yesterday when I'd shown Hollis to the bathroom. I'd seen it with my own two eyes. And the matching bra was still hanging right next to where my thong had been. I *always* wore sets, *always* washed them together, and *always* hung them next to each other to dry. But now...it was gone.

I couldn't stop shaking my head. I had to tell someone. So I grabbed my robe from the bathroom hook, filled my coffee mug to the brim, and headed next door. I hadn't checked in on Bree in a few days, anyway.

The door opened.

"*He stole my underwear*!" I marched inside.

Bree's face wrinkled. "What? Who?" She closed the door and followed me into the living room.

"My new boss. I had four sets of underwear and bras hanging in my bathroom, and this morning my black lace thong is missing."

I'd been so absorbed in my stupid story that I didn't even notice Bree didn't look so hot. Her skin was pale, and she leaned on the couch like she was dizzy.

I walked over and grabbed her arms. "Are you okay? You don't look so good."

"I'm fine. It's just...the doctor changed my medication, and it makes me feel a little lightheaded, I think."

"Well, come on, let's sit you down." I made Bree take a seat on the couch and crouched in front of her. "Should we call the doctor? What can I do? And why don't you have your oxygen on?"

She waved me off. "No. I'm fine. Don't call anyone. I think...I must've gotten up too fast. That's all it was. And I was just heading into the kitchen to make some tea, so I took my oxygen off because I don't wear it near the stove."

I looked around for the tubing to her oxygen machine that snaked through the house, and found the end with the nasal cannula slung over the arm of a chair.

Grabbing it, I helped her put it on. "Sit and relax. Let me make you the tea."

I went to the kitchen, boiled water in the kettle, and steeped Bree a cup of her favorite peppermint tea. I served it to her in the living room in her favorite Tiffany teacup, which she displayed, but never actually drank from.

"I don't get collecting china and not using it. You love this set, why not use it?"

She sipped. "I guess I don't want to break it."

I arched a brow. "Do you often break cups?"

She smiled. It made me feel a lot better. "No."

"Okay then. From now on, you eat and drink on your china. Take it from me, your pretty little china wants more than to be admired. It's useful, too, if you give it a chance."

I watched while Bree drank her tea—maybe a little too vigilantly.

"I'm fine. Stop waiting for me to keel over."

"Are you sure we shouldn't call the doctor? It couldn't hurt to call your pulmonologist."

"No. I just needed to sit down for a minute."

I looked her over. Her color had definitely improved, and she didn't look like she might pass out anymore. "Okay. But take your time getting up from now on. Anyone who knocks at your door can wait for you to get there or go screw themselves."

Bree smiled sadly. "Maybe I'll get a welcome mat that says that."

"Don't tempt me to have one made for you."

She chuckled. "So what were you saying? Your boss took your underwear?"

"Oh. Right. Yup."

This was typical Bree—changing the subject from her health. She hated to dwell on her illness. The first chance she got, the focus was always pushed back to me. At least today my story might cheer her up. "So get this, Hollis—Mr. Grumpy-stick-up-his-ass—*stole my underwear.*"

"You...slept with your boss already?"

"No!"

"So how did he get your underwear?"

"Hailey had a last-day-of-school party at a friend's summer home in Connecticut. We hitched a ride to the house after school, but bossman had to come pick us up after work. He dropped me off next door, and Hailey came in to use the bathroom. Hollis had to go, too, so he used the one in my bedroom. You know how I hang my bras and underwear over the shower curtain after I hand wash them? Well, after he left, my black lace thong was missing."

"Are you sure he took it? That doesn't sound like Hollis, from what you've told me. Maybe you put it away in a drawer or it's in the laundry or something."

I shook my head. "I checked. And I'm positive I saw the set there when I flicked on the light and showed him the bathroom last night. Plus, he was acting weird after he came out. In fact, I was teasing him and asked if he'd played with my underwear while he was in there, and he got all flustered. I thought it was because he'd touched them...but this morning I realized it was because he'd *stolen* my thong. Mr. Uptight walked out with my underwear hidden in his pocket, Bree."

I clapped my hands and fell back against the couch. Telling the story made me as tickled as I'd felt when I'd realized what had gone down. I would be amused thinking about it for a long time to come.

"What are you going to do? Pretend you don't know?"

I sat back up. "Is that medication also making you delirious? You know me, Bree. I'm not going to let it pass. I'm going to use it to torture the hell out of the man."

Bree shook her head. "But he's your boss."

I shrugged. "So? He started it. If it's okay to steal my panties, it's okay to call him out on it. Plus, he's totally fun to screw with."

"Why do you think he took them? Is he lonely?"

"Honestly, I have no damn idea. If he's lonely, it's certainly not because he can't get a date. The man is ridiculously good-looking. Even at the party today, the mothers were all getting hot and bothered when he walked in."

Bree got quiet. I knew what she was thinking. But it wasn't like that—not with Hollis, anyway. "Stop worrying. I don't want to torture him the same way I did the guys I met working for Soren. Hollis is different. I'm pretty sure he's attracted to me, and that actually pisses him off."

"Maybe he's different in a good way," Bree countered. "Maybe he's the kind of guy who wears a lot of armor because he's protecting a fragile heart."

I scoffed. "Not so sure about that. I think it's more like he hasn't had time to get laid in a few weeks and wouldn't mind boinking the nanny. But he's smart enough to know that might not end well and then he'd have to find a new one. Hence, rub one out while wearing the nanny's panties over his face."

Bree looked skeptical. "Just don't get yourself fired."

I smiled. "Who me? Never."

Baaa!

When Hailey and I walked into the apartment Monday afternoon, Huey greeted us. We looked at each other and smiled.

"Does that drive your uncle nuts?"

Her smile widened. "Pretty much."

We laughed.

"Go take a shower and get that sticky stuff out of your hair. I'll get dinner started, but I'll save the chopping until you're done so you can help."

"Okay."

Hailey and I had gone to MOMA today. And we took a walk through Central Park so I could show her Bethesda Fountain—which we'd seen in two paintings. During our walk, we passed a cotton candy vendor, and Hailey suckered me into buying her some. It was a breezy day, and her long hair blew into the pink fluff half a dozen times, making a clump of her hair sticky.

In the kitchen, I put the water on to boil and then heard the bathroom door close. Since I had a few minutes, I decided to do a little snooping. Hollis had acted like his normal, abrupt self this morning, and since Hailey was up early, I didn't get a chance to ask him about my underwear. But maybe I would be able to find them—then I'd know for sure.

I listened at the bathroom door to make sure the shower was running and then went to Hollis's bedroom. The door creaked as I opened it. I'd peeked inside last week, curious to see what his lair looked like, but I'd never actually stepped in.

Feeling a morsel of guilt, I crossed the threshold. I was invading Hollis's privacy. Then again, how much more invasive can a person get than swiping undies? I had every right to be in here. *Tit for tat.* Though, seeing as he stole my panties and not a bra, I was thinking he was more of a *va-jay-jay-for-tat* man.

I looked around. A king-sized bed with a carved wood frame was the centerpiece of the room—very masculine, with luxurious-looking bedding. *I bet those are soft and comfy.* I had the strongest urge to find out, roll around in the center of the navy-and-cream-striped plushness. *Another day, Elodie.*

I tapped my pointer finger to my lip. *Hmmm...* Where would I stash my spank-bank material if I were a panty thief? I went to the obvious place first—the bedside nightstands.

The one on the left side was pretty barren—some batteries and a few old remotes. But the one on the right side was pretty full—a box of condoms, Visine, a pocket watch, a small notepad, two old wallets, a phone book, a few pens, and some other boring miscellaneous stuff. *No panties.*

I shut the drawer. Hailey wouldn't be in the shower that long, and I didn't want to get caught, so I needed to hurry up. I slid my hand under the mattress, checked under the bed, opened each of the dresser drawers and did a quick rummage through, and I even checked out his massive walk-in closet—*no thong*. I let out a sigh of defeat.

Maybe he didn't steal it? Could it have been somewhere in my apartment and I'd overlooked it? Maybe I was wrong after all? I was just about to shut off the light when the bed caught my attention once again. *Hmmm*. It was worth a shot.

I walked around to the side where the end table was full—figuring that was where he probably slept—pulled back the bedding, and lifted the pillow.

Bingo!

Oh my God!

Oh my freaking God!

My eyes bulged.

My thong.

My freaking thong was under his pillow.

Though I'd been looking for it, I was shocked to actually find it. *Especially under his pillow.*

I stared at it for the longest time, unsure what the hell to do. Did I leave it? Take it? It wasn't like there was proper etiquette for stealing back your lingerie from a panty thief. I had no idea what to do.

"Elodie!"

I jumped, hearing Hailey's voice.

Shit.

Shit.

Shit.

I quickly dropped the pillow and pulled the comforter back over it before bolting to the bedroom door. My heart raced in my chest as I walked down the hall toward the bathroom. "Hailey?"

"Can you get me a bottle of conditioner out of the hall closet?" she yelled from behind the bathroom door. I pressed my hand to my chest, relieved at not having been caught. "I forgot to bring it in with me, and there's none left in here."

"Yes. Sure. Hang on a second."

I grabbed a bottle of conditioner from the closet and knocked on the bathroom door. "Coming in, kiddo."

I set it on top of the toilet. "I'll just leave it right here."

"Thanks."

I walked back out of the bathroom and pulled the door shut. *God, that was close.*

Now I knew I had a few minutes before Hailey would be finished in the shower, and I could fix the comforter and figure out what the hell I was going to do.

With my heart still beating out of control, I walked back into Hollis's bedroom. I stayed in the doorway for a long moment, staring at the bed and trying to figure out how to handle this situation. Then it hit me—seriously, like a lightning bolt. I knew *exactly* how to handle it.

I stepped inside and shut the door behind me, making sure to lock it. Walking over to the bed, I pulled back the comforter and snatched my clean black thong from underneath the pillow. Then I unbuttoned my pants, shimmied them down my legs and stepped out. I slipped off the hot pink silky thong I had on today and put on the black lace one Hollis had stolen. Smiling, I left my pink one under the pillow.

I bet you enjoy these more, perv.

Hollis was in a mood when he came home that night. I tried to act like it was business as usual, despite not being able to stop thinking about the panty situation.

He didn't even acknowledge me as he headed straight for the cabinet, took out a glass, and poured himself wine.

"Lasagna is warming in the oven," I said.

Hollis took a long sip then simply grunted to acknowledge he'd heard me say something.

He still wasn't making eye contact with me.

Was he feeling guilty, perhaps? I started to second-guess what I'd done to mess with him—for a millisecond. Then I snapped back to reality, reminding myself that he'd stolen my damn panties in the first place and had therefore asked for it. *He* started this.

He loosened his tie. His hair was a bit unkempt. One thing about Hollis, he was even sexier when he was mad.

He took another sip of his wine and finally asked, "Any reason you're sticking around? Something you need to tell me about Hailey?"

"No. Not at all. Hailey's great. She's cleaning up her room. I'm sure she'll tell you all about what we did today." After a few more seconds of awkward silence, I said, "Have a good night."

"You too," he said, massaging the tension in the back of his neck.

Awkward. Awkward. Awkward.

As I walked out the door, I realized I was sort of jealous of my own undies and the fun they might be having tonight without me.

CHAPTER SIXTEEN

Hollis

Ever wish you could go back and change something you've done? A stupid mistake made on impulse that had lasting repercussions?

I have many regrets in life. But if I could change only one thing, it would be the moment I ever thought it was a good idea to slip Elodie Atlier's thong into my back pocket.

Apparently, I believed I could get away with murder that night. Instead, I opened a huge can of worms I wouldn't be able to get myself out of. I certainly never thought she'd taunt me about touching them the second I walked out of her bathroom. Perceptive thing, she is.

At this point, I suspected she knew I did more than touch her lingerie. Was there a chance I might have gotten lucky and the theft had gone unnoticed? I suppose. But the *not knowing* was driving me crazy. The uncertainty kept me agitated all day and unable to focus on my job. Basically, I was now paranoid, as if I'd committed a crime and knew the police were going to show up at my door any minute.

But as the evening wore on, I calmed down somewhat. Hailey told me all about their day at the museum over dinner. Elodie's lasagna was phenomenal. After a couple of glasses of wine and a full belly, I felt a bit less on edge.

I decided to assume that even if Elodie suspected I'd taken the thong, there was no way she could prove it. That seed of doubt would always exist. Eventually, this whole situation would blow over.

Later that night, as I lay in bed, though, I realized how depraved I really was. Because as much as I regretted taking her thong, I kept thinking about the fact that it was under my pillow. I wanted nothing more than to take it out again and use it for inspiration as I jerked off. *What's one more time?*

Yes, I'd in fact masturbated with her panties over my face last night and was now considering an encore.

I'd convinced myself that if the opportunity arose and I could get back into her house, I could return them— maybe slip them behind a radiator in the bathroom or something. It would be like this whole thing never happened. So, taking them out *one more time* would harm no one. Right? No one would ever know.

In the end, though, I rolled over and decided against it.

I can't.

But after several minutes of lying there staring into space, insomnia won. I finally succumbed to the fact that I would need a release to fall asleep tonight. I slipped my hand under the pillow and pulled the thong out.

My heart went from racing excitedly to skipping a beat when I noticed the silky fabric. The hot pink color. This was *not* the same thong.

This. Was. NOT. The. Same. Thong.

I stared at it in my hand as if it were alive.

What the fuck now, Hollis?

How did she know to look under my pillow? What was she doing in my bedroom? I wanted to give her a piece of my mind for trespassing. How dare she snoop when I was at work?

But she had me exactly where she wanted me, because I couldn't even address it to reprimand her.

I was madder at myself than Elodie. I'd caused this. Why? Because I was impulsive, horny, selfish—and a goddamn panty snatcher, apparently.

I opened my bedside drawer and threw the hot pink thong into it before slamming it closed. So much for sleeping now.

I stared at the drawer as if I'd stuffed a body in a trunk. Elodie could have taken her black thong back and left nothing behind. She could've snapped a photo to taunt me. Instead, she opted to leave another one. She was enjoying this little game, messing with me, capitalizing on my sexual attraction to her.

She wants me to have it.

I opened the drawer slowly and took the thong into my hands, threading the silky fabric through my fingers. I brought them to my nose and took a deep whiff in. *Ohhhh.* Fuck. Me. Whereas the other pair had just come out of the wash, smelling like detergent, these smelled like a woman. She'd worn these. There was no debate left. I got up and double-checked that my door was locked.

Then I returned to bed and lay back, placing the panties over my face. Taking out my rigid cock, I stroked it hard, simultaneously breathing in. If I was going to hell for something, at least this would be worth it. And getting off to her actual scent—knowing she'd taken these off for *me*, knowing they'd been up against her pussy today—made me crazy.

It didn't take long. I came fast and hard, all over my abs. One would think it had been days since I'd last jerked off, when in fact it was last night.

But as the high of my orgasm wore off, I started to come back to reality. I was back to seeing myself as a filthy pig lying here with her panties on my face. I crumpled them up, threw them in the drawer, then slammed it shut again.

The following afternoon, my concentration level at work was even worse than the day before. Once again, I hadn't been able to look Elodie in the eye when I left for work this morning. I'd taken her damn panties out again when I woke up at the crack of dawn, took care of business, then left them under the pillow exactly where I'd originally found them. I wanted her to think maybe I'd done nothing at all with them, maybe I'd never found them, maybe I'd redeemed myself and no longer wanted anything to do with her.

I knew I was kidding myself. I'd had aftershave on, and she'd smell me all over them.

Maybe a part of me wanted that, too. I was sick.

Addison's voice snapped me out of my thoughts. "Hello? Earth to Hollis!"

I'd been twisting a pen around in my hand when she interrupted my rumination.

I threw the pen down. "What?"

"We've been waiting for you in the conference room for nearly a half hour. Did you forget about the two o'clock meeting?"

Shit. I totally forgot. "Sorry. I'll be right in."

For the entire meeting, Addison kept staring at me, squinting...assessing. She'd known me a very long time and could see through anything.

After we left the meeting, she cornered me in my office.

"What the hell has gotten into you now, Hollis?"

At first, the thought of Addison knowing what was going on seemed mortifying. But the truth was, I could use her unbiased opinion on how to handle this situation. In the end, I was Elodie's boss, and what I'd done was beyond inappropriate. So from both a professional and personal viewpoint, I needed input.

"Today is your lucky day, Addison."

"Oh? Why is that?"

"Because I'm about to give you blackmail material you can hold over my head forever."

"Uh-oh. What did you do? And please tell me this has to do with Elodie." She grinned. "I've been waiting for some juice."

I braced myself and began to tell her the story.

⌒

Addison was all too amused. "You dirty dog. This is better than I ever hoped. Although I don't know who's worse, you or her."

"Skip the taunting. How do I handle this?"

"I'm just kidding. This isn't a real problem, Hollis. It's all in good fun."

"You don't see a problem with this? If I stole your underwear, you could sue me for harassment, and it would ruin my career. How is this any different?"

"Well, you definitely took a risk. But I think you did it in part because you know there's a reciprocal attraction there. You're comfortable with her. And you also stupidly assumed you wouldn't get caught."

I sighed. "Okay, so what now?"

"Just see where things go. Why do you have to have a plan?"

"Because I can't even look at her."

"Well, you need to get over that. You're both adults, and clearly she's enjoying this."

I pulled on my hair. "This is such a fucking mess."

"Why? Why is it a bad thing? It's innocent fun. Although, I don't expect it will end up innocent."

"I've already explained the ramifications of getting involved with her. Have you not heard anything I've been saying?"

"Oh, that's right. If things don't work out, *Hailey* could get hurt."

"Precisely."

"This has nothing to do with the fact that *you* could get hurt, too, right?"

I paced. "Now you're overanalyzing."

"Am I?" She crossed her arms. "I think you see Elodie as exactly the type of woman you would want in your life if you weren't so damn scared to let someone in. I think that's why you're afraid of messing things up. It's *not* only about Hailey."

I stopped moving. Her words shook me, but I was unwilling to accept that she was right.

When I didn't say anything, she added, "We've had many drunken conversations, Hollis. You told me yourself once that the only two women you've ever loved—your mother and Anna—disappeared on you. You said you'd never make the mistake of getting attached to anyone again. If you thought you could just have meaningless sex with Elodie, and that would be it, you'd be running *toward* this situation and not away from it. You see the potential for something more here. And that scares you."

Speaking of running away, I needed to get the fuck out of this conversation.

I walked back over to my desk and rustled some papers. "I'm behind on some admin stuff."

"See? This is what you do. You run away before you have to deal with things that hurt." She stopped in front of my desk and leaned into it until I had no choice but to look at her. "Stop letting your past determine your future, Hollis. Allow it to make you a better person, not a bitter one."

I shut my eyes briefly. "I get what you're saying. But even if I didn't have whatever issues you think I have, anything more than a business relationship with Elodie is not a possibility because of Hailey. So this isn't open for discussion."

After Addison left, her words haunted me. I knew she was right.

Still, I was unwilling to accept the possibility of something more happening with Elodie. I needed a distraction. That meant I needed to get off on something other than Elodie's underwear.

Hailey had a sleepover on Friday night. I'd have the apartment to myself for the first time in a while. I picked up my phone and sent a text to someone I knew would be a sure thing with no strings attached.

Hollis: My place Friday night?

CHAPTER SEVENTEEN

Elodie

I was shaking. Literally shaking. *What's wrong with me?* I'd started this game, but now I was nervous.

Hollis and I hadn't said a peep to each other this morning. I couldn't tell if he was embarrassed or angry at me for what I'd done. And he wouldn't look at me long enough so I could figure it out.

Hailey and I had ended up having a busy day, so I'd had no opportunity to venture into Hollis's bedroom to check things out. I'd taken her to buy clothes at Justice using her uncle's credit card. We then went to Dylan's Candy Bar and loaded up on sugar before returning to the apartment.

Now that we were back, Hailey had gone to her room while I worked in the kitchen, prepping dinner.

She entered the kitchen several minutes later and asked, "Would it be okay if I went downstairs to Kelsie's?"

Kelsie was the only kid around Hailey's age who lived in the building. I looked over at the clock. It would be about an hour and a half until Hollis came home. Since I knew her leaving would give me the opportunity to snoop like I'd been dying for, I was all for it.

"Is her mom going to be home?"

"Yeah. I heard her say it was okay."

"Just an hour. I want you home before your uncle gets back."

"Alright."

"Actually, I'll walk you downstairs."

It wasn't that I didn't trust her. But I knew the type of stuff I'd pulled when I was around her age. At the very least, I needed to make sure she was going where she said she was.

Once I made sure Kelsie's mother was really home, I returned upstairs to the empty apartment.

My heart raced as I made my way into Hollis's bedroom.

I went straight for the pillow and lifted it to find my hot pink panties exactly where I'd left them the day before. Could he have not seen them? I pondered that—until I smelled them. They reeked of his musky scent. Could it be from the pillow? I wasn't sure. All I knew was that my thong now smelled like Hollis. And that turned me on very much. I squeezed the muscles between my legs. I'd teased him about being a perv, but who was the perv now? That was all I could think as I sat there on his bed, sniffing my own damn underwear.

I didn't know what to do. Did I continue this game? Or did I stop it and let him make a move if he wished to continue?

In the end, I slipped off my panties again. Except this time, I placed them in his bedside drawer. Make him look for them. Change things up.

The following day, Hailey and I rode bikes around the neighborhood and took lunch to Central Park, where we rollerbladed.

I'd specifically planned activities that would require Hailey to take a shower when we got back. Actually, we both had to shower. I went first.

After I got out and changed, Hailey went in.

Baaa. "Anna's home!" Huey squawked as I waited to hear Hailey turn on the water.

Once I heard it running and was confident she was in full shower mode, I snuck into Hollis's room.

I peeked under the pillow first. *Nothing.* I opened the drawer where I'd put the royal blue thong yesterday, and sure enough, there it was in the same spot I'd left it. I lifted it to my nose and was thrilled to find it smelled like Hollis's cologne. This was it: proof. There was no way he hadn't touched them.

Busted.

Our little undie switcheroo game continued throughout the week. I had to admit, I was getting impatient. I kept waiting for Hollis to acknowledge what was happening, to say something—anything—and he never did. Neither of us budged. I guess I was secretly hoping it would lead to something more. But having a kinky underwear fetish and wanting a relationship were two different things, I supposed.

When Friday rolled around, I was more frustrated than ever. That afternoon, I dropped Hailey off across town for a sleepover.

Before heading home to Connecticut for the weekend, I decided to return to the apartment to clean up some dishes we'd left in the sink and feed Huey. Since Hailey was gone, I'd be able to skip out early and wouldn't get to see Hollis when he came home from work. I had mixed feelings about that, but in the end, I opted not to stick around.

Before leaving, I took off my yellow thong and placed it under his pillow. I vowed this would be the last one. If nothing came of this, I wouldn't continue the game.

I boarded my train back to Connecticut and was almost home when I panicked. As I rummaged through my purse, I realized my phone was nowhere to be found. Had I left it at Hollis's place? That was unlike me, but my head hadn't been on straight today. There was no way I wanted Hollis to have access to my phone! I'd always been too lazy to program a security code. That meant he would be able to look through all of my photos, some of which I'd taken years ago, when I was still married to Tobias. I used to sometimes send him a nude selfie to be a tease when I knew he was in a faculty meeting. And I had thousands of old pictures stored from previous cell phones that had been transferred over the years.

Shit. I needed to go back.

By the time I caught another train and made it back to the city, it was after 7PM. As I walked into Hollis's building, I wondered if maybe I'd luck out and he wouldn't be home. I knocked, but there was no answer, so I decided to let myself in.

After turning the key and opening the door, I got the shock of my life to find Hollis standing in the living room—with a woman.

She had long reddish hair and was dressed in business attire. The top buttons of her black satin blouse were undone to reveal just the right amount of cleavage. Her lips were painted red.

They were both holding glasses of wine.

This is a date.

I've walked in on Hollis's date!

More than pissed, I felt...devastated.

His eyes nearly popped out of his head when he saw me enter.

"Oh...uh..." I stammered. "I'm sorry."

"What are you doing here?" he snapped.

"I think I left my phone. I was on the train and had to turn back."

"You should've called or...knocked or something."

Is he serious?

"I did knock, but apparently you were too busy to answer! Anyway, I didn't think it was a big deal. I was hoping you wouldn't be home."

"Next time please don't use your key after hours."

My ears burned. I couldn't believe he was treating me so rudely. *Fuck him.* Not to mention, he was planning to give this bitch *my* orgasm—the one I'd *earned* by playing this little game all week.

I lifted my chin. "Who's this?"

"This is Sophia." He turned to her. "Sophia, this is Elodie, Hailey's nanny."

"Hello," she said, looking me up and down.

"Pleasure to meet you," I said, my tone bitter.

I pushed past Hollis and ventured down the hallway without permission.

"Excuse me," he said to her.

He followed as I went from room to room. "What the hell do you think you're doing?"

"I told you. I'm looking for my phone."

"You can't just barge in here like this."

Without stopping, I said, "Are you kidding me? I spend more time in this house than you do."

I finally spotted my phone on the bathroom sink... I didn't remember bringing my phone into the bathroom at all.

Did he take it in here?

Has he been looking at my photos?

Rage filled me.

No way I was letting him fuck that woman with my panties beneath them.

I barged into his bedroom and tossed his pillow aside to retrieve my thong. I felt around the sheets. There was nothing there. It was gone.

"Hollis, where is it?"

He tugged at his hair. His jaw ticked. But he said nothing.

"I'm not leaving without my underwear!" I shouted.

At that moment, we both turned and noticed Sophia standing in the doorway.

She didn't look happy. "What the hell is going on?"

"Sophia, I'm really sorry about this," he pleaded.

"Yeah. So am I," she huffed. "Goodnight, Hollis."

Her heels clicked against the marble floor as she marched down the hall to the foyer. After we heard the front door slam, silence filled the air.

Huey's voice rang out in the distance. *Baaa!* "Anna's home."

"Are you happy now?" Hollis finally said.

"No, I'm not. Because I don't have my underwear."

"Do you see how ridiculous this situation is?"

"Actually, I don't. You've been fucking with my mind all week—using me to get your rocks off. Then, I innocently come back here to retrieve my phone—which you probably looked through—to find you getting ready to fuck someone else."

"How is it any of your business who I fuck under my own roof?"

"It is my business when you've been playing with my mind."

He took a few steps toward me. "You started the game, Elodie."

I pointed at his chest with my index finger. "Are you smoking crack? *You* started this by stealing my damn underwear."

"That was a mistake," he muttered. "It was just a prank."

"A prank..."

He swallowed and said nothing.

I snapped my finger facetiously. "Oh! Because thirty-year-old men in suits who work on Wall Street go around pranking people like little children all the time." I blew a breath up into my hair and held out my hand. "Look, just give me my panties back, and I'll be on my way."

He wouldn't say anything.

"Come on, Hollis."

He bit his bottom lip and said, "I can't."

"Why?"

"Because they're not here."

"Where are they?"

"They're...in the laundry."

"The laundry?"

His voice was low. "Yes."

"Why are they..." I stopped when I figured it out.

He gritted his teeth. "I came home and saw them, and...I... Anyway, I thought I had until Monday to get them back to you."

I felt my eyes widening. Was I horrified or completely turned on by the fact that he'd used my panties to jerk off? I mean, I knew that's what he did with them; I just didn't know he did it *with* them. I guess this was new.

In a sense, I guess I couldn't fault him. I'd led him on to do exactly what he did. I was just frustrated that he'd chosen to not see me as anything more than this game. He'd invited Sophia to spend the evening with him—not me. And that spoke volumes.

I looked down at my feet. "I thought maybe this was...leading to something. Then I walk in and find you with her." Laughing angrily, I said, "I've been kidding myself. To be honest, I'm hurt, Hollis. And I feel like a fool for feeling this way."

I let out a frustrated breath and walked out toward the door.

He followed me. "Elodie, wait..."

But I kept on going.

On the subway ride home, it bugged the crap out of me that I'd found my phone in Hollis's bathroom, because I didn't remember bringing it in there. If I'd learned anything about the infuriating man, it was that if my gut said something was awry, it probably was.

I wondered if he'd been checking out my photos, maybe collecting a little spank-bank material for his jerk-off session before his big date. That was the part that upset me most—the thought that he used me to get off before his actual date. I'd thought I'd put my job with Soren behind me, but apparently my only use to any man was my looks. My cheeks heated with anger.

Yet I couldn't help but be curious what photo might have done it for him. I wasn't even sure what was on my phone anymore. I looked around the subway car; no one was sitting next to me or would see my phone. It would be the perfect time to scroll through, so I clicked to my photo app. The very first picture stopped me in my tracks.

What the hell?

I lifted my cell for a closer inspection.

At first I couldn't make out exactly what it was; all I saw was tan skin. But then I turned the phone sideways, and I gasped. *Oh my God!*

Oh my freaking God!

I knew those clothes and that hand. Hollis had used my phone to take a selfie—a close-up of his lower half. The picture was shot from the belly button down. His dress shirt was hanging open, revealing killer abs and a deep-set V, and his slacks were unzipped with one hand pushing down the band to his boxer shorts. It didn't reveal his dick, but it was sure as hell close. The entire photo was all taut skin, veins, and little bit of neatly trimmed hair right above where his shaft would be.

My mouth hung open. It was, without a doubt, the most erotic photo I'd ever laid eyes on, and I was most definitely in a state of shock that he'd taken it. After a few very intense minutes of studying every nuance of the shot, I swallowed and finally managed to snap out of it. I needed to swipe and see if he might've left me something else. Unfortunately that was the only one—not that anything more was needed.

I had no idea what to make of this new revelation. I suppose his plan had been to up the ante in our little game. If I could leave something enticing behind, so could he.

But now things had changed; our game had been cut short by an abrupt ending. Which begged the question—what should I do with this now? Other than the inevitable—adding it as material for my own version of a spank bank: the rub club.

CHAPTER EIGHTEEN

Hollis

"**A**re you and Elodie mad at each other?" Hailey asked.

Mad wouldn't exactly be the right word. Maybe *pissed off, infatuated, displeased, obsessed, angry, captivated*—though none of the things I felt about my damn nanny were appropriate to share with my niece.

"No. Why do you ask?"

"Because you barely said two words to each other this week, and when she made me dinner, she only made enough for me and didn't leave you anything to eat."

Oh, yeah, that.

I shook my head and held up a hand to get the waitress's attention so I could order more coffee. "We're just busy, and it's not Elodie's job to cook dinner for me."

My niece squinted. She was street smart, even at her age. She knew bullshit when she heard it. But I wasn't about to explain the disaster I'd gotten myself into to an eleven year old.

"You know what I think happened?" she asked.

"No. But I'm guessing you're about to enlighten me."

"I think she likes you, and you were a jerk to her."

My fork had been halfway to my mouth, and I froze. Seeing my reaction, my niece grinned from ear to ear. *Son of a bitch.*

Luckily, the waitress walked over and interrupted our heart to heart.

"I'll take another coffee, please." I looked at Hailey. "Would you like more chocolate milk?"

She nodded to the waitress. "Yes, please."

I'd definitely noticed the addition of the word *please* to Hailey's vocabulary the last few weeks. I wished I could say it was my doing, but it wasn't. Elodie had been making good headway with her. Even this morning, Hailey had set an alarm to wake up early and then gotten herself ready for me to take her to sign up for some hip-hop lessons she wanted to take. A few weeks ago, her idea of an alarm was me yelling at her to get out of bed seven times.

Hailey finished off her chocolate chip pancakes in silence. I was relieved she'd seemed to drop the discussion on Elodie.

"Do they...let kids visit their parents when they're in prison?"

Shit. Can we go back to talking about Elodie?

"I believe they do, yes. I think it depends on the reason the person is in prison. But I don't know all the rules."

She took the straw out of her almost-empty chocolate milk glass and lifted it to her mouth, tilting her head back to drink the last few drops. "So is my father allowed to have visitors?"

"I'm not sure."

Her eyes had been looking anywhere but at mine. She took a deep breath and met my gaze. "Can you find out and take me to visit him if it's allowed? Please?"

I didn't know the right answer here. Should I take an eleven year old to a prison? Or would that scar her for life? Although maybe it would be worse to keep her from the only parent she had known for that long—even if he was a total loser. This was a decision I should definitely run by Elodie.

"Your dad is in Ohio, so it's not like it's a simple trip. Can you give me a day or two to look into it and think about it? I'll be honest, I'm not sure that's the best environment for you to see your father in."

Hailey frowned. "I've seen him in worse. How do you think he found his way home when he was high? Sometimes I'd have to get him from those abandoned buildings where all the people sleep on dirty mattresses on the floor."

Jesus Christ. I knew my half-brother struggled with drugs and stole cars, but I didn't realize his daughter had to scoop him out of crack dens.

I nodded. "Give me a day or two. Okay?"

"Okay."

Monday night Elodie was readying to make her now-usual rapid departure when I walked in. She pulled her purse to her shoulder, said goodnight to Hailey, and started for the door.

"Ummm, Elodie? Can I speak with you a moment, please?"

She stopped and turned back to face me. The corners of her mouth curved down.

I nodded toward the front door. "I'll walk you out." I looked over at Hailey. "I'll be back in a few minutes. Why don't you get started on your homework?"

Her brows drew together. "Uhhh...because it's summer, and I don't have any?"

I shook my head. "Just go watch TV for a few minutes then."

Elodie walked ahead of me to the door. Her ass swayed back and forth in a pair of tight jeans. This woman—she was Eve, and that ass was my shiny apple.

Once we got to the hall, she folded her arms across her chest and waited for me to speak.

I cleared my throat. "Hailey asked me if I could take her to visit her father in prison. I wanted to get your opinion on how I should handle that."

The stern mask she'd been wearing for the last week and a half slipped down. "Oh. Wow. That's a tough one."

I nodded. "I hate the thought of bringing her to a prison, of her having to see him in that environment. But, as she's reminded me, she's seen her father in worse conditions. And the bottom line is, he is her father. The way he dumped her here and disappeared like he did—I have to wonder if she wants to see for herself that he's okay."

Elodie looked down at her feet, seemingly lost in thought. When she looked up, I realized it was the first time she'd made eye contact with me in more than a week. "I don't think I ever told you about my father."

When I'd interviewed her, she'd said something about a shitty childhood—it was her justification as to why she was the right person for the job. But we'd never discussed anything in detail.

"You've mentioned you had a difficult time growing up, like Hailey."

She nodded and stood a little taller. "Both of my parents are alcoholics. *Raging* alcoholics. Or *were* raging alcoholics. Well, technically, I think my mother is still a raging alcoholic—I'm not sure. We aren't that close, and I don't really want to know. But I guess that's irrelevant to the story. Anyway, my dad was a cop, and most of his friends were cops that drank too much, too. Birds of a feather and all."

She shrugged. "He would think nothing of drinking all afternoon at a friend's barbecue and then driving us home. I knew right from wrong, but I guess I also figured he was a cop—so that made it okay for him to break the law. The day before my twelfth birthday, we were on our way home from one of those summer barbecues, and my dad was swerving all over the road. He'd had way too much to drink and ended up wrapping our car around a tree. My mom suffered a broken leg and a few broken ribs. I was sitting behind her in the back seat and somehow walked away with nothing more than a few scratches and bruises. But my father didn't have his seat belt on. He went through the windshield and was thrown over a hundred feet. He broke his neck and was instantly paralyzed."

"Jesus. I'm sorry."

"Thank you. He was in the hospital for a long time. They actually arrested him and arraigned him there. My mom wanted me to visit him with her, but I was too mad at what he'd done—what they'd both done. Not to mention that I was mortified at school because it was all over the news: disgraced police officer drives drunk and almost kills his family."

"Did you visit him?"

Elodie shook her head. "Nope. I was stubborn." She smirked. "I know you'll have a hard time believing that."

I smiled. "Yeah. Seems totally out of character now. Because you're so easy going."

"Anyway, paraplegics are at risk for a lot of health problems related to being immobile. Thrombosis is one of them. One night, he apparently had some swelling in his arm. The next morning he was dead from a blood clot."

I closed my eyes and nodded. "And you'd not visited him in the hospital."

"He was there for five weeks, and I never went."

"Do you regret it?"

She nodded. "I'm not sure why, but I do. I wish I'd gone even once. Maybe it would've helped to have my last memory of my father be him sober and suffering the consequences of his actions. I don't know. But I've always regretted it."

"I guess I have my answer then."

Elodie leaned forward and pushed the button to call the elevator. When it arrived, she stepped inside and looked at me sadly. The doors started to close, and I just couldn't let her go without saying something.

I stuck my hand out and stopped them from sliding shut. "I'm sorry about the mess I made between us. I was wrong to take your underwear. And I was wrong to speak to you the way I did last week when you walked in on my date. You didn't deserve that."

She nodded. "Thank you. And I'm sorry I kept the game going and then got mad and ruined your date."

I reached out my hand as a peace offering. "Friends?"

She hesitated, but eventually put her little hand in mine. "Sure."

"Thank you." I nodded and released my hold on the elevator doors.

This time, Elodie stopped them from closing. "Hey, Hollis?"

Our eyes met.

"You know what I'm *not* sorry about?"

"What's that?"

"The photo you left on my phone. It's *come* in *handy*." She let go of the elevator doors and stepped back, flashing me the wickedest grin right before they closed. She wiggled her fingers. "'Night, Hollsy."

The next morning, Hailey was up early again. Apparently, she and Elodie were spending the day doing a photography tour of graffiti around the city. She sat at the kitchen island, eating a bowl of cereal.

I set my empty coffee mug in the sink. "So I thought about what you asked me. I'll take you to visit your dad if you want."

Hailey grinned. "Elodie gave you permission, huh?"

The little shit. "Have you ever heard the saying *Don't bite the hand that feeds you*?"

"I have. But Elodie feeds me most nights, remember?"

I grabbed my wallet and cell phone from the dining room table. "Don't be a smartass, Hailey. You know what I mean."

She jumped down off the stool she was sitting on and walked over to me. Pushing up on her tippy toes, she surprised the shit out of me by kissing my cheek.

"Thank you, Uncle Hollis."

I nodded. "You're welcome."

She went back to her bowl of Honey Nut Cheerios. "So when can we go?"

"I'll need to make flight arrangements. But visiting hours on the weekends are all day. So we'll probably fly down on Friday night and come back Saturday after the visit."

"Can Elodie come?"

"Elodie doesn't work on weekends."

"But if I ask her to come and she agrees, is it okay?"

It was a bad idea for me to be spending any time outside of what I had to with Elodie. Though, I had to admit, she had a special connection with Hailey and would know better than me how to handle things if she got upset.

I sighed. "If you want her to come and she's able to, yes, we can take Elodie."

"Dope."

Yeah, I am. You can say that again.

CHAPTER NINETEEN

Hollis

We wound up booking a Saturday afternoon flight and planned to see my brother on Sunday morning before flying back that evening. I'd considered sending a car for Elodie, so she could meet us at the airport, but then decided the least I could do was pick her up since she was coming with us on her day off.

Hailey and I left the city early, in case we hit traffic anywhere. Plus, parking at LaGuardia with all the construction was going to be a bitch. We pulled up at Elodie's house almost a full forty-five minutes earlier than planned.

Hailey started to get out of the car and noticed I hadn't moved. "Aren't you coming in?"

After the shit I pulled last time, I wasn't risking it. "I have to answer a few emails, so I'll wait here. You go ahead, and let her know we're early. Tell her she doesn't need to rush."

"Okay."

I watched Hailey skip up to the door and Elodie open it. They talked for a minute, and then the two of them looked over at the car. I waved and held up my phone. Even from the curb, I could see the smirk on Elodie's face—no doubt she knew why I wasn't coming inside. But whatever... Better safe than sorry.

About ten minutes went by. I was in the middle of answering a long email when a black BMW pulled to the curb in front of me. A man got out and started to walk toward Elodie's door.

Who's this douche?

He didn't have anything in his hands like he was delivering something, and he was dressed pretty nice. He also walked up to the door without any hesitation about where he was going. I watched from the car like a hawk.

The man knocked, and Elodie opened the front door with a smile on her face. Seeing who was there, it immediately wilted. I reached for the car door handle, but managed to stop myself from opening it.

Elodie put her hands on her hips and said something. The guy then took a turn speaking, and whatever he said pissed her off. She started to wave her hands around, and I heard her voice rise, even though my windows were up.

Fuck this. I got out of the car and was at her front door in five long strides.

"Is there a problem here?"

The guy turned and looked me up and down. "Who are you?"

"Hollis LaCroix. And you are?"

"Elodie's husband."

Elodie's lips twisted. "*Ex*-husband. And he was just leaving. You can ignore him, Hollis."

Her ex thumbed his finger at me. "Who the hell is this guy?"

"He's none of your business, that's who he is. And I have nothing to say to you. So *go home*, Tobias."

I folded my arms over my chest and widened my stance. "You heard the lady."

He scoffed at me. "What are you going to do, punch me?"

My hands were already balled into fists. Sure, why not? *Give me a reason, asshole.* "Why don't you just listen to what your ex-wife is saying and take off? Obviously you're not welcome here."

Hailey came to the door. "Who's this?"

Elodie answered. "This is Tobias. My ex-husband. Would you mind rolling my suitcase out from the bedroom, Hailey?"

My niece shrugged. "Sure."

Elodie stepped outside and pulled the door closed behind her. "As you can see, we're on our way out. So why don't you send me an email if you need to talk to me."

He sighed. "It's about Bree."

"What about her?"

"My mother asked me to speak to you." The douchebag glanced over at me. "Can we speak in private, please? It's a family matter."

Elodie blew out a deep breath. "Fine. But we need to get on the road." She turned to me. "Would you mind waiting five more minutes, Hollis?"

I didn't want to leave her alone with this guy, but Elodie obviously didn't feel she would be in danger. I nodded. "Hailey and I will wait in the car."

"Thank you."

Hailey brought the suitcase to the door, and I picked it up and loaded it into my trunk. Elodie's ex-husband seemed like a real dick. Rather than wait inside the car, I leaned against the driver's side door, keeping my eye on the house. Hailey did the same thing right next to me. Looking over at her protective stance, I realized how comical we probably looked, both standing guard with our arms folded across our chests. Though I didn't give a shit.

"Did you see that?" Hailey said.

"What?" My eyes had been glued to the front door. I couldn't have missed something.

"Next door. The blinds moved, and I saw a woman. I think she's watching us or something."

"Oh. That's probably Elodie's friend Bree. She lives next door. I'm sure she's just keeping an eye out, making sure everything is okay."

Two minutes later, *I* saw the blinds move next door. Her friend was definitely watching us. But not long after, Elodie's front door opened, and her ex walked out. I stretched my spine straight.

He gave me the evil eye as he passed, but said nothing while he walked back to his car and got in.

Elodie walked down the front path with her purse. "Sorry about that."

"Is everything okay?"

She looked back at her friend's house and frowned. "Not really. Would you mind if I took five more minutes?"

166

"Not at all. Go do whatever you need to do. We were early."

"Thank you."

I gave Elodie privacy this time and got into the car while she went next door to her friend's. Fifteen minutes later, she opened the passenger door to my car. Her face was puffy with tears.

"Elodie?"

She shook her head and looked forward. "Not now."

"You want to take a few more minutes? Go inside and wash up?"

"No. I just want to go."

I nodded and started the car.

Hailey went to the newsstand across from the gate to look at magazines. Elodie had been quiet the entire trip to the airport.

"You want to talk about it?" I said softly.

"About Tobias? No. But about Bree? Maybe."

I shifted in my seat to give her my attention, while still keeping an eye on the newsstand. "Whatever you want."

"I've told you my best friend is sick. Bree had been part of an experimental treatment for her condition. She has lymphangioleiomyomatosis."

"That's a mouthful."

She nodded. "It's an incurable lung disease. She doesn't talk about it much, doesn't want to burden me with the details. Which I think is stupid, but that's who she is. It's important to her to not disrupt my life—so she plays down how she's feeling. Tobias's mother, Mariah, is married to Bree's father, and yesterday Bree told her father that she'd stopped the experimental treatment. It's making her really sick and dizzy, more out of breath than usual. But the new drugs were basically a last hope. Bree won't listen to her dad, so Tobias came to talk to me to see if I could intervene. His family doesn't know our marriage ended poorly. We told them we jumped into things too fast and realized we were better off as friends."

I nodded. "I understand. And I'm sorry about your friend. Did your talking with her help any?"

She shook her head. "She promised she'd think about going back to the treatments. But I know her, it was just to get me out the door."

I thought about what I'd gone through with my mom at the end. The treatments had made her so sick. "My mom had cancer. She died when I was nineteen after multiple rounds of chemo. At the end, she chose to stop all treatments and enjoy the days she had left. It was really hard to accept. There're just some things in life we can't change. So *we* need to change to deal with them. And that's much easier said than done."

Elodie looked over at me and nodded. "Thanks, Hollis. And thank you for coming to check on me when you saw Tobias at my door."

Her eyes were glassy, and I knew she was fighting back tears. I put an arm around her shoulder and squeezed her. "Of course. Anytime. We're friends, remember? That's what friends do for each other. Well, that and sniff each other's panties and leave obscene selfies."

Elodie laughed and wiped a tear from her eye. "We have a fucked-up friendship, Hollis."

I smiled. "We have from the very start. I don't think we can do it any other way."

The flight to Ohio was uneventful, and I'd booked us adjacent rooms at a hotel in downtown Cleveland. Hailey and Elodie were in one room, and I was in the other, only a door separating us.

The three of us went to dinner at a five-star seafood restaurant within walking distance of where we were staying and opted to return to the hotel right after.

While Elodie and I were keen to relax, Hailey seemed to have different plans.

"The pool is open till ten!" she announced just as we were approaching our rooms.

"Guess we're going swimming?" Elodie said.

I lingered at my door. "You two brought bathing suits?"

"Of course. What fun is a hotel without swimming in the pool?" Hailey asked, as if my question was stupid.

"I sort of like just lying in the bed, watching TV with some snacks myself," I said.

"That's cuz you're old, Uncle Hollis."

That made me chuckle.

"Apparently, everyone came prepared but you, Hollsy." Elodie winked.

Something about that wink made me wish I could smack her on the ass.

They retreated to their room to change. My plan was to hang out and watch some HBO while they were gone. That is, until they came over to say they were heading downstairs.

Elodie's tight stomach and ample breasts peeking out from her bikini taunted me. I would be crazy to stay in my room when I could spend the next hour gawking at her. I couldn't touch, but I could still look, right? That sounded a hell of a lot better than HBO.

"Maybe I'll join you."

Hailey was confused. "You're gonna swim?"

"No. But I'll hang out, maybe read the paper."

Once downstairs, we used the room key to access the indoor pool area. It was heated and felt like a sauna. I'd purchased a USA TODAY down in the lobby and threw it on one of the tables before settling into a white plastic chair.

Elodie removed her shorts and dove into the pool. Hailey jumped in right after her.

It was hard not to watch the way Elodie's breasts bounced as she played with Hailey in the water. I had my paper in front of my face, but I did more peeking over it than reading.

The other day, I'd made the mistake of looking through the photos in her phone when she'd left it at my apartment. I came across a selfie she'd taken of herself in a bra and undies and must have gazed at it for a half hour straight. I felt guilty afterward. That's when I'd snapped that photo of myself, right before destroying her panties by jerking off with them.

Despite the immense fun I'd had with our game, I was still certain we couldn't take things any further. Nevertheless, I grew increasingly sexually frustrated by the day.

Elodie emerged from the pool and took a seat next to me. Her blond hair was wet and slicked back off her face. She ran her hands through it to remove some of the tangles.

She looked out at Hailey, still swimming away. "I'm really glad she's having a good time tonight. I'm sure tomorrow is going to be stressful for her."

"Well, thanks to you, she's having a good time. Not sure she'd be having so much fun if it were just the two of us. Thank you again for agreeing to come."

"You're welcome." She was quiet, then turned to me. "It's been good for me, too. I didn't exactly have wild plans this weekend."

"Are you feeling better than you were this morning?"

"Definitely."

I smiled. "Good."

She looked away, almost seeming uncomfortable with our eye contact, a little bashful, which was uncharacteristic—but adorable.

"Thank you for dinner. It was really good," she said.

"If I'm counting, I probably owe you a hundred dinners by now."

"Until I stopped making them for two."

"Yeah, that sucked, by the way. But I understand."

"You deserved it."

"I know."

We shared a smile then sat in comfortable silence while we continued to watch Hailey in the pool.

After about an hour, Hailey was shivering with a towel wrapped around her when she announced that she wanted to go back upstairs.

Back in our rooms, I could hear the shower running next door and decided to take my own. Gazing for so long at Elodie's body had gotten me more worked up than usual. My orgasm was intense in the shower. And yet, it wasn't enough. I honestly didn't know what I was going to do with this crazy attraction to her. I wished I could rid myself of it or bottle it up, put it away, and lose the key. But it wasn't that simple when she was around almost every day. It felt like I had all of this sexual energy and nowhere to put it.

After my shower, I threw on a clean black T-shirt and some gym pants. I normally slept in my boxer briefs, but I wasn't sure if I would see Elodie again tonight. I turned on the TV and grabbed some pretzels I'd bought at the airport. I was just starting to get into a movie when Elodie sent me a text.

> **Elodie: Hailey is out like a light. Wish I could fall asleep, too. She totally crashed. That swimming did her in.**

It did me in, too, just in a different way.

Was she hinting for me to invite her to hang out in my room, or was she just giving me an update?

Without thinking it through, I typed.

> **Hollis: I'm awake if you want some company.**

CHAPTER TWENTY

Elodie

I wasn't expecting him to invite me next door. Don't get me wrong—I was hoping he would, but Hollis rarely put himself in a position to be alone with me. So this was surprising. Although, Hailey was sleeping just over the wall, so I suppose he knew nothing could happen.

I quietly creaked open the door that connected our rooms before closing it.

Hollis stood by the window, looking down at the evening traffic on the street below. He turned around, seeming a bit tense.

"Hey." I grinned.

He rubbed his hands together. "Hi."

I looked over at the television. "Did I interrupt your movie?"

"Nah. I hadn't gotten into it yet."

I took a seat in the corner chair. I didn't dare lie on the bed.

His eyes glossed over my legs, and his jaw ticked. I was wearing short sleep shorts and a T-shirt. I'd caught him checking me out numerous times at the pool, too. I loved catching him looking at me.

At this particular moment, he looked hotter than ever with his hair wet from the shower. He smelled like the aftershave I remembered from my panties. Just the thought of our game made my pulse race.

But it was like foreplay that had led to nothing. That whole experience was the polar opposite of what I encountered when I was with him—a relationship that was *friendly* at best.

Hollis moved over to the bed and kicked his legs up. He lowered the volume on the TV and said, "Your ex-husband seemed like a real douche."

The fact that he'd brought up Tobias right now sort of surprised me.

"I didn't think he was a douche for many years. I was quite smitten. He was my professor, after all. I had a lot of respect for him at one time. The whole person-of-authority thing can be very alluring. Student-teacher. Employee-boss. You know how it is."

Hollis cracked a slight smile, but he didn't touch my comment as it might have related to him.

He cleared his throat. "How often does he show up at your house unannounced?"

"He does it from time to time. A part of him still looks at it as his house. I try not to let him get to me anymore, though."

"Shouldn't he give you more privacy than that?"

"Well, there isn't much to see lately. It's not like he's going to find me in any compromising situations."

Hollis stared for a bit then asked, "Why has it been so long since you've been with anyone?"

My eyes widened. "Have you tried online dating, Hollis? It's bad. I don't want someone who's just after a quick fuck, even if that's all I need sometimes. It's frightening out there. There are diseases and scary people. I don't know. Sometimes I just don't think I was made for this."

"You were made to be with one man..."

"Yes. I have a lot to give someone, the right person. But I'm too apprehensive to take the necessary steps to find him, I guess. I suppose I thought I *had* found him in Tobias. But I was wrong. So now it's like starting from square one."

I decided to move the focus off me and satisfy some curiosity of my own. "You don't think you'll ever settle down?"

He blew out a breath. "No. I've made the decision to remain single. I had a bad experience in the one serious relationship of my life, and I haven't had the desire to put myself in that position again."

Wow. There was definitely a story there.

"Do you want to talk about it?"

"I'd prefer not to."

"Okay. I understand."

God, I was so curious. Seeing that vulnerability peek through made me *more* attracted to Hollis. He wasn't as cold as I'd originally thought; he was likely just protecting his heart.

I played with some lint on the arm of the chair and asked, "So, that woman from the other night...when I interrupted you... She knew exactly what she was there for? No expectations?"

"Yes. All the women I associate with are clear on the fact that I don't want anything more than a sexual relationship. I'm open with every person I meet."

"Do you meet them online?"

"Typically, no. I mostly meet women while out and about at social events."

I nodded.

"Of course, given my current responsibilities, there aren't as many opportunities as of late." He lifted his brow. "Any more questions?"

I don't know what came over me when I asked the next one. But it was the one thing I needed to know.

"Do you want to fuck me, Hollis?"

His eyes went wide. "What kind of a question is that?"

"I didn't mean now." A nervous laugh escaped me. "It was...more of a general question. I'm just curious what would happen if circumstances were different."

"I think that question is irrelevant given that we *are* in this situation."

"I'm genuinely curious if you just enjoy flirting with me or if I would be your type."

"You're not the type of woman I would want to get involved with—not for a lack of desire, but because you're...too good for me."

"How so?"

"You deserve a man who wants to settle down, who wants to give you more than a quick fuck. I'm not that man."

"Are you attracted to me?"

"You know the answer to that, Elodie."

"I do?"

"Haven't my actions made it extremely clear that I find you attractive?"

I didn't even know where I was going with this conversation anymore. I just wanted to see what he would say. So, I asked, "What if I told you I just wanted to have sex with you, nothing more?"

"Is this still a hypothetical question?"

"Of course. This whole conversation is hypothetical," I said, not believing my own words.

"Alright... Hypothetically, if you told me you just wanted to have sex and nothing more, I probably wouldn't believe you based on everything you've told me about yourself thus far."

"You would think I wasn't being truthful."

"Yes."

I uncrossed my legs and leaned in. "Can we stop being hypothetical for a moment?"

"Yeah."

"I don't want to want you in an inappropriate way, Hollis. You're my boss, and nothing good could come from crossing the line in our relationship. That wouldn't be good for Hailey."

"I totally agree."

"But that game really got to me. Finding you with that woman...it upset me, made me jealous. I realized the game had gone to my head."

I needed to stop myself because I was revealing too much.

"I don't even know the point of this conversation," I said. "I'm sorry. I'm rambling."

"You're good. I don't mind. I appreciate your honesty. The truth is, I took things way too far with you.

It was a game I never should have started, no matter how tempting. I'm sorry if I led you on in any way. It was a mistake. And I take full blame."

Ouch. Well, that certainly wasn't the response I'd hoped for.

I was horny and frustrated and had a massive crush on my boss, who'd pretty much just admitted he was playing games with me and had no serious intentions.

I felt like a complete and utter fool. Was I secretly holding out hope that I could change him? Or was I just so attracted to him that I didn't care about anything other than getting to have him?

Hollis had been playing a *game* with me. And I'd used it as evidence that things might have been moving between us, when it was always only a game. It was clearer now where we really stood.

I lifted myself off the chair. "I think I'm going to hit the sack. I'm starting to feel tired all of a sudden."

He stood up from the bed. "Okay. I'll probably follow suit."

"Goodnight."

He lifted his hand. "'Night."

Ugh.

Totally awkward.

Back in bed, I tossed and turned, feeling like crap and wishing I'd never broached the subject. He'd completely crushed my hope for anything between us.

The next day, a glass partition separated Hailey from her father. Hollis and I gave her space as she sat across from his brother. Stephen looked like a gaunt version of Hollis. Even though they were *half*-brothers, I could definitely see a resemblance.

He and Hailey were just wrapping up their visit when I heard him say to her, "Put your hand against the glass."

She did as he said. "I love you, Daddy."

"I love you, too, Hailey. Thank you so much for coming all this way. I promise when I get out of this place, you're gonna have a whole new dad. I'll never let you down again."

Given his history, something told me that promise needed to be taken with a grain of salt.

"Okay," she said.

She stood up from the seat and walked over to me. I gave her a hug. I was so proud of her for being brave and wanting to come here.

Hollis went over to his brother, and they spoke privately for a few minutes while Hailey and I waited.

As we exited the prison, it was evident something was bothering her.

We were almost to the car when I stopped. "What's wrong, Hailey?"

"I'm just thinking about something my dad said to me."

"What is it?" Hollis asked.

"He kept saying how he's finally learned his lesson, that being in jail has helped him see the light, and he can't wait to come home so we can be together again."

"Why did that bother you?"

"I don't want to live with him, Uncle Hollis...ever again. It's not that I don't love my father. But I don't think I could trust him. I feel safe with you. Can he really make me go back with him?"

Hollis paused, looking over at me. "That's complicated, Hailey. Technically, he can, but..."

"Can't you do something?"

He seemed at a loss for words.

She looked like she was about to cry. "Do you not want me forever?"

Hollis bent so he was eye level with her. He placed his hands on her cheeks. "That's not it at all, Hailey. I promise if it were up to me, I'd have you with me permanently. You've given me purpose. Having you around has changed my life, but it's all been for the better. Taking care of you makes me very happy. Don't ever doubt that, okay?"

She sniffled, and then nodded. "Okay."

That squeezed my heart. Say what you might based on some of his actions, but overall, Hollis was a good guy.

"The law doesn't always keep someone's best interests in mind, though," he told her. "If the courts were to deem your father fit to parent you once he completed his term, there wouldn't be anything I could legally do." He wiped her eyes. "But I promise you this: I will do everything in my power to keep you with me, okay? And if I can't, you won't be able to get rid of me. I'll be over there every day to make sure you're okay."

Before he was transported to Ohio on an outstanding warrant, Stephen had lived with Hailey in New York. Assuming he would choose to go back there, Hollis being able to check in on her daily wouldn't be out of the realm of possibility.

"What about Elodie?" she asked.

"What about me, sweetie?" I smiled.

"I don't want you to lose your job if I have to go back to Dad's."

"Oh, don't worry about that, honey. There are plenty of things I can do. I'll find a job."

"Trust me. She's very versatile," Hollis cracked.

I gave him the evil eye, which transformed into a smile. He smiled back.

His response surprised me. "I'll try to keep Elodie with you if I can. Even if you're with your dad, I'll pay to keep her with you, provided Elodie can stay."

My eyes met his. Then I turned to her. "You won't be able to get rid of me, Hailey. Even if I'm not being paid, I'll still be in your life. I promise, okay?"

I knew that assurance meant somehow Hollis would always be in my life, too. He wasn't going anywhere, so something had to change.

This was a reminder that I needed to move on from these feelings, move on with my life, despite him being in it.

Hailey let out a relieved breath. "I feel better now." She sighed. "I know my mom is looking down and happy I have you guys."

I knew Hailey's mom had died of a drug overdose when she was little. It always broke my heart. But despite her mother's decisions while on this Earth, Hailey spoke of her fondly, as if her mom were an angel watching over her now.

"You and I have more in common than you think," Hollis said, placing his hand atop her head. "I know how hard it is to lose your mother. I know I had mine for much longer than you had yours, but losing her has never gotten any easier for me, no matter how old I am."

CHAPTER
TWENTY-ONE

Hollis – 12 years ago

Anna rubbed my back. "Can I get you anything to eat? You haven't eaten all day."

"No, thank you."

It was the day after my mother's funeral. Yesterday had been exhausting, having to deal with everyone's sympathies, having to actually talk to people while in this condition. But nothing was worse than the eerie quiet of today—the day after. No more *I'm sorrys*, no more noise, no more food deliveries. The quiet was deafening. And the harsh reality had hit: my mother wasn't coming back.

I'd given up everything to stay home and take care of her while she was sick. I'd turned down the UCLA baseball scholarship because it would have meant leaving her. And it wasn't just me who'd given up the opportunity to attend UCLA. When Anna realized I wasn't leaving my mother, she'd stayed here and attended the local college with me. While I felt a lot of guilt over that, I couldn't imagine what it would have been like if Anna had left on top of everything else.

With Anna by my side, my life had become about taking care of my mother. And I would do it all over again. Now that my mother was gone, I was supposed to have all of the freedom in the world. Yet I felt numb. I didn't know who I was, if not my mother's son. Despite this new freedom, in a strange way, I wasn't sure what I'd do with my life now. I'd have to figure out a way to pick myself up and start over.

I sat in Mom's bedroom and looked around at all of her things, the clothes hanging in the closet, the bunny figurines on the dresser. Easter was always her favorite holiday. She'd have the entire house decked out in pastel-colored eggs, little furry chicks, and bunny figurines. Easter was going to be tough this year.

Every day was going to be tough.

I knew eventually I would have to pack this stuff away so I could sell the house and move on with my life. There was only one thing I was sure of: moving on involved taking the next step with Anna. She was my family now.

"Let's move in together," I suddenly said.

Her eyes widened. "Where did that come from?"

"It comes from the fact that I love you. I want us to start our lives together. Mom would want that."

Anna and I had planned to get an apartment together in California before our move was canceled. She'd continued living with her father while commuting to school.

"Are you sure?" she asked.

"Of course, I am. It's long overdue."

Before she died, my mother encouraged me to someday sell this house and use the money to buy Anna an engagement ring, along with a place for Anna and me to call our own. I planned to fulfill those wishes.

"I would love nothing more than to move in with you, baby," she said.

"It's settled, then."

The brief high that came from thinking about shacking up with Anna was quickly replaced by another wave of emptiness.

She could see that my fleeting moment of happiness was gone.

"What can I get you?" she asked.

"Why don't you go home?" I told her. "You've been by my side for three days straight. You need a break."

"I don't want to leave you."

"It's okay. I promise, I'll be fine."

"Are you sure?"

"Yeah. I'm positive."

She embraced me. "I love you so much. I'm just gonna check in on my dad. I'll come right back tomorrow morning."

Anna was about to get up off the bed when I placed my arm on hers to stop her.

"Thank you for everything." I wrapped my hands around her cheeks, pulling her in for a kiss. Her warmth comforted me. Maybe tomorrow I could bury myself inside of her and forget this pain.

"You know you're not alone, right?" she said. "You have me."

That was probably the only thing I could count on. Anna had been my rock throughout my mother's illness, and now in the aftermath of her death. Anna was my everything.

But right now, I did need to be alone. I'd somehow managed not to lose control yesterday, kept my tears at bay at the service because I didn't want prying eyes witnessing my grief. Being back in the emptiness of this house, staring at the bed where my mother took her final breaths with hospice by her side, was proving more difficult than I'd imagined. I needed to let go, and I wanted to do it alone.

As soon as Anna left, I collapsed onto Mom's bed. Her pillow still smelled like her perfume. I buried my head in it and finally wept.

Screw this. I jumped out of bed, conceding to the fact that I couldn't sleep. Throwing on my clothes, I decided to get some air.

I put one foot in front of the other and eventually ended up at the hospital. Not the most obvious place to go in the middle of the night, but nevertheless, here I was. Even though Mom wasn't here anymore, it felt like this was where I needed to be. I'd gotten so used to visiting that it sort of felt like home, though it would surely be different now.

I headed down to the pediatric unit and wandered the desolate halls. The door to one of the rooms was open. I noticed a kid who was wide awake and sitting up in bed. I'd definitely never seen him here before. He must have been new and looked about thirteen.

He turned when he noticed me standing there.

After a few seconds, he asked, "Who are you?"

Who am I?

That was an interesting question, since lately I'd been trying to figure that out.

"I'm Hollis."

"What's up?"

"Nothing. I'm lost, I guess."

"Pretty sucky place to get lost. Are you sleepwalking or something?"

"Something like that."

He gestured to the chair next to his bed. "You should sit. Take a load off."

I shrugged. "Alright."

The second my ass hit the seat, there was a loud vibration from beneath it that resembled the sound of flatulence. I shot up and saw it: a deflated whoopee cushion.

Little bastard.

The kid started cracking up. "I've had it there all day, and you're the first one to fall for it."

"I guess I should check where I sit from now on. Glad I could entertain you, though."

"I gotta entertain *myself*, dude. No one else is gonna amuse me here, least of all those volunteers who come in and *try* to be funny. They're not. You can't make me laugh when you're *trying* to make me laugh, you know? That's so lame."

I nodded. "I get that."

"You know what makes me laugh? Stuff that's not supposed to be funny, but just is—like the look on your face when you sat on that whoopee cushion, a split second of complete shock. Wish I could've snapped a photo of it."

"I'm sort of glad you didn't."

"It's the same thing when someone is laughing and accidentally farts. Not funny for them—at all—but *really* funny for me."

I was glad I'd taken one for the team if it meant brightening this kid's spirits.

"How about when someone trips?" I said. "Somehow that's funny, even though it's not supposed to be."

"Falling down a flight of stairs? Even better."

"You're a little sadistic, you know that?" I chuckled. "What's your name?"

"Jack."

I lifted the flattened whoopee cushion off the seat and sat back down. "Nice to meet you...I think."

"What are you really doing here?"

"My mother used to be at this hospital. And I'd sometimes come down and hang out here. Old habit."

"Where is your mom now?"

I hesitated, not wanting to upset him. "She passed away."

"I'm sorry."

"Thanks."

"So you come back here and visit because you feel sorry for us?"

"Well, this is the first time I've been back, but no, just the opposite. I come here because I've met some really cool people. Being here also reminds me a little of my mom. But I came tonight because I wanted company."

We spent the next hour playing a video game where Jack got to take out his sadistic side—on fake people this time.

When I looked over at the clock and saw it was 3AM, I stopped the game. "I better let you get some sleep."

He sat up. "Will you come back sometime?"

"You're not gonna play any more tricks on me, are you?"

Jack smiled. "I can't promise that."

Making him feel better made me feel better. Maybe this was how I'd be able to take my mind off losing Mom—by continuing to spend time here with the kids.

"How does tomorrow sound?"

CHAPTER TWENTY-TWO

Elodie

Benito was funny.

I'd forced myself back to one of the online dating sites I'd used before, and he'd been the first guy to message me. Seeing his picture pop up on my phone, my immediate thought had been *Ugh, I'm done with pretty boys.* So I'd told him that. Which led to him sending me photos of his toes and an entire conversation about how ugly his feet were. Honestly, they really were pretty damn fugly.

But he'd made me laugh with his self-deprecating humor, and over the last few days, he'd sent me photos of his other flaws—a jagged scar on his abdomen from a mountain biking accident (though I really only noticed how defined his abs were), a birthmark shaped like Australia on the top of his ass (that was pretty damn defined, too), and a section of his arm that oddly didn't grow hair.

But the overall package was an attractive one, small flaws and all. Not to mention that I'd stalked his

Instagram and watched a video of him dancing some Latin dance—those hips don't lie.

My phone buzzed with an incoming message.

Benito: I sliced my finger using a table saw this morning. Needed a few stitches. It looks pretty gnarly. Do I need to send photos to continue pleading my case?

I smiled and had started to text back when Hailey came out of her room. She stretched her arms over her head, and her eyes dropped to my phone for a moment. "Who are you texting so early?"

"First of all, it's ten o'clock, sleepyhead. And second of all, it's personal, so none of your beeswax."

She rolled her eyes. "It's a boy."

"Well, if it *were* a member of the opposite sex I was talking to, it would be a man, not a boy."

She shrugged. "From what I can tell, most men just grow taller and wider. They're still little boys."

I shook my head and chuckled. *Wise beyond her years.*

It felt sort of awkward to admit I was talking to a man. But if I expected her to share things about boys with me, I couldn't be that closed off.

I set down my phone and picked up my coffee mug. "His name is Benito."

She frowned.

"What? You don't like the name?"

"No. It's not that." She avoided making eye contact and walked into the kitchen. Opening the refrigerator, she spent a few minutes hanging on the door and staring into it.

I walked over. "Are you waiting for something to magically appear in there? Want me to make you banana nut pancakes?"

Her stomach growled loudly, and I laughed. "I'll take that as a yes. Go sit. You can peel the bananas and mash them for me."

I grabbed two bowls from the cabinet and took out the flour, sugar, baking soda, eggs, and cinnamon. Setting one of the bowls in front of Hailey, I handed her three bananas and a spoon to use to mash.

"So what's the deal? You made a face when I said I was talking to a guy named Benito. Does the name remind you of someone you don't like or something?"

She peeled each banana and let them drop unceremoniously into the bowl. "Are you dating the guy?"

I watched her expression. "No. Well, not yet. But I might. I'm thinking about it, I guess."

She frowned again. "I thought you thought my uncle was cute."

I froze. "Why would you think that?"

She started to mash up the bananas with the back of the spoon. "You guys are always looking at each other."

"Well, he's my employer, so of course I'm going to look at him."

She rolled her eyes. "You know what I mean. You *look look* at him, and he *looks looks* at you. You both do it when you think no one is watching. But you're so obvious."

There was no point in trying to escape the truth. "Your uncle is a nice-looking guy. It's hard not to notice, Hailey. But it doesn't mean anything."

"Why doesn't it?"

I sighed. She asked good questions—hard ones, but good. "Well, just because two people are attracted to each other doesn't mean they're right for each other in a couple sort of way."

"Is Benito attractive?"

"Yes."

"So what does he have that Uncle Hollis doesn't?"

I shook my head. "It's not that your uncle is missing anything. We just don't want the same things, so we're not compatible as a couple."

"What does he want?"

Uh...how do I extricate myself from this one? I couldn't very well say, *your uncle just wants to* dirty fuck *me, like most asshole men.* Though—I looked at her—she was a really beautiful girl. It was probably a lesson she should learn to save her some naïve heartbreak. But that was a conversation best had a few years from now.

I poured flour into a measuring cup and emptied it into the bowl, then slid everything to the other side of the counter so I could sit on the stool next to her.

"I told you I was married before. As much as I was sad about the way my marriage turned out, I'm still hopeful that maybe the right guy is out there for me. For a long time, I wasn't. But that's changed lately. And I think that a lot of it is because of you, actually."

"Me?"

I nodded. "I want a family someday. You reminded me of that. So while I'm a little scared to go back out there into the dating world, I think I need to do it now. It's sort of time."

I'd thought I'd explained it so well, but one look at Hailey's face told me I hadn't. Her shoulders slumped, and she stared down at her hands. "So Uncle Hollis doesn't want a family?"

"Oh God, no. That's not what I meant at all. He wants you. I'm certain of that. You heard him the other day when he said he would do everything in his power to keep you or stay in your life. He loves you and wants you to be his family."

"I don't understand, then. You want a family. He wants me. Why can't *we* just be a family?"

The fear in her voice made my chest hurt. "It's complicated, sweetheart. And I think I'm muddying things up by explaining stuff wrong. But the bottom line is, I adore you. Your uncle adores you. And my dating someone else will have no bearing on any of that."

Luckily, that seemed to satisfy her—either that or she'd grown bored of the conversation. Hailey finished mashing the bananas and moved on to asking if we could go ice skating today. It was summer in New York City and going to be in the eighties this afternoon. But I was so anxious to change the subject, I'd say yes to just about anything.

"Sure. Let me see if I can find a place."

"What's up, bossman?" After work, I decided to stop by my old job. I walked into Soren's office and planted my ass on the other side of his desk.

He folded his hands behind his head and leaned back into his chair. "Well, look what the cat dragged in. Did Richie Rich figure out you're nuts and fire your ass already?"

"No. Well, yes." I shook my head. "I mean, I'm pretty sure he knows I'm nuts, but he didn't fire me."

Soren squinted. "He knows you're nuts and hasn't fired you? So he's trying to get in your pants, then?"

I sighed. "I wish."

His brows jumped. "Hot for the new boss?"

"I think I really need to get laid."

Soren wrinkled his nose and waved his hands at me. "Don't tell me shit like that. You're like my sister."

"Well, that's sort of why I'm here. I want my big brother to do a little background check on a man I'm thinking about going out with."

"Your boss? The Hollis guy?" He scraped his boots off his desk and sat up in his chair. "No problem."

"Thanks. But actually, it's not Hollis I want you to check out."

"No?"

"No. His name is Benito. I met him online. He seems nice enough, but you know... He could be a serial killer."

Soren picked up his reading glasses and shook his head. "What the hell are you meeting men online for? Meet them the old-fashioned way."

I arched a brow. "You mean hire them to be my secretary and not tell them sucking my dick is part of the job until after they start?"

"You got some mouth on you."

I tilted my head toward the door. "I noticed Bambi has been replaced. I'm guessing things didn't turn out well. *Again.*"

He grumbled something under his breath.

In the two years I'd been with Soren, he'd had at least a dozen secretaries, most of whom he'd slept with.

"This Benito got a last name, or what?"

"Del Toro."

"Benito Del Toro. Like the actor?"

"No, that's Benicio. I know. The name is a little unfortunate. But he's a few years older than me, so his mother named him before the actor became famous. Could be worse though. His name could be Jeffrey Dahmer."

"He live in the boroughs?"

"Brooklyn Heights."

"I'll take care of it. Give me till morning."

I smiled. "You're the bestest boss...and *since I'm here*...why don't we order from that Chinese place I love? I miss the food. And I miss you buying it for me even more."

Soren shook his head. "You expect me to buy you dinner even after you quit on me?"

"You miss buying me food, and I know it."

He opened his drawer, reached in, and tossed a menu at me. "Call it in. I'll take my usual."

"He was *literally* a fucking boy scout. Even has a credit score in the eight hundreds." Soren called the next morning just as I walked up the stairs from the subway.

"Oh, wow. Okay. So no skeletons, then?"

"Nope. One car accident—ironically, while parking a few years ago. So you two should probably stick to public transportation. Owns his condo and his car outright. Same job for nine years. One sister—lives in bumfuck Nebraska. Mother died last year, and up until then, he'd been paying for her nursing home."

I attempted to cross the street at a green light but had to stop abruptly when a cab made a sudden turn and nearly ran over my toes. The jerk blew the light only to get stuck in the crosswalk.

I banged on the trunk of his car. *"Watch where you're going, asshole!"*

Soren chuckled. "Not sure why we bothered to check out this guy's background. Pretty sure if he pisses you off, you'll kick his ass."

"Thanks for looking into him, Soren."

"Anytime, kid. Better safe than sorry. And stop by more often, even if it's just to bum a free meal. Office isn't the same without you torturing me."

I smiled. *Such a softie behind the badass.* "I will."

I managed to navigate the two-block walk to work without getting into any more fights with cabs. While I waited for the elevator, my phone buzzed in my purse. I dug it out again and smiled seeing the name on the screen.

Benito: Good morning. Might today be the day she says yes?

There really was no reason not to go out with Benito anymore. Anyone Soren couldn't find dirt on was squeaky clean. Plus, he was funny and handsome and seemed genuinely interested in getting to know me. Unlike a lot of guys, he asked me questions about myself, rather than telling me how great he was. Yet I still couldn't bring myself to say yes to a date for some reason.

Though I didn't want to say no anymore either. So I put off responding for now. I slipped my phone back into my purse and stepped onto the elevator.

Hollis's apartment was quiet when I walked in, except for Huey's greeting. *Baaa!* "Anna's home!"

I still cracked up every time he made that sound. "Hi, Huey!"

He nodded his head rapidly. I swore he understood me, though no one else seemed to agree.

Hollis walked out of his bedroom and down the hall, taking long, rapid strides. At first, I assumed he was running late and in a rush. But the stony glare he flashed when he saw me made me second-guess that.

"Is...everything okay?"

"Why wouldn't it be?" he snapped.

"*Okey dokey,* then." I dropped my purse on the dining room table and went to the kitchen to get myself some coffee. I kept a discreet eye on Hollis through my peripheral vision.

He struggled to close the cuff on one arm of his dress shirt, and I could see he was getting angrier by the second. Eventually, he gave up and let out a string of curses. He grabbed his suit jacket off the back of a chair, swiped his wallet and keys from a bowl on the kitchen counter, and marched toward the front door without another glance in my direction.

I just couldn't help myself sometimes. I called after him in a sing-songy voice. "You have a fabulous day, too, Hollis!"

He glanced back with a hardened face and opened the front door. I sipped my coffee, expecting to hear the door slam shut, but instead he stopped in the entranceway. He stood in silence, looking up at the ceiling for a solid sixty seconds before turning around. If the moment he took was supposed to cool him off, it definitely hadn't worked. Because the look on his face now was almost murderous.

"It's inappropriate for you to be talking about your dates with Hailey."

My brows furrowed. "What dates?"

His jaw ticked. "Benito?"

My mouth formed an O. *That date.*

If eyes shot daggers, I'd be pretty damn holey right about now.

"She's eleven and impressionable. The last thing she needs to hear about is you sleeping around."

Sleeping around? *How dare he assume?* I set down my coffee, and my hands flew to my hips. But before I could rip into him, he walked out and slammed the door shut behind him.

Un-freaking-believable.

So un-freaking-believable.

That man had some balls insinuating that I would discuss anything inappropriate with Hailey. Someone had obviously pissed in his Cheerios this morning. I needed to give him a piece of my mind. The jerk could've still been waiting at the elevator, so I headed for the door. Of course, the elevator that normally crawled had to be fast when I wanted it to take its sweet time. Hollis was already gone, though the hallways smelled like his aftershave. Which only pissed me off more because my damn body reacted to the scent.

Fuming, I went back into the house and in search of my cell. I thumbed off a four-paragraph angry rant, telling Hollis exactly what I thought of him and his accusations. But as my finger hovered over *Send*, a thought crossed my mind. Why send a text when I could do something much more vengeful?

I deleted what I'd typed and, instead, called up the last incoming text I'd received.

Benito: Good morning. Might today be the day she says yes?

I typed back.

Elodie: Today is absolutely the day. I'd love to go out with you, Benito. How's Friday night at seven?

CHAPTER
TWENTY-THREE

Elodie

Hollis: **It's going to be a late night at the office. I'm stuck in a meeting.**

I read the text and sighed. I'd already been on edge all day about my date tonight. Sadly, a part of me hoped I'd have to cancel.

Elodie: How late?

Hollis: Probably ten. I'll have a car service take you home.

Benito and I were meeting at a restaurant downtown at seven. I needed to let him know since it was almost five o'clock already. I switched over to my text string with him and started to type. But I got a funny feeling.

Nah...Hollis didn't even know about my date. It couldn't be.

I started to text Benito again and then stopped. Hailey had gone into her room to change.

"Hailey?" I called.

"Yeah?"

"Is there any chance you mentioned my date tonight to your uncle?"

She walked out to the living room. "Last night I asked him if we could go to that hibachi place I like tonight and take my friend. He said yes, and I asked if I could also invite you. But before he could answer, I remembered you had plans, so I told him to forget it because you already had dinner plans tonight with Benito."

That asshole.

It could very well be a coincidence and he had an *actual* meeting that was running late, but I knew in my gut he didn't.

"Okay, thanks."

"Was I not supposed to say anything?" Hailey asked.

"No, it's fine, honey. You didn't do anything wrong. But your uncle is going to be a little late tonight. So why don't you go downstairs to Kelsie's apartment and see if she wants to go to dinner with us soon. We'll go to the hibachi place without your uncle."

"But what about your date?"

I smiled. "Benito and I can meet later or another night."

While Hailey went down to her friend's apartment, I decided to do a little investigating. Hollis never answered his own phone, so I called the office, knowing I'd reach his assistant, Laurel.

"Hi, Laurel. It's Elodie. Would you be able to give me the phone number for Hailey's pediatrician, please? I want to set up her school physical appointment."

"Sure, Elodie. No problem. Hang on a second." I heard the keys on her keyboard clack a few times and then she returned. "It's 212-555-0055."

"Great thanks."

"Did you want to talk to Hollis, too?"

"No, it's fine. He's probably in a meeting or something."

"No, actually his afternoon meeting ended early. He should be able to make it home at a normal time for a change."

"Oh wow. That's great," I lied through my clenched teeth. "But I don't need to speak to him. Thanks for the information. Have a great weekend."

"You, too."

I swiped my phone off and sat in the living room, stewing. He'd been an asshole to me all week, but this crossed a line. I was furious, but also salivating at the thought of ripping him a new one when he got home later.

Shit was about to get real between us.

It worked out perfectly.

When Hailey and I walked Kelsie back to her apartment after dinner, Kelsie asked if Hailey could sleep over. Normally, I'd check with Hollis for something like that, but not tonight. If Hailey was at a friend's, he'd expect me to go home, of course, and I had no damn intention of doing that. Not until he and I had a little conversation.

The door handle jingled at about nine forty-five, and my blood started to pump with fury. Over the last few hours, I'd calmed down, but the anxiousness came barreling back with a vengeance. I stood in the living room and waited.

Hollis walked in, saw me, and quickly diverted his gaze. The bastard couldn't even look me in the eyes. "Sorry I'm so late."

I waited until he walked into the kitchen to put his wallet and keys in the bowl on the counter, like he always did. Then I followed.

He glanced over at me, and his eyes quickly read my face. "Is everything okay?"

"No."

For a second, he seemed genuinely concerned. "Where's Hailey?"

I took a step toward him. "She's fine. Downstairs with Kelsie. Her mother said she could sleep over."

His brows furrowed. "Okay. So what's the problem?"

I took two steps more toward him. "*You.*"

"Me? What the hell did I do? I just walked in."

I closed the distance between us and jabbed my finger into his chest with each word. "You. Didn't. Have. A. God. Damn. Meeting."

There was always the possibility that he could've had a dinner meeting his assistant didn't know about. But any small doubt I had about the game he was playing flew out the window when I saw the guilt written all over his face.

He looked away. "What are you talking about?"

I pushed up on my tippy toes and looked into his eyes. "You *knew* I had a date tonight. There was no meeting. You just wanted to ruin my night like I ruined yours."

He tugged at his tie and walked around me, striding toward his bedroom.

I followed in hot pursuit. He wasn't getting off that damn easy. "How old are you? I ruined your date unintentionally because I forgot my phone. And you go and do this *on purpose*?"

"Go home, Elodie."

His attitude made me even more irate. He wasn't even going to apologize. Did he think I would turn around and walk out the door, feeling like our score was settled now? Not a fucking chance.

Hollis walked to his dresser, pulled the tie from around his neck, and started to unbutton the cuff of his shirt.

"I'm not going anywhere! You owe me a damn apology."

He struggled to undo his cuff, and after ten seconds of trying to open the button, he yanked, and the cufflink went flying across the room. He stared down at his wrist for a minute, and I watched as his chest heaved up and down. When he finally looked at me, there was so much anger in his eyes.

"What would you like me to apologize for, Elodie?"

"For ruining my date!"

His jaw flexed, and he took a step toward me. I backed up. My heart raced out of control.

"An apology would mean I'm sorry it happened. And I'm not. Not in the fucking least."

My eyes widened. "You are *such* an asshole."

He kept walking toward me, and I kept taking steps back. "What does that say about you? You must like assholes, Elodie."

"*Screw you*. I don't like you *at all*!"

"No?" His voice turned eerily calm. "So you don't *like me*, but yet you want to *fuck* me."

"I don't want to fuck you. Go to hell, Hollis!"

He laughed bitterly. "I'm already there. Apparently, hell is a place where the devil is a woman with an attitude that would send any normal man running the other way."

"You owe me an apology!"

He closed the distance between us, causing my back to hit the wall behind me.

Hollis ducked down so we were at eye level and spoke with his nose inches from mine. "Let's see. What do I owe you an apology for? Jerking off to your panties? Or maybe coming so hard in the shower to visions of your face that I can barely see straight afterward? Or could it be wanting to beat the crap out of every asshole guy named *Benito* in the city of New York? Which is it, Elodie? Will one big, fat apology do?"

There had been very few times in my life that I'd been left speechless, but right now I had no idea how to respond. My jaw hung open, and my heart felt like it might come through the wall of my chest.

Hollis's eyes dipped to my lips, and I felt my knees go weak.

He growled. "*Fuck this*."

Before I could register what was happening, he wrapped his big hands around my face, tilted my head, and planted his lips over mine. It took a few heartbeats for the shock to wear off. But when it did, all hell broke loose.

My hands threaded into his hair, and I yanked as hard as I could. He growled and responded by grabbing the backs of my thighs and lifting me, guiding my legs to wrap around his waist. His firm chest pushed against mine, and if it hadn't felt so incredibly good, it might have concerned me how rough we were getting. Hollis ground his hips between my parted legs, and I could feel how hard and hot he was. *Oh God.*

We didn't kiss—that would be too tame of a word to describe what was raging between us. We assaulted each other with our mouths. He bit down on my bottom lip until I tasted metal seeping onto our joined tongues. I dug my nails into his neck so hard I pierced the skin. My clit was throbbing; tomorrow it would be bruised from the way he grinded against it. Neither one of us could get enough. We wanted rougher, faster, harder, *more.*

I distantly registered that my back had left the safety of the wall behind it. We fell onto the bed together, limbs crashing and bodies colliding. The anger we'd both had five minutes ago hadn't dissipated one bit—it had just redirected to this.

Abruptly, Hollis tore his mouth from mine and stumbled to his feet. I panted, gulping mouthfuls of air, and lifted my hand to cover my swollen lips. Was he stopping? I was about to scream bloody murder if he thought he could leave me here gasping and drenched like this.

But then I realized why he'd jumped up so fast. I must've missed the first warning sounds.

"Uncle Hollis? Are you here?"

Shit!

Not wanting Hailey to see me all disheveled, I ran to Hollis's master bathroom and closed the door. It seemed like the most sensible thing to do with no time to think.

I placed my ear on the door and listened to their conversation.

"Why do you have lipstick all over your face?"

I cringed. *Shit.*

Hollis played dumb. "I do?"

"Yeah. Look in the mirror."

"Wow. You're right," he said. "What are you doing home?"

"Kelsie threw up, so her mom thought it was best if I didn't spend the night. She walked me upstairs, and I used my key."

"Ah. Okay. Well...that was probably the right decision."

"So, why do you have lipstick on your face?"

Figures she wouldn't drop it. How the heck was he going to get around this? Moreover, how the heck was I going to escape this bathroom?

Hollis finally answered, "It's a long story I'd rather not get into, okay? I don't owe you an explanation for everything."

"Hmmm. Okay. Whatever."

I chuckled to myself.

Hailey was definitely skeptical, although I doubted she suspected this had anything to do with me.

"It's late. Why don't you go to your room, try to get some sleep."

"Okay. 'Night, Uncle Hollis."

"Goodnight, sweetheart."

There was a long moment of silence. I assumed he was waiting for Hailey to fully disappear. In the distance, I could hear the door to her bedroom shut. Hailey had a habit of always slamming her door, and this time was no different.

The bathroom door opened, and I got a look at Hollis's face. He did have my lipstick smeared all over his mouth. His hair was a wild mess, too. Not to mention, his erection was still straining against his pants. He looked totally hot and fuckable. I wondered if he would have been inside of me right now had Hailey not come home.

Speaking of which, my panties were soaked. Clearly my body had been preparing for something big.

His eyes landed on my bruised lips as he said, "We have to sneak you out."

I nodded and walked out of the bathroom.

Tiptoeing across the floor and through the foyer, I made my way to the door. He followed me out to the hall and closed the door behind him.

He spoke quietly. "That was really close. She almost walked in on us."

"Well, she didn't, thankfully."

Hollis looked pained. "I shouldn't have attacked you like that."

"No need to apologize. I quite liked it, actually."

He ran his hand through his already-messed-up hair. "Look...clearly I'm confused. My feelings for you are carnal, and sometimes they feel...uncontrollable. That doesn't change the fact that it shouldn't have happened. That was a close call, but I'm thankful it stopped us from making a mistake we can't take back."

That pissed me off.

"So, you would've slept with me and then called it a mistake? What would've happened, Hollis? You would've gotten your fill, gotten to experience the thrill of sex with me, and then told me it could never happen again? You were going to *fuck* me."

"I don't know what would have happened. Clearly, I'm not thinking with my brain."

That's for sure. "Do me a favor, Hollis. Stay out of my life, okay? It's one thing if you don't think it's a good idea for us to be anything more than business associates. But if that's the case, don't manipulate things—like you did making me late for my date tonight. That's not fair. You can't have it both ways."

Hollis neither confirmed nor denied intentionally ruining my date with Benito.

He simply said, "I won't interfere in your life."

"Thank you."

Then he let me walk away without stopping me. I wished he had. I wanted him to prove me wrong, to admit he had feelings for me, that he was so jealous of the prospect of me dating someone else that he couldn't help but interfere.

But instead, in typical Hollis fashion, he closed up, once again making me feel like I was the crazy one for believing there could ever be something between us.

———

Sometimes Bree had trouble sleeping and stayed up late. I wondered if she'd be up for a visit tonight. So I texted her, and she responded that I should come over. She told me to use my key to let myself in.

She was sitting on the couch when I entered her house. She looked like she'd lost more weight. The fact that she'd stopped the experimental treatments was starting to show. I didn't like this one bit.

She coughed. "What happened tonight?"

I spent the next several minutes making myself a cup of tea and telling Bree the whole story of my humiliating encounter with Hollis and the near-miss of Hailey finding us.

"So, wow. He definitely likes you."

"Did you not hear anything I just told you? He used the whole experience to reiterate what a *mistake* it would be if we ever crossed the line. It was like he felt Hailey's arrival was a warning of danger from God."

She shook her head. "He's just scared, Elodie. It's so clear to me. He obviously has feelings for you that go beyond the physical if he went through the bother of sabotaging your date. He just hasn't admitted it to himself, let alone you."

"See, I don't see it that way. He's egotistical. It's not so much that he wants me for himself. He just wanted to get me back for walking in on *his* date. He was angry and frustrated at my calling him out on his behavior, and *that* led to the lapse in sanity that was our make-out session. It's rare that we're ever alone, and I honestly think for him, it was just sexual."

"I don't know if I believe that." Bree covered her mouth as she coughed again.

"Are you okay? Can I get you some water?"

She held out her hand. "I'm fine." Yet she continued to hack.

My friend was such a trooper. I hated that she had to live with that horrible disease. I poured her some water anyway and handed it to her.

"Okay," I said, examining her face to make sure she was good before continuing to vent. "The worst part is, I had to cancel a date with a perfectly good man who *does* want to spend time with me."

"How did the guy take it? What's his name again?"

"Benito. I told him I had no choice, that my boss never came home to relieve me. Hopefully, he doesn't think I'm making it up."

"I'm sure he'll jump at the chance for a rain check this weekend. But honestly, be careful how fast you move with anyone else. I still feel like things with Hollis could change. He seems extremely weak when it comes to you, and I would hate for him to come around, only to find you with someone else."

"Well, that would be *his* problem."

"Except that I think it's Hollis *you* really want. I don't think you'd even be pursuing the online dating thing if it weren't to escape your feelings for him."

She was right. And that sucked.

"It doesn't matter what I felt for him...and I say *felt* in the past tense because after what he pulled tonight, I'm more determined than ever to get over it."

I looked for more logical excuses to push past my feelings for him.

"And you know what else? He's a workaholic. I'm looking for a family man, someone who'd put me and my child first. Even though he was forced to take Hailey in, Hollis isn't naturally that type of guy. It's becoming more obvious by the second that he's all wrong for me."

CHAPTER TWENTY-FOUR

Hollis – 7 years ago

Anna and I were getting ready to go out to dinner when I decided to bring up something that had been on my mind.

"I've been thinking more and more about starting my own company," I said as I helped put her necklace on.

She turned around to face me. "Really?"

"Yeah." I straightened her gold charm. "I realized working at the firm will eventually end up burning me out. I'm making great money now, but I don't want to do these sixteen-hour days forever—not if we're gonna have a family someday. I need more flexibility, need to have my nights and weekends back. I need to start planning for that."

She adjusted my collar. "Well, I can't complain about the prospect of you having more free time. As of right now, you're married to your job."

"I don't want to be married to my job—I want to be married to *you*." I leaned in and kissed her before rubbing her shoulders. "I was actually considering asking Addison to be my partner. What do you think?"

"Wow." Anna stared off to ponder that. "Actually, I think you guys would be great together—if you don't kill each other."

"We may bust each other's balls, but I trust her. And she's smart as a whip. She's probably the only person I could imagine going into business with."

"I think you'd make a great team."

I was thrilled and relieved that Anna was on board with this. "Then let's do it."

Leaning in to give her another kiss, I heard something that gave me pause.

"Anna's home!"

Our attention turned to the bird Anna had brought here the other day. He sat in his cage in the corner of the room.

"Did he just say 'Anna's home?'" I asked.

Then he did it again.

"Anna's home!"

She laughed. "I didn't even realize he knew my name."

Something occurred to me. "The other day when you walked in after your shopping trip, I looked at him and said, 'Anna's home.' It must have stuck."

Anna volunteered at a bird sanctuary and for some reason had decided to bring this particular bird home to live with us. Since he was from Australia, she thought it would be funny to name him after the Aussie actor Hugh Jackman. But he didn't look like a Hugh to me, so we called him Huey for short. I wasn't too keen on living with this thing, having to clean its cage and whatnot, but she'd insisted. I couldn't fight it.

We were headed out the door when he did it again. *"Anna's home!"*

She laughed. "That's going to drive you crazy, isn't it?"

"Nah. I'll never get tired of hearing your name, even if it does come out of that annoying little guy."

A few weeks later, Addison met Anna and me to look at a rental office space for the firm we planned to start. Addison had taken me up on the offer to partner together, and the future was looking bright.

A realtor took us to a space downtown that was small, but perfect for what we had in mind. The price was right, and we couldn't find one reason not to take it.

The agent clapped her hands together. "What do you say? Shall we head back to my office and draw up the papers?"

Addison and I looked at each other before she nodded, giving me the go ahead to say, "We'll take it."

Anna stood on her tippy toes to hug me. "Congratulations! This is so exciting."

"After we do the paperwork, shall we go celebrate?" Addison asked.

"That sounds like a great idea, but we'll have to take a rain check. Anna and I have to go to the hospital tonight. Adam's mother called me today. Apparently, he was readmitted."

Her excitement faded. "Oh, I'm sorry to hear that."

I let out a deep sigh. "Believe me, so am I."

Adam looked worse than I'd ever seen him as I wheeled him into the lounge to start a game. We sometimes played in his room, other times out here for a change of scenery. I tried not to ask him too many questions about his health because I didn't want to alarm him by seeming overly concerned. Based on his gaunt appearance, though, it was obvious enough that he wasn't doing well.

When Anna excused herself to go to the ladies' room, Adam shocked me by saying, "Hollis, stop the game for a minute."

I immediately put down my controller and muted the volume. "What's up?"

Nothing could have prepared me for what he said next.

"I'm not gonna make it this time."

My heart dropped to my stomach. I hadn't been expecting him to confide in me, and certainly not with news like that. As I stared at his pale skin, I tried to comfort him, even if I knew it was in vain.

"You don't know that."

"I do. And you know what the sad part is?" He laughed almost maniacally. "I'm still a fucking virgin at nineteen who's never even had his first kiss! And I'm gonna die that way."

What could I possibly say to that?

"Are you saying you want me to kiss you?"

God only knows how he managed to smile, but he did.

"On second thought, I'm good."

Anna returned, and in her presence, he no longer seemed interested in talking.

We went back to playing our game until a nurse came and interrupted, insisting that Adam needed his rest and should return to his room.

Anna and I lingered in the lounge after the nurse wheeled Adam back.

"What's going on? You look upset," she said. "Is it the way he looks?"

I shook my head. "I'm fucking devastated, Anna."

"He's not doing well, is he?"

"He just confided in me that he doesn't think he's going to make it this time."

She stared down at the floor. "It sucks that he's lost hope. How does someone live each day knowing they're going to die? I can't even comprehend it."

"He told me he couldn't believe he was going to die a virgin who's never even kissed a girl. I felt terrible. What the hell do you say to something like that?"

She placed her head on my shoulder. "What *did* you say?"

"I made a dumb joke, offered to kiss him myself."

Anna smiled sympathetically.

"It got him to smile at least."

We sat in silence for a while before I finally stood up. "We might as well get going."

"Should we say goodbye to him?"

"We should let him rest," I said. "I'll come back tomorrow."

We were on our way out when Anna stopped, just before we made it to the elevators.

She looked anxious and said, "Wait right here, okay?"

"Why?"

"I'll be right back."

Anna ventured down the hall toward Adam's room. Even though she'd told me to wait, I couldn't help my curiosity, so I followed her.

He was, in fact, awake and sitting up alone.

Standing just outside the doorway, I watched as Anna sat at the corner of his bed and pulled him to her. Adam didn't question it. He just laid his head on her chest and closed his eyes. After about a minute, he looked up at her and to my shock, Anna lowered her head to his. My heart beat out of control as I watched her place a long, firm kiss on his lips. It only lasted a few seconds, but for Adam, I was sure the memory would last a lifetime. His mouth spread into a wide smile after.

Mine did too.

CHAPTER TWENTY-FIVE

Elodie

My Saturday plan was to sleep in, go shopping for a new outfit at the mall, treat myself to a mani-pedi, and then go home to get ready for my date with Benito tonight. Thankfully, he hadn't written me off for canceling on him.

Anyway, those *were* my Saturday plans. That is, until my phone rang as I was getting up to start my day.

When I saw it was Hollis, I almost wondered if he was calling to apologize about last night. I should've known better.

My tone was cold as I answered. "Hello?"

"Elodie...I'm sorry to bother you on a Saturday."

"What's up?"

"Hailey was invited to an opera tonight, if you can believe that. Her friend's parents have tickets. They're going to the performance, and then she's going to sleep over at their place across town. She has nothing to wear. They want her in a dress. I told her not to bother you, but she really wants you to go shopping with her. Any chance I could pay you double time to take her out for a couple of hours today? Feel free to say no."

Feel free to apologize to me for being a dick last night.

I didn't answer right away. A part of me wanted to blow him off. I just couldn't do that to her, though. But I wasn't going to free up his morning on my day off, either.

"I'll tell you what, I was already going to the mall near me to buy myself an outfit. She and I can shop for a dress there. Maybe you could drive her out here?"

He didn't hesitate. "Yeah, I could do that. Probably not worth it for me to come all the way back to the city, though. I'll take some work with me and find a place with WiFi until you're done."

"Okay. Whatever. Westshore Farms Mall at one o'clock? We can meet inside the main entrance."

"Got it." He paused then said, "Elodie?"

I let out a breath. "Yeah?"

"Thanks for doing this."

Hollis and Hailey were right on time. I'd gotten to the mall a few minutes early, probably because the idea of seeing Hollis made me anxious. Standing around the house and waiting had been driving me nuts.

"I'm so excited to shop!" Hailey beamed and gave me a hug.

Hollis, on the other hand, didn't seem that excited. He looked freaking amazing, though, dressed in a pale blue collared shirt left untucked from his jeans. His sleeves were rolled up, leaving his tanned, muscular forearms on full display. He looked like something out of a Ralph Lauren catalog.

He gazed up at the two levels above us. "I can't remember the last time I was at a mall."

"There's a Starbucks on the first floor with WiFi."

"Yeah. I think I'll head over there." He turned to Hailey. "How long do you think you'll be?"

She scrunched her nose. "You can't rush perfection, Uncle Hollsy."

"Right." He chuckled.

Once we separated from him, Hailey and I went to three different places before we ended up at the big department store. We visited the Juniors' section first to pick out a handful of dresses for her. Then we headed over to the Women's department and selected a few outfits for me to try on. We took them to the dressing room and planned to model the clothes for each other.

I entered a stall and Hailey took the one next to me. We'd tell each other when we were ready, then meet in the common area to show off our outfits.

When I tried on the last one, I exited the stall to find she wasn't in the common area. Instead, I could hear her talking outside the dressing room.

"Hailey?" I called.

"Out here!" she said.

I walked out. "What are you..." I lost my words at the sight of Hollis standing in the middle of the Women's department.

He swallowed hard as he took me in. I happened to be wearing a striking red dress that pushed my breasts together nicely. If I'd had to choose an outfit for him to catch me in, this was it.

"What are you doing here?" I asked.

"Hailey told me she needed me."

She looked at him. "Well, you have to pay for my dress, right?"

That's total bullshit.

I called her out. "You know I have your uncle's credit card."

She blushed. "Okay, you're right. I wanted him to see how pretty you look."

Fairly certain I was the one blushing now.

Hollis's eyes traveled up and down my body. "She does...look very pretty."

"She's going on a date. He's picking her up at eight." She laughed. "That rhymes."

I'd never told her I was going on a date tonight, let alone what time Benito was supposed to be picking me up.

Lifting my brow, I asked, "How did you know that?"

"A text from him popped up on your phone." She shrugged. "Anyway, I'm gonna go change out of this."

Hailey skipped away to the dressing room.

I was just about to head back in myself when Hollis's voice stopped me.

"Wait."

I turned around, and before he could say anything, I said, "I hope you know I was specifically trying not to advertise what my plans were tonight."

He slipped his hands into his pockets. "I know."

I crossed my arms. "What were you going to say?"

"I just wanted to say thank you again for this. After the way things ended yesterday, you could have easily told me to fuck off."

"I'm doing this for her, not you."

"I know that. But thank you for not taking my mistake out on her."

"Mistake, yeah. Every time you've gotten close to me, you chalk it up to one big mistake."

"That's not what I meant." He looked down at his shoes then back up at me. "Look, I'm sorry about yesterday. Clearly I don't know how to handle myself around you."

I laughed angrily. "I'd better go before she hears us."

When Hailey and I returned, holding the two dresses we'd chosen, I was surprised to see Hollis still waiting for us. He looked like a fish out of water, deep in thought, staring off into a rack of Diane von Furstenberg wrap dresses.

The three of us moved to the register, and Hollis stood close behind me while I paid for Hailey's dress with his credit card and used my card to pay for my own. When he breathed out, I could feel it on the back of my neck; that's how close he was.

That simple breath brought back the memory of what it felt like when he devoured my lips, how amazing it was to be ravaged by him in the least gentle of ways.

Hollis was quiet as we walked back out of the mall. When we got to the parking lot, he still seemed lost in his own mind.

He scratched his head. "I can't seem to remember where I parked."

"Well, that's unfortunate," I said. "I'm right over there. I guess I'll see you guys on Monday."

Hailey gave me a hug. "Thanks again, Elodie."

I squeezed her. "Have the best time at the opera. Let me know how it is. I've never been."

She pulled back. "Really?"

"Most kids don't grow up getting to do such fancy things. And many adults don't get to, either. You're very lucky."

"I know." She smiled.

I smiled, too. I knew Hailey appreciated the life she'd been given as of late.

We both turned to Hollis, who still looked like he was trying to figure out which direction to go. He really had forgotten where he'd parked.

"Drive safe back to the city," I said.

"If we can find the car!" Hailey laughed.

I left them before I knew whether they'd reunited with Hollis's vehicle.

Thoughts of him flooded my brain the entire ride back to my house. I really wished I knew what had happened to make him so guarded, so afraid of intimacy.

I shook my head. I wasn't supposed to be analyzing Hollis. I was supposed to be looking forward to my date with Benito.

When I got home, I realized I'd never responded to Benito's text about picking me up at eight, the one Hailey had seen on my phone.

I typed out a response.

Elodie: Sorry for the delay. Eight is great. Looking forward to it.

Benito: Me too. I still can't believe you finally agreed to meet :-) Do you like sushi?

Elodie: I love it.

Benito: I know this great place not too far from you. There's a jazz bar around the corner that has really good drinks, too. Maybe we could hit that after.

Elodie: That sounds perfect.

Benito: Can you text me your address?

After I typed out my address, I second-guessed whether it was safe to have him pick me up here. But then I remembered his background check was clean and decided not to stress over it.

It was four o'clock. The time would fly by before I knew it. Even though I never had a chance to get the mani-pedi I'd originally planned for today, I thought helping Hailey pick out her first nice dress was a much better use of my time.

I thought about the fact that she would be spending the night at her friend's, since the opera was on the other side of town. That meant Hollis would have the place to himself. He'd likely be calling one of his concubines to fix the mess he'd started with me the other day. The thought of him taking out his sexual frustrations on someone else really irked me.

And here I am thinking about Hollis again.

Why? Why couldn't I rid my mind of him for one

night?

Deciding to take a relaxing bath to clear my head, I filled the tub and threw a bath bomb into the water. Slipping inside the bubbles, I took my time as I applied a face mask before shaving my legs carefully. While I was pretty certain there wouldn't be any sex with Benito on the first date, I had to prepare for the unexpected.

Once out of the tub, I slipped on my black lace panties and immediately, of course, thought of Hollis. This, after all, was the thong that had started our infamous game. Pretty sure I selected this particular one as an extra *fuck you* to him tonight.

After blowing my hair out and applying my makeup, I put on the red dress I'd chosen and tilted my head as I looked at myself in the mirror.

There was still a ton of time before Benito would be here. I decided to pour a glass of wine. My palms were sweaty, and my heart was racing. It had been a damn long time since I'd been out on a date.

At seven forty-five, my doorbell rang.

Holy shit. He's early.

My heart now pitter-pattered as I dumped the remainder of the wine into the sink. I straightened my dress and rubbed my lips together before taking one last look at myself in the hallway mirror.

I'm ready for this.

Or so I thought.

But when I opened the door, it wasn't Benito standing there.

CHAPTER TWENTY-SIX

Elodie

My racing heart came to an abrupt halt at the sight of Hollis on my front porch. I hated the effect the man had on me. The wine I'd just consumed burned in my throat, threatening to come back up, and I swallowed to speak.

"What are you doing here?"

He dragged a hand through his hair. "Can I come in?"

I folded my arms across my chest as my initial shock started to turn to anger. "What for?"

"I need to speak to you."

"That's not a good idea. My date is going to be here any minute."

Hollis's jaw flexed, but he did his best to keep his voice steady. "It will only take a second."

Last week, him getting angry at the mention of my date would have thrilled me. But I was done playing games. He didn't get to be angry, and he certainly didn't get to be possessive, because I wasn't his. Lord knows I'd given him ample opportunity, and he'd made it clear that anything that happened between us was a mistake. I was *no one's* mistake.

I straightened my spine. "Say what you have to say right here. And do it fast. You've already ruined the first plans I had with Benito. There's no way I'm letting you mess up tonight, too."

Hollis looked down and just kept shaking his head. After a long minute of watching and waiting, he finally spoke.

"I'm sorry." His voice was barely a whisper.

"For what?"

"For making you miss your date the other day." He looked up and caught my eyes. "For acting like a jealous asshole."

I sighed. I wanted to read into his admission of jealousy, to take it to mean he had feelings for me. But a strong physical attraction doesn't equate to feelings, and I was done getting my hopes up.

"Fine. Apology accepted. Is there anything else?"

Hollis looked back and forth between my eyes. As we stood there staring at each other, a car slowed and pulled to the curb.

Shit. Benito.

I held my breath while he parked and began to get out of the car. Hollis looked over his shoulder and back to me. My hands trembled, but I wouldn't let either of these men see me like that.

"Don't go," Hollis whispered.

Benito shut the car door and started up my walkway.

I felt tears well up in my eyes. "Give me a reason not to, Hollis. Not with your mouth or your body, but something from the heart—words, feelings, anything."

The pain in his face was palpable. But I'd let him do this to me more than once. I needed more than jealousy and physical attraction. I'd take something minimal even, just to assure me I wasn't going to take this risk alone.

Benito's footsteps grew louder.

"Hollis? Do you have anything more to say?"

He continued to watch me as my date walked up and stood next to him. I had no choice but to acknowledge the man.

I put on my best fake smile. "You must be Benito."

"I am." Benito looked over at Hollis with his eyes trained on me.

The entire thing was awkward.

"Ummm... This is my boss, Hollis."

Benito stuck out his hand. "Oh. Good to meet you."

Hollis turned, leveled him with an icy glare, and dropped his eyes to Benito's hand. He made no attempt to reciprocate the greeting.

Instead, he looked back to me. "Can we have a moment, please?"

I couldn't let him do this. I just couldn't. He'd had his chance, and again he'd left me dangling.

"We can talk about it Monday morning when I get to work." I turned my attention back to my date. "Hollis was just leaving. Would you mind coming in for a minute, Benito? I just need to get my purse."

"Umm...yeah. Sure."

It didn't get much more uncomfortable than this. I nodded at Hollis. "Have a good weekend."

Opening the door, I walked in, and Benito followed. Once he was inside, I held the door open and waited a few more seconds. Hollis stared at the ground.

I frowned. "Goodbye, Hollis."

Saying those words and shutting that door were oddly some of the hardest things I'd ever had to do. But I needed to do it. My relationship with Hollis wasn't healthy, and I deserved more than he would ever give me.

Benito looked at me. "Everything okay with your boss?"

I took a deep breath in and out. "Yeah. We just have differing opinions on how some things need to be handled. He'll get over it." Though I wasn't so sure I would. "I'm sorry about how he acted. He can be a real asshole sometimes."

Benito laughed. "No problem. I've had those bosses before. The trick is to nod a lot, then stand firm and do what you think is right."

I forced a smile. "Yeah. Would you excuse me for a minute? I need to use the ladies' room before we go. There's wine and water in the fridge, if you don't mind helping yourself."

"Thank you. Take your time. I was early."

I went to the bathroom and immediately stepped into the bathtub so I could peek out the window. The blinds were shut, so I adjusted them enough to see outside. It broke my heart to see Hollis getting into his car. He buckled himself in and started it, then stared up at the house for a long time. Then, he pulled away.

The entirety of what had happened began to bubble up, and I felt tears stinging my eyes. Every emotion raced through me—anger, sadness, disappointment, grief, relief. It became too much to keep bottled in, and my shoulders began to shudder as tears streamed down my face.

God damn you, Hollis.

God damn you.

In truth, I was angrier that he'd left than I was that he'd shown up at all. The man had a way of getting my hopes up despite all the pessimism I felt. And each time I fell for it, he crushed me, leaving me feeling like a fool once again.

I closed my eyes and took a few deep, cleansing breaths in and out. Once I steadied myself, I looked in the mirror. My face was red from crying, so I blotted on some skin-toned cream contour that hid anything. It was too bad they didn't make this stuff for your insides. After I was done, I relined my lips in a bold red that matched my dress and spritzed on some perfume.

I had no desire to go on this date anymore. But I'd be damned if I was about to let Hollis ruin another night for me.

I was going to have a great time, even if it killed me.

Benito was actually more handsome in person. He was tall, with naturally tanned skin, almond-shaped eyes the color of honey, and great bone structure. He had an amazing smile that he shared often and a hearty, contagious laugh. If he hadn't been unknowingly competing with Hollis LaCroix, I would have been thrilled about meeting a guy like him.

"How about some dessert?" he said.

I had eaten too much bread and drank two glasses of wine to calm my nerves. I'd been almost full before dinner even arrived.

"I'm pretty stuffed."

He flashed a boyish smile. "So am I. I'm stalling because I'm not ready for our evening to end."

How novel, a man who tells you what he feels.

That should've made me want to stay out longer, but I just wanted to go home and get into bed. I'd been struggling to put on a happy face ever since we left my house. Benito was great company; I just couldn't enjoy it tonight. And for that, he deserved some honesty.

"You're a great guy—"

Benito interrupted. He covered his heart with one hand like his chest hurt. "No, don't say it."

"Say what?"

"You were about to give me the *but* speech, weren't you?"

I smiled sadly. "Sort of. I'm a little out of it tonight, and even though we just met, I feel like you know that."

He nodded. "Your boss threw off your evening. I get it. It happens."

What a nice guy. "Thank you for understanding. Do you think maybe we could skip dessert and try this again another evening?"

"Sure. I'd like that. I'll get the check."

I felt lighter after acknowledging I wasn't myself tonight. Letting my guard down allowed me to be in the moment. We left the restaurant, and maybe it was only because I knew the date was ending soon, but I felt more relaxed than I'd been all day. Benito and I chatted as we waited for the valet to bring his car, and the conversation continued to flow freely during the drive to my house. When we pulled up alongside a young guy driving a clunker that had the rearview mirror duct-taped on, we laughed about our first cars.

"I had no air conditioning in mine, and a giant hole in the passenger floor," Benito said and shook his head. "The hole was perfectly round and looked like the previous owner had cut it out with a circular saw or something. I had the biggest crush on this girl named Angie my senior year. A few days after I got my car, I pulled into the gas station to fill it up, and there was Angie with a car full of her friends. I tried to play it cool, but it was the first time I'd actually pumped gas. Angie came over to talk to me, and I got completely distracted and forgot to take the nozzle out of the gas tank when I was done."

I covered my mouth and laughed. "Oh no. And you pulled away with it like that?"

Benito nodded. "I did. It had a quick release on top of the handle, so it didn't make too much of a mess, but the tug of the hose line set off some kind of alarm. The entire gas station, inside and out, flashed lights and a high-pitched siren blared."

"Was Angie still there?"

"Oh yeah. Laughing her ass off with her friends. The following day in school I admitted to her that I'd been trying to act cool and hadn't known what the hell I was doing."

"What did she say?"

"Crazy enough, she agreed to go out with me. It was a good lesson. I learned honesty gets you much farther with women."

"You learned that pretty early compared to a lot of men. How long did things last with Angie?"

Benito pulled off the highway at my exit. "One date. It was pouring the night I took her out. I drove over a big puddle, not thinking about the hole I had in the floor on her side, and a giant spray of dirty water came through the bottom of my car." He laughed. "She was soaked. The thing was like a geyser, I swear. I learned a second lesson that night. Women will only put up with you being an idiot once."

We laughed, and Benito navigated through the side streets on the way to my house. I'd really relaxed. It was too bad it hadn't happened on the way to our date, because he was good company. We made the last left, turning onto my block, and my heart skipped a beat.

Hollis's Mercedes was parked outside my house again. When we pulled closer, I saw that he wasn't waiting inside it. His imposing frame sat on the steps of my front porch. He stood when we slowed, and my date noticed him for the first time.

"Is that..."

I nodded. "My boss."

Benito pulled to the curb and put the car in park. We looked over at the porch once again. I was relieved Hollis had waited there and didn't come over to us.

"Do you want me to tell him to take a hike?"

Yes.

No.

Maybe?

I shook my head. That would most definitely not be a good idea. "No, I'm fine."

Benito's brows drew down. "Is he...more than your boss?"

I sighed. "It's...sort of...complicated."

He frowned. "Okay."

"I'm really sorry about tonight. You are such a nice guy, and I didn't mean to ruin our date."

"It's fine. Another night, maybe?"

He'd said it to be polite. In that moment, both of us knew there wouldn't be any other nights. I leaned over and kissed him on the cheek.

"Sure. Thank you so much for dinner, Benito."

He nodded. "I'm going to stay until you go inside."

"Thank you."

Butterflies swarmed in my belly as I strode up the walkway. I freaking *hated* what this man did to me. He made me feel inside-out.

"Are you happy?" I said quietly as I approached. "You ruined my date with a perfectly nice guy. Probably the first one of the species I've met in years."

Hollis looked down. "I'm sorry."

I rolled my eyes. "No, you're not."

Digging my keys from my purse, I unlocked the front door. Hollis waited as I walked inside. "Benito is a gentleman. He's going to sit there and make sure everything is okay. So you need to come in."

He nodded and followed me inside. I waved to Benito before shutting the door.

"I'm going to need wine for this." I walked to the refrigerator. "Would you like a glass?"

"No, thank you."

I poured almost to the brim and took the seat on the chair across from the couch, not wanting to sit too close to Hollis. He sat across from me and watched as I sucked half the glass down in one big gulp.

"Go ahead." I shrugged. "Say whatever it is you need to say. It's been a long evening, and I'm tired."

I waited forever for him to pull his thoughts together—at least it seemed like a long time.

Hollis dragged a hand through his hair, which looked like he'd been doing that a lot tonight. A five o'clock shadow peppered his sharp jaw, and it pissed me off that I sat there thinking how good messy looked on him.

"I'm not the right man for you, Elodie."

I set my wine down on the coffee table and stood. "I don't need a gentle letdown, Hollis. You wasted a trip to Connecticut."

"Sit," he barked.

I folded my arms across my chest. "No."

"God damn it, Elodie. I don't want to have a battle of wills with you. We both know you'll win. Can you just sit the hell down and give me five minutes?"

His admitting I'd win softened me. "Fine. Five minutes."

Hollis waited until I sat and then looked away. "Thank you." He blew out an audible breath. "As I was saying, I'm not the right man for you. You've been hurt, and yet underneath all that armor you wear, you still believe Prince Damn Charming is out there. I'm no Prince Charming."

I tilted my head. "Well, at least we agree on something."

Hollis chuckled. He took one more deep breath and finally looked me in the eyes. "You deserve Prince Charming. But I'm a selfish enough bastard that I don't give a shit what you deserve."

My heart fluttered. My head knew it was dumb, and that the other shoe was probably about to drop, but I had no real control over the giant muscle in my chest.

"Can you just spit out what you want to say? The push and pull is exhausting."

"I want to try, Elodie."

I had to be misunderstanding. "Try what?"

"To be together."

I squinted at him. "You mean, you want to fuck me?"

"No. Yes. No. Well, of course, I do. But that's not what I'm trying to say."

"So what *are you* trying to say?"

"I want to...I don't know, date you?"

Well, this was a turn of events I hadn't expected. I couldn't help but be suspect.

"You want to date me?"

"Yes."

"And what does that entail?"

"I don't know. Dinners. Spending time together..."

"What if I said I won't have sex with you? Would you still want to date me?"

His brows rose. "Forever?"

I smiled. "No. Not forever. But...I'm not sure I believe you want to date me, Hollis. I think you're frustrated and know that's the only way it's going to happen between us. It's a means to an end for you."

He frowned. "Not to be a dick, but if getting laid was all I wanted, that isn't too hard."

I wanted to believe him so badly, but it wasn't that easy. "Why? Why the sudden change of heart? The other day our kiss was a giant mistake, and you regretted it. Today I go out with someone else, and you miraculously figure out you want to date me?"

Hollis leaned forward on the couch and looked directly into my eyes. "I'm not going to lie to you. That probably is what got me off my ass. But does the reason I pulled my head out of my ass even matter?"

I searched his eyes. He seemed so sincere... Yet so had Tobias when he said his vows at our wedding. This man could easily crush me. But let's face it, I'd already given a piece of my heart to him, and it was going to happen whether I dated him or not. I suppose I might as well get a few good dates out of it.

"Fine. But I want to eat at the restaurant in the Mandarin Hotel. When I worked for Soren, I had to meet assholes at the Aviary bar there, and the restaurant always smelled so good. It's out of my price range."

The corner of Hollis's lip twitched. "Done. Anything else?"

Hmm... As long as he was asking...

"I've never taken a carriage ride through Central Park."

"We can do that."

"Or gone ice skating in Rockefeller Plaza."

That lip twitched again. "It's July, but maybe at Christmastime."

My heart swelled. Christmas was a good five months away. That simple answer told me he wasn't planning a short fling—not intentionally, anyway.

"Anything else?" He raised a brow.

I tapped my finger to my lip. I'd been teasing, but something important did come to mind. "We don't tell Hailey what's going on between us—not at first, anyway. She already wants us to be a family, and I don't want to disappoint her if things don't work out."

Hollis's mouth formed a straight line, but he nodded. "That's fine."

I picked up my wine and drank a sip. "I guess we have a deal then."

Hollis's eyes sparkled. "Not yet. You haven't heard my terms."

My brows jumped. "Your terms?"

He smirked. "That's right. Don't I get terms?"

"I guess that depends on what they are."

Hollis reached out and took the wine glass from my hand. He lifted it to his lips and proceeded to gulp the remainder. Setting it on the table, he extended his hand to me.

I hesitated, but eventually placed my hand in his. The second I did, Hollis yanked hard, and I was out of my chair and onto his lap. He cupped my cheek. "Number one. No other men. Especially not Benito."

I pretended to deliberate and then shrugged. "I guess so."

He scooped a hand under my ass and squeezed. *Hard.* "Cute. Number two, if we're not going to be having sex for a while, you'll need to wear something other than lace panties."

I pulled my head back. "You don't like my lace panties?"

"I love them. But since I'll have to take care of myself for the time being, you'll be leaving your panties behind at the end of our dates. The lace can be chafing."

My eyes widened. I couldn't believe he'd just told me he rubbed my panties against his dick so hard that it chafed him.

"I'll need to amend my conditions, please."

He arched a brow.

"I'll need some new panties. I only have one or two pairs that aren't lace."

Hollis flashed a wicked grin. "That would be my pleasure."

I wrapped my arms around his neck. "Are we done?"

"No. I have one more condition."

"Shoot."

He looked me up and down. "Don't wear this dress on any of our dates."

I pouted. "You don't like my dress?"

"Just the opposite. I fucking love it. If you wear it, I won't be able to stop myself from ripping it off you and fucking you up against the wall at some point."

I swallowed. *Oooohhh. Up against the wall. That sounds really good.*

Hollis growled. "I need a fourth condition."

"What?"

"Don't look like that around me."

"Like what?"

"Like you really want me to fuck you up against the wall."

My eyes softened.

Hollis pulled me against his chest and pressed a sweet kiss to my forehead. "Are we good?"

I nodded. "I think so."

'Then I better go."

"Go? Why?"

"Because your ass is sitting on my dick, and I'm going to try to break rule number one in the next five minutes if I don't, sweetheart."

Sweetheart. I liked that.

Hollis brushed his lips with mine. "Tomorrow night. Seven o'clock."

I smiled. "Okay."

"Get some sleep."

I walked him to the door.

"Be careful driving."

He'd made it a few steps out of my house when I called after him. "Hollis?"

He turned back.

I reached under my dress and slid my panties down my legs. Stepping out, I picked up the black lace thong and tossed it at him. "Sorry. You'll have to deal with a little chafing tonight."

He caught my thong and lifted it to his nose, taking a deep whiff. "Mmmm... Missed this."

The sight of him smelling my underwear was so damn erotic. Apparently Hollis might not be the only one handling himself tonight.

Seeing my face, he winked. "I'll pick you up some batteries when I get your new panties."

CHAPTER
TWENTY-SEVEN

Hollis

"**C**an I help you, sir?"

A clerk caught me in the act of rubbing a pair of silk panties along my cheek. *Yeah. That isn't fucked up.* Seriously, what had my life come to?

I'd gone to a high-end lingerie store to make good on my promise. I hadn't originally planned to use my face as a testing mechanism. I'd just gotten carried away, imagining Elodie in them.

"No, thank you."

"Are you looking for something in particular?"

"Uh...*soft* panties, particularly thongs," I said in a low voice.

She walked to the other corner of the room. I followed her, briefly looking over my shoulder.

The woman opened a drawer and took out a lavender silk thong before handing it to me. "This is definitely our softest material."

Threading it through my fingers, I said, "I'll take one in every color."

She leaned in and whispered, "Are they for you?"

Caught off guard, I said, "For me?"

"Yeah. You know, some men actually like to wear them on the downlow."

She thinks I'm a cross-dresser?

"No. They're for my..." I hesitated.

What the hell was Elodie to me? She wasn't my girlfriend, but she was more than a friend or a casual fuck.

"They're for my nanny." I laughed at the word I'd ultimately settled on. Well, it was the truth, I suppose.

"Your nanny?"

"Yes." I laughed. "A gift."

"Well, she's a very lucky girl. I used to nanny for a couple on the Upper West Side. I certainly never got fancy underwear."

She put together a rainbow pile of thongs and carried them over to the register. She wrapped them in tissue paper and stuffed them into a pink bag.

Looking down at my credit card, she said, "Well, Mr. LaCroix, I hope your nanny enjoys her soft panties."

"Oh, *we* will." I smiled.

That afternoon, after I returned from my impromptu Sunday lingerie jaunt, Hailey called me from her neighbor friend's apartment. She was supposed to be spending the day with Kelsie and sleeping over. It was the first time I'd ever specifically asked her to check with a friend to see if she could spend the night. What can I say? I was desperate to be with Elodie.

"What's up?" I asked.

"Change of plans tonight. I can't sleep over at Kelsie's anymore."

Shit. "Why not?"

"Kelsie's aunt went into labor. They have to drive to New Jersey."

Well, there goes my babysitting. I was supposed to pick Elodie up at seven. I'd made reservations at the restaurant she wanted to go to in the Mandarin Hotel and arranged for a carriage ride afterward. Hailey, of course, wasn't supposed to know. Now what? I wasn't going to be able to find a sitter on such short notice. I chuckled to myself. *Maybe if you weren't dating the damn sitter, Hollis, you wouldn't have this problem.* Anyway, I'd been looking forward to seeing Elodie all day. I didn't want to have to wait till next weekend.

"What time are you coming back?"

"They're leaving soon. Probably in about fifteen minutes."

I sighed. "Okay, kiddo. See you soon."

Letting out a frustrated breath, I picked up the phone and dialed Elodie.

She picked up. "Hey."

My tone seemed less than happy. "Hey."

She could sense something was off. "What's wrong?"

"So...I have a little problem."

"Are you standing me up?"

"Fuck, no."

"What happened?"

"I have Hailey tonight. Her plans fell through."

"I thought she was sleeping over at Kelsie's."

"She was. But they had a family emergency. So she's on her way back in a few minutes."

Elodie blew a breath into the phone. "Shit. Okay. Well, that sucks. But it is what it is."

Think. "I know you said you didn't want Hailey to know anything. I think that's wise...but I still really want to see you."

"Well, what choice do we have?" She sighed. "We can't."

I rubbed my chin. "Maybe we can."

"How?"

"Can you come to the city?"

"Of course, but she's going to suspect something if I come over on a Sunday."

I wracked my brain for a solution. "I'll take her out somewhere. You can show up and pretend you just happened to run into us. I'll take her shopping to get stuff to make dinner here. We need to go shopping anyway. When she sees you, I know she'll beg you to come back home with us."

"I've been telling her I want to check out the new gourmet place downtown, Victor's Market," she said. "Maybe I can have an intense urge for pickled artichokes that prompted me to board a train to the city on a lazy Sunday?"

"Perfect. Whatever. She'll buy it if we make it look coincidental. How soon can you be here?"

"Ninety minutes?"

⌒

I spotted her before Hailey did. Elodie had a shopping basket hanging from her wrist as she perused the bread aisle. Her long, blond hair was tied into a low ponytail. Her little ears were exposed, and they looked bitable.

I wanted to bite her fucking ears now? *Jesus*. This woman made me lose my mind.

Our eyes finally met. We shared a smile as Hailey continued to be distracted by a cheese sample.

Elodie approached and pretended to be shocked to see us. Her jaw dropped. "Hollis?"

I acted surprised. "Elodie? What are you doing in the city on a Sunday?"

Hailey's head whipped around. "Oh my God! What?" She ran to Elodie and gave her a hug.

"Hey, Hailey! What a surprise to run into you guys."

"Why are you here?" Hailey asked.

"Well, I had the worst craving for pickled artichokes and warm brie. So, since I had nothing better to do today, I decided to come into the city and stock up on my favorite things."

"You're gonna carry all that food home on the train?"

"Well, I limit myself to one big bag."

Hailey looked up at me. "Uncle Hollis is going to make homemade Margherita pizza for us tonight. We came to get dough, and fresh basil and stuff."

Elodie gave me a look like she was impressed.

I shrugged. "I'm not the greatest cook. But pizza I can handle."

"Then we're gonna watch the new Marvel movie after."

"That sounds like so much fun." Elodie grinned.

Hailey bounced up and down. "You should come have dinner with us and watch the movie."

Bingo. Thank you, dear niece.

Elodie feigned hesitance. "Oh, I don't know. It might be too late for me to get home at a decent time if I come over. It's a work night, after all. I have to be ready for you bright and early in the morning."

Hailey sulked. "I guess that's true."

Elodie and I shared a knowing look. Neither of us had been expecting Hailey to give up so easily.

What now? "I'd be happy to drive you back after dinner," I said. "I'm sure Hailey wouldn't mind the ride."

"Great idea, Uncle Hollis." She turned to Elodie. "See? Now you have to come."

"Well, how can I say no to dinner, a movie, and door-to-door chauffeur service?"

A woman near us was eating something chocolatey on a stick.

Hailey fixated on it. "Where did you get that?" she asked.

The lady pointed. "Sample table in that corner."

"Be right back!" Hailey said, booking it over there.

Elodie shook her head. "She's got a one-track mind."

"I can certainly relate to that."

She blushed. "You were *very* determined to see me."

"You look beautiful."

"Well, I thought I had a date with a very handsome, sometimes obnoxious man tonight. I'd gotten myself all dolled up."

"I hope you know he had big plans for you...the Mandarin Hotel restaurant, a carriage ride, the whole nine."

"I might have gotten a little carried away with my requests. I hope you don't think I truly care where you take me. I'm thrilled just to be with you. Hanging out at home is great."

Her use of the word *home* made me a tad uneasy. It was a reminder that I needed to think before I entered into something serious. But right now, I couldn't think of much else besides her lips. My eyes were glued to them.

"You want to get a sample?" she asked.

"All I want to fucking taste are those lips." Checking to make sure Hailey wasn't looking, I leaned in and attempted to do just that, keeping my eyes in my niece's direction the entire time.

When Hailey suddenly turned around, I pushed back and muttered, "Shit."

"It's gonna be a long night." Elodie smiled.

The kitchen was covered in flour. We'd opted to wait to clean up the mess until after we ate. Elodie cleaned the counter while I hand-washed a few dishes.

Hailey dried each plate as I handed it to her. "When are we starting the movie?"

"Probably in about ten minutes."

When she finished the last one, she said, "Can I go to my room until then?"

"Yeah. Sure."

Elodie was still wiping the counter down when Hailey's door slammed shut.

I waited a few seconds, then came up behind Elodie, pulling her into the small utility closet off the kitchen.

It was nearly dark in there, but just enough light from the kitchen seeped in through the slats in the door.

She panted as she looked up into my eyes.

I lowered my mouth to hers and emptied all of my breath into her. We kissed as if we were both starved. She pulled my hair as I grabbed her ass. Tasting the hint of wine on her, I moved my tongue harder and faster to taste everything else. Lowering my head to her neck, I sunk my teeth into her flesh.

That's when she knocked me out of my trance, pulling back. "We'd better go back out."

I rested my mouth on her skin then grunted. I peeked out before opening the door to make sure the coast was clear.

She followed and then went back to nonchalantly wiping the counter.

She glanced over at me and blushed. That made me want to kiss her all over again.

"It's kind of fun sneaking around," she said.

"I feel like a fucking kid." I laughed. "I've been waiting to do that all freaking night."

"I made sure not to wear lipstick, hoping you would." She winked.

"Well, your lips are pretty damn red right now. I did a number on them."

We continued to stare at each other, wanting more than we could have right now, knowing Hailey could come out at any minute.

Her soft, fair skin was begging to be bitten again. My inability to focus on anything tonight besides touching and kissing her was eye opening. It was like now that I'd given myself permission to touch her, I couldn't keep my hands off. Maybe it was a good thing Hailey was with us tonight. We might have taken things too far. Or at least I would have *tried* to.

I was just about to steal one more kiss when Hailey's bedroom door opened, demonstrating that we were only ever just seconds away from getting caught.

CHAPTER TWENTY-EIGHT

Elodie

My lips were still sore from our closet kiss. Hollis was so hot for me tonight—it was driving me absolutely insane.

"Can we make popcorn?" Hailey asked.

"What's a movie without popcorn?" I smiled. "I'll get it started."

A few minutes later, Hailey shut off the lights in the living room. I placed the gigantic bowl of popcorn in my lap. Hailey sat on one side of me. It surprised me that Hollis chose to sit on the other side of me rather than next to Hailey. That might have made her suspicious. But honestly, I was glad he'd taken the risk. If I couldn't touch him and kiss him tonight, I at least wanted to be near him.

The side of his leg was right up against mine. The heat from his body penetrated my clothing. I could feel his desire without him having to say or do anything beyond this subtle contact.

I was dying inside, wishing he could just take me to his room and ravage me. I tried to focus on the movie, but it was hard when all I could think about was when I'd get to feel his mouth on me again.

Our hands brushed against each other in the popcorn bowl. From time to time, I'd catch him looking at me instead of the movie. And I could feel him slowly inching closer to me, if that was even possible. I knew neither of us was really focused on the television.

Hailey suddenly stood up. "Can you pause it so I can go pee?"

"Sure," Hollis said as he grabbed the remote. His eyes followed her down the hall.

When the bathroom door shut, Hollis placed his hand on my thigh and nudged me toward him as he enveloped my mouth in his. He groaned into my lips, the sound of starvation satisfied. His tongue against mine made the muscles between my legs contract.

In the distance, the toilet flushed. He ripped himself away from me before grabbing a throw pillow and placing it over his crotch. He laid his head back as if nothing had happened and tried to act casual as Hailey returned to her spot.

She plopped down on the couch. "Okay. Press play."

Hollis did as she asked. We went back to watching the movie as if he hadn't just rocked my world with those ten seconds of fucking my mouth with his tongue. I seriously wanted to escape to the bathroom and relieve the ache between my legs. It wasn't going to be satisfied any other way tonight, because as soon as this movie ended, Hollis would have to drive me home. I wondered if the batteries in my vibrator still worked. I hadn't used my little friend for some time, but tonight I might need it.

When the movie ended, Hailey turned to me.

"It's kind of dumb for us to take you all the way home when you have to come back early in the morning. Why don't you just spend the night?"

I turned to Hollis. "I'm not sure your uncle is comfortable with that."

"I'm happy to drive you home if you'd prefer to sleep in your own bed, but we do have a guest room. You're welcome to stay."

Hailey got up to grab a drink and Hollis mouthed, "Say yes."

I chuckled.

When Hailey returned, I said, "You know what? It's late. I think I'll take you up on your offer. I'll just wear the same clothes tomorrow."

"I'm sure Uncle Hollis has a T-shirt you can sleep in." Hailey bounced. "This is so cool. We're having a sleepover with Elodie!"

Hollis flashed me a quick, mischievous smile.

Excited about my spending the night, Hailey insisted we paint our nails before bed. She also asked Hollis again for a T-shirt I could borrow. When I put it on, it went to the middle of my thighs. It was basically a dress.

I didn't want her to sense anything strange— namely that I was anxious to get back to Hollis—so I took my time hanging out with her and acted as normal as possible. She finally yawned and announced she was turning in.

I gave her a hug. "I'll see you in the morning, kiddo."

I'm sure Hailey assumed I was walking down the hall to the guest bedroom. Instead, in my long T-shirt and bare feet, I searched the apartment for Hollis. The kitchen was empty, and he wasn't in the living room.

I peeked into his bedroom and saw he was just emerging from the bathroom. He'd changed into a fitted, white T-shirt and sleep pants. His feet were bare.

He spotted me in the doorway.

Wiping the moisture out of his hair with a towel, he said, "Come here, you."

Hollis took me into his arms, and I became completely lost in him. Straight out of the shower with a fresh coating of aftershave, he smelled so damn good. That was to be expected. What wasn't to be expected was the rampant beat of his heart.

I still wasn't sure what Hollis was doing with me, what his intentions were. But his heartbeat may have been my first real clue that this wasn't a game to him anymore.

"How come you showered? I feel dirty now."

"I had to...relieve some tension. But to be honest, I don't feel like it did much."

Hollis definitely still seemed tense. We both clearly wanted the same thing on a physical level, but we couldn't go there tonight.

That left us not really knowing what to do with each other.

"I love you in my shirt," he said.

I rubbed my arms. "Thank you for letting me borrow it. It's so soft."

He stepped back. "That reminds me. I bought you something."

My brow lifted. "Yeah?"

He reached under his bed and took out a pink bag. I recognized that it was from La Vivienne, a pricey lingerie store. He looked uncharacteristically shy as he watched me open it.

Inside were silk thongs in a rainbow of colors.

"Hollis, these are so...expensive."

"The woman at the store swore they were the softest."

"Yeah, but you must've paid three hundred dollars for undies you're just gonna end up wrecking."

"It'll be worth it." He winked.

"Want me to try one of them on?"

"You don't have to."

"But do you want me to?"

"Fuck, yes," he said immediately.

I slipped out of the red lace ones I was wearing, leaving them on the floor. Hollis stared down at them.

Then I carefully ripped the tag off a pair of cream-colored panties and slipped them on.

"These feel amazing."

Hollis's pupils were dilating. I knew he wanted to see them on me, but his long T-shirt was covering my bum.

"You wanna see?"

His chest rose and fell. "Yes."

I slowly lifted the T-shirt and turned around, exposing my backside. "How do they look?"

He didn't say anything. I couldn't see his face, but I could hear his breathing become even more labored.

He cleared his throat. "Worth every penny."

"You like them?"

"Like? *Like* is not a strong enough word, Elodie."

I turned around to the sight of him with an erection. I inched closer and wrapped my arms around him, pressing my abdomen against the hot bulge in his pants.

Running my fingers through his damp, lustrous hair, I said, "You're a beautiful man."

"I'm glad you think so."

"I've always thought so."

I loved being able to touch him like this. I knew there was so much more to Hollis than his physical beauty. He was complex. I so wanted to know more about his past but was always afraid to broach that subject for fear of upsetting him.

Still, a huge part of me was terrified to take the next step without knowing the story of what had made him so guarded when it came to love. It seemed like necessary information at this point.

I took a chance and asked, "Will you tell me what happened with Anna?"

Hollis's jaw flexed. Our eyes met, and he seemed to be searching for the answer to my question.

Eventually, he nodded. "Why don't we go out to the living room? If we stay in here, I won't be able to focus on anything but your ass in that underwear."

I smiled. "Okay."

CHAPTER TWENTY-NINE

Hollis – 6 years ago

I was sweating.

The last time I was this nervous was the day I had to stand up to give my mother's eulogy in front of a packed church. I shouldn't be sweating now. I'd never been surer about anything in my life than asking Anna to marry me. We'd been together nearly ten years. We'd lived together the last five. She was the best thing that ever happened to me, and I had no doubt she would say yes.

Over the last few months, she'd given me subtle hints that she was ready. Well, as subtle as Anna Benson could be. We'd pass a jewelry store, and she'd point out a setting she liked. When Addison got married a few months ago, she'd mentioned on multiple occasions that she couldn't believe *she* was getting married instead of us. Granted, Addison married her asshole husband after only two months of dating—so not many people could believe she was getting married.

But I understood what Anna meant.

The time was finally right. My new business had taken off. Addison and I had earned the equivalent of our annual salaries at our old firms in the first three months of our partnership. Anna and I had moved to a nicer apartment, and I could finally afford to get her the ring she deserved.

I took said ring out of my pocket and looked at it one more time. *Eighteen grand.* I'd never shelled out that much money at once. Even the down payment on my new car had only been ten. But my girl was worth it. I'd have spent more if I thought she wouldn't be afraid to wear it.

The elevator doors opened, and I stepped off and walked to our apartment. I stopped in front of the door, pausing before going inside. She had no idea what was coming tonight, and I'd figured out the perfect way to ask her.

I took a deep breath in and blew out a loud exhale. *Screw it. Here goes nothing.*

I opened the door.

"Anna's home!" *Squawk!* "Anna's home!" *Squawk!* "Anna's home!"

I chuckled. Her bird was about to be the wingman in my proposal. "What's up, Huey?"

Anna was in the kitchen unloading the dishwasher. "Hey. You're home early."

I leaned in and kissed her. "I thought we could go out to dinner tonight."

"Oh, okay. I took out chicken to make, but it will keep for another night."

"I made a reservation for six." I left out that the reservation was also for *seven people*—I'd invited her father, and Addison and her new husband, as well as Anna's good friend from work. Her father knew what was going down tonight, because I'd already spoken to him to ask for his blessing. But Addison and the others had no idea. I'd made up some story about celebrating a new account I'd landed.

"Where are we going?"

"It's a surprise."

She smiled. "You have to at least tell me what to wear."

"Something sexy."

She rolled her eyes. "You'd say that if you were taking me for pizza."

I took the plate she'd removed from the dishwasher out of her hand. "Go get changed. I'll finish unloading."

"Okay. But we have to let Huey out before we go. So would you shut all the windows when you're done?"

Bingo. I'd been counting on her insisting on taking care of the bird before we left. "Sure."

Anna liked to let Huey stretch his wings and get some exercise every day. We'd developed a little routine. When I got home from work, we'd shut the living room windows and the doors to all the bedrooms, and I'd put a treat in the bird's mouth. The little shit flew around for a minute and then would land on Anna's shoulder and turn the treat over to her. He'd only eat it if *she* gave it to him. Tonight, the treat he'd deliver was going to be one hell of an expensive one.

While Anna was in the bedroom changing, I closed all the windows in the living room and shut the doors to the other bedroom and my office. Then I slipped the ring box from my inside jacket pocket and tied the diamond ring to one of Huey's treats, before stashing it back in my pants pocket.

When Anna came out, she looked gorgeous with her hair down and wearing a sexy, curve-hugging, light pink dress. Pink was her favorite color, but right now it was mine, too.

"You look beautiful."

She smiled. "Thank you. Are we ready to let Huey out? It's after five thirty already."

While I'd been nervous before I walked in, suddenly everything felt right. "I'm ready. Let's do this."

Anna walked over to the cage and let Huey out, and he did his usual routine—flying around and then coming to me for a treat. I made eye contact with him as I pulled the treat with the ring tied to it from my pocket. *Don't fuck this up, buddy.*

I held my breath while he fluttered his wings and circled the room with the treat in his beak. Anna was busy filling his water bowl and didn't notice anything unusual. When she finished, it was time for Huey to have his treat, so he made his usual landing on her shoulder.

The ring dangled from a little string.

She took the treat, still completely unaware as I knelt down on one knee.

Time seemed to move in slow motion after that.

Anna saw the ring.

Her jaw dropped open.

One hand flew up to cover her mouth.

She turned to find me.

It was time. So many years in the making.

"Anna, I've loved you since kindergarten. But my love for you grew along the way. You're still my best friend, but now you're the woman I want to spend the rest of my life with. You already have my heart. Will you do me the honor of taking this ring, too?"

CHAPTER THIRTY

Hollis

Elodie covered her mouth when I got to the part of the story where I'd gotten down on one knee. Oddly enough, it was a lot like the face Anna had made that day.

"What did she say?"

It was still difficult to talk about the shit that went down, even after almost six years.

I cleared my throat. "She started to cry. I assumed it was happy tears. Until she began to shake her head and told me she'd met someone else."

"What a fucking bitch."

Her honest reaction made me crack a smile for the first time when I thought of anything to do with that day. "Long story short, we argued. I went to the bedroom to get my wallet and stormed out of the apartment. Anna followed me, and while she was gone, Huey flew out the open window in our bedroom because I'd left the door open. He still had the treat with the ring tied to it. He cruised around outside for a while and then found his way back in. But somewhere in his travels, he dropped the treat...along with the ring tied to it."

"Jesus. That's insane." Her eyes widened. "Oh my God. You once said he cost you eighteen grand. That's what you meant?"

I nodded. "The ring probably landed on the street near the building and someone picked it up. At least it was someone's lucky day. Anna looked for it for days."

"I hope it made her feel like shit."

I chuckled. "Anyway. Damn bird cost me eighteen grand. Anna moved out a few days later, leaving him behind because her new place didn't accept pets. The vet said Huey is probably about ten, and the breed can live as long as ninety years. So I only have another eighty years of him yelling *Anna's home* to remind me of that shit every day."

"How long were you and Anna together?"

I frowned. "We were friends since we were kids. Things changed to more when we were teenagers."

"Wow. Okay. Well, thank you for sharing that. I can understand why you're not a super fan of Huey a little better now."

After that, we spent a few more hours talking. It was probably the longest time I'd ever spent talking to any woman since Anna and I split. While my past wasn't a subject I wanted to rehash, it hadn't killed me to talk about it like I'd always felt it would. And in the end, I was glad Elodie knew.

I woke with an aching hard-on.

This wasn't unusual, of course. Waking with a woody a few times a week had been a regular occurrence since the age of ten. But this wasn't your basic, run-of-the-mill morning glory. My cock was so stiff it felt like I could have hammered a nail with the damn thing. Though today's wood had less to do with a natural bodily function and more to do with the woman whose ass was pressed up against my crotch.

Elodie and I had fallen asleep on the couch together last night. The sexual mood from earlier in the evening had been sufficiently dampened after I'd told her about Anna. But neither one of us had wanted to separate and go back to our respective rooms. I woke with my body wrapped around her, one leg draped over her hip, keeping her tucked close.

I didn't have my watch on, and I had no idea where my cell phone was, but morning had started to break outside the living room windows. It had to be close to six o'clock. I attempted to untangle our bodies without waking Elodie, but one of my arms was underneath her, and she stirred when I gently lifted her to free myself.

Her eyes fluttered open.

"Sorry," I whispered. "I was trying not to wake you."

She stretched her arms over her head and flashed a goofy smile. "Well, you did a pretty shitty job of that, didn't you?"

I chuckled—a ball buster even at the crack of dawn. "I'm going to jump in the shower to get ready for work. Why don't you go to the guest room and go back to sleep? Hailey won't be up for hours, and it's probably best she thinks you slept in there."

Elodie nodded. "This couch is pretty uncomfortable, anyway. The metal frame was jabbing into my spine half the night."

I gripped her hip and pressed my front against her back. "That's no metal frame, sweetheart."

"Oh!" She giggled. "Oh my. That must be uncomfortable."

"You can say that again."

It would have been so easy to free my cock from my pants, lift the flimsy T-shirt she had on, and slide between her legs. But it wasn't the time or the place for that. Not to mention, the ball was in her court as to how fast we went with things. She needed to trust I wasn't in this just for the sex, which meant I couldn't push until she got there.

So I cleared my throat and extricated myself from behind her. Standing, I offered a hand to help her up.

Elodie was eye level with my crotch. She stared at the obvious bulge in my pants and licked her lips.

"Jesus Christ," I grumbled. "Don't do that."

She looked up at me, wide-eyed. "What?"

"Look at me like you're hungry for my cock."

Elodie blushed and bit on her lower lip. "I was thinking... My condition was no sex. But we didn't exactly define sex, did we? Maybe I could..."

I looked up at the ceiling and let out a string of muttered curses before crouching down to look into her eyes. "Your throat would be sore from how hard I want to ram my dick down it right now. Plus, unless you want Hailey walking out and finding me with two fistfuls of your hair and my ass pumping into your face like a wild animal, I think it's best I go take that shower, and you take your ass to the guest room."

Her jaw hung open.

I leaned in and whispered in her ear. "Better close that sexy mouth before I'm not such a gentleman."

I opened the door to the guest room, trying to be as quiet as possible in case she'd fallen asleep.

"Feel better?" Elodie smiled. She was lying in the middle of the bed, her blond hair splayed out across the pillow.

I had taken care of myself in the shower—the quickest jerk off session in the history of jerk off sessions—but no, I didn't actually feel better. I felt like I could explode at any minute.

"Not really."

She leaned up on her elbows. "The offer is still good if you want a little help getting some relief."

I dragged a hand through my wet hair. "You're the devil. You know that?"

She giggled. "At least you *can* relieve yourself. I need a little toy for that."

Any relief I'd gotten from finishing myself off in the shower was long gone as I pictured Elodie using a vibrator to get herself off. I felt my cock swelling in my slacks.

"Were you serious when you said not all sex was off the table?"

"I was. I'd be happy to help you take the edge off before you go to work."

Without breaking our gaze, I reached behind me and grabbed the doorknob. The clank of the lock bolting shut echoed through the room. "Slide down to the edge of the bed." My voice was thick and gruff.

Elodie pulled back the sheet covering her and shimmied down the bed. Her eyes were hooded as she waited, assuming I was accepting her offer. But the only thing that could possibly come close to satisfying my appetite was a taste of her.

"Lie back and open your legs."

Her eyes widened, but she did as I asked.

I walked to the bed, tugging at my tie to loosen it, and knelt before her. "Spread wider for me, Elodie."

I reached up and gently rubbed two fingers over the soft fabric of the panties I'd bought her.

So soft.

So fucking in the way. With a quick flick of my wrist, I tore them from her body.

Elodie gasped, and I wasted no time diving in. My face burrowed into her pussy. I couldn't control myself enough to start slow and let it build. There was no teasing, fluttering of the tip of my tongue over her sensitive skin. Instead, I licked from one end to the other, and my tongue tunneled inside of her. Her pussy tasted so sweet, and she was so fucking wet and tight. I needed more. Pushing on her knees, I stretched her legs wider. Elodie began to writhe beneath me and dug her nails into my scalp. If I'd had any concern that she might not enjoy the roughness of my actions, that was thoroughly put to bed when she yanked at my hair and pressed me farther into her.

"*Oh God.*" Her back arched off the bed.

I lifted one hand and pressed it against her flat stomach, holding her down. I completely devoured her, licking and sucking, delving my tongue deep inside of her until she began to say my name over and over.

"Hollis. *Oh. God.* Yes. *Hollis.* Like that."

She grabbed hold of my ears, and I knew she was on the brink. Her juices covered my entire face, and if I could have drowned in them, I would have died the happiest man on the fucking planet. I licked my way up to her clit and sucked hard. She moaned. So I slipped two fingers inside of her and pumped in and out. Her tight muscles clenched down, and she started to come. And come...long, hard, and *loud.* It was the first time since I was a boy that I thought I might cream my pants without any friction.

After, Elodie lay on the bed with one arm slung across her face, and the back of her hand covering her eyes. She panted. "*Holy shit.* That was..."

Feeling like a king—hell, I felt like the pride of the whole damn jungle—I smiled and rose from my knees to hover over her on the bed. "Feel better?"

She peeked one eye open. "I'm on birth control."

Not exactly what I'd expected her to say. But *fuck me.* I wanted to come inside her more than I could remember ever wanting anything.

"Well, then it's too bad actual sex isn't on the table."

"I'd like to amend my rules."

I arched a brow. For a second, it almost felt like I was the one in control here. "And what if I'm not amenable to your rule changes?"

Elodie hooked a hand around my neck and pulled me down for a kiss. I fucking loved that she didn't give a shit that I'd just eaten her out and had the taste of her on my tongue.

"If you're not amenable, I'm sure I can find someone else," she said. "Benito is probably available."

My eyes darkened. The thought of any man coming anywhere near her made me crazy. She saw my face and smiled knowingly.

"You're going to pay for that comment, smartass."

"I hope so. When?"

I dropped my head and chuckled. "You sound as desperate as I feel."

"It's been *two years*, Hollis. We need a whole night."

I couldn't agree more. Although something in the pit of my stomach told me a whole night wouldn't scratch the surface with this woman. A *whole year* might not be enough to get my fill of her.

"Let me see what I can do. Hailey asked if the girl who had the pool party could sleep over. Maybe I'll call her mother and suggest they do one night here and then one there."

Elodie squinted. "*I'll* call the mother. I didn't like the way she looked at you when you came to pick us up the day of the party. That woman wants to see you naked. DILF, remember?"

I liked that we were on the same page. Normally, a jealous woman would be a complete turn off to me, but for some reason, I loved Elodie jealous. I wanted her possessive, because I felt the same way about her.

"It doesn't matter who wants to see me naked. Because there's only one woman I have any interest in getting naked for."

"It's about time." Addison plopped down in the guest chair on the other side of my desk. Staring out the window, I hadn't even noticed her walk into my office.

"What?"

She smiled. "You're banging the nanny. It took you long enough."

My brows drew together. "What the hell are you talking about?"

Addison sighed and rolled her eyes. "You've been softening for weeks. I was in the hall when you walked in this morning. The new receptionist was texting on her cell phone. Again."

"And..."

"You smiled at her and said good morning instead of firing her."

"You're out of your mind."

Addison arched a brow. "So you didn't get laid last night."

Technically, I hadn't. I lifted a stack of papers on my desk that didn't need straightening and straightened them. Looking away, I said, "I didn't sleep with Elodie. Not that it's any of your damn business."

Addison's face changed to surprised. Her eyes widened, and she clapped her hands together. "Oh my God. You're falling for her, and you didn't even sleep with her yet."

"Don't you have any work to do? I looked at the new client roster. Your team isn't exactly pulling in big numbers this quarter. Maybe you should spend some time riding them and get off my ass."

Her answer was a giant, ear-to-ear smile. "I'm so happy for you, Hollis."

I shook my head. "Be happy somewhere else. I have actual work to do."

"It's been a long time since Anna. You deserve some good in your life."

Normally, any mention of my ex left a sour taste in my mouth. But this morning, I was too busy savoring the taste of Elodie to let anything else seep in. If I closed my eyes and breathed deep, I could still smell her on my face. I inwardly laughed at what Addison would've said if I'd suddenly done that—closed my eyes, took a deep whiff, and flaunted a satiated smile.

I looked over at my business partner. She wasn't going to get the hell out of my office unless I gave her something. So I tossed the pen in my hand on the desk and gave in a little.

"It's not going to end well."

Her brows drew down. "Why do you say that?"

"Hailey is already pretty attached to her. When things go south, she's going to suffer."

Addison's eyes roamed my face, and then she shook her head. "There's just so much wrong with that last statement that I don't even know where to begin."

"Stop psychoanalyzing everything. Not everything someone says has a deeper meaning. I have a legitimate concern when it comes to Hailey. She's a kid, and someone has to protect her. God knows her fuckwad of a father left her swinging in the wind."

"Hollis, it's not your concern about Hailey getting hurt that's odd. What did you just say to me? Think about it."

I shrugged. "I have no idea. But I'm guessing you're about to enlighten me."

"You said, *when things go south, Hailey's going to suffer.*"

"So?"

"What does *when things go south* look like to you?"

Did she really need it spelled out for her? I thought it was pretty damn clear. "Hailey's not attached to many people. When Elodie leaves, she's going to be hurt. What part of this is so hard for you to understand?"

Addison frowned. "The part that you're so certain she's leaving. Not every woman is going to abandon you. But if you go into this relationship with the ending to the story already written, everything you do will be leading you in that direction."

I knew she was staying because I hadn't left yet. That was typical Addison. Normally, it would be a business issue I was struggling with—a client asking me to do something I wasn't sure about, or something going on with an employee that didn't sit right with me. We'd air things out in the morning, generally disagree, and then hours later, on my way out for the night, I'd stop at her office and together we'd find a middle ground on how to handle things.

Only today it wasn't about business.

I took the seat across from her, on the other side of her desk, and leaned back into the chair. "So how do I change it?"

Addison slipped her glasses from her face and tossed them on top of a stack of papers. "You allow yourself to give things a real chance."

"And how the hell do I do that?"

"Well, you have to start by changing your outlook. It's not going to happen overnight. But you need to believe that happiness is a possibility for you. Start small. Think of something you're thankful for and express it in some way. It doesn't have to be grandiose. Just accept things you're thankful for and acknowledge them as positive instead of waiting for them to turn negative."

"Okay."

"Also, use positive words. Instead of saying *this is a disaster,* say *we'll work it out.* And make plans in your personal life that are more than a few days in the future—maybe a trip next month with Elodie, or even tickets to a play in the fall with Hailey. It'll show them you're thinking long term."

I sighed. "Okay. I can do that."

"It's going to take time, Hollis. Just take small steps and try not to worry about the ending. Instead, enjoy the journey."

I arched a brow. "When did you become the freaking Dalai Lama?"

Addison smiled. "Right after my second divorce, when I decided it was time for me to actually be happy."

CHAPTER
THIRTY-ONE

Elodie

I'd been anxious all day.

Anxious to see Hollis, since the last time I'd seen him he'd had his head between my legs.

Anxious about whether he'd come home with a change of heart about us.

Anxious because he hadn't texted me more than a few words all day.

So when I heard the key jingling in the lock of the front door, I jumped a little.

"Hey." I stood in the living room, feeling unusually awkward.

Hollis walked toward me, his eyes roaming my body with each step. The air began to crackle as he glanced around the living room. "Where's Hailey?"

"Shower. She just went in. We painted today, so she might be a while. Her hands got as much color as the canvas."

Hollis hooked one large arm around my waist and pulled me flush against him. His neck bent, and he brushed his lips over mine. "Good. I haven't been able to stop thinking about this mouth all day."

All the anxiousness rushed out of me in one giant sigh. I wrapped my hands around his neck. "I've been thinking about your mouth, too. Mostly how talented it is."

He arched a brow. "Is that so?"

I nodded with a goofy grin. "I'm glad we amended the rules."

"Me, too." His eyes swept over my face. "I got us tickets to an art show I thought you might like. A client of mine owns a gallery."

"Oh, wow. That's nice. When is it?"

Hollis brushed a lock of hair behind my ear. "Labor Day weekend."

Warmth spread through my chest. "Okay. Thank you. That sounds great. I have some plans for us, too."

"Yeah?"

I nodded. "I spoke to Lindsey Branson today, Megan's mother. Megan's coming over tomorrow to hang out with Hailey."

"That's good."

"And apparently the Bransons have a boat and are going to Block Island next weekend. They invited Hailey to go with them—for the *entire weekend*."

Hollis's eyes darkened. "I like your plans better than mine. Actually, I have only one problem."

"What's that?"

Hollis leaned into me. "I have to wait until next weekend to be inside you." He started to kiss my neck and gave me goose bumps.

"I could feel your mouth between my legs all day today. You're so good at that."

"And I could taste you all day." He whispered, "I need more, Elodie...in the worst fucking way."

My back was up against the counter as he slipped his tongue into my mouth. He sucked on my tongue the same way he'd worked my clit this morning. The muscles between my legs clenched. I could feel how hard he was through his trousers.

"I want you," I panted.

"I'm losing my mind," he groaned.

I could feel his erection growing as he rested his mouth on my neck. "You tasted so much better than I ever imagined. I can't wait to fuck you."

Gripping his hair, I pulled him closer and pushed my tongue into his mouth.

My eyes moved to the side.

Hailey.

Oh my God.

Oh no!

We'd gotten so carried away that we hadn't noticed Hailey standing in her towel, watching us from the hallway.

Hollis was oblivious, his face buried in my neck, when I pushed him off of me.

"Hailey..." I said, my heart beating out of my chest.

Hollis froze. Either it was the shortest shower ever, or we'd gotten lost in each other.

Hailey looked just as stunned as we were.

No one said anything. This was one of the most awkward moments of my life.

To make matters worse, Hailey wasn't amused. In fact, she seemed very uncomfortable.

"I'm...just gonna go to my room," she finally said before disappearing down the hall.

We stood stunned, watching her walk away.

When she was out of sight, Hollis buried his face in his hands. "Fuck."

I panicked a little. "Should I go talk to her?"

"We both need to talk to her."

"I can't believe this."

We waited a bit, assuming she was getting dressed. She never came out. It became clear that she was intentionally staying in her room. I was at a loss. Considering she'd always been pushing for something to happen between Hollis and me, I wouldn't have expected her to be so upset about having caught us.

"I think we'd better make the first move here," I told him.

"Okay, but before we go in there, let's talk about how to approach this."

"There's no time. I think we have to wing it. Just answer her questions honestly," I said.

Hollis nodded and followed me down the hall to Hailey's room.

A lump formed in my throat as I knocked. "Hey, can we come in?"

After a few seconds, she said, "Yeah."

I'd never seen Hollis look so uncomfortable. His body was stiff as a board as he sat down on the edge of her bed.

I took a seat on the pink shag carpet and crossed my legs. "Are you upset?"

She wouldn't look at us. "I'm not upset. It was just weird to see you like that—not because I don't like you guys together. But because...you didn't tell me."

I blew out a relieved breath. So this was about her being kept in the dark?

"It feels like you're hiding it from me or something," she said.

Hollis shut his eyes. "I'm sorry, Hailey. This is my fault. I handled it all wrong."

"We both did," I was quick to add.

Hollis took the lead. "We didn't want to say anything to you, because we don't want you to be hurt if it doesn't work out between us. It's all very...new."

"It doesn't *look* new."

She had a point. Hollis had practically been mauling me. We looked very comfortable with each other.

Hollis's face turned uncharacteristically red as he said, "Elodie and I really...enjoy each other's company."

"You think?" she taunted.

Now I felt flushed. "But our priority is you."

She turned to me. "I like you guys together. I just don't want you to hide things from me."

Nodding, I said, "I get it."

"But what if it doesn't work out?" she asked.

"What happens between Elodie and me has nothing to do with your relationship with Elodie. Or my relationship with you, for that matter."

She crossed her arms. "So, if something happens, Elodie is still going to come here every day?"

He blew out a breath. "I can't speak for Elodie, but I would never keep you from someone you cared about."

"But you won't even *talk* about Anna when I ask you. I didn't know who she was. Dad had to tell me. I was curious because of Huey saying her name. If you won't talk about Anna, how do I know the same thing won't happen with Elodie?"

Seemingly at a loss for words, he shut his eyes.

When he didn't respond, I spoke up. "Life is about risks, Hailey. No one can say exactly what's going to happen with anything. All we can do is try as best we can not to hurt each other. We don't *want* to hurt each other...or you."

"Were you gonna tell me?"

"Of course," I said.

"I've always wanted you guys together, but it was weird to find out that way."

"And that was my fault," Hollis said. "No more secrets, okay?"

Hailey looked to me, then to Hollis. "Okay."

"I'll see you in ten minutes for dinner, kiddo," Hollis said as he got up and exited the room.

I gave her a hug on my way out. "I'll see you tomorrow."

Hollis and I walked together to the door.

He spoke low. "What a clusterfuck."

"She's way more perceptive about you than I ever imagined."

"The connection she made about Anna..." he said. "It caught me off guard. But she's right. If I couldn't talk about that situation, what's to make her believe I could handle seeing you every day if things went south between us? We need to make sure we're not kidding ourselves here, Elodie."

This situation was the perfect excuse for Hollis to doubt us again.

My guard went straight up. "And how exactly do we not kid ourselves, Hollis?"

"I'm not sure. Maybe we need to slow down a bit."

Are we seriously back at this place?

279

"Is this about Hailey or about you? I honestly don't know."

His jaw ticked, but he didn't respond.

I lowered my voice. "You want to fuck me. You've made that very clear. But I think you're still not sure if you're ready for more. *Wanting* to be ready and actually being ready are two different things. You're always looking for an excuse to back away." I turned toward the door. "I have to go."

I opened it and addressed him one last time. "This is never going to be risk-free, Hollis. There's always going to be a chance I could hurt you or you could hurt me. We have to decide if being with each other is worth the risk."

He said nothing as I walked away.

I headed straight to Bree's house when I got back to Connecticut. I hoped she was in the mood to talk.

She looked even more gaunt than the last time I'd seen her.

"Have you eaten today?"

She straightened in her chair. "Yeah. Mariah brought me some taco pie. I had a little."

"How long ago was that?"

"This afternoon."

"Can I make you something?"

"No." She coughed, covering her mouth with her hand. "Tell me what happened tonight. You seem upset."

"Hailey caught Hollis and me making out in the kitchen."

"Shit. Okay."

"We had to have a talk with her and explain everything. She was a little weirded out, and that surprised me."

Bree sighed. "Well, as she gets more attached to you, I suppose the fear of losing you is more pronounced."

"Did I tell you I finally got Hollis to open up to me a little about his past relationship?"

Bree shook her head no and downed her water.

"This girl—her name was Anna. She was his long-time girlfriend. Anyway, she broke his heart, out of left field. He hadn't seen it coming. He's been reluctant to get involved with anyone since. She's the reason his bird, Huey, says nothing but 'Anna's home.'"

She wiped her mouth with her sleeve. "Wow."

"Anyway, Hailey alluded to the Anna thing. She's more aware than we thought that her uncle has trust issues, and I think she's just as scared as I am that things won't work out."

"She sounds like a smart girl."

"Well, now that she knows, it's a wake-up call that I really do stand to get hurt here. We've gotten caught up in our sexual attraction, but if he has trust issues—and let's face it, so do I—is it smart for me to sleep with him and get even more attached? Not to mention, he immediately started acting weird again toward me after she found out."

Bree fell into another coughing fit.

"Let me get you some more water."

I ran to the fridge and filled her glass before handing it to her.

She drank some, and then looked up at me.

"Listen, Elodie. I want you to hear me out, okay?"

I sat down on the ottoman across from her. "Alright..."

"I would give anything to have the dilemma you're experiencing. You're asking yourself if you should take a chance on the possibility of love. I don't have the opportunity to take such a chance. I'm not saying this to make you feel sorry for me, just to give you a different perspective—your problem is a good one to have. There's only so much thinking you can do about something before you've totally wasted your life away. Just do what feels good and stop overthinking everything, for the love of God."

I'm such an idiot. All I do is come here and complain to Bree about problems that are solvable. Meanwhile, she's suffering from an incurable disease.

Idiot.

Idiot.

Idiot.

"I promise to try to heed your advice. Thank you as always for listening." I knelt next to her. "Please tell me what I can do for you, Bree."

"Actually, there is something..."

"Anything."

"I was wondering if you'll be around this weekend."

This weekend.

I was supposed to spend it with Hollis. In any case, my friend came first.

"Of course I can be around. What's up?"

"Well, I'm not sure how things are going to go for me in the next few months. I've been talking to my father about going to the lake house in Salisbury. I'd really like the whole family to be there. Unfortunately, that means Tobias." She laughed a little. "Do you think you'd be able to come up with us?"

"Of course. Absolutely."

"Great. We can all drive up together in my Expedition. Lord knows it needs to be driven before it disintegrates into the ground from lack of use."

I tried to lift her spirits. "We'll have the best time. We can hit a couple of the antique stores while we're there."

"Basically, we'll just avoid Tobias together." She laughed.

I smiled, even though I felt like I was crying inside. "Exactly."

CHAPTER
THIRTY-TWO

Hollis

I scrunched up my tenth piece of paper in as many minutes and tossed it into the trash. My focus today was nonexistent.

As usual, Addison was onto me.

She marched into my office holding two coffees and placed one on the desk. "What did you do, Hollis?"

"Why do you always seem to think you know what's going on with me?"

"Because I know you better than you know yourself. Now, spill. What did you do to fuck things up with Elodie now?"

I crumpled one more piece of paper and aimed for the trashcan. "Hailey caught us kissing. We were forced to tell her we're dating much sooner than we were ready for."

She nodded. "Okay, but might that be a good thing? It saves you from having to hide it from her."

"No. It was too soon. The verdict is still out on us.

How can we explain it properly to her when we don't even know what's happening ourselves?"

"How did Hailey take it?"

"Not well. Now she's worried I'm going to fuck it up and she's going to lose Elodie."

"So don't fuck it up."

"Gee, thanks. You're brilliant."

"It really *is* that simple, Hollis."

I thought ahead to this weekend and wondered if our plans were even still on. "We were supposed to have the whole weekend to ourselves...take the next step."

She smirked. "Shag like monkeys?"

"I was trying to be more tactful."

"So, what? Now you're not sure?"

"She's not the type of woman you mess around with. I can't have it both ways. And I need to decide which way I'm going before I take it any further."

Addison walked around toward me and started rummaging through my drawers.

"What are you doing?"

"Taking out a legal pad. We're going to nip this in the bud right now." She grabbed a pen and drew a line down the middle of the yellow, lined paper. "Pros and cons of going all-in with Elodie. There's one rule, though. The cons cannot be reflections of yourself or 'what-if' questions. We're only listing Elodie's traits. So, something like 'afraid to get hurt' can't be a con or 'afraid to hurt Elodie', 'afraid to hurt Hailey.' Those are all reflections of your self-doubt and don't really exist other than in your head."

She clicked the pen. "I'll start. She's obviously gorgeous." She jotted it down. "Great for Hailey." She paused to think. "Makes you smile like a giddy fool when you don't even realize it—technically not a trait, but I do think it's relevant."

After writing it all down, she looked at me. "Cons?"

The most ridiculous shit that held no significance came to mind.

Wears abrasive underwear.

Can't park for shit.

Nothing I could think of had any relevance or changed the fact that Elodie was fucking perfect for me.

I wracked my brain, trying to come up with at least one legitimate con. But there were none. Every single negative thing I could think of was exactly what Addison had described: a reflection of my own fear.

"I have another pro," I said.

"Oh?"

"No one else can have her if we're together."

"Well, technically that one is a reflection of your insecurities and not a trait, but I'll let it slide and add it." She chuckled. "So that's it? No cons?"

I tapped my pen, then threw it across the desk in frustration. "No cons."

Addison was enjoying this way too much.

"Stop laughing, Addison." I opened the coffee she'd brought me.

"Congratulations, Hollis. I just saved you months of useless rumination that would have led you to the same conclusion. You want to be with her, she makes you happy, and honestly, that's enough."

She looked me straight in the eyes and her expression turned serious. "It really *is* enough, my friend."

That evening, I was determined to make things right with Elodie.

When I walked into the apartment, I noticed she looked sad as she wiped down the kitchen counter.

I threw my keys on the table. "Hey."

She looked up. "Hi."

"Can we talk?" I asked.

"Actually, I have to talk to *you*."

Feeling a bit anxious, I said, "Alright..."

She put the washcloth aside. "After yesterday, I don't even know if we were still on for this weekend, but I won't be able to see you, in any case."

Shit.

"Why not?"

"My friend Bree is not doing well. She requested that her family get together for a weekend away at their summer home up north. Since I'm like family to her, I need to go too."

"Wow. Okay. Of course, you need to be there."

The timing obviously sucked. After a lot of self-reflection this afternoon, I felt like I'd finally gotten my shit together. But she was in no mood for my shit. She had far more important things to attend to, and whatever was going on with us needed to take a back seat.

I placed my hands on her shoulders. "Are you okay?"

"It wasn't until she requested this trip that I realized just how serious it was. I know that sounds stupid because I'm with her all the time. But I guess I haven't wanted to believe it. She thinks she isn't going to make it even a few more months, and this trip proves it. It's hard to accept. I've been in denial."

"Believe me, I understand. When my mother was sick, I'm pretty sure denial got me through."

She smiled. "Yeah. I know you understand."

"I'll be here all weekend if you need to talk while you're there."

"Thank you."

"Where's Hailey?"

"She's in her room doing her summer reading."

I leaned in and placed a gentle kiss on her lips.

She sighed. "I'm just hoping I don't kill my ex-husband during the trip."

My body went rigid. I'd completely forgotten her friend was also the stepsister of Elodie's ex-husband. A family vacation meant he would be there, too.

Great. Elodie would be feeling needy and vulnerable and surely doubting my feelings for her based on my behavior this week. And he'd be right there to pick up the pieces, possibly manipulating her. I didn't trust that he wouldn't try to get her back. It was a vibe I'd gotten from him that day he'd showed up at her place while I was there. That guy was trouble.

I wanted to open up to her right then and there, tell her I was sorry, that I was ready to take the next step. But despite my jealousy, this was not the time for that. She was upset about her friend. I'd have to let her go and pray I could make things right when she came back.

CHAPTER
THIRTY-THREE

Elodie

The lake house was even more peaceful than I remembered.

The two-hour drive up north had turned into almost three and a half due to rush-hour traffic and a backup from an accident. So it was late by the time we arrived, and Bree was ready for bed the minute we walked in. She always seemed so exhausted lately.

The two of us were sharing a room, so after I helped her set up her oxygen machines and made the beds with fresh linens, we talked until she could barely keep her eyes open.

Bree's dad and stepmom were in the bedroom across from us, and they'd turned in for the night about an hour ago. Tobias's bedroom was at the other end of the house, and he seemed to have disappeared, too, which I was immensely grateful for.

But I couldn't fall asleep. So I walked down the back stairs to go sit on the dock and get some fresh air by the lake.

My mind felt so jumbled. Between watching how weak Bree had become, being back up at the lake for the first time since Tobias and I had split, and the unsettled state of my relationship with Hollis—I just couldn't relax.

The lake was serene in the dark, as flat and reflective as a mirror, with only the soft ripple of the water lapping against the rocks along the edge. Sounds of what I thought might be a giant frog croaking in the distance alternated with an owl above the bristle of the trees. They almost seemed to be having a conversation.

I sat in a wooden Adirondack chair on the edge of the dock, took a few deep breaths, and shut my eyes.

Fresh air in, unhappy thoughts out.

Fresh air in, negative energy out.

Fresh air in, shoulders relaxed while exhaling.

After a few minutes, my mind started to clear a little. I felt the tension in my neck ease, and my hands, which I hadn't noticed were balled into tight fists, bloomed open. Everything seemed easier to deal with.

Until I heard the sound of footsteps walking down the stairs.

"There you are."

My eyes flashed open at my ex-husband's voice. Whatever tension had started to wane immediately came back.

"Is everything okay with Bree?"

"She's fine. I went to your room to look for you, and she's sound asleep. I was wondering where you'd snuck off to. Then I remembered how much you loved it out on the dock. Remember the night we brought a blanket out and—"

I cut him off. No way was I taking a walk down memory lane right now. "Did you want something, Tobias?"

He stepped closer, crouched down, and put his hand on my arm. "I was hoping we could talk."

I pulled my arm back. "About what?"

"I don't know." He shook his head. "Anything. The weather. Work. Politics. Whatever you want."

"My ability to make small talk with you ended the afternoon I found your dick inside your student."

It was dark, but the moon lit the lake enough that I could see Tobias flinch. *Good.*

He sighed. "There's not a day that goes by that I don't regret what I did."

"You know how you avoid having those regrets?"

"How?"

"You don't shit on the people who care about you." I stood and started to walk toward the stairs. I'd made it up two steps when I decided I *did* have something to talk about with my ex-husband. Turning around, I marched back to where he stood and folded my arms across my chest.

Something had been eating at me for a long time. "Why?" I said.

His brows furrowed. "Why what?"

"Why did you cheat on me? I was a good wife. I kept a nice home and cooked you meals. We never really argued. I thought we had a good sex life, even. You seemed to get off, and I can't remember a single time I turned you down when you were in the mood. I even dressed up and answered the door in those cheap naughty nurse outfits you liked so much."

"My therapist thinks I'm a sex addict."

I scoffed. "Sex addict? Therapist?"

"Yes, it's a compulsive disorder, no different than someone who washes their hands all the time or checks if they've locked the door. It's a disease."

"Really? Okay, well, people who need to wash their hands all the time or check if the door is locked—do they go to someone *else's* house to wash their hands or check if the neighbor's door is locked? Because I might believe there's a disorder that makes you obsessive about sex— but that doesn't explain why you couldn't just bang your willing wife more."

Tobias frowned. "You're simplifying something that's more complicated than that."

"Actually, I think you're making something pretty simple more complicated than it is. You cheated because you're an asshole. And even after two years, you still can't own that. You know why? Because *you're an asshole*. Maybe you have obsessive-compulsive asshole disease. Why don't you ask your therapist to treat you for that? I hear an enema might help."

"You're lashing out because you still care." He took a step toward me, and I put both my hands up and took a step back.

"Don't," I warned.

"You should come to my therapist with me. I think it would be good for us."

"No, Tobias. First of all, there is no *us*. Second, you don't need a therapist to treat you for some bullshit disease. You simply need to man up and grow some morals. And third, I'm not lashing out because I care. I'm lashing out because I hate cheaters. You've robbed me of happiness these last two years, and some stupid bitch has the man I care about too nervous to try a relationship because she cheated on him. Cheaters are basically the bane of my existence."

My ex-husband had the audacity to sound perturbed. "What man you care about?"

I huffed and turned back to the stairs. "Go to bed, Tobias."

The next morning during breakfast, Bree asked if we could all go sit on the back porch when we were done eating. Mariah, Bree's stepmom, and I cleaned up the kitchen while Richard, Bree's dad, and Tobias headed outside. We told Bree we'd join them as soon as we were done.

Not ready for the conversation we were about to have, I spent a solid minute drying a single plate. "Maybe we should take all the dishes out of the cabinets and wash them. The house wasn't used over the winter, and they're probably pretty dusty."

Mariah finished rinsing the last plate in the sink and shook the water off before placing it on the drying rack. She turned to face me, leaning her hip against the basin.

"I know this is hard. But think of how much harder it is for her. We have to try to keep it together through everything she wants to say today."

I shook my head. "I don't think I can."

She smiled warmly. "You can. Though I've only been part of this family a few years, I can say without a doubt that you're one of the strongest women I know. A storm makes a tree grow its roots deeper so it can keep standing. That's what you'll do, what we'll all do. We dig in and hold tight as a family. All together."

A lump formed in my throat. Leaning on people hadn't exactly worked out for me in the past—my own family, Tobias... Every time I'd grown the courage to trust someone and allow them to bear a little of the weight, they'd crumbled when I leaned.

But I'd do whatever it took to help my friend. I just needed to stand strong on my own and be there for her. Breaking down today would only make it harder.

"Thanks, Mariah. I guess we shouldn't keep her waiting anymore."

Mariah and I went out to the back porch and joined everyone else. Once we were settled, Bree took a folded paper from her back pocket and began to open it. She cleared her throat. "I thought it was time we discussed my final wishes."

I knew why she'd asked us all here for the weekend— her reasons were obvious—but hearing her say the words *final wishes* made it so much more real. Tears welled in my eyes. There was no way I'd get through today dry.

Bree looked at each one of us before she began. I was in awe of how strong she could be.

"Last week when I went to my doctor, I signed a DNR form." She raised her long-sleeve shirt to reveal a bracelet I hadn't noticed on her wrist. "I'm sure you all know what that means, but I wanted to make sure you knew that *I also know* what it means. This bracelet tells any emergency responder or physician that I do not want to have prolonged life-saving treatments performed on me. I'm choosing not to be resuscitated in instances where my heart stops, or where I might need long-term intubation."

Tears streamed down my face, and Mariah reached over and handed me a tissue.

Bree looked at me sadly. She actually felt bad for *us*. Talk about being selfless.

"I'm so sorry I need to do this, and that it's causing you pain. But I believe it'll be better in the long run if everything is clear. It would be far worse for you all to be unsure of my wishes and have to make decisions on my behalf you aren't certain about. I also don't want you to think I might've signed documents like the DNR in haste. I want to make sure you know I've thought long and hard about my decisions."

Of course, this made perfect sense. It was the responsible thing to do. Though that didn't make it any easier. I felt so distraught, so utterly gutted, that when Tobias reached over and took my hand, I didn't have the wherewithal to pull it away. Instead, I clutched it right back.

"Dad is my executor. My estate is fairly simple and straightforward. All of my remaining savings will go the Lymphangioleiomyomatosis Research Foundation. I have a safety deposit box, which has a few things in it I'd like each of you to have, and he'll make sure to distribute those."

For the next twenty minutes, my best friend went on to talk about pain management, donating her organs, her funeral plans, and a half a dozen other things that I heard, but didn't really process. She talked so long that she had to take multiple breaks to catch her breath. By the time she finished, she'd worn herself out so much that she needed to lie down and rest.

I went with her to the bedroom to make sure she was okay.

Bree sat on the edge of the bed and patted the spot next to her. "We're never going to have these depressing discussions after today. But things needed to be said."

"I understand. And I'm amazed at how brave you are, holding it all together while you do this. You're incredible, Bree."

She took my hand in hers. "I need you to do something for me. I didn't want to discuss it in front of Tobias."

"Of course, anything."

She smiled. "I was counting on you saying that."

"What do you need?"

"I need you to promise me you'll fight for true love."

"I don't understand."

"I worry about things—like my dad not going to church after I'm gone, because he blames God. So I made him promise he'd go to services every Sunday for a year after I'm not around anymore. I figured if he could get through that first year, his faith would help him find his way the rest of the time. And I worry you've given up on love because so many people have disappointed you in your life."

I sighed. "I want to give you anything that will make you happy. But I'm not sure how to promise I'll fight for something that may not exist, Bree."

She frowned. "Do you trust me?"

"Of course, I do."

"I mean, *really* trust me. Blindly. Enough that you can believe something I say to be true, even if it doesn't make any sense to you?"

I thought about it. "I think so."

She looked me in the eyes. "Good. Real love is out there, because I've experienced it. I don't talk about my ex a lot because our breakup was difficult for me. But I've been loved by a man and loved him back in a way that was pure and true. So I can tell you, without any hesitation whatsoever, that real love exists."

"I believe you experienced that. But how can you be certain there's someone out there like that for everyone?"

She looked down at her hands for a minute before looking back up at me. "Faith. I have faith."

I wanted to believe what she said, if for no other reason than to put her mind at ease. But I also didn't want to lie to her. So I offered what I could. "I promise you I'll try. I promise I'll fight for love if I experience it—that I won't run the other way if things get tough. Can that be enough?"

Bree smiled. "That's all I can ask for. You're so stubborn. I know if you commit to me that you'll fight for something, you'll get it. All I needed was that commitment. So it does put my mind at ease."

I smiled. "Okay, crazy lady. Whatever makes you happy."

Bree squeezed my hand. "I'm going to lie down. I expect you to go on out to the living room and get your ass good and drunk while I take my nap. Maybe tell off my asinine stepbrother as a way to vent some of your anger. I think you deserve it."

She really was amazing. I started to get up and then sat back down and pulled her close for a long, tight hug.

"I love you, Bree."

"I love you, too, Elodie."

CHAPTER THIRTY-FOUR

Elodie

'd never been more drained than when I got home Sunday evening. The weekend at the lake house had sucked out all my energy, even though we did nothing but sit around for two days.

What I needed was a nice, long, hot soak. I filled the bathtub and tossed in my favorite Lush bath bomb, called Sex. It was supposed to have some sort of powerful ylang ylang aphrodisiac, but I just liked the jasmine smell and how the soymilk in it left my skin feeling soft.

I undressed and lifted one foot into the warm water, but as I attempted to shift my weight and fully get in, my doorbell rang.

Jesus. You've got to be kidding me.

I wasn't expecting anyone, so I figured it was probably someone trying to sell me something I didn't want, or worse, someone trying to preach to me about their damn religion. I hesitated with one foot in the water and considered ignoring it, but then I worried it might be Bree and grabbed my bathrobe off the hook on the back of the bathroom door.

I pushed up onto my tippy toes to peek through the peephole and was surprised to find Hollis standing on my welcome mat. I hadn't heard from him all weekend, and it looked like he was alone, though he should've had Hailey with him.

I cinched the belt on my robe and opened the door. "Hollis? What are you doing here?"

His eyes raked down my body and took in my exposed legs. My robe was pretty short.

He cleared his throat. "Hey. Can I come in?"

I looked over his shoulder to check inside the car. "Is Hailey with you?"

He shook his head. "She called this morning and said the Bransons wanted to stay another night. So she won't be home until tomorrow."

"Oh." I stepped aside. "Sure. Come in. I was just about to get in the bath. Let me turn the water off."

Hollis nodded.

Inside the bathroom, I twisted the faucet off and lifted the lever on the drain release. I took a look at my reflection in the full-length mirror and deliberated changing from the skimpy silk robe I had on into something more appropriate.

But then I decided against it. Hollis might be here to let me down gently. The least I could do after being jerked around for so long was make him eat his heart out a little. I didn't even bother to put on panties.

He was staring out the window when I returned to the living room. He seemed lost in thought.

"So, what's going on? Did you come from the city? You must've hit a lot of traffic at this time?"

He turned to face me. "I drove out this morning, actually."

My brows drew together. "Did you have a meeting or something?"

He shoved his hands into his pockets and looked down as he shook his head. "I wasn't sure what time you'd be home. I drove out right after Hailey called this morning."

"You were parked outside when I pulled up?"

"No. I went into town to grab something to eat. You must've come home while I was gone."

"But it's almost six o'clock. You sat outside all day?"

He nodded.

"Why didn't you call?"

"I didn't want to interrupt your time with your friend. I didn't know when you'd be leaving."

It was a little crazy to drive all this way to park in front of my house and wait, but his reason for not calling was also thoughtful and sweet. Hollis had so many rough edges, yet every once in a while he showed a soft side. And that soft—however rare—eclipsed all of the hard.

I sat down on the couch. "Thank you. But you could have called or texted."

Hollis took a seat on the couch, a few feet away from me. "How was your weekend? How is your friend?"

I sighed. "She wanted to talk about her final wishes and arrangements and stuff."

He nodded. "That must've been tough."

"It was. And she did it for us. She wanted to make sure we knew what she wanted, not for her sake, but so it relieved us of any difficult decisions we might have to make. In fact, the entire weekend was really to make sure we were going to be okay after..." I trailed off, unable to bring myself to say the words.

Hollis scooted closer on the couch and took my hand. "I'm sorry."

I swallowed and nodded. "Anyway, I don't think I can handle rehashing the weekend, so I'd prefer to change the subject. Why don't we talk about what you came here for? What's going on?"

He moved in closer. "I came here for you."

Maybe it was a self-protective mechanism, but instinctively, I moved back. "For me?"

"If you were anywhere else but with your friend who needed you this weekend, I would have driven to you—never mind driven, fucking *walked* if I had to."

He ran his hands through his hair, making a beautiful, tousled mess. He seemed uncharacteristically nervous. "I've counted every minute you've been gone. Holding this in has been difficult."

My heart rate sped up. "Holding what in?"

"I wanted to say this before you told me about going to the lake with Bree. You'll remember I came home from work that night wanting to talk. But then you told me you were going away, and I realized that given the situation, this needed to wait. You had to focus on her. But I can't wait anymore, which is why I came up here."

I crossed my arms. "What is it?"

"I'm done fucking things up, Elodie." Hollis looked up at the ceiling and paused, as if to gather his thoughts. "I spent this whole week trying to find one legitimate reason, other than my own fear, as to why I can't go all-in with you, and I couldn't."

Despite his candor, my guard was all the way up tonight. Maybe it was the emotional toll of the weekend. Seeing Tobias was a reminder of my own poor judgment in the past and how easy it was to be hurt by someone you thought you knew.

But more importantly, my sense that life was short was stronger than ever now. I had no tolerance for games or bullshit anymore.

"So, you're looking for reasons *not* to be with me?"

He shook his head. "I didn't mean it like that. I'm not *hoping* for a reason not to be with you. I was trying to...I guess...somehow ensure I don't end up getting hurt. But I finally had an epiphany. I realized I can *never* guarantee that. I can never guarantee we won't hurt each other. It's not something you can rule out a hundred percent, because nothing is guaranteed in life. In the end, it comes down to whether I need you more than I care about the possibility of getting hurt. And that answer is *yes*. I need you. So fucking badly."

My heart began to crack open a little, despite my best efforts to keep it closed. He was telling me everything I wanted to hear, but I wasn't going to fully open my heart to him until I was one hundred percent convinced he meant what he was saying.

My experience with Hollis thus far had trained me to tread very carefully.

"How do I know you're not going to backtrack again? Seriously, Hollis, I can't take it even one more time."

I thought back to my conversation at the lake with Bree. "I made Bree a promise this weekend. All she asked of me is that I fight for true love. Can you believe that? I would have given her anything she wanted. But out of all of the things she could have wished for, my finding true love, true happiness, matters to her most. And she understands that the biggest impediment to finding it...is myself."

Hollis nodded. "She sounds amazing, and wise."

"She is." I sighed. "Anyway, I promised her I would try, that I would fight for love if I ever experienced it, that I wouldn't run the other way if things got tough."

It hit me in that moment that what I needed from Hollis was exactly what Bree wanted from me. "I need you to make me that same promise—that you won't run if things get difficult, that you will fight for us. If you can't do that, I can't be with you. I can't handle the back and forth. You're not the only one with abandonment issues. I feel like I'm always holding my breath for the other shoe to drop. And the fucked-up thing is, that feeling gets stronger when things are going well between us. Thus far you've proven my fears are warranted. I just... want to be able to exhale."

He looked truly pained. "I'm sorry I've let my issues ruin the best thing that's happened to me in a very long time. I understand why you're not able to trust what I'm saying right now. My word means nothing. I get that. It's actions that count."

He pointed to his chest. "But if you could see inside of me right now, you would know there is no doubt left, no more hesitation. I'm ready to do this, Elodie. But proving that is going to have to happen day by day. And I'm up for the challenge. In fact, it starts now."

"What exactly are you starting?"

He looked at me with an intensity I'd never witnessed in him before. "Being the man you deserve."

CHAPTER THIRTY-FIVE

Hollis

I wasn't leaving her tonight unless she insisted I go.

"Why don't you go have that bath you were trying to take before I got here?"

"Are you leaving?"

"No. Not going anywhere. I'll be right here when you get out."

She pondered a moment. "Okay. I'll try not to take too long. Help yourself to anything in the fridge."

After Elodie disappeared into the bathroom, I noticed she had a pile of dirty dishes in the sink. Rolling up my sleeves, I turned on the water and began washing. When I'd finished, I grabbed a broom and swept. After that, I grabbed her Swiffer and mopped the floor. When that was done, I wiped down the counters. I took all my nervous energy out on the kitchen.

Not to mention, it was about damn time I'd helped her with something. This woman spent every day taking care of Hailey—and me. I wanted to take care of *her* tonight, show her just how much I cared about her. And not just tonight, but *every* night.

It must have been at least forty-five minutes before Elodie emerged from the bathroom. She wore a long T-shirt under her robe, and her legs were bare. Her damp hair cascaded down her shoulders.

She looked around at the sparkling kitchen. "You cleaned?"

I threw the towel I was holding over my shoulder. "Yeah."

Her skin reddened. She actually seemed a bit embarrassed.

"I'm not normally such a slob. I got home from the city too late before we had to leave for the lake. That's the only reason the dishes were—"

"Whoa. Hang on, I wasn't thinking that at all. I was just trying to help. In fact, the whole time you were in there, all I've been able to think about is that it's about damn time I did something for *you* for a change."

"Well, thank you."

She smelled so damn good, like coconut and vanilla. It must have been her shampoo.

I placed my hand on her cheek. "Tell me what you're thinking."

"I feel better. That bath definitely helped me decompress. I did a lot of thinking in there, too."

"About?"

"About this past weekend and about you."

There was something I had to know. "Did your ex try anything on you up there?"

She blew out a breath. "He tried to reel me back in a bit, take advantage of my vulnerability. But it didn't work. He told me the only reason he cheated on me was because he's a sex addict. Can you believe that? I'm not buying his crock of shit, but it did get me thinking about you."

My stomach sank. "Please don't tell me you think I would ever do that to you."

"No, actually. You've been with a lot of women, but you're not a cheater, and you were always open about your intentions. I truly believe you're a different kind of person than he is. You're a better person—more afraid to be hurt than capable of hurting someone else. You're more worthy of a second chance than he could ever be." She sighed. "I can't say no to you, Hollis. Because your reasons for being cautious are actually honorable." She paused. "We need to try—for real this time."

I responded by taking her hand and placing it on my heart. "Feel that. I've been worried you'd already written me off for being an asshole. I promise you won't be sorry."

My happiness was quickly curtailed when she said, "I don't think you should spend the night, though."

I couldn't say it didn't disappoint me. But I had to respect her wishes.

"Okay, baby. That's alright."

"I think I'm just going to go to sleep, if you don't mind."

"It's only seven thirty. You're ready to turn in already?"

"Yeah. It's been a really long weekend. But will you tuck me into bed?"

Well, that sounded painful—tucking her into bed before taking to the road for my long, *hard* journey back to the city. At the very least, I wanted to lie next to her, breathe in some of that delicious scent as I fell asleep.

But it didn't look like that would be happening. I had to respect her decision and not push.

"Yeah, of course," I said.

I followed Elodie into her bedroom. It had a calming atmosphere with soft lighting and a feminine aura. Basically, it was heaven, and I didn't want to leave.

I thought I'd known what torture was before—when she told me I would have to go home tonight. But apparently I knew nothing about torture.

She took off her robe, followed by her shirt, letting her creamy breasts spring free. I took in her perfect, light pink nipples, shocked. I hadn't expected her to undress in front of me. But then again, maybe it shouldn't have been surprising.

Because this was my bold Elodie we were talking about, the same woman who'd taunted me for days with her panties. She was most definitely an expert in cock teasing. And that was exactly what she was doing to me right now.

Speaking of panties, she slipped out of them. It was official. She was trying to kill me. She then slipped under the covers before I could examine every inch of her like I wanted to.

I swallowed. "You always sleep naked?"

"Yes."

My heart was palpitating. "I see."

She held the sheet over her breasts. "Thank you for understanding that I need to be alone tonight. Come here and tuck me in?"

I walked over to her slowly. Kissing her on the lips would only make things worse; I wouldn't want to stop. So I opted for a gentle kiss on her forehead.

But before I could blink, she'd grabbed my face and planted a real kiss on me, a deep, sensuous one with her tongue down my throat. Tasting her and knowing she was naked under that sheet drove me mad.

My dick practically weighed me down as I ripped myself away and forced my feet toward the door. The strain of my cock against my jeans was embarrassingly obvious. I wondered if I'd have to park at a rest stop and jerk off on the way home.

The only thing more difficult than leaving at this point would be staying.

"Well, goodnight," I said. "I'll see you tomorrow."

Just as I was about to turn around and go, she hopped up. "Oh my God, Hollis. Come here. I'm just messing with you."

Huh? "What?"

"I don't want you to go home. I want you with me. I was egging you on. I have no intention of letting you walk out of here tonight."

This was a game?

Well, shit. I'd never been more grateful for a *game* in my entire life. I couldn't even be mad at her.

It felt like I expelled all the breath in my body when I said, "Thank fuck."

"I was teasing you. I thought you liked it when I did that." She winked.

"You're gonna pay for that," I warned.

She tossed the sheet aside, exposing her fully naked

body. "By all means, make me pay, Hollsy." She flashed a mischievous grin.

Her beautiful blond hair splayed across her chest, barely covering her nipples. Her taut stomach. Her bare pussy.

Her bare pussy.

Fuck. Yes.

She must have waxed the landing strip she'd had before. God, she was so perfect.

I ripped my shirt off and walked to the bed. Kneeling on the mattress, I watched as Elodie reached for my belt and undid it. She gazed down at my crotch like she wanted to devour me. I undid my pants and tossed them aside, leaving only my dark gray boxer briefs between us.

"You're so hard," she said as she pulled me on top of her, her bare skin now pressed against me. "I couldn't let you go home like that. Not after you waited all day for me. I had to stop myself from masturbating in the bathtub just thinking about you on the other side of that door."

Note to self: watch her take a bath in the near future.

"I feel like I've had this erection for months, Elodie. You have no idea how badly I want you right now. But I'll wait as long as you need."

That was certainly easier to say now that I knew the wait was over.

I could feel her heat through my boxers. After her little bedtime-routine naked tease and now this, my dick felt like it was going to explode. Matter of fact, if she chose to move under me right now, I couldn't guarantee I wouldn't cream my boxers.

I took a moment to let this sink in. Gorgeous Elodie. Naked beneath me.

It had taken us so damn long to get here, but it was all worth it. The future may not have been certain, but one thing was: I was about to fuck her so good.

Our lips smashed together, and as the intensity of our kiss grew, I had no idea how I would stop from losing it once I felt her warm pussy around my cock. But there was no way I could blow—literally—our first time together. I had to find a way to pace myself.

As I lay on top of her, Elodie slipped her hands into my boxers and squeezed my ass. That made me crazy. She moved my underwear down my legs, and now my cock was right up against her pussy. I lowered my mouth to her breast and sucked hard on her nipple as I rubbed my slick cock over her clit.

She'd told me before that she was on the pill. That was essentially permission to slip inside her raw. And I wanted nothing more than to do just that. I could hardly contain myself, and so I didn't. I pushed inside of her in one hard thrust.

She flinched.

I immediately froze. "Are you okay?"

"Yes. Yes...it's just been a while. Don't stop."

She felt so tight around my cock. I moved in and out of her as ripples of mind-numbing pleasure coursed through my body. My lips hovered close to hers the whole time, though my mouth was agape from the sheer intensity of how damn good it felt to be inside of her and how hard I was trying not to come.

She gyrated her hips under me, meeting my thrusts with rhythmic precision and taking everything I was giving her.

"Please forgive me if I come too soon. I swear to God, Elodie. I've never felt anything so good. You're fucking amazing. I have to find a way to do this every day with you."

She was so incredibly wet. She had her hands wrapped around my neck and her legs around my back. I looked down at her face. Her eyes were shut tight, her mouth open. She looked like she was in ecstasy, totally in a zone, and it pleased me that I was the one putting her there.

I began to fuck her harder as she squeezed her muscles around me. My cock was so deep inside of her now. It felt warm and safe, yet at the same time like I'd taken my first hit of a drug that would have me hooked for life.

I moved my hips faster as I felt her contract. When she suddenly moaned, I realized she was climaxing. I couldn't believe she'd lost it before I did. Shaking and pulsating, she screamed in pleasure as she came. I would have been willing to bet her friend next door could hear it; that was how loud she was.

I finally let myself go, unloading an endless stream of cum into her and mentally claiming her as mine as I experienced the most intense orgasm of my life. I didn't slow down until every last drop had emptied out of me. The movement of my hips finally stopped just before I buried my head in her neck and kissed her softly.

Within a minute, I felt ready for round two.

Elodie panted. "So freaking worth the wait."

Fucking her was everything I'd imagined it to be and more. If this woman wanted me, there was no doubt in my mind that she had me for life.

For life.

I'd really just thought that? I waited for the panic I was certain was about to hit.

But then I felt soft lips against my cheek, and I pulled back to look down at the woman beneath me. Elodie had the goofiest ear-to-ear smile on her face. The front of her blond hair was glued to her head with sweat, and the back stuck up and out all over the place. She looked a mess, but a beautiful and thoroughly fucked *hot* mess. She also looked truly happy. And you know what happened then?

I smiled back at her.

That panic I'd been waiting for never came.

CHAPTER
THIRTY-SIX

Elodie

I had to slap my hand over my mouth to stop from cracking up when Hollis turned his back to me.

We had taken a bath together. I'd needed the long soak after all the exercise we'd gotten in bed last night. Muscles ached that I hadn't even realized I had. I couldn't count the number of times we'd had sex. All I knew was it had been a *long time* since I felt this satisfied.

I'd drawn the bath while Hollis was still sleeping, and he'd surprised me by joining after I'd settled in. But when we were done, I'd lied and said all of my towels were in the laundry and handed him one of my furry winter bathrobes to dry off. I don't know how I kept a straight face as I encouraged him to put it on—telling him the inside had more moisture-wicking ability than the outside.

Now I had this gorgeous, normally stern, wound-too-tight, six-foot tall, masculine man standing in my bathroom wearing a bright pink fuzzy robe. He turned around and caught the gigantic smile on my face.

His initial reaction was to return the smile, but he'd already gotten to know me pretty well. He knew the difference between my happy smile and an amused one, and the progression of his own smile halted as he squinted at me.

He looked around the bathroom. "There's no linen closet in here. Where do you keep your towels?"

I tried my best not to laugh. "In the closet right across the hall."

Hollis's eyes dropped to my smile, and then he examined my face some more. Without another word, he opened the bathroom door, stepped into the hall, and swung open the linen closet.

Ten fluffy, clean towels greeted him.

He stood with his back to me, looking into the closet for a long moment. Then he very calmly closed the closet door and turned around to face me. The smile on his face could only be described as wicked. It shot straight to between my legs.

He arched a brow. "Are you enjoying yourself?"

I arched one back and a little chuckle escaped. "I am."

He took a step toward me, and, instinctively, I took one back. Seeing me retreat turned up the volume on his already mischievous smile.

"Nervous I might get even?"

My face should've cracked from how wide my smile stretched. "Nope. Not at all."

He took another step toward me.

I took another back.

His eyes sparkled...right before he lunged at me. I yelped and laughed as Hollis bent down, leaned his shoulder into my belly, and lifted me up and into the air in a fireman's hold. He swatted my ass while I kicked and giggled.

"I couldn't help it. You look so cute in pink."

Hollis marched out of the bathroom and maneuvered his way down the hall. "You like games, do you? I'm all for it, but it's my turn to pick the next one we play."

I continued to laugh as he walked us into my bedroom and sat down on the edge of the bed. In one fluid motion, he lifted me up and off his shoulder and brought me down across his lap so I was bent over one of his knees.

He applied firm pressure to my back when I tried to get up.

"What do you think you're doing?"

"I told you. It's my turn to pick the game."

My head hung nearly to the carpet, and I had to crane my neck to look up at him. "And what exactly is this game? Because I seem to be bent over your knee with my ass almost exposed."

Hollis smirked. "Oh yes. Let me rectify that." He lifted the hem of my short, silky robe and exposed my entire ass. "*Now* we're ready to play."

I probably should've felt nervous in such a vulnerable position, but instead I felt kind of turned on. Hollis's wicked grin was so damn sexy, and I loved how powerful and in control he looked right now. Only *this* man could rock a pink, furry robe.

"Let me up," I said.

He ignored me. "My game is sort of like Jeopardy—except you don't get points for correct answers. You get smacks for getting things wrong."

"You're out of your mind."

"First question: favorite body part on your master, Hollis?"

"My master?" I scoffed. "Gee, let me guess, would the right answer be *his dick*?"

Hollis swatted my ass hard enough that it stung. He made a playful buzzing sound. "*Bzzzt.* I'm sorry. You failed to use proper form. The correct answer is *What is Hollis's dick*?"

I snorted. "You're insane."

"Next question. When Hollis takes a bath or shower next time, what will you give him to dry off when he's done?"

I couldn't help myself. "What is my red silk robe?"

He swatted my ass again. In the same exact place, and a little harder.

"Ow!"

"*Bzzzt.* Incorrect answer. Did I fail to mention that like Jeopardy, the stakes go up as you answer?"

"Let me up, you nut job!" I tried to sound pissed, but it's impossible to pull off when every word comes out of a smiling mouth.

"Final question. This is worth double, so pay close attention." He paused and smoothed his hand over the part of my ass he'd smacked. "Will you ever screw with Hollis again?"

I braced for it this time. I actually *wanted* to feel his big hand on my ass again. "Yes! Yes! I definitely will!"

His hand connected with my ass in two swift smacks. The first one stung, but the second was hard enough that it would definitely leave a handprint.

Yet I wasn't pissed off at all. Instead...

I was hornier than hell. *Again.*

Hollis lifted me to standing. He still had that gleam in his eye as he sat on the bed, watching to see what I'd do, how I would retaliate. But I didn't want to get even; I wanted to mount him. I was practically dripping and oh-so turned on. I took a step back so he could have a full view and slowly untied my robe and let it fall to the floor. Turning around, I bent over enough to rest my hands on my knees and pushed my ass out so he could get a good look at his handiwork, then gazed back at him over my shoulder.

I watched his pupils dilate as he stared at where he'd smacked. The spot was warm, so I figured he could probably see the entire outline of his hand raised in a bright red welt.

He gaped and swallowed. "*Jesus Christ.* That's fucking hot."

I couldn't agree more.

I turned back around and tilted my head coyly. "It's my turn to pick the game now, right?"

His eyes jumped to meet mine. Hollis was smart. He wasn't sure if I was screwing with him again.

"That depends on what you have in mind."

I opened my legs and straddled his knees as he sat on the bed. Licking my lips, I smiled. "My game is ring toss. Guess who's gonna play the part of the stick?"

Hailey was coming back soon. She'd kept in touch with Hollis to let him know what time they were leaving Block Island so he could pick her up when she returned. It had worked out pretty damn amazingly well that we'd had a whole night together alone, *and* didn't have to rush this morning. Hollis had done some work from my place, but for the most part he'd taken the day off—though he was currently standing in my dining room, talking to his partner on the phone. He looked over at me as he spoke.

"Because I wasn't home last night or this morning. I'm at Elodie's house. I stayed here last night, if you must know."

Hollis pulled the phone away from his ear, and I heard Addison screeching. He shook his head and rolled his eyes, but his voice was playful. "Don't hold your breath. You just got as much as you're going to get out of me."

I finished loading our breakfast dishes into the dishwasher and decided it was time I finally got dressed. On my way to the bedroom, I stopped in front of Hollis under the pretense of kissing him, but then I snatched his cell phone from his hand.

"Hi, Addison. It's Elodie. Why don't we have lunch soon, and I'll fill you in on everything you want to know."

She laughed. "That would be awesome. Not only because I'm nosy as shit, but because I'm positive he hates the thought of us going to lunch together."

I looked at Hollis, who didn't look too pleased, and nodded. "He sort of looks like he sucked on a lemon, so I think you're right. How does next weekend sound?"

"That sounds perfect."

"Great. I'll see you then."

I handed the phone back to Hollis and strutted off toward the bedroom. Hollis came in as my arms were behind my back, clasping my bra.

"I don't like the two of you together."

"Why not?"

"Because she's nosy, and once she gets into my personal business, I'll never be able to get her the hell out."

I walked into my closet and grabbed a powder blue tank top and a pair of white shorts. "You need someone who cares about you in your personal business, Hollis. We all do."

"I do just fine on my own."

I pulled my shirt on and walked out of my closet shaking my head. "Really? How long has it been since you had a relationship again? Six years now?"

Hollis took the white shorts from my hand and knelt down on the floor in front of me. He opened them so I could step in and then pulled them up to my hips and reached for the zipper. The small gesture of helping me dress made the inside of my chest feel all warm. When he wanted to be, Hollis was really sweet and thoughtful. He didn't seem to have to try. He naturally wanted to take care of me.

After he buttoned my shorts, he stood and snaked his hands around my waist, locking them behind my back. "Drive with me to pick up Hailey and then come home with us. Stay at my place tonight. I'm not ready to let you go yet."

That warm feeling in my chest turned to goo. "What about Hailey?"

He shrugged. "What about her? We already spoke to her. She knows something is going on between us."

I wrapped my hands around his neck. "She knows *something* is going on. But I don't think it's a good idea that she sees us in the same bed so soon. She's impressionable, and we're setting an example for her—that includes how fast you jump into bed with someone."

Hollis dropped his head and groaned. "I want you in my bed."

I smiled. "And I'd like to be there. But I think it's important that we put Hailey first, instead of our libidos."

"Fine. Come home with me tonight and stay in the guest room. You've done that before. I'll tell her I picked you up before coming to get her today because I have an early day tomorrow. She sleeps late. She won't know what time I leave."

I bit my lip. It was a tempting offer, but I wasn't so sure we wouldn't wind up in Hollis's bed. Neither one of us had much self-control around the other.

I needed some assurances. "Okay. But *no* sneaking into the guest room. She caught us once already, and I definitely don't want her to walk in on us naked and doing the dirty."

"Fine."

Hollis agreed to that way too soon. Something was up.

"Why did you agree without an argument?"

"I'll do whatever it takes to get you to come home with me."

"So you're not going to try to get in my pants later? Why do I not believe you?"

He smiled. "I figured you're probably sore anyway. I should give you a break."

My gut said he was full of shit, but I gave him the benefit of the doubt. I nodded. "Okay. I'll come home with you."

Hollis planted a chaste kiss on my lips and moved his mouth to my ear. "Plus, we already determined that *sex* doesn't include oral, and I can't wait to put you on your knees and watch you suck my cock later."

⌒

"I want to run next door to check on Bree before we go. This weekend was really hard on her. Plus, I'd love for her to meet you, if she feels up to it."

Hollis smiled. "That would be nice. I feel like I know her already from everything you've told me."

"I'm sure she feels the same way, too." I looked at the time on my phone. We had about fifteen minutes until we needed to leave to pick up Hailey, and I'd already packed an overnight bag. "I'll be back in five."

I slipped on a pair of flip-flops and walked next door. It took Bree a few minutes to open the door. Once she did, she smiled, even though she didn't look so hot. Her skin had a tint of gray to it, and I heard the hiss of air from her nasal cannula. Her oxygen was turned up pretty high this morning.

"How are you feeling?"

She opened the door wider so I could come inside. "I used to feel like a thirty year old with a sixty year old's lungs. But today my entire body feels like it's seventy."

I felt her forehead. "Are you sick? Do you have a fever? Do you need to go to the doctor?"

She smiled sadly. "No. It's just the progression of the disease. This is all normal."

"The trip this weekend was too much. We should have all come over here."

She shook her head. "No. I wanted to be at the lake."

Bree took a seat in her reclining chair, and I sat on the couch across from her. I'd come over to check on her, but also to tell her about Hollis, and at the moment that felt incredibly selfish.

"Why aren't you at work?" she asked.

"I...uhh...Hailey was at her friend's house for the weekend and decided to stay another night. I'm actually going to take a ride with Hollis to pick her up in a little while."

Her brows furrowed. "Hollis? He's coming here to pick you up?"

I didn't want to lie to her, but I also didn't want to rub my good fortune in her face. "He, ummm...came over last night, and we talked."

"Oh?"

"We're going to give things a try—a relationship, I mean."

"Oh. Wow. That's..." She coughed a bunch of times. "...good news. That's great news."

I nodded. "Yeah. But I feel like an idiot talking about my blossoming romance when you're so sick."

"Nonsense. I want you to be happy. You know that."

We talked for a few minutes, and then I realized Hollis and I needed to get on the road. I reached over and took her hand. "I have to run, because we need to pick up Hailey at two o'clock. But call me if you start to feel worse. Please."

Bree nodded, though I knew she wouldn't call anyone if her health declined, which really sucked. She struggled to get up from her chair.

I told her to stay put, but Bree, being Bree, insisted on walking me to the door.

I mentally debated asking her if she felt up for a visitor, and when we got to the door, I figured her health wouldn't likely be getting any better. I also knew she truly wanted me to be happy, so maybe meeting Hollis might bring her a little comfort.

"Would you...want to meet Hollis before we go pick up Hailey? He's next door, and I could bring him by to meet you really quick."

Bree frowned. "Not today. I'm sorry. But let Hollis know I'm rooting for him, okay?"

I kissed her cheek. "I will. And I'll text you later to check in."

She nodded.

I went back home feeling deflated. Hollis took one look at my face and pulled me against his chest for a hug. He kissed the top of my head. "She's not doing well, I take it?"

I swallowed a salty lump in my throat and shook my head. "She's not really up for visitors."

"Of course. Another time."

I held on to him for a minute, and then pulled my head back. "I almost forgot—Bree said to tell you she's rooting for you."

"Oh?"

"She's been rooting for you from the get-go. She seemed to sense that we should be together."

"You have a smart friend."

I smiled. "I do."

Hollis motioned toward the door. "Come on. We have a few minutes before we need to leave to get Hailey. I saw a little flower shop when I went into town yesterday to get something to eat. Why don't we go pick her up some flowers, and you can drop them off before we go?"

God, I loved relationship-Hollis. He was so thoughtful. "You're the best. Thank you."

"No reason to thank me."

I stretched up and brushed my lips with his. "Maybe. But I'll do it anyway—later, after Hailey is sleeping...*on my knees.*"

CHAPTER
THIRTY-SEVEN

Hollis

The sun was setting as we pulled up to Megan's house. When Hailey entered the car, she seemed surprised but happy to see Elodie.

She leaned into the front seat from the back. "Are you coming home with us?"

Elodie looked back at her. "Yeah. Hope that's okay?"

"Yeah, of course, it is!"

I was relieved to get this response from Hailey. Not that I could've changed anything at this point, but her feeling more comfortable meant one less complication.

"How was Block Island?" Elodie asked.

"So much fun, except I barfed on the boat on the way there."

"Oh no!"

"What did you guys do this weekend?" she asked.

"We hung out a little at my place in Connecticut," Elodie answered.

"I told Megan you guys were dating, and you know what she said?"

I raised my brow and looked at her through the rearview mirror. "What?"

"She said that meant you were probably boning while I was away."

Elodie and I looked at each other, and she cringed.

"I assume you know what that means?" Elodie asked.

Hailey's face turned red. "Yeah."

I had to put a stop to this conversation. "Elodie and I are adults, Hailey. What we were doing is no one's business but ours. And your friend shouldn't be saying such inappropriate things to you. I don't want to hear that kind of stuff again. Not sure Megan is a very good influence if she's saying things like that to you."

"She was just joking. Please don't stop letting me hang out with her. I'm sorry."

"I won't do that, but think about what you say before you say it, okay?"

She sulked. "Okay."

"I was only with your uncle part of the weekend," Elodie said. "I went to my friend's lake house. Remember I told you I was going away?"

"Oh yeah. I forgot about that. How is she?"

"Unfortunately, she's not doing that great. But I'm glad I got to spend the time with her there. Then Hollis came to visit me when I came home from the lake."

"And now you're coming home with us. Are you moving in soon?"

Elodie shook her head and laughed. "No."

"Elodie and I are taking things slowly," I said. "But she's going to be spending *a lot* more time at the house."

If I had my way, that would mean every night. So not *technically* moving in, but...

Hailey seemed happy about that revelation. "Cool."

Elodie turned to face her. "You're okay with that?"

"Of course, I am. I love you."

I knew they were close, but I'd never heard Hailey say that to Elodie before.

"I love you, too," Elodie said without hesitation.

"Do you love Elodie, Uncle Hollis?"

Leave it to my niece to put me on the spot. I was definitely falling hard for Elodie, but I wasn't sure how to answer the question.

I finally responded, "I think it would be very easy to fall in love with Elodie."

I realized that wasn't exactly an answer. Thankfully, Elodie seemed to like it, as she reached over for my hand.

"I'm sorry I was weird when I first found out about you guys," Hailey said.

"I think that was a normal reaction," Elodie said. "I totally understood."

After a short time of driving in silence, I decided to announce, "So, I was thinking of taking the day off tomorrow and hanging out with you guys. How does that sound?"

"Oh my God. What?" Hailey squealed.

"Is it that shocking?" I chuckled.

"Yes!" they both said at the same time.

Elodie laughed. "You've never taken a day off since I've known you. And now you're taking two in a row."

"I know. I think it's time I started putting other aspects of my life ahead of my job. So I've decided I'm calling in again." I rolled my eyes. "Believe me, Addison's going to have a field day. She'll be thrilled to fill in for me."

Elodie had gone straight to the guest room after the three of us stayed up late watching a movie. So much for the girl earlier who'd promised to thank me on her knees. Elodie had also been a girl scout about not showing affection toward me around Hailey all night.

But now that my niece was asleep, my focus switched to tainting Elodie's good intentions. I knew we shouldn't risk getting caught in the act, but I wasn't sure I had any self-control. My ability to stay away from Elodie was much weaker now that I'd gotten a taste of being with her. *Addicted* couldn't even begin to describe it.

I was determined to get Elodie into my room, come hell or high water. As I lay here *alone*, I took out my phone and sent her a text.

Hollis: I'm pondering changing the color scheme in my bedroom. Can you come in here for a sec and give me your opinion?

Elodie: I would, but I'm afraid if I step foot into your room, I'll never leave.

Hollis: That's the idea. ;-)

Elodie: I sort of figured it was. Which is why I am staying put.

Hollis: Actually, what I'm really pondering is the thought of you on your knees at the foot of my bed giving me head.

Elodie: That rhymes.

Hollis: Do you like that?

Elodie: Rhyming? Sure.

Hollis: I'm also pondering you on my cock grinding your hips while I suck on your lips.

Elodie: LOL

Hollis: Also...this might sound crass, but I'd REALLY like to slap your ass.

Elodie: Well, aren't you the creative one when you're horny...

Hollis: My version of nursery rhymes. ;-) Remind me why you're down the hall and not in my bed again?

Elodie: Because now that we're actually here and she's in the next room, I've chickened out.

Hollis: How is it possible that I miss you already? I just saw you...what... twenty minutes ago? I'm already twitching.

Elodie: And you're taking the day off tomorrow again! I can't believe that. Have I mentioned how much I love sweet, romantic Hollis?

She'd used the word *love*.

Hollis: Not sure my intentions right now are purely romantic. By the way, did you just say you LOVED me?

There was a long pause before she retracted her statement.

Elodie: Don't worry, I didn't mean LOVE love. Don't want to freak you out. LOL I just meant I really like this sweet side of you.

I decided to tease her.

Hollis: Is there another meaning for love? Because I'm pretty sure you said you loved me.

Elodie: I just meant I love the man you are lately.

Hollis: That sounds an awful lot like you love me.

The three little circles danced for a while. I assumed she didn't know what to say, or that I'd made her uncomfortable by calling her out.

Hollis: I'm teasing you, Elodie.

Elodie: I thought maybe I freaked you out.

Hollis: That's because a text doesn't allow you to see someone's face. If you could see me, you'd see how big my smile is at the moment. The only thing freaking me out is the fact that you're right down the hall, and I can't touch you. And if you don't come down to my room right now, I'm coming to you, which is not ideal since you're right next to Hailey's room. Which is it going to be?

Elodie: Are you serious?

Hollis: Fuck Yes. Watch me.

About a minute later, my door creaked open. Elodie stood at the entrance in a long T-shirt.

"Took you long enough. Come here, beautiful."

She shut the door carefully before walking over to me. "I just don't want her to wake up and see me in here."

I pulled her into me as I sat at the edge of the bed. "We'll be really quiet. We need to start practicing that anyway. Her waking up is a chance I'm willing to take. She already thinks we're—in her words—*boning*, thanks to Megan. So, I'm getting blamed for it without reaping the benefits, at the moment."

"Yeah, that's unfortunate."

Squeezing her ass, I said, "What's unfortunate? My not reaping the benefits or Megan's choice of words?"

"Both? Anyway, you reaped the benefits just this morning."

I nuzzled her neck. "It's not enough."

Her breaths were shaky as she bent her head back. "Hollis, what have you done to me? I've never felt like this in my life. I'm so screwed if you ever break my heart."

That will never happen.

Somehow I knew that. If things with us didn't work out, it wasn't going to be me that ended it. My hesitation was always about my fear of her leaving me, never the other way around.

The words burst from me. I didn't expect them to come out. But they did.

"You said you love the man I am when I'm with you. I love the man I am when I'm with you, too. But more than that, I love *you*, Elodie. I love you so fucking much. And I'm sorry if that freaks you out a little, but it's the truth, and I thought you should know." I swallowed, somewhat shocked by my own candor.

In the distance, Huey squawked. *Baaa!* "Anna's home!"

It was as if the universe had given me the reminder of Anna to test me. But it didn't change a thing.

Elodie looked just as shocked as I was at my admission. "How can you be sure so soon?"

"Soon? Just because I only now got my shit together and put aside my fears doesn't mean I'm only now figuring out that I love you. I'm pretty sure I've loved you for the majority of the time I've known you. And that's what scared the crap out of me."

Her eyes watered as she let my words sink in.

She grabbed my face. "Oh my God, Hollis. That really was what I meant in the text. And then I backtracked, because I was afraid you weren't there yet."

"I'm here, Elodie. I'm very much here. And I somehow knew you felt that way about me, too, even when I was teasing you." I looked in her eyes. "I love you."

Her chest rose and fell. "I love you, too."

Elodie straddled me. We started kissing, and the next thing I knew, I was inside her. Both of us were still sitting in the exact same position, fully clothed, just with our underwear pushed to the side now, as she rode me slowly, passionately—and ever so quietly.

CHAPTER
THIRTY-EIGHT

Elodie

"You sure you're okay with me meeting up with Addison?"

I didn't want to upset Hollis when things were going so well.

He came up behind me as I scrambled some eggs and kissed the back of my neck. "Of course. It's good for you to get to know her."

It was the weekend after Hollis and I had declared our love for each other. I'd spent every night this past week with him, except one. I'd insisted on going home to check on Bree and spent Thursday night in Connecticut—not to mention, I was all out of clothes.

Addison and I had decided a Saturday lunch worked best, given her schedule, so I'd be meeting her later today. Even though my initial interest in lunch with her had been to mess with Hollis, I did want to get to know the person who was such a big part of his day-to-day life.

I poured the eggs out onto two plates. "I'm sure there's a part of her that wants to make sure my intentions are in the right place with her best friend."

"Nah. Believe me, Addison has been a huge supporter of you from the very beginning. She's not going to grill you. She just wants to talk to you, maybe rank on me a little for fun. Trust me. You're good."

⌒

Addison and I met at a cute little restaurant in Midtown. Even though it was the weekend, she was dressed to the nines in a crisp, collared shirt and pencil skirt. I didn't know her exact age, but Addison looked about Hollis's age.

"You're so dressed up. I'm relieved I wore a nice outfit."

"It's just a habit. I always think I'm going to run into a client. You look lovely, by the way, Elodie."

"Thank you."

After we sat down, I opened my menu and said, "It's so nice to get out like this. I don't do it nearly enough."

She played with her string of pearls. "Why don't you?"

"Much of my time is spent with Hailey. By the time I get home, I'm exhausted. Well, when I used to go home."

"*Home* lately is with Hollis, I take it?" She grinned.

"Yeah, at least as of the past week."

"And now it's *Hollis* exhausting you after hours?"

I chuckled. "Only in a good way."

The waitress came by and took our order. I opted for salmon over salad, while Addison ordered a burger with Swiss.

After, Addison leaned in and said, "I hope this doesn't come off as strange, but can I just tell you I prayed for you?"

I didn't quite understand. "Prayed for me?"

"Yes. I asked the good man or woman above to bring someone like you into Hollis's life—someone he would find attractive and appealing enough to hang everything up for. It had to be the whole package. Someone who would be worth taking the risk of getting hurt. It had to be someone special, who wouldn't give up on him. I knew he wanted someone like you before he did. It was actually at my wedding that I wished for you."

"Really?"

"Well, my *third* wedding. Let me back up a bit." She laughed. "Third time was the charm for me. I'd been through two short-lived, failed marriages before I decided my happiness was going to come first. Both of my exes were critical people who never really supported my career, or supported me in general. With my first two husbands—both of whom I met on Wall Street—it was always a competition, never a true partnership. They never had my back."

"I'm sorry."

"Oh, don't be. Everything worked out the way it should." She smiled. "I met my husband, Peter, when we shared a cab. Sounds like a typical New York love story, right? Except Peter was the driver. He saw me so upset one night after a fight with my now ex-husband number one. He turned off the meter and kept driving us all the way to the Jersey Shore. We stayed up talking all night. We remained friends but didn't get together until my second marriage was over. So, I basically made the same mistake twice before I saw the light. One day I just woke up and realized it had been Peter for so long. I was ignoring the fact that he was perfect for me. As soon as the papers were signed after my second divorce, I was all-in and never looked back."

"Wow. That's a great story."

"And I *know* that this is it for me. Peter's the one. When you know, you know."

I couldn't agree more. "Oh, I know what you mean."

"I hadn't told Hollis about my friendship with Peter while I was married. I kept that whole thing secret and sacred. But once Peter and I started dating and they actually met, Hollis could see how happy I was. He never approved of my first two marriages. He knew both of those men through the industry prior to my relationships and could always see through them, even when I didn't."

"I love your effortless friendship with Hollis. He speaks so highly of you. And I'd love to meet Peter."

"We'll have to go out for drinks, just the four of us one night."

"That would be so much fun."

At that moment, my phone rang.

I looked down at the screen. "It's Hollis."

She waved her hand. "Take it."

I answered, "Hey."

His deep voice vibrated in my ear. "Is she being good?"

I glanced at Addison, who was beaming. "Yes. We're having a very nice time. She just told me the story of how she met Peter."

"We all met in vehicles. They met in a cab. And we met when you crashed into me."

"Very funny. I think we both know what *really* happened there."

He laughed. "Okay, I'll stop crashing your party. Just wanted to hear your voice and annoy Addison at the same time. Make sure she knows I'm watching her."

"You're crazy."

"I know."

After I hung up, our food arrived, and we dug in.

Addison's mouth was full when she pointed her fork at me and said, "Anyway, getting back to my original point. Peter and I had a destination wedding in Greece. He's Greek, actually, but born here. We only invited close family and friends. During our dance on the beach in Mykonos, I spotted Hollis watching us. And I could have sworn I saw a look of longing on his face. I came to the conclusion that he knew he was missing his life by building so many walls. He just didn't know how to change. And that made my heart ache. So, I prayed for you that night. And it took a little while, but you came along."

Wow. "Addison, that's really poignant. I hope I can live up to your expectations."

"Are you kidding? Hollis is already ten times less wound up. You've already done your job, as far as I'm concerned. And I got to keep my Bentley on top of it all."

"Your Bentley?"

She winked. "Just a little bet we had going."

It took us over two hours to eat lunch, because neither of us seemed to be able to shut up long enough to get more than a few bites in every now and then. While I'd started out a little nervous, things were ending better than I could have expected. Addison was warm and accepting, and it was evident she loved Hollis very much. We fought over who paid for lunch and walked out of the restaurant arm in arm.

"So are you heading back to Connecticut or staying here in the city?"

"I told Hollis I'd come back to his place for the night."

She smiled. "He can be a little on the possessive side, can't he?"

"It's okay. I'm a little on the possessive side, too. We've both been burned before, so we might hold on a little tighter this time."

Addison shook her head. "His ex is lucky I never got my hands on her after what she did to him."

I smiled. "I'm sorry he's been hurt. But if I ever ran into her, I'd have to thank her. Her loss is totally my gain."

Addison hugged me. "For the record, Hollis was wrong after all. He told me I was going to think you were great. But you're freaking awesome."

"Honey, I'm home," I teased as I let myself into Hollis's apartment. He was on the couch with his bare feet propped up on the coffee table and a book in his hands.

He set it down on his lap and waited for me to come to him. Of course, Huey greeted me with his usual *Baaa!* "Anna's home".

"Hi, Huey. *Elodie's* home." I walked over to Hollis and leaned down to kiss his lips. "Did you miss me?"

When I went to stand up, he grabbed the back of my knees and pulled me onto his lap.

"I did. Let me show you how much." He nuzzled my neck and palmed one of my breasts through my shirt.

I giggled. "Where's Hailey?"

"She went downstairs to Kelsie's so they could pack a bag for Kelsie to sleep over. So give me that mouth and let me cop a cheap feel. We don't have very long."

Hollis slipped a hand behind my neck and pulled my lips to meet his again. Our kiss heated up as fast as always. I wound my hands into his hair, and his tongue swept away thoughts of anything but my desire for him.

We hadn't done very well at keeping things private. Hailey had caught him grabbing my ass in the kitchen the other day, and also caught us making out in the elevator one night when the doors slid open on their floor. It was just so easy to get lost in each other. Which, of course, was why neither of us heard the front door open this time either.

"Ugh. Get a room, you perverts," Hailey groaned on her way to her room with Kelsie.

I could tell from her voice that she was more teasing than upset. But regardless, she'd caught me off guard, and my reaction was to jump out of Hollis's lap. Unfortunately, my attempt at standing failed, and I wound up flat on my ass on the living room floor.

Hollis chuckled and extended his hand. "Smooth."

"Shut up." I rubbed my ass as I got up. "That was your fault. I tried to give you a nice peck on the lips. But *noooo*...that wasn't enough. You had to be greedy."

"I can't help it when I'm around you. I *am* greedy. I want your body in my hands at all times." He stood and kissed my forehead. "Sit. I got you that wine you like. I'll get you a glass, and you can tell me all the horrible things my business partner told you about me, so I can deny them."

Hollis came back with two wine glasses and sat down next to me on the couch. He set his glass on the coffee table, scooped up my feet, and started to take off my sandals.

"So how did it go?"

"It went great. I really love her."

"Good. I'm glad. Because while she's a giant pain in my ass, she's a good person and my best friend. But don't tell her I said that."

I sipped my wine. "I won't. But I'm pretty sure she adores you as much as you adore her. Though both of you seem to like to pretend you get on each other's nerves. On the train here, I realized I never asked either of you how you two met."

"We've known each other since college. She was Anna's macroeconomics TA. They became friends."

"Oh, wow. It didn't sound like they were friends anymore."

Hollis tossed my shoes on the floor and began to massage my feet. "They definitely aren't. Anna met her first, and the three of us became friends. Addison was a year ahead of us, but she and I had the same major, so the three of us would often study together. After we graduated, we went to work at competing firms. When I decided I wanted to go out on my own, I suggested we do it together." He shrugged. "When shit went down with Anna, she might've been as pissed off as I was. The two of them may have been friends first, but if things hadn't gone wrong with Anna, there's no doubt whose side of the church Addy would've been sitting on."

"I like that your best friend is a woman."

Hollis dug his thumb into the arch of my foot, and I felt my entire body relax. "Oh yeah? I like that your best friend *isn't* a man. Pretty sure I'd hate you hanging around another man all the time."

I laughed. "Are you saying you'd feel threatened?"

"Nope. I just prefer the only dick swinging around you to be mine."

"I feel bad for Hailey when she starts dating. You're a little on the protective side."

Hollis's fingers stopped moving. "Dating? We have a long time until that happens."

"Not really. I was into boys by the time I was thirteen. Went to the movies alone with Frankie Hess at fifteen."

"I don't like Frankie Hess."

I chuckled. "Well, Hailey's Frankie Hess better hope someone besides her uncle answers the door when he comes to pick her up."

"Someone else? I assume that means you, right?"

Things between Hollis and me were pretty much perfect, but I still liked to screw with him to keep it real. I shrugged. "Or whoever you're dating by then. We are talking a few years down the road."

I pretended not to notice the scowl on his face. "And where are you planning on being then?"

If I looked at him, I'd crack up. So instead I sipped my wine and reached to set the glass down on the coffee table next to his. "I don't know. Maybe I'll look up Frankie and see what he's doing these days."

I was flat on my back with Hollis hovering over me faster than I could finish yelping. "I'm joking." I laughed.

"Joking, huh? You're in some mood. First you tell me Hailey's going to be dating in the next two years and then you taunt me by talking about another man."

I giggled. "Frankie was *fifteen*."

He snuggled into my neck. "Don't care. What's mine is mine, and I don't like to think of it belonging to anyone else, before or after me."

"*Neanderthal*," I teased. But the truth of the matter was, I loved hearing Hollis refer to me as *his*.

He pulled his head back and looked down at me. "If it makes me a caveman that I want to lock you up and fill your belly with my babies, then so be it. Where's my club? I might use it to beat Frankie's ass."

My face softened, and I reached up and cupped Hollis's cheek. "You want to have babies with me?"

He seemed confused by my question. His brows drew together. "Of course, I do. Don't you?"

Having kids wasn't something I'd ever felt was necessary before. Tobias and I had never talked about it. But when I looked into Hollis's eyes, I could see our future including little gorgeous Hollis babies.

I stared at him for a long time before answering. "I think we'd make a nice little family."

Hollis ran his thumb along my lip. "Sweetheart, I hate to tell you, but we already *are* a nice little family."

That night we ordered a pizza with Hailey and her friend. Then Hollis and I watched a movie in his room so the girls could take over the living room. It was such a simple day, but my heart was full as I rested my head on his chest. Watching some old *Die Hard* movie he'd picked out, I felt content for the first time in—well, really forever.

I propped my head on my fist. "I do want to have a baby someday...have a baby with you."

Hollis pointed the remote at the TV and muted the sound. "That's good, babe. I'm glad we're on the same page, even if you're just figuring it out and I've known for a while."

I smiled. "I didn't have the best home life. So having a family someday wasn't a given for me, I guess."

Hollis pushed a lock of hair behind my ear, and his thumb lingered, stroking my neck. "Ours will be different. I promise."

"I know."

"By the way, as long as we're on the subject, you keep saying *someday*. And the way you say it makes it sound like *someday* is a long way off. Just giving you fair warning, we don't have to have kids next week—I'm open to whenever it feels right for you—but you and me living under one roof, you not having to sneak across the hall, me locking down the formality of you being here and being mine? Those aren't so far off."

Warmth spread through my chest. I could *not* love this man any more. It should've scared me how fast things were moving. I'd been practically living here the last few weeks already, and now he was talking about making it permanent...making *us* permanent. But I wasn't scared. Love was risky, but I was certain Hollis LaCroix was worth taking a chance.

I took a deep breath and smiled. "Okay."

He looked into my eyes for reassurance. "Okay?"

"Yeah. I'm good with that."

I didn't so much fall asleep that night as I floated. I'd never been happier. My life with Hollis seemed like a fairy tale, almost too good to be true.

But when I woke up abruptly at nearly two in the morning, realization struck me fast.

Fairy tales are just stories made up by other people. And they *are* too good to be true.

CHAPTER THIRTY-NINE

Elodie

"Oh my God...." My heart raced in my chest, yet the rest of my body felt paralyzed.

Hollis shot up from sleeping. "What's going on? What's the matter?"

I held my cell to my ear and spoke to Mariah. "Where is she?"

"At Bridgeport Hospital. I know it's late, but I promised you I'd always let you know if she took a turn."

I climbed out of bed and ran across the hall to the guest room where I kept my clothes. My legs were shaking. "Is she stable?"

Mariah's voice cracked. "An ambulance brought her in. She coded on the way to the hospital, but they brought her back. During all the commotion, an intern forgot to check for a medical bracelet and they... intubated her."

"But she didn't want that."

"I know. It was an honest mistake. It must be shocking for them to see such a young woman's health on the line, and they probably just did what they could to save her. It was wrong, but…she's still with us."

"I'm on my way."

When I turned, Hollis was behind me, already dressed and with his keys in his hand.

I looked at him, and he grabbed my hand. "Come on. I called Kelsie's mom and said we had an emergency. She's coming up to stay with the girls. Let's get on the road."

Ten minutes into the ride, Hollis finally spoke. I'd been so lost in thought as I stared out the window that I forgot we hadn't yet discussed the call or anything that had transpired. He reached over to my lap and took my hand. Threading our fingers together, he brought our joined hands to his lips and kissed the top of mine. "You okay?"

I shook my head. "No."

"Do you know what happened?"

"All her stepmother told me was that she stopped breathing in the ambulance." Tears started to stream down my face. "She's been so weak lately."

Hollis squeezed my hand. "But she's stable now?"

"They put a tube down her throat, even though she didn't want that. Someone made a mistake, apparently."

"Shit."

I returned to staring out the window as Hollis navigated the city. The streets were so empty. I looked at the clock on the dashboard. Two thirty in the morning. That explained why it was still dark out, and the roads were so desolate in Manhattan.

"I wanted her to meet you," I whispered.

"I will. If she's anything like her friend, she's tough, and she'll pull through this."

348

The drive to Bridgeport was normally about two hours, but Hollis was flying.

"You know," he said, "when my mom was sick, I remember watching the news at night and getting pissed off at some guy who had robbed an old woman at gun point and pistol-whipped her unconscious."

I looked over at him. He glanced at me and back at the road.

"That asshole was walking around perfectly healthy, and my mom was lying in bed, fighting for her next breath. It just made me angry."

I hadn't thought of the fact that Bree's plight could bring up some heavy feelings for Hollis. "I go back and forth between angry and upset," I told him. "Angry is easier to deal with."

Hollis smiled. "I never would have guessed that."

Even at the darkest time, he could cheer me up. I squeezed his hand. "Thank you for jumping in the car without asking a single question."

"Of course. I wish there was more I could do than just drive you. I wish I could carry the weight you have on your shoulders."

"Having you next to me makes me feel like I'm not carrying anything alone anymore."

"I'm glad. Because you're not."

We arrived at Bridgeport Hospital in record time. Hollis pulled in and stopped at the parking lot entrance. "Want me to drop you off at the front door and meet you inside?"

"No. If you don't mind, I'd rather park and go in with you. I'm nervous about what I'm walking into."

"Of course."

Hollis parked, and we walked hand in hand to the hospital's front entrance. The doors were tall and wide and loomed ahead ominously. Each step made the lump in my throat grow.

"Do you know where she is, or do we need to go to the front desk to ask?"

"Tobias texted me a little while ago and said she was moved to the ICU. She's in bed three."

We rode the elevator up to the fourth floor and followed the signs to the Intensive Care Unit. When we came to a set of closed double doors, there was a button to push to open them, and a hand sanitizer dispenser on the wall right next to it. Hollis and I both squirted some Purell into our palms, and then I took a deep breath.

"You ready?" he said.

I forced a small smile. "No, but let's go in anyway."

Hollis used his elbow to push the button on the wall, and the double doors creaked open. The room was large, with a dozen or so beds positioned around the outer rim and a large nurses' station in the middle. We walked to the nearest available nurse. "Can you tell me where bed three is, please?"

She pointed to a corner of the room where the curtain was closed and frowned. "There's some family in there now, but you can join them."

"Thank you."

Hollis put his hand on my back. "Do you want me to wait here?"

"No. If you don't mind, I'd really like you to stay with me."

"Whatever you want."

He guided us over to bed three. The curtain around the area hung a foot or so from the floor, so I could see three sets of feet. I assumed they belonged to Bree's dad, stepmom, and Tobias. When we got close, I felt a wave of relief to hear machines beeping. I'd been terrified we took too long to get here.

I turned to Hollis and let out a ragged breath. "Machines. I hear the machines."

He smiled. "That's good."

Someone must've heard us, because the curtain suddenly slid open. Mariah stood at the foot of the bed, blocking my view of Bree. She turned around, took one look at me, and pulled me to her. I got my first glimpse of my best friend over her stepmother's shoulder.

A tube was down her throat, taped to her face to hold it in place. And a loud machine positioned next to the bed simulated the in-and-out sound of breathing. Her skin was so pale, and she looked so tiny and young. My chest hurt so badly.

Mariah released me, and I looked over at Bree's dad and Tobias. Neither one of them seemed to be paying any attention to me. They were too busy staring over my shoulder.

"Oh, I'm sorry. This is..."

"Hollis," Bree's dad interrupted.

I looked between them, confused. "How did you know his name?"

It felt like there was some sort of staring contest going on that I wasn't part of. Everyone seemed to have their attention fixed on the man behind me. Yet they all said nothing.

I turned to Hollis.

He was staring wide-eyed at my friend lying in the bed.

"Hollis?"

He ignored me.

"Hollis?"

I knew she didn't look good, but Hollis looked like he'd seen a ghost. Maybe it was too much, asking him to come see her like this. His mom had probably been in the ICU, too.

I touched his shoulder. "Are you...okay?"

He shook his head. "What the hell is going on?"

"What are you talking about? This is my friend Bree."

He turned and stared at me. "You mean *Anna*."

Anna.

Anna?

It took several seconds to even begin to register what he was talking about.

My heart beat faster and faster as I slowly pieced this together.

He'd just called Bree...*Anna*.

My eyes widened. Brianna was Bree's full name. But it couldn't be...

Bree is Anna? Hollis's ex, the one who'd broken his heart?

My Bree?

I took one look at his face, and there was no more questioning it.

Bree is Anna.

The room seemed to sway, and a feeling of unreality overtook my body. This made no sense, and even though there was no longer any doubt, I needed him to confirm it.

"Hollis? Bree is your ex-girlfriend, Anna?"

Unable to take his eyes off her, he nodded.

My ex-husband interjected, "What the hell is going on?"

There was no easy way to say it. "Hollis is my boyfriend. I had no idea he ever knew Bree. He'd always referred to his ex as Anna, and I don't think of Bree as Brianna. I didn't know anyone called her Anna."

Bree's father closed his eyes and began to shake his head.

Mariah's eyes were wide. "Well...that's quite a coincidence."

"Only a few people called her Anna when she was younger. That's what her grandmother called her," Richard said. "She stopped going by it as she got older. She preferred Bree. But she was always my Anna growing up."

Tobias gave Hollis a dirty look before announcing to Richard, "I need to get some air."

After Tobias left, I breathed out a small sigh of relief. His presence only made a bad situation worse.

Hollis still wasn't saying anything. The room was eerily quiet aside from the sound of the machines keeping Bree alive.

Suddenly, he walked over to her bed and pulled a chair up next to her. The rest of us watched Hollis stare down at her incredulously. He placed his hands on his head and pulled at his hair as he continued to take her in. Then, as if a switch flipped, he got up out of his seat and swiftly exited the room.

"Excuse me," I said as I rushed after him.

Hollis escaped down the hall, finally stopping at a water bubbler. With both hands, he leaned against it, breathing in and out as if he were about to hyperventilate.

He finally looked over at me. And as our eyes met for the first time since this nightmare began, neither of us had words.

There simply were none.

CHAPTER FORTY

Hollis

I finally forced the words out. "I don't understand. Make me understand, Elodie."

She shook her head. "I don't understand, either. I really don't."

"You didn't know about this?"

Her expression went from concerned to angry. "What, you think I tricked you or something? Of course I didn't know!"

I immediately regretted my assertion. This was so damn confusing. "I didn't mean to imply you were being deceptive. I just don't understand how we could not have known this. She's your best friend."

Elodie kept shaking her head. "She's never once mentioned you to me, Hollis. I knew she'd experienced heartbreak several years ago. She alluded to an ex-boyfriend. Honestly, I don't know if that was you or someone else, but I swear to you, Hollis, she never once mentioned your name or said a thing when I mentioned you, either."

Taking a deep breath in, I tried to find my bearings. Every second we wasted out here trying to figure this mystery out, Anna was in there fighting for her life. I didn't care how badly she'd hurt me or how jarring this revelation was—none of it mattered right now.

She's dying.

Anna was dying.

What *did* matter was that Anna be surrounded by those she loved in what could be her final hours. I didn't know whether she'd ever really loved me, but a part of me would always love her. That's why I'd been so devastated all these years. Up until Elodie, Anna had been the love of my life.

I snapped myself out of my thoughts. "We need to get back in there."

Elodie wiped her eyes. "Yeah. Let's go."

Entering that room a second time was no easier, no less shocking. Anna had always been small, but she looked exceptionally frail and fragile, though with the same beautiful face I'd always remembered. Seeing that tube down her throat physically hurt me, especially knowing it was against her wishes.

You're so brave, Anna.

My instinct was to try to save her, to do something, but it was clear there was nothing any of us could do right now except pray. I couldn't remember the last time I'd asked God for help. Honestly, after my mother died, I'd lost faith that anyone out there was listening to my prayers. This was the first and only time since then that I'd felt compelled to beg for mercy.

Please don't let her suffer like this.

Memories of Anna flashed through my mind. She'd been my rock at the worst of times during my mother's illness. That was what always stuck out. No matter how things ended between us, I'd never forgotten that or stopped appreciating it. Seeing her in this state was the worst kind of deja vu. It felt like the cruelest of life's jokes.

Richard must have noticed the continued horror on my face because he took me aside.

"Hollis, son, I know how much Brianna meant to you. I'm sorry you had to find out like this."

God, if this was difficult for me, I could only imagine how he felt. Anna was always a daddy's girl.

I asked a dumb question. "How are you possibly handling this?"

"Well, you know...." He hesitated and his eyes filled with tears. His voice trembled. "She's my little girl."

"Yeah," I whispered.

I wasn't the type of guy who easily embraced another man, but in that moment I didn't hesitate to wrap my arms around Richard. Fuck, we were consoling *each other*. Richard always used to make me feel like I wasn't good enough for his daughter. I eventually realized it wasn't a reflection on me, but more of how much he loved her and felt she deserved the absolute best. I'd just begun to earn his trust when Anna suddenly ended things with me.

After we let each other go, my eyes returned to Anna.

I'd had so much anger in my heart toward her over the years. But in this moment, all I wanted was a miracle. She was a damn good person who didn't deserve this fate. In my heart, I knew the situation was dire and expecting a miracle was a long shot. But I couldn't give up hope.

I looked over at Elodie, and my pain magnified. I was supposed to be holding her hand through all of this but could hardly sustain myself. I only hoped she would understand.

Richard walked to the door. "I'm gonna get some water."

Needing another breather, I said, "I'll go with you."

As we walked down the hall together, I asked, "Do you remember how long after our breakup she was diagnosed?"

Richard blinked. "I don't, Hollis. But it probably wasn't long. Even after she discovered she had this disease, she was absolutely fine for a long time. Things really only got bad the past few years."

"What happened to the guy she was with?"

The one she left me for...

He blinked as if to try to remember. "It didn't last," he said.

She'd devastated me for a relationship that didn't even last? Did he leave her when he found out about her illness? And how long had Richard himself been married? Anna's mother had died when she was a baby, but he hadn't had a girlfriend that I knew of. And he just *happened* to marry a woman whose son Elodie married? I had so many questions, but this wasn't the time to ask them. I'd asked enough for now.

Richard drank from the water fountain. I placed my hand on his shoulder as we walked back to the room.

Upon my return, Elodie's eyes met mine, and the sadness in them was palpable. I was sure she could see the same feeling in mine. We held each other, despite the awkwardness of Richard and Mariah watching us. Elodie burst into tears in my arms. As much as I might have needed to, I couldn't cry. Still stifled by my shock and confusion, the build-up of emotions inside of me wouldn't come out.

A doctor finally came in to talk to Richard.

"The next twenty-four hours are going to be critical," he said. "I really wish I could tell you one way or the other how things are going to go, but we just don't know. Right now, she's completely reliant on the machines. We'll test the waters tomorrow to see if she can breathe on her own. But we're not going to try anything tonight."

"What would you say the chances are of a full recovery?" Richard asked.

The doctor's face was grim. "It doesn't look likely. Given your understanding of her disease and the prognosis, I'm not telling you anything you don't already know. That doesn't make this any easier. I know that. I'm so sorry."

It was incomprehensible that Anna could die so young, that her father would have to say goodbye. It was painful enough losing a parent. I couldn't imagine losing a child. I chose to focus on what losing Anna meant to Richard because I couldn't even fathom what it meant to me. I hadn't spoken to her in years, but she was never far from my mind. She was the person who'd impacted my life the most.

And yet I'd had no idea what she'd been going through all these years. If I had, my attitude toward her certainly would have been different. I'd been filled with such disdain for her; meanwhile, she'd apparently been suffering the majority of the time.

The sun was starting to come up by the time Elodie and I left, vowing to return in a few hours.

Tense silence filled the air during our ride home. We were both too exhausted and distraught to talk. But at one point, I needed to ask her a question, even though I knew she didn't have the answer.

"How did she not say anything to you when you've been talking about me to her?"

"I don't know, Hollis. I've mentioned your name numerous times. Is it possible she thought it was a coincidence and never considered that you were the same Hollis?"

I shook my head. "I can't imagine she wouldn't have at least questioned it. My name is not a common one, and she knew my niece's name. We were together when my half-brother's girlfriend gave birth, though I don't think the two of them ever met. None of this is making any sense."

And it doesn't look likely that we'll get the chance to ask her.

Elodie noticed I was driving toward Connecticut. "Where are you going? You're taking me home?"

I hadn't realized I was taking her home and not back to the city with me. But the truth was, I needed to be alone tonight. I wanted to be there for her. I really did. I wanted to be a better and stronger man than this, but I just couldn't.

"I need to be alone tonight. I hope you can understand that."

"I'm not sure I do, Hollis. I think we need to lean on each other right now, not push each other away."

She was right. But I needed to process this without having to worry about how my feelings might impact her. Maybe that was selfish. But I couldn't be around anyone right now, not even her.

As I pulled up to her house, I shook my head. "I'm sorry. I know I'm not handling this very well. Maybe this will sink in at some point. I'm just not there yet."

After a moment, she seemed to soften. "I'm sorry for making you feel bad about it. I understand."

Elodie said nothing further before she got out of the car. I waited until she was safely inside before taking off.

Exhausted, I had every intention of going back to the city to get some much-needed sleep. But after seeing a sign on the side of the road, that wasn't where I ended up.

CHAPTER
FORTY-ONE

Elodie

It was almost dawn, and I hadn't slept a wink. I'd been sitting up on my couch and staring into space, trying to make sense of this. Wracking my brain, I'd ruminated over all my communications with Bree about Hollis. I was desperate to figure out whether she knew *my* Hollis was *her* Hollis.

The pain in his eyes tonight was something I wouldn't soon forget. It was clear that a part of him still loved her. And I wasn't going to lie and say that knowledge didn't have a profound impact on me. Then again, *I* loved her. So much. So how could I blame him?

Anna had left Hollis for another man. Bree always referred to the love she lost. Was that the other man? Or was it Hollis? She never wanted to talk about it.

Was it possible she'd figured out the truth about who I'd fallen in love with and felt badly for having hurt him, so she never said anything to me? Maybe she wanted to give him a chance at love without interfering, because she knew how much she'd hurt him.

That was just one theory. The questions in my mind were endless. And I knew we might never get the answers we needed.

Filled with urgency, I rushed up off the couch and grabbed my keys, which included the one to Bree's house.

Running next door, I let myself in. I knew I had no right to trespass, but my need for answers was desperate. I also missed my friend. Being in this empty house without her was eerie. My eyes wandered over to her ever-present water glass on the table next to the chair she sat in. Knowing she might never return was heartbreaking.

I ran up the stairs and started going through her drawers and closets, in search of anything that could provide me answers. My tears fell as I kept coming up empty, more devastated with each passing minute. I sifted through all the things she might never get to enjoy again, like the clothing hanging in her closet. Concert ticket stubs littered the top of her bureau. She loved music and live shows. She might never see another one.

Life is so unfair.

My eyes landed on a stack of photo albums in the corner of her closet.

My hands shook as I grabbed them and took them back downstairs to the living room. Sitting on the couch, I inhaled a deep breath and opened the first one. It mostly contained photos of Bree as a child. In one image, she was so thin and small it reminded me of what she'd looked like today at the hospital, shriveled and childlike.

The second photo album featured photos of her teenage years. It didn't take me long to stumble upon the one I'd been looking for: the first photo of Hollis and Bree. *Anna.* They were at the beach, and Hollis had his arm around her. Bree wore a bikini and Hollis had on board shorts. They looked happy as could be with the sunshine bearing down on them.

It was surreal to see them together, my best friend and my boyfriend. They loved each other. Or at least Hollis loved her. That was evident from the way he smiled at her in the next picture I came upon. They were sitting under a tree. It was a candid shot, as if someone had happened to notice the way he was looking at her. *God, this hurts.*

Hollis had an innocence about him in these photos that no longer existed. By the time I met him, he was hardened by loss. The guy in these photos was most definitely long gone. I kept turning the pages. More photos of them together. Some of them kissing. Lots of them laughing. A prom photo. Graduation. They'd been through a lot together. I wondered if they'd been each other's firsts.

Why, Bree? Why did you keep this from me? I'd opened up to her so much about my attraction to Hollis, about my developing feelings. Had she not made the connection, or was she hoping it wasn't true so as not to disrupt my life?

She hadn't wanted to meet him that weekend he'd stayed over in Connecticut. I remember feeling like that was odd, even though I'd chalked it up to her poor health. Did she suspect something and not want to find out the truth? Or did she *know* the truth?

I had to wonder if things with Hollis and me would ever be the same again. Could we survive this?

I closed the photo album. These questions had to take a back seat for now. Because Bree was fighting for her life. Did anything else really matter?

The hallways of the hospital were quiet, except for an older man singing a Johnny Cash song as he mopped the floor outside the elevator on the fourth floor. It wasn't quite 7AM, but the ICU had no visiting hours, and I couldn't sleep. I thought Richard might be here, though I didn't expect to see anyone else this early.

Arriving at the closed double doors, I rubbed some Purell into my hands and pressed the button to open them. The nurses' station was subdued, and I stopped when I saw the same woman who had been checking on Bree before I left.

"You're back quickly," she said.

"I am. I couldn't sleep. How's she doing?"

The nurse offered a sad smile. "Brianna's about the same. I just took her vitals and made sure she was comfortable a half hour ago."

Brianna.

I wasn't sure I'd ever get used to that. The name sat like a weight on my chest because of all the implications...Bri*anna. Hollis's* Anna. *Oh, God.* I rubbed at my breastbone. *Huey's Anna,* too.

"Okay. Thank you. Is it alright if I visit with her now?"

"Of course. We're going to change shifts in a little while, so you and your brother will need to step out for about an hour then. But right now is fine."

"My brother?"

She lifted her chin toward the opposite side of the room where Bree's bed was. "He's been here for almost a half hour already. Doesn't look like he slept much either."

I followed her line of sight, expecting to see Tobias, and a lump formed in my throat.

Hollis.

He sat beside Bree's bed. His hair stuck up all over the place; one look and I knew he'd spent the last few hours tugging at it. But what was he doing here so early? It was a two-hour drive each way back and forth to the city, and we'd only left in the middle of the night. He couldn't have gone home and back. I felt like I might get sick. Had Hollis dropped me off at home so he could rush back and be alone with Bree?

That thought brought so many emotions—sadness, confusion. I hated myself for feeling it, but there was definitely some jealousy mixed in, too.

I watched from a distance, unsure what to do. Did I go over and join him? Go sit in the waiting room and give him some time alone? Leave and come back?

After a few minutes of attempting to figure out the right answer, I realized there really was none for this situation. So I took a deep breath and decided to go over and check on him. I'd ask him if he wanted to be alone. I didn't want to hide that I was here, and I also needed to see my best friend—even if just for a few minutes.

Hesitantly, I walked toward Bree's bed. My feet felt so heavy as I approached. Hollis's back was to me, so he didn't see me coming. But when I got within a few feet, I heard his voice, and it stopped me in my tracks.

"I broke a promise I made to you." He reached up and took one of her hands in his, and my chest constricted so tight it felt difficult to breathe. Yet I stayed frozen in place.

"I realized it when I was walking through the hospital last night on my way out and saw the signs for the pediatric oncology unit. Do you remember the night you made me promise I'd never stop my visits? It was the night Adam died."

Hollis went quiet for a long time. I should have backed out, given him some privacy. But I just couldn't move. He let out a loud rush of air before continuing.

"You were his first kiss. And his last." He shook his head and gave a dry chuckle. "I was jealous of that kiss. Don't think I ever told you that. You gave a dying thirteen year old who had a crush on you his first and last kiss of his life, and I was jealous of him in that moment. How's that for possessive and fucked up?"

He cleared his throat. "The night Adam died, you made me promise I'd never stop visiting the pediatric oncology unit to play video games. But I did. I stopped after you walked out on me. I still sent a check at Christmas every year, to make sure the unit could get new games and stuff, but I stopped going, Anna. We're all made of good and bad. But when you left, you fucking took all the good parts of me with you. I didn't even realize I could get those parts back until recently. I'd thought they were gone forever." He paused. "Anyway, last night, instead of going home, I wound up at a twenty-four-hour Walmart. I picked up some games and a new gaming console and brought them up to the unit here in the hospital. The nurses were nice and let me hook it up.

And I met Sean while I was doing that. He's fifteen, in for his second round of chemo, but he's in pretty good spirits. Kicked my ass in Grand Theft Auto."

He squeezed Bree's hand. "I think I stopped going because I was so pissed at you. Last night, meeting Sean brought back a lot of memories. Memories of both of us sitting in that pediatric unit playing with those kids. Memories of you being by my side every damn day when my mom was sick."

He shook his head, and I felt tears sliding over my cheeks. "I don't know what happened between us. But I remember how much you were there for me. And I'm going to be here, Anna. Right by your side, like you were always there for me."

A nurse walked up behind me and touched my shoulder. Startled, I jumped.

"I'm sorry. I thought you saw me. Would you like me to bring over another chair? So you can both sit with Brianna?"

Hollis turned around, and our eyes locked. "Elodie."

"I...I need a moment."

I practically ran out of the ICU. Once I was in the hall, I saw an illuminated Exit sign to the left, so I rushed in that direction. A door led to a stairwell, and all I wanted to do was hide and be alone. I managed to make it down one flight before I had to stop and sit on a step because I was crying so hard I could barely see.

I wasn't even sure what had upset me.

Was it the story Hollis told Bree, and the realization of how deeply he'd loved her, or the fact that my best friend was lying on her deathbed?

Both, I guessed. It was just too much to handle at once.

Luckily, very few people took the stairs at seven in the morning. So I sat on that step for a long time all by myself and let it all out. Eventually, when I had no more tears left, I walked down to the first floor and re-entered the hospital. I wandered around, not quite sure where I was going, until I noticed a sign for the chapel.

The tiny sanctuary had only a half dozen pews on each side and an aisle that led to a simple altar. The room was dark and empty, and I didn't bother to turn the lights on. Instead I took a seat in the back row and said a few prayers quietly with my eyes closed. It was the most peace I'd had in the last twenty-four hours, and I felt my shoulders drop and some of the tension in my neck unfurl.

I decided to stay and try to relax a bit. I was in no rush to go face Hollis at the moment. But after a little while, the lack of sleep and exhaustion must've caught up with me, because the next thing I knew, a man was waking me up—a man wearing a collar.

"What time is it?" I rubbed my eyes.

The priest smiled. "It's about ten o'clock. I saw you in here a few hours ago and figured you needed some sleep. But there's a daily mass that's going to start in about twenty minutes. So I wanted to wake you now so you didn't wake up in the middle of it."

"Oh. Sorry. Okay. Thank you. I'll get out of here. I hadn't meant to fall asleep."

"There's no rush. Can I ask what you're at the hospital for? Are you visiting someone?"

I nodded. "My best friend. She's very sick."

"I'm sorry to hear that."

"Thank you."

"Would it be alright if I sat down with you for a few minutes?"

"Of course."

I'd been sitting at the end of the pew, so I scooted over to make room, and the priest took a seat.

"Will your friend be in the hospital long?"

I frowned. "I think so. Unless...."

The priest nodded even though I couldn't complete my sentence. "You know, no one cares for the caretaker. Everyone is naturally focused on the patient, but the caretaker has an important role. You need to rest and tend to your own needs in order to be able to do the job of being by the side of your loved one."

I sighed. "Yeah. I know. Last night was just so shocking."

"What's your friend's name?"

"Bree...Anna. Her name is Brianna."

"And your name?"

"Elodie."

The priest held out a hand to me. "I'm Father Joe. Shall we say a prayer for Brianna together?"

"Oh. Yes. That would be great." I put my hand in his and closed my eyes.

The priest recited a few prayers and then added, "Dear Heavenly Father, today I ask that you look down with compassion on our friend Brianna, who has been confined to a bed of sickness. Please send comfort and healing. We pray for Your gracious kindness to strengthen and heal, whatever the problem is that has caused this illness in her body. And we pray for strength for her family and friends, especially Elodie, that they may hold her hand with courage and love in her time of need. In the name of the Father, and of the Son, and of the Holy Spirit. Amen."

I made the sign of the cross and opened my eyes. "Amen."

Father Joe smiled warmly at me. "Would you like to say confession? Many people find it helps take some of the weight off their shoulders. You're carrying enough when you're taking care of a sick loved one."

I smiled. "You said you have a mass to give soon. Not sure there's enough time for me to tell you all the things I've done wrong since the last time I've been to church."

Father Joe laughed. "Why don't you give it a shot, if you feel up to it. I'm sure it can't be that bad."

"Well, I've definitely lied on a few occasions."

"Okay."

"And I might be lying again right now, actually. Because I'm pretty sure it was on more than a few occasions. In my last job, I used to manipulate men into compromising positions in order to enhance their wives' divorce settlements."

The priest's brows shot up. "Sorry. We're not supposed to show any emotion, but that's one I hadn't heard before."

I chuckled. "Yeah, those weren't my finest moments. But anyway, I definitely lied a lot. I also curse like a sailor and use the Lord's name in vain occasionally. Oh, and I'm divorced. But my ex-husband cheated on me and is a jerk, so I think I should get a free pass on that one."

"Alright. Anything else?"

"I don't think so. Oh, wait. Premarital sex is a sin, right?"

"It is."

"But I love him. So that should count for something, too, right?"

Father Joe smiled. "Say four Hail Marys and two Our Fathers."

"Okay." I started to shut my eyes and then changed my mind. "Can I ask you something?"

"Of course."

"Is it possible to love two people at the same time?"

"That's a big question." He was silent for a long time. "I think it's possible to love many people at the same time. But I don't think it's possible to love two people in exactly the same way."

"But can a man fall in love with someone new, if he never stopped loving the person he was in love with first?"

"There are some people who come into our lives and take a little piece of our hearts when they go. So they'll always have that love with them. But the heart is resilient and will eventually heal itself. Though the new heart isn't the same as the old heart, and that's why we never love two people the same way."

"I guess."

"Are you worried about the man you're with now?"

"It's a long story, and it's incredibly selfish for me to even be thinking about it now, but yes."

"I see."

"He loved a woman, and she broke his heart. Like you said, she took a little piece of it with her when she left."

"Do you love him?"

"I do. So much so that it scares me."

Father Joe smiled. "That's how you know it's real—if it scares the heck out of you. I'm not personally that well versed in relationships of the man-and-woman kind, obviously. But I've counseled a lot of couples in my forty years of the priesthood. My advice would be to give this man some time. Perhaps he's feeling just as scared as you are right now."

I sighed and nodded. "You're right. Time. We definitely need some time. I should probably say those prayers and get going now, before your mass starts. But thank you for talking to me."

"Anytime, Elodie. I'm here from eight to six or so every day. But if I'm not here..." He pointed to the cross hanging over the small altar. "He is. So come by and talk to either of us whenever you need to."

CHAPTER FORTY-TWO

Hollis

"**H**ow are you holding up, son?" Richard walked into the small waiting room outside the ICU while I was waiting for my coffee from the vending machine to finish brewing.

"I've been better. You?"

He smiled sadly. "Same."

I slipped the cardboard cup out of the machine and sipped. My face scrunched up, and Richard chuckled.

"Looks like coffee," he said. "Smells like coffee, too. Tastes like shit. Though you *look* like shit. So it's a match."

"Thanks," I grumbled.

"Were you here all night?"

"I left to drive Elodie home and run an errand, then came back."

He took a dollar from his pocket, and the vending machine sucked it in. "This has gotta be hard on you both."

"It's definitely not something I saw coming."

Richard frowned. "I'm sorry about that." He took a deep breath and pushed the button to add cream and sugar to his coffee. "I spoke to the pulmonologist on the phone a little while ago. He's going to come in about two o'clock and talk to us. Said he's bringing the neurologist at the same time, and wants to discuss prognosis. He didn't sound too optimistic."

I rubbed the back of my neck. "Okay. I'll head out before then so you can have some privacy."

"I wasn't telling you so you would leave. I was telling you so you could be there. Bree would want us all to be together at a time like this."

"Not sure Anna—Bree—envisioned I'd be around again. But I appreciate that."

Richard sipped his coffee. "You might not have been together anymore, but you were always in my daughter's heart, Hollis."

She had a funny way of showing it. But this wasn't the time or place for bitterness.

Instead, I nodded. "I'll be there when the doctor comes. Thank you."

"Can you let Elodie know about the time, too?"

"Yeah, sure. I'll get in touch with her."

She'd disappeared after she saw me sitting with Anna early this morning. I was sure she'd put two and two together and figured out I couldn't have gone to the city and back. She probably thought I'd lied to her when I dropped her off—saying I needed to go home. But I really hadn't *planned* on coming back. Then I saw a billboard for the pediatric oncology unit of the hospital and suddenly my car was crossing three lanes of traffic to turn off at the next exit for a Walmart.

It was difficult to plan anything when things could change from one minute to the next. Thankfully, Addison had taken Hailey *and* control of the business, so someone with a brain had the reins, at least.

After we finished our coffees, Richard went to sit with Mariah. I wanted to give him some alone time, so I decided to go for a walk outside and get some fresh air. I figured I'd call Elodie and tell her about the doctors coming at two o'clock.

But when I walked out the front doors of the hospital, I was surprised to find Elodie sitting on a bench.

"Hey. What are you doing out here?"

She forced a sad smile. "I don't know. I wasn't ready to come back upstairs yet, but I also didn't want to leave."

I nodded. "Can I sit?"

"Of course." She inched over on the small bench. "I checked in with Hailey a little while ago. She sounded good. Apparently she asked Addison to take her to Home Goods, and she's spending the day redecorating your office since she's at your work today."

"Great." I chuckled. "Can't wait to see what that looks like."

We fell quiet. There was so much to say, yet nothing felt right. The silence stretched into awkwardness until I finally remembered I did have something to tell her—about the doctors. Only when I went to speak, she also started to talk.

We smiled and both said, "You go first"—again, at the exact same moment.

I held out my hand indicating the floor was hers, so it wouldn't happen a third time.

"I was just going to say I'll pick up Hailey tonight from Addison's and stay with her, if you want to spend the night at the hospital again."

I frowned. "Elodie, I didn't intend to come back last night when I dropped you off. I really did plan to go home."

"It's okay. You don't have to explain."

"No, I *need* to explain. I don't want you to think I lied to you."

She nodded. "Okay."

"But don't worry about Hailey. Addison said she would keep her a few days. She'll be fine. She loves Addison."

"Are you sure?"

"Positive. And besides, if one of us had to leave to go get her, it would be me, not you. You belong here."

"So do you."

I shook my head. "I don't know where I belong these days."

Elodie's face told me she'd taken that to mean something more than I'd intended.

"I didn't mean—"

She stopped me. "It's fine. What were you going to tell me?"

"I spoke to Richard, and he said the doctors want to talk to him at two o'clock. He wanted us both to be there."

"Oh, wow. Okay." She looked at her watch. "That's an hour. I should probably go grab something to eat. I don't remember the last time I ate, and all the coffee I drank is making me jittery."

She didn't ask me to join her, and that made me sad, though I understood the need to be alone. "Alright."

Elodie stood. "There's a bagel shop about a mile up the road. Would you like me to bring you back anything?"

"No, thank you."

She looked at me awkwardly and raised her hand in a wave. "Okay. See you up there, then."

I watched her walk away like a damn idiot. In my heart, I knew I should've grabbed her and held her in my arms before letting her go. Yet I couldn't. And I hated myself for that.

"So, Dr. Rashami and I have spoken at length," the pulmonologist, Dr. Marks, said. "And we've also consulted with Dr. Cowan, the staff ICU doctor who has been monitoring Brianna's care since she arrived."

All of us were lined up on one side of the bed—me, Richard, Elodie, Tobias, and Mariah. The two men in white coats stood on the opposite side of the bed.

I looked down at Anna. This morning I'd asked a nurse if she could hear me when I spoke, and she'd said sometimes people remember things they heard when they were in a coma, and other times they didn't. I got the feeling that whatever was going to be said now might be scary to Anna if she were listening, and I didn't want her to suffer any more than she had to.

So I spoke up, even though it wasn't really my place. "Do you think we could have this conversation somewhere else? The waiting room, maybe?"

Dr. Marks nodded and pointed to a door a few beds away. "Of course. Let's do that. Why don't we go into the isolation room? It's empty today."

We moved into a small, private room, and the doctor closed the door behind him.

"So, like I was saying, the two of us have conferred and spoken to the other members of Brianna's care team. As you know, we did a high-definition CAT scan, some x-rays, and ran blood work. Basically, we've learned that Brianna's LAM, her lymphangioleiomyomatosis, has progressed, causing blockages of the small airways and damage to her lung tissue. She also has a blockage in her lymphatic channel that has caused a good amount of fluid to collect in her chest and abdomen—fluid that shouldn't be there."

"So what do we do?" Tobias asked.

"Well, the fluid in her chest and abdomen can be drained. But that requires a surgical procedure. And even if we were to do that, there's a good chance they would fill back up again. However, we know because of Brianna's advance directive, that she did not want any lifesaving actions taken if she was to enter a state where she was unable to make her own health decisions."

"So what will happen if we do nothing?" Richard's voice shook as he spoke.

"Her lungs will continue to fill up and... Well, there's no easy way to say this, but it needs to be said so you can make the right choices. She'll basically drown in her own body."

Mariah broke into a loud sob. Her husband put his arm around her and pulled her to his chest.

The doctors looked at each other. "We believe the right thing to do would be to turn off the ventilator before we reach that point."

"Can she breathe on her own?" I asked.

The pulmonologist looked down and then back up. He cleared his throat. "No, that's not likely."

Everyone in this room knew the right answer. Anna had made her wishes crystal clear, so there was nothing to discuss. Yet two hours passed, and we were no closer to coming to a solid conclusion on the next step. The problem wasn't figuring out what Anna would have wanted; the problem was that no one was ready to let her go.

I'd never use the term "pull the plug" in jest again as long as I lived.

Despite what we all knew in our hearts, the burden of officially making the decision and giving the go-ahead to her doctors lay in the hands of her father.

After a long period of silent rumination, Richard finally shook his head and said what we were all thinking.

"There's no way around it. We need to respect her wishes. We have to let her go." He pressed his fingers to his eyes to squelch the tears that came with that confirmation.

We all seemed to nod silently at once. It wasn't necessary to confirm it aloud even one more time. The thought of having to take her off life support was killing me. And I hadn't seen Anna in years. I couldn't imagine what this felt like for her father or Elodie. I could feel tears building in my eyes, but I refused to release them. Out of all of these people, I didn't have the right to be crying right now, didn't have the right to upstage their sadness.

At one point, Richard went to speak to her doctor, and when he returned to the room, he looked absolutely devastated. I knew he'd given the go-ahead to turn off the ventilator.

Later that night, the hospital staff came in and did just that. It was quick, but the wait that ensued was excruciating.

A nurse escorted Anna's grandmother in. I wasn't sure how Nana Beverly had gotten to the hospital, because no one in this room had left to get her. She had to have been in her nineties now.

As the family held vigil around Anna, the stress of waiting for her granddaughter to die became too much for Bev. This couldn't have been good for her own health. But I could understand her needing to say goodbye despite that.

Elodie wrapped her arms around Beverly and escorted her out of the room. I followed to make sure everything was okay.

"Someone needs to take her back to the nursing home," Elodie said. "They sent a driver to bring her here, but I don't think she should go back alone in this state."

I was the best candidate to leave the premises, considering I wasn't sure Anna would've wanted me here in the first place. I offered to drive Beverly back, not knowing whether Anna would be alive when I returned.

Nana Beverly definitely didn't remember me, and I was fine with that. So distraught, the poor woman cried the entire drive. But somehow, focusing on Beverly helped keep my own feelings from spiraling out of control.

After I walked her inside the facility and saw to it that she was safely in her room, I rushed to my car to get back to the hospital.

I'd just fastened my seat belt when my phone lit up.

Elodie.

I picked up. "Hey. I was just heading back. What's going on?"

There was a long pause.

My heart dropped.

Finally came the words I dreaded.

"She's gone, Hollis."

CHAPTER FORTY-THREE

Elodie

The days after Bree stopped breathing were a blur. I say *stopped breathing*, because it was really hard for me to use the word *died*. *Died* sounded so final.

I spent every waking hour helping Richard in any way I could: picking an outfit for her to be laid out in, ordering flowers, helping to arrange the after-service meal. While Bree had handled some of her arrangements prior to her death, no one person alone had the mental energy to handle the tasks that remained. So we had to do it as a team.

Hollis, like the rest of us, was still in shock. I hadn't seen or heard from him in a couple of days, aside from quick check-in texts I initiated. As much as I needed him right now, I knew we also needed to give each other space to grieve.

Adding to the devastation of her final hours was the fact that Hollis hadn't made it back in time to see her take her last breaths. She might not have been able to hear us, but saying those last goodbyes gave us some solace. Hollis missed a good portion of that because Bree succumbed pretty quickly.

When he'd arrived back at the hospital that night, his eyes were visibly red. I knew he'd had a good cry in the car after my phone call. I would probably never fully understand how he felt. I'd had my own close relationship with Bree, but nothing as intimate as Hollis had. With her gone now, neither he nor I would get the closure we needed. We'd never know whether she knew I was dating him before she died—whether we had her blessing, or whether she would have been upset.

Anytime I caught myself analyzing that fact, I reminded myself that right now the focus had to be on laying her to rest. And at the moment, I was doing what I needed to keep things moving: making a photo collage of her to be displayed at the funeral. I'd purchased two large canvas boards that I planned to cover with photographs. Sifting through albums in her bedroom, I removed the photos I felt best represented her life from childhood to adulthood. There were even a couple photos of Hollis and Bree when they were kids. I definitely stared at those the longest. I'd never seen photos of Hollis as a child until now. His hair was lighter, but he had the same beautiful face.

Richard had sent around an email to close family and friends asking if any of us wished to speak at her funeral. He asked us to "reply all" to the message so all the recipients could stay in the loop as to who was doing what.

I replied that it would be my pleasure to speak. Hollis indicated that he wasn't sure how Anna would feel about him giving a speech, so he offered his help in any other way that was needed. He didn't know I knew this, but Richard told me Hollis had insisted on covering the entire cost of the funeral. Richard had refused the money, but I knew Hollis would find a way to pay for it.

Because of Bree's wishes, the family opted to skip a wake and planned just one service at the church, as opposed to a funeral parlor. The service would be followed by a burial. Her casket would be situated on the altar, surrounded by candles and flowers. She'd be put up on a pedestal, which was what she deserved.

Both Hollis and I arrived at the service early, but separately. He was dressed in a dark suit and pacing in front of the church when I arrived. I was certain he was reluctant to go in. As was I.

He spotted me as I approached.

"How are you doing?" I asked.

"I should be asking you that question," he said.

"Pretty sure the answer is the same for both of us." I adjusted his tie. "We're early."

"Yeah, I didn't want to risk getting stuck in traffic. I've been here for a while."

"How is Hailey?" I asked.

"She misses you, but she's doing great. She's really taken to Addison's dogs. She and Peter have a big day planned—dog park and giving the mutts baths. I'm certain she'll start begging me for one soon."

"Not sure how Huey would like that. We wouldn't want him to start barking, too."

Hollis cracked a reluctant smile, probably just to appease me. This was certainly not the time for jokes, although I was desperate to feel anything but this pain.

"Anyway," I said, "I'll have to find a way to thank Addison for taking over for me."

He looked down at his watch. "Why don't we go inside?"

Hollis placed his hand on the small of my back as we walked into the church together. That slight touch gave me an ounce of comfort, as did how packed the church was. Addison was seated in the back pew and smiled sadly at both of us as we passed. I hadn't even thought about her coming, but of course, she had—they were all friends at one time, and she and Hollis were thick as thieves.

The photo collages I'd made were displayed in the foyer, surrounded by white hydrangeas—Bree's favorite flower. Hollis stopped to take in the images.

His eyes landed on the two photos of himself and Bree as kids. "Who put these together?"

"I did."

I hoped he wasn't mad, since I hadn't checked with him to see if it was okay to use photos of him.

His eyes hadn't left them. "Where did you find these?"

"In her closet."

"I'm surprised she still had them."

"She kept a lot of albums. She also collected concert ticket stubs, from, like, every concert she ever attended."

"She loved going to live shows."

Hollis leaned on the table for support and let out a deep breath. He shook his head.

"What are you thinking right now?" I asked.

He kept staring at the photos. "I just regret all of the years I didn't speak to her, that I never checked in on her long enough to even know she was sick."

"The way you handled it was understandable given the circumstances. That's what most people would have done."

He refused to accept that. "No. First and foremost, Anna and I were friends. That was how we started at a very young age. I wish I'd had a little more respect for that. I should've put my feelings aside and contacted her to make sure she was okay. That's what friends fucking do. Not sure I can ever forgive myself for being so egotistical."

"You don't know whether she would have been forthright if you had. She never wanted people to perceive her as sick. She never talked about it until she had to." Looking over at a photo of Bree and me, I said, "We all look back and wish we could have done things differently. When we lose people, we think about all the things we should have said or done. Like, I wish I hadn't wasted so much of her precious time venting about my problems. She never seemed disinterested, even though she had so much of her own stuff going on. I never really thought anything would happen to her, as sick as she was. I'm still waiting for this to sink in."

"I've been struggling a lot with the question of whether she'd want me here," he said. "I basically abandoned her after she broke up with me. She would never expect me to be here, Elodie, even though I feel like I really *need* to be here."

"I'm certain she'd want you here, Hollis."

His eyes met mine. "I guess we'll never know."

***

Bree was laid out in a pink chiffon dress I'd chosen from her closet. Her attire was one of the things she hadn't planned, so I did my best to pick out something I thought she'd like. Pink was her favorite color, and the dress had been hanging in her closet with the tags still on; she'd obviously intended to wear it but never had the chance. She looked beautiful, albeit a bit different with all the makeup they'd put on her.

I did the best I could to eulogize Bree without crying. I spoke about how important her friendship was to me, how she always made time for me, how she never stopped being a friend even when she was at her sickest. It was difficult reading while having to watch her father break down. And Hollis had his eyes on the floor the entire time I talked.

As I stepped down after my speech, I noticed Hollis stand up from his pew and begin walking toward the podium. All eyes were on him, because this wasn't part of the itinerary. To my utter shock, he situated himself in front of the microphone and started speaking.

"I first met Brianna Benson in kindergarten—Anna, to me. These boys were teasing me because I'd pissed my pants during recess. And Anna overheard. She proceeded to scream at the top of her lungs until she scared them away, totally freaked them out. It was the most fantastic thing I'd ever witnessed in my life at the time." He closed his eyes and smiled. "I was so indebted to her that I stole a ring from my mother's jewelry box that night and gave it to Anna the next day—not with romantic intentions but as true payback."

He glanced over at Bree's dad. "Richard probably remembers that. Anna showed him the ring, and he realized it was real and worth hundreds of dollars. So Anna gave it back. I was grounded for a week when my mother found out. That was the end of my career as a jewel thief but the beginning of my long friendship with Anna. I'd make an ass of myself several more times through the course of our friendship. There's that old debate about whether boys and girls can really be friends. We proved you could—for a very long time. Then I went and ruined it because I fell in love with her."

He laughed slightly. "That wasn't hard to do at all. Our friendship as we knew it ended when that happened. But we had more wonderful years together. She helped me through some of the most difficult days of my life when my mother was sick. That's why I'll always regret not being there for her during her own darkest days, which unfortunately I didn't know about." He looked down and swallowed to compose himself. "We lost touch over the years. Ironically, our relationship started with a ring and ended with a ring. But how or why it ended is not a story for today. It doesn't matter why Anna and I disappeared from each other's lives. What matters is the huge light she shined upon mine for the years we had together. What matters is my hope that she hears this from wherever she is so she understands how very much she meant to me and will always mean to me. And what matters is that all of you understand this: if someone means something to you, you shouldn't let your ego allow you to erase them from your life. Because someday, you may not have the chance to tell them all the things you wish you could. In honor of Anna, go home tonight and think of anyone you care about that you might not be in touch with. Take it from me, put aside your pride and let them know you're thinking about them."

He looked over at the casket. "I know I wish I had."

The dinner after the service was held at Anna's uncle's restaurant. While Hollis and I sat next to each other during the meal, we didn't talk much. I was still reeling from the emotional toll of this day, especially after Hollis's speech. I was relieved that people weren't talking and laughing as you often see at get-togethers after funerals. The mood all around was somber, as it should have been.

"I'll be coming back to work on Monday," I finally said. "So you can let Addison know."

"Are you sure?"

"I think returning to work will be good for me. I really miss Hailey."

"She'll love that."

I didn't want to hear Hollis tell me he wasn't ready for me to resume sleeping over at his house, that he wasn't ready to go back to the way things were. So I decided to beat him to the punch.

"Since I'm right next door, I've let Bree's dad know I'll handle cleaning out her house. I can go in each night and make some progress. They told me to take my time, that they're in no rush, but it's still a lot of work. So,

I'll be heading back to Connecticut in the evenings to handle that."

"Of course. That has to be done."

And that was that.

Hollis hadn't given me much eye contact today. I wasn't sure if that was because he thought seeing the pain in his eyes would upset me.

When he finally looked at me, I said, "I'm proud of you for getting up there and speaking today. I know it wasn't easy."

"I wasn't expecting to."

"I know that."

"I don't even remember what I said."

"It came from your heart, unrehearsed and authentic. It was better than something planned."

"After you got up and spoke, I realized it was the one chance I had to publicly acknowledge her. I would've been stupid not to take it. I just hope she heard it."

"I believe she did," I said.

I reached under the table for his hand. Thankfully, he didn't resist. He brushed his thumb along mine. It felt bittersweet, since it was the first time we'd touched like this in so long.

I wondered whether Hollis and I could ever get back to the place we'd been before. Would the ever-present mystery of what Bree knew continue to haunt us forever? Would I ever get over witnessing just how deeply he'd loved her, and would he ever get over the fact that I'd been so close to the woman who'd broken his heart? Only time would tell.

But I knew he needed space. He still hadn't processed much of this. And to a certain extent, neither had I.

CHAPTER FORTY-FOUR

Hollis

The Monday after the funeral felt nothing like a typical Monday. I'd been up since 4AM. and had already had three cups of coffee, even though I couldn't stomach breakfast. This would be my first day back at the office, my first day back into a life that was the same on the surface, but otherwise forever changed.

The door opened, and Elodie let herself in. It seemed like business as usual, aside from the massive ache in my chest. I'd missed her like crazy. I just didn't know how to fall back into the place we were before all of this happened. It somehow didn't feel right to be celebrating life, to be happy, at a time like this. I didn't know how to be anything but miserable at the moment.

Normally, I'd be rushing out the door with my stainless to-go coffee mug. But today, I leaned against the counter—in no rush to leave but unsure of what to say.

"How are you?" she asked.

"I'm alright. How are you?"

"I've been keeping myself busy. Happy to be here, though."

"Me too. I'm happy you're back."

Elodie glanced over toward Hailey's room. "She's still sleeping, I assume?"

"Yeah."

"I thought maybe she'd be awake and excited to see me."

"She must not have missed you that much," I teased.

She grinned hesitantly. "Richard told me what you did. That's amazing."

Since Anna's father had refused to let me pay for her funeral as I'd requested, I donated a large sum of money to start a foundation in her honor for people affected by the same lung disorder.

"It seemed like the logical thing to do."

"I know she'd be very grateful...and I want you to know I'd be honored if you'd let me help run it."

"Of course. We need all the help we can get. I'll add you to the correspondence."

"Thank you," she said.

For some reason, at this inopportune moment, a flash of Anna's smiling face entered my mind. True understanding that she was gone seemed to come in waves, alternating between denial and bursts of harsh reality.

I closed my eyes. "Imagine what it's like to know you're going to die—essentially dying a slow death. Imagine the bravery needed to endure that. I still can't believe she had to live like that for so long."

I'd managed to not break down throughout the funeral and after, but for some reason, it finally started to happen at this moment—the worst possible time because I didn't want Elodie to have to see me cry, given the complexity of the situation.

"I'm sorry. I have to go. I'm late," I said before rushing out the door.

Elodie didn't have a chance to react.

As soon as I got to the sidewalk below, my first tear fell.

"Well, you look like shit." Addison planted her ass in a chair on the opposite side of my desk.

I tossed the pen in my hand into the air and scrubbed my hands over my face. "Rough morning."

"Rough few weeks, I'd say. How's Elodie holding up?"

"Okay...I guess."

Addison frowned. "You don't *know* how she's holding up?"

"She's been busy. She spent the last few days doing some stuff for Anna's family—helping clean out her house and stuff."

"Why aren't you right next to her, helping her?"

"She needs some time."

Addison arched a brow. "*She* needs some time, or *you* do?"

"We both do."

"Why?"

"What the hell do you mean, why? Isn't it obvious?"

She folded her arms over her chest. "No, it's not."

"We both experienced something traumatic. We're not machines. It takes time to work through that."

"But you're a couple. Why aren't you working through it together?"

I felt fucking lost. I wanted to be there for Elodie. I just didn't know how. It felt wrong to touch her and hold her—but I didn't know why.

Addison's face softened. "If this hadn't ended the way it did. If you would have just found out Elodie and Anna knew each other, would that have changed anything between you and Elodie?"

I thought about it. Though I felt unsure about how to act around Elodie these days, I was sure about one thing: I loved her. I *fucking loved* her.

"No, it wouldn't have changed anything. I guess there would have been an adjustment period. It's not like it would have been simple to hang out with the two of them together."

"You want to know what I think?" Addison asked.

"Not really. But that's never fucking stopped you."

"I think you're a big chicken shit."

I blinked a few times. "Excuse me?"

"You heard me right. I think you're a big chicken shit. For years you've been avoiding a relationship— fucking your way through Manhattan—because the last woman you loved left you. You *finally* meet a woman who's worth risking your heart for, and then *bam*... It all bubbles back to the surface, and you retreat."

"You don't know what the hell you're talking about. We both need time, Addison. This was her best friend and my Anna."

She shook her head. "She wasn't *your* Anna anymore, Hollis. But she is *your* Elodie. At least for now. So get over yourself—Elodie is not going to hurt you like Anna did. And you know what, if I'm wrong and she winds up hurting you, wouldn't some years with Elodie be better than living without her?"

Living without her. Those words made my damn chest hurt.

"Are you done?" I picked up my pen and looked down at the stack of papers on my desk. "Because if you are, I have some work to do."

Two nights later, I was sitting in my office at 7PM, staring at the framed photo Hailey had put on my desk. Her "redecorating" had included adding two cow-patch-patterned pillows to my leather couch, a white shaggy throw rug under the coffee table—I was certain the throw rug was from the bathroom aisle and should've been in front of a tub—and a few framed pictures on my desk, one of which was a selfie she'd taken the day Elodie and I picked her up from her friend's house in Connecticut. Elodie and I were sitting in the front seat, leaning in, and Hailey sat in the center of the back seat between us. It was a cute picture. That was also the day after Elodie and I had slept together and the night I'd told her I loved her. Elodie and Hailey had big smiles on their faces, but I was looking at Elodie. The shot really captured how we were feeling that day—happy, in love, and without a care in the world.

What a difference a damn week can make.

A knock at my office door startled me.

Looking up, my brows drew together. "Richard? What are you doing here?"

He stood in the doorway. "Mind if I come in?"

"No, no, of course not." I stood and held out my hand to shake. "It's good to see you. How are you?"

His eyes roamed my face. "Better than you, from the looks of it."

I sighed. "I've been working a lot. Catching up after being out for a while."

He made a face that said he knew I was full of shit, but he didn't call me out on it. He took a seat across from me.

"It's been tough," he said. "It's never easy to lose a child, but Anna...she was my little girl." His eyes welled up. "I know every father thinks his little girl is special. But mine really was. Do you know I've had chocolate-covered fruit delivered every day this week from her? It's always been my weakness. I don't even know how she arranged for that to happen. That's the kind of person she was—always thinking of other people and making sure they were okay."

That was the Anna I'd known years ago. But it wasn't my place to tell a father his daughter only thought of herself when it came to the end of our relationship.

So I nodded. "She was a good person."

Richard reached around to his back pocket and pulled out an envelope. He held it up. "She wanted me to give you this...after. I don't know if I agree with some of the ways she went about things, but her secrets were mine to keep. And for that, I owe you an apology, Hollis."

"What secrets?"

He stood and tossed the letter on the desk. "It's all there. I didn't read it. But she told me what she wrote, and I think it will explain a lot." He held out his hand. "Elodie is an amazing woman. I'm glad you two have each other. I hope things work out for you. I expect an invitation to the wedding when they do. Take care of yourself, Hollis."

And just like that, he turned and walked out of my office.

I stared down at the white envelope in the center of my desk with Anna's familiar handwriting across the front of it: *Hollis.*

What the hell is going on?

CHAPTER FORTY-FIVE

Elodie

"Are you and Uncle Hollis mad at each other?"

I frowned. "No, sweetie. Why do you ask?"

"Do you not want to be boyfriend and girlfriend anymore?"

I'd been peeling a cucumber for a salad and set down the knife to give Hailey my full attention. She sat on a stool on the opposite site of the granite counter.

"No, we haven't broken up, if that's what you're asking."

"But you might?"

I sighed and walked around to her side. Taking her hand, I guided her to hop down from her seat. "Let's go sit in the living room and talk."

We sat on the couch, and Hailey played with a strand of her hair—something she did when she was nervous. I put my hand under her chin and lifted so our eyes met.

"Uncle Hollis and I lost someone who was close to us. We're just sad."

At least that's what I hoped. Though the last few days, I'd started to lose some of my confidence that we'd get through it.

Hailey nodded, but it looked like she had more to say, and for some reason I didn't think it had to do with Hollis and me being a couple. "Hailey, have you ever lost anyone close to you?"

She shook her head. "Is what your friend had contagious?"

"Oh God, no. Definitely not. Bree had a rare disease called lymphangioleiomyomatosis. Not only is it not contagious, but so few people have it that there have only been something like four hundred documented cases in the United States."

"Wow."

"Yeah."

Hailey still had that look on her face.

"Is there anything else you want to know?" I asked. "We can talk about anything."

She looked away for a moment. "What happens to you when you die?"

That was a tough question to answer. But I knew Hollis and his brother had been raised Catholic, so I gave the answer I thought they'd want me to. In truth, it was what I'd believed for most of my life. Though the last few days, I'd been questioning everything.

"Well, your soul goes to heaven, and you're freed of any sickness and pain you had here on Earth."

"So Anna isn't sick anymore?"

I smiled. That was the one belief I'd held on to tightly. "No, she's not."

"That's good."

"It is. I'm glad she's at peace now."

"What if...Uncle Hollis got sick?"

"Oh honey, Uncle Hollis is very healthy. You shouldn't worry about that."

"But Anna was healthy, too, right? Before she got sick."

She had a point. And I knew from personal experience what it felt like to be uncertain of what would happen to me if my alcoholic mother didn't wake up one morning. Even before my dad died, I'd always felt alone. When nothing in life feels secure, you tend to think about your next move an awful lot.

I looked at Hailey. We'd only known each other for a few months now, but I loved her with all my heart. "If something happened to your uncle Hollis—which it's not going to—I'd ask your father for permission to have you come live with me."

Her eyes lit up. "You would?"

I cupped her cheeks. "Yes, I absolutely would."

Hailey visibly relaxed. "Thank you."

"There's absolutely no reason to thank me. I'd be lucky to have you, kiddo."

The doorbell rang at almost eight o'clock. Hollis had texted only a half hour ago that he wouldn't be home until late tonight. I hadn't expected him so soon, but thought he must've forgotten his key. But when I looked through the peephole, a man I didn't expect to see stood on the other side of the door.

I opened it. "Richard? Is everything okay?"

He smiled warmly, but looked tired. "Yes, sweetheart. I'm good. Could I come in?"

I stepped aside. "Of course. Of course." I assumed he'd come to see Hollis. "Hollis is working late tonight. He's not home yet."

"I figured that. I just left him at his office."

My forehead wrinkled. "You went to see him at work?"

Richard nodded. "I had to drop off something."

"Oh. Okay."

He looked around. "Hollis's niece lives here with him, right?"

"Yes. She's in her room with a friend. Did you want to meet her?"

"No. No. I just hoped we could talk for a minute in private."

"Oh. Of course. Can I get you something to drink? Water or maybe wine?"

"I'd love a glass of water. From the tap is fine."

I walked to the kitchen and Richard followed. He took a seat at the counter where Hailey had been earlier. I filled a glass with ice and filtered water from the refrigerator door.

Passing it to him, I watched as he guzzled almost the entire glass and then made a loud *Ahhh* sound. "I miss New York City water. Damn Connecticut water doesn't taste the same."

I smiled. "Fewer rats in the sewer system. Connecticut's so fancy."

Richard reached around to his back pocket and took out an envelope. He put it on the counter in front of him. "Listen, sweetheart, I'm going to cut to the chase.

I know you're a straight shooter and don't like smoke blown up your ass."

"Okay… Thank you, I think."

"Bree wanted me to give this to you. She owes you some answers, and I think you'll find them in here." He pushed the envelope in front of him across the granite.

"She wrote me a letter?"

He nodded. "I don't have to tell you my daughter loved you like a sister. You're the one good decision that bum of a stepson I have ever made. His loss was my baby girl's gain. You were good for her soul, Elodie."

Tears welled in my eyes. "She was good for mine, too."

He lifted the glass and finished off the last of the water. "I'm going to get out of your hair. We don't need to slice open the fresh wounds that are only starting to heal. We'll do that at the lake house in a few months. I think we should get together on Bree's birthday in November, talk about all the good times. It'll be easier then."

I smiled. "I'd like that a lot."

He got up and walked to the door. As he opened it, he turned and looked me in the eyes. "Don't be mad at her. She meant well."

I had no idea what he meant. *Why would I be mad at Bree?*

Richard drew me into a bear hug and held me for a long time. Then he kissed the top of my head. "Love finds us all in different ways. It's not important how it happens. It only matters that it's real. Take care of yourself, sweetheart."

My hands shook. I didn't know why I was so nervous. The worst thing that could happen had already happened. But I knew in the pit of my stomach this was about Hollis and me. We were on such shaky ground already; I needed to brace for more impact. I picked the envelope up and put it back down three times.

Preparing myself, I decided to text Hollis so he would know what he was coming home to. There was a good chance I was going to be a wreck after reading this.

I picked up my phone and texted.

Elodie: Richard just came by. He dropped off a letter Bree wrote me.

I watched my phone, anxious as the message went from *Sent* to *Delivered* to *Read*. A return text came seconds later.

Hollis: He came by here today. I got one, too.

Richard *had* said he'd been to Hollis's work to drop off something. Of course, he had a letter, too.

CHAPTER
FORTY-SIX

Hollis

I poured two fingers of the scotch I kept in the office for special occasions, sat down on the couch, and opened the envelope. Just seeing her handwriting knocked the wind out of me, and I had to take a few deep, calming breaths. When that didn't do shit to steady me, I gulped back the contents of the glass in one giant swallow.

Let's get this over with.

Dear Hollis,

In eleventh grade, you said something that has stayed with me to this day. Your mom was back in the hospital. She was dehydrated from how sick the medicines had made her, and she'd gotten a horrible infection from the chemo port. She was in a lot of pain, and it killed you to see her like that. It killed me, too. I had to go home, and we stood in front of the hospital for a long time holding each other. You were crying, and you said,

"I wish I had the strength to make her believe
I don't need her—so she could let go."

You knew the constant fighting to hang
on was difficult and painful for her, but she'd
never stop because of you. Sometimes in life,
people need help letting go.

Since you're reading this letter, I'm gone
now. But you let me go before today, and
that's what I wanted. What you deserved. You
took care of your mother for so many years,
selflessly sacrificing your life to be by her
side. I couldn't let you do that for me, too. You
deserved so much more—to be free.

So I lied, Hollis. There was never any
other man. Three days before you proposed,
I was diagnosed with my illness. I'd been
trying to find a way to tell you, and in that
moment, when I looked at you down on one
knee, I realized what telling you would mean.

I knew I had a long battle ahead of me,
one that would inevitably end before I was
thirty. So I made a rash decision. I told you
I'd met someone else so you'd move on.

But over the years, I kept tabs on you,
and I realized you weren't really doing that.
So when I found out Hailey had moved in with
you, and then I miraculously stumbled upon
an ad for a nanny—an ad with the mailing
address of your firm—it was fate.

Elodie is an amazing woman, and
somehow I just knew you two would hit it

off, if I could get her to apply. Everything else happened on its own—the car accident where you met, you hiring her, the beautiful way you two fell in love.

I'm sure you're both confused right about now. I can't even imagine the moment when you figured out your Anna was Elodie's Bree. So I feel I owe you both an explanation, along with an apology.

I'm sorry I lied to you.

I'm sorry I lied to Elodie.

I'm sorry I made you think I didn't love you enough to be faithful.

I'm sorry I made you doubt your trust in women.

True love means wanting the best for someone, and for you, that didn't include me.

Take good care of yourself, Hollis. And take good care of my girl. You deserve each other.

Always,
Anna

It took me a full hour before I could even get up from the office couch. I read the letter over and over, fearing I'd missed something of importance. But the entire thing was important—every single word. It was the most *important* message I'd ever received in my life, so precious and sacred, never to be repeated, never to be clarified. This was it. Her final words.

The first read-through was certainly shocking. But the more I read it, the more everything clicked. For the first time since Anna walked out of my life, it all made sense.

When I arrived at my door that night, I paused before opening it. I knew Elodie had received a letter, too. I assumed she was in a similar predicament of confused emotions.

When I finally entered, I saw her sitting alone on the couch.

She got up fast and ran to me, taking me into her arms. The tension in my body dissipated as I allowed myself to be held by her without retreating. I'd resisted her far too much in the past several days. At the very least, we needed this right now.

We held each other for a long time before she finally let me go and said, "I can't believe it."

I let out a deep breath and nodded. "But it's the first time anything has ever made sense to me when it came to her. Even when I saw her lying there in the hospital, it never occurred to me that she could've known about her illness before she ended things with me all those years ago."

Elodie stared off. "I've been thinking back to some of the conversations she and I had when I was dating you. I don't understand how she could've endured listening to me go on and on. That took a lot of strength."

"Everything she did took strength. Handling the stuff about us was a drop in the bucket compared to surviving every day on this Earth knowing she was going to die young."

I closed my eyes. That got to me the most: the courage it took to live like that.

Elodie seemed more concerned about me than herself as she placed her hands around my face. "Are you going to be okay, Hollis?"

She didn't realize that even though this news was hard to grasp, it brought me comfort to know my lingering emotions over Anna all these years hadn't been in vain.

"Reading her letter was jarring, but it's brought me a strange sense of peace," I said. "I'd been so conflicted about whether she would've wanted me at her funeral, conflicted about why I was so devastated to lose someone who had apparently betrayed me. It's going to take a while for this to sink in, but I'm more okay today than I was yesterday, if that makes sense. I thought we'd never get answers, that we'd have to live with uncertainty forever. Now we know everything."

"Yeah." She sniffled. "We do."

We moved over to the couch, and Elodie rested her head on my chest. I wrapped my arm around her as we sat in silence. I didn't want her to leave tonight. I wanted to sleep next to her and bury myself inside her to forget about the pain of this day.

But I wanted those things to comfort *myself*.

I still didn't feel right about jumping back into things with Elodie until I was ready to give *her* everything she deserved. Just when I'd started to think I might be able to try again to pick up my life where it had left off, this new bomb had dropped. Even though it had brought me some peace, it also brought new emotions that had to be dealt with, namely grappling with the realization that Anna never stopped loving me. She'd died knowing I loved someone else. Despite the fact that she'd orchestrated that, I knew it had to be painful for her.

Hailey walked out into the living room. "Are you two okay?"

"Yeah, we're fine," I told her.

Her face said she knew that was bullshit.

"No more secrets, guys, remember?"

Elodie looked up at me and mouthed, "Can we tell her?"

I nodded.

"Sit down, Hailey," Elodie said.

She took a seat on the chair across from us.

Elodie sat up. "Today we both received letters from our friend Brianna."

"She wrote you from heaven?"

Elodie shook her head. "No. She wrote us before she died."

"Oh. What did she say?"

"She admitted something neither of us ever knew."

"What?"

I spoke before Elodie had to explain it. "Apparently, she found out about her illness just before she ended things with me all those years ago. And so the reason I believed we'd broken up all these years wasn't true."

"She lied?"

"It's complicated, but she didn't want me to have to suffer knowing she was sick and watching her die, the way I'd had to with my mother. So she pretended to choose to leave so I...wouldn't love her anymore."

Hailey looked down at the floor. "That's so sad."

"I know," I said. "It's a prime example of selflessness."

410

"What did she write to you, Elodie?"

"Well, she actually told us both something that's really pretty unbelievable. She was the one who set me up to apply for this job. She somehow knew it was your uncle's listing and planned the whole thing so I would meet him. She hoped we would fall for each other."

Hailey's eyes moved back and forth as she processed that information. "I always thought God sent you. But it was Anna? She's better than God."

Elodie smiled. "She's basically an angel, both while she was here and beyond."

"So if she wants you guys together, why are you so sad?" Hailey asked.

Elodie looked at me. That answer wasn't a simple one.

"I guess we're still trying to accept how hard it must've been for her," I said.

Hailey got up from her seat and gave me a hug, which was rare. "Thank you for telling me." Then she hugged Elodie, too.

Talking it out with Hailey had actually helped lessen the tension a bit.

Yet as much as I wanted Elodie to stay the night, I let her walk out the door—again.

CHAPTER FORTY-SEVEN

Hollis

In the weeks that followed, I did something I'd never done in my entire career: I took actual time off. The only thing was, no one knew about it—besides Addison.

I needed the time to myself, to think and let everything that had happened in the past month sink in.

So, I'd leave for "work" in the morning, letting Elodie think I was going to the office. Meanwhile, I'd wander the city, eating in various diners or buying meals for the homeless. One afternoon, I went to a Yankees game. Another day, I visited Anna's grave to give her a piece of my mind for ever believing it was better for me to spend those years without her. Then I bent down and kissed the gravestone, making sure she knew I understood the decision she ultimately made.

As I got to the end of my self-imposed hiatus, I found myself longing for Elodie more and more. Given that school had started again for Hailey, there was no reason Elodie couldn't have been by my side during this time off.

My last stop on Friday afternoon felt like the right place to end my "staycation."

When I entered the pediatric oncology unit of the hospital, I went straight to Sean's room. I'd been visiting him every day since I started playing hooky from work. So when I walked in today and his belongings were gone, the walls bare, I froze.

A woman came up behind me. "Can I help you?"

"Yes, I was looking for Sean."

"He changed rooms, but he's still here. He's meeting with his therapist right now. I'm his mother."

Relief washed over me. "Ah. I see."

I'd nearly had a heart attack thinking that something had happened to him; I couldn't take another goddamn loss.

She tilted her head. "And you are?"

"I'm Hollis...a friend of his."

"You're the guy who bought the video game console. Sean said someone close to you was in the hospital here, and you stop in every day to take a break and play some games with him."

"Yes. That's me."

"That's so nice of you."

"It's been my pleasure. Sean is a great kid."

"Would you like to sit for a bit? Why don't I grab us coffees?"

"Sure. That would be great."

"How do you take it?"

"Black."

"Okay. Be right back."

She disappeared for a couple of minutes, leaving me to sit alone in the common area outside Sean's old room. Someone wheeled a little kid with a shaved head past me. Being here always put things in perspective.

Sean's mother returned with two steaming coffees in Styrofoam cups.

I took one. "Thank you."

"I'm Kara, by the way."

"Nice to meet you. Do you live close by?"

"We rent an apartment around the corner from here to be closer to him. Our house is an hour away in New Jersey."

"I assume you're here every day?"

"Yes. In fact, next weekend will be the first time I won't see my son for a few days. My husband and I are going to Aruba to renew our wedding vows. We're doing it for Sean. He's too sick to go with us, but he insisted we take this trip."

"Is that right?"

"He said he was sick and tired of our depressing asses and wants us to go live life a little."

"*Depressing asses*. That's pretty funny."

"That's my son for ya. He said the only thing worse than being stuck here is watching *us* stuck here all the time as well. My husband and I don't leave his side for too long. But you know, I never saw things from his perspective until recently. He admitted that the worst part of being sick wasn't even the illness, but the burden he felt he was placing on us. Can you believe that?"

My thoughts immediately went to Anna.

"Yeah." I stared off. "I actually can."

"So...we're going away for Sean, renewing those vows and living it up for a weekend in Aruba. He'll be with us in spirit. And we're gonna take lots of photos and send them to him. That's the one thing he insisted on. He said, 'You'd better promise to take pictures, Mom and Dad. Don't go all the way to Aruba and not document it. Don't be dumb.'" She laughed.

I grinned. "He's an amazing kid."

"It took me a long time to agree to go. I didn't feel like I could go away and enjoy myself when he's so sick. But he said, 'Just because I'm sick doesn't mean you and Dad can't enjoy your life. Because if not, it's three people dying, not one. You can still laugh, Mom. You can still get dressed up and do all the things you used to do. Every day that passes where all you do is sit here and watch me really hurts, because it makes me feel like your life stopped for me.'"

Wow.

That hit close to home.

"Are you okay?" she asked, likely seeing the effect her words had on me.

"Yes. What he told you just really resonates with me."

I thought about all the things I'd be missing if I continued to endlessly mourn Anna. I wasn't guaranteed an infinite amount of time on this Earth myself. No one was. Elodie had been so patient with me. It was time to let myself feel all of the things my soul had been yearning to experience again. My brain had been the one putting a stop to it, and that needed to end.

"I'm more than okay, Kara—more okay than I have been in a long while. Because I'm pretty sure someone very special to me who recently passed away led me to this spot to hear you say what you just did."

Suddenly, I couldn't get to Elodie fast enough.

I stood up. "Thank you. Please tell Sean I'll be back to visit him soon. In fact, I'll come keep him company when you're away next weekend."

"I most certainly will. And that sounds great. He'll appreciate that."

The cool fall air hit me as I exited the hospital. It had been raining on the way in, but the sun was now peeking out. I looked up at the sky. There was a rainbow—a rarity over the city.

"Beautiful girl," I whispered. "There you are."

I weaved through the crowded streets with my eyes focused on the colorful beams of light. "I get the point now," I told her. "I heard you loud and clear. I'm gonna start doing this life justice in your honor and enjoying the gift you gave me—Elodie. And I promise to take lots of pictures."

CHAPTER FORTY-EIGHT

Elodie

I'd never cleaned so much in my life. Hollis's apartment was spotless because I'd been taking all my nervous energy out on it. It had been a couple of weeks since we'd received Bree's letters. I knew her intent was to bring us closer, to let us know we had her blessing. Yet for Hollis, it wasn't that simple. He still needed to come to terms with the fact that everything he'd thought he knew was a lie.

I'd been giving him as much space as I could, but it was frustrating. I missed him. I missed his touch. I missed his attention. Maybe that was selfish, but I did. I felt lonely and wanted him back.

But you can't force someone to get over something that's haunting them. They need to do it on their own terms.

Just because I understood his behavior, though, didn't mean I wasn't starting to lose patience. The one thing no amount of reflection or time could do was bring Bree back. So why not try to get *our lives* back?

417

The door burst open, and I nearly dropped the broom I'd been holding because it scared the shit out of me. Hollis wasn't due home for another couple of hours, and Hailey had gone to a friend's house after school for a sleepover.

"What are you doing home?"

"I am *finally* home." He was out of breath as he said, "I'm so sorry I've been stuck in my head for so long."

It was as if my Hollis had come out of a coma. He rushed to me and brought me into an embrace.

Thank you, God.

Speaking into his chest, I breathed him in and said, "You don't need to apologize."

"Yes, I do. You needed me, and I failed you." Hollis pressed his lips against mine, and my entire body came alive.

After he kissed me hard, he said, "I've missed you so much. I've just been afraid to admit it, afraid to feel things I perceived as selfish. Not to mention, I've been lying to you for two weeks."

My heart started to palpitate. *Lying?* "What do you mean?"

"I haven't been working in the office. I've been wandering the city, eating at every greasy spoon I could find—just doing nothing. I can't remember the last time I did that. I didn't want to tell you because I felt like I should've asked you to come with me. But I needed to be alone. I needed to not work and just...be."

Wow. "Where else did you go?"

"Lots of random places. A Yankees game, the park—I played video games with Sean at the hospital, and I visited Anna's grave. But I finally found the light at the end of the rainbow, so to speak. Today I went to the pediatric oncology ward, and it's a long story, but something important finally clicked while I was there."

"What was that?"

"It's okay to smile in the midst of darkness. It's okay to be happy—our loved ones want that. I'm not gonna feel sorry anymore for loving you, Elodie. I'm not gonna feel sorry for fucking you hard up against the wall tonight. I'm not gonna feel guilty for any of it."

Practically leaping into his arms, I wrapped my legs around him as we kissed. It felt incredible to be in Hollis's arms like this again.

"You're really back."

"And I'm not going anywhere ever again. I promise," he groaned. "I want so badly to slip inside you right now. But it was poor planning on my part. We need to leave."

"Now? Why?"

"Our ride is going to be here in a few minutes."

"Our ride? Are we going somewhere?"

"Yes."

"Why aren't we taking your car?"

"I think we need a change of pace for tonight."

I smiled. "Okay."

When we stepped outside, I was shocked to find a horse and carriage right out front. He remembered what I'd told him about my fantasy date.

"I promised you a ride in one of these a long time ago, before I botched that date night. I'm making up for it now. I'm making up for a lot of things."

Hollis took my hand and helped me in.

I leaned my head against him, and we enjoyed the ride while the sun began to set. The smell of the horses was quite...*robust.* But that didn't stop my bliss. Things were quiet aside from the sounds of traffic and hooves clicking against the concrete.

Hollis turned to me at one point and asked, "Elodie, can I have your attention?"

"Of course."

He swallowed, seeming nervous. "I don't want you to believe for a second that my being distant had anything to do with doubts about you. The love I had for Anna is different than the love I have for you. And the knowledge that she still loved me when she ended things all those years ago doesn't take away from how very much I love you."

"Thank you for clarifying that. Although I never felt like it was a competition."

He placed his hand on my chin and directed my eyes toward his. "My feelings for you are unprecedented, Elodie. I do love Anna, and I always will, but most of all, I love her for bringing me you. I don't want to waste a single day more contemplating the meaning of anything. I just want to be the man you deserve and show you every day how much you mean to me."

Those words would have been enough to last a lifetime, but then he stunned me by reaching into his pocket and taking out a ring box.

"What is that?" I covered my mouth. My heartbeat accelerated. "What are you doing?"

He opened it, displaying a massive diamond set between two smaller stones.

"I know this seems crazy—to go from being so withdrawn to this—but hear me out," he said.

Truly shocked, I placed my hand on my chest. "Oh my God, Hollis."

Is this really happening?

"Today when I was leaving the hospital, on my way home to you, I saw a rainbow. I believe it was Anna, her presence. I kept walking toward it until it finally disappeared. And the moment I couldn't see it anymore, I realized I was in front of a jewelry store. Was it a sign? I don't know. But here's the thing: I didn't care if it was a sign. I was looking for any excuse at that point to do what I've wanted to do from the moment we first got together. I don't want to waste any more time. I want to start a life with you, Elodie. I want to rub your feet while you watch Turkish soap operas I don't understand. I want to sleep next to you every night. I want to go all-in. This ring isn't about rushing out and getting married tomorrow. This is about my commitment to you, a reminder when you look down at it that my heart belongs to you, fully and wholly, and not to anyone else. I don't want you to ever question that again."

His hand trembled a bit. "So...will you marry me... someday...when you're ready?"

Tears sprang to my eyes as I nodded with great enthusiasm. "Yes! I will marry you...someday... tomorrow...or today. Whenever you want me."

Our lips smashed together, but the moment was interrupted when the carriage stopped short. The horses had nearly crashed into the back of a cab.

The driver shouted back at us, "Everything is okay! Near miss, but we're fine!"

"We're used to accidents," Hollis cracked. "In fact, that's how we met. She crashed into me."

"Actually..." I corrected. "He *backed* into me."

EPILOGUE

Hollis – 2 years later

There was a knock at the door. As Elodie went to answer it, I admired the jiggle of her ass.

"Are we expecting someone?" I asked.

"Not that I know of."

When she opened the door, a man stood there with a huge bouquet of flowers.

"Delivery for you, ma'am."

"Oh wow. Thank you."

After the door closed, she placed the flowers on the kitchen counter and read the note to herself. She laughed before handing me the card.

> *Elodie, you've come a long way. You went from trapping bad men to creating future good ones. Belated congratulations on your son.*
>
> *—Soren*

P.S. If you ever want to come back to work for me, I'd make a great babysitter.

"Fat chance of that ever happening, you dick." I laughed and tossed the note.

I could never imagine letting my wife go back to that line of work. I'd end up in jail.

"Well, that was very nice of him, anyway," she said.

Our three-month-old baby son lay on his stomach atop my chest. He stretched his little neck to see all around him. Ben—short for Benson, Anna's last name—had my brown hair and nose but Elodie's eyes. He was a true mix of us. I'd taken two weeks off to be with them, and today was the last day of my vacation. I wouldn't have minded spending every day with these two and not ever going back to work again. Gone were my workaholic days. Now I ran out of the office when the clock struck five most nights to get home to my family.

We still lived in the same apartment but had converted the guest room into a nursery. Not only were we adjusting to life with a newborn, we were now dealing with a teenager. Hailey still lived with us, and hopefully that would be the case forever. After my brother was released from prison, he disappeared. He'd written us a letter, though, shortly before his release, asking if we'd be willing to take Hailey indefinitely. I was totally relieved. I didn't want to have to fight him. And although she worried about her dad, Hailey was thrilled to live with us permanently.

Speaking of the devil, Hailey waltzed into the living room. My eyes widened when I got a look at what she was wearing—a cutoff shirt.

"Where do you think you're going dressed like that?"

"To the movies."

"With whom?"

"Kelsie."

Somehow, I was skeptical. "That's it?"

"And Evan."

"Evan?"

"Elodie knows."

I looked at my wife. "Care to explain?"

"I've met Evan and his mom. He's a nice kid." Elodie shrugged. "I told her she couldn't go alone with him, though. She had to bring Kelsie along."

This can't be starting already. "How old is he?"

"Fourteen," Hailey answered.

I thought back to the chronic masturbator I had been at that age and cringed.

"Go put on a different shirt," I ordered.

She huffed, but she returned to her room. It was a rarity that she didn't argue with me.

After Hailey left for the movies, Elodie and I continued hanging out with our son on the floor. He had one of those playmats with toys hanging from it, and he was now kicking his legs around. Both of us were concerned because the poor little guy hadn't pooped in days. We were on what we'd dubbed "poop watch." If he didn't go tonight, we planned to take him first thing in the morning to the pediatrician.

After about an hour of floor time, we noticed baby Ben got the look on his face that usually meant he was about to push something out.

"Oh my gosh! This might be it!" Elodie beamed.

Ben's face turned beet red, and it looked like his eyes were bugging out of his head. He grunted.

"It's happening," I said.

And then came the sound of the explosion.

Elodie picked him up off the floor and ran to the nursery to assess the situation.

Several seconds later, I heard her yell from down the hall. "Ben made the motherlode! The *motherlode!*"

I ran to the room and said, "Let me do the honors."

"No, I'm just so relieved he did it that I don't even mind changing it."

She handed me the dirty diaper, and I disposed of it in the pail.

Elodie got him changed and dressed in a clean sleeper. She handed him to me, and I lifted him up in the air as we danced around with him. This was what my life had come to—dancing in celebration of a bowel movement. I wouldn't have had it any other way.

We returned to the living room with our freshly changed son, who surely must have felt lighter after that.

Baaa. "Ben made the motherlode!"

"Did you hear that?"

Elodie walked over to the bird's cage. "Huey, what did you just say?"

He was silent.

Just when she'd given up and turned away, he squawked. *Baaa.* "Ben made the motherlode!"

"Oh, man." I laughed. "Are you serious?"

"You think it will stick?" she asked.

"Well, his last saying only lasted an entire decade."

I hoped Anna was looking down right now and laughing her ass off.

ACKNOWLEDGEMENTS

We are eternally grateful to all of the bloggers who enthusiastically spread the news about our books and persist even as it becomes harder and harder to be seen on social media. Thank you for all of your continued hard work and for helping to introduce us to readers who may otherwise never have heard of us.

To Julie – Thank you for always being one click away. We are so lucky to have your friendship, daily support, and encouragement.

To Luna – Our right hand woman. We know we can count on you for anything and appreciate your friendship and help so much.

To our agent, Kimberly Brower – We're so excited for the year ahead and are grateful that you will be there with us every step of the way. We are so lucky to call you a friend as well as an agent.

To Jessica – It's always a pleasure working with you as our editor. Thank you for cleaning up our manuscripts so nicely.

To Eda & Julie – Your eagle eyes and attention to detail is so appreciated. Thank you for helping make Hollis and Elodie the best that they could be.

To Elaine – An amazing editor, proofer, formatter, and friend. We so appreciate you!

To Letitia – Thank you for your patience with this one!

To Brooke – Thank you for organizing this release and for taking some of the load off of our endless to-do lists each day.

Last but not least, to our readers – We keep writing because of your hunger for our stories. We love surprising you and hope you enjoyed this book as much as we did writing it. Thank you as always for your enthusiasm, love and loyalty. We cherish you!

Much love,
Penelope and Vi

OTHER BOOKS BY
PENELOPE WARD &
VI KEELAND

ABOUT PENELOPE WARD

Penelope Ward is a *New York Times, USA Today* and *#1 Wall Street Journal* bestselling author.

She grew up in Boston with five older brothers and spent most of her twenties as a television news anchor. Penelope resides in Rhode Island with her husband, son and beautiful daughter with autism.

With over 1.5 million books sold, she is a twenty-time *New York Times* bestseller and the author of over twenty novels.

Penelope's books have been translated into over a dozen languages and can be found in bookstores around the world.

Subscribe to Penelope's newsletter here:
http://bit.ly/1X725rj

OTHER BOOKS BY PENELOPE WARD

The Day He Came Back
When August Ends
Love Online
Gentleman Nine
Drunk Dial
Mack Daddy
RoomHate
Stepbrother Dearest
Neighbor Dearest
Jaded and Tyed (A novelette)
Sins of Sevin
Jake Undone (Jake #1)
Jake Understood (Jake #2)
My Skylar
Gemini

ABOUT VI KEELAND

Vi Keeland is a #1 *New York Times*, #1 *Wall Street Journal*, and *USA Today* Bestselling author. With millions of books sold, her titles have appeared in over a hundred Bestseller lists and are currently translated in twenty-five languages. She resides in New York with her husband and their three children where she is living out her own happily ever after with the boy she met at age six.

OTHER BOOKS BY
VI KEELAND

All Grown Up
We Shouldn't
The Naked Truth
Sex, Not Love
Beautiful Mistake
EgoManiac
Bossman
The Baller
Left Behind (A Young Adult Novel)
First Thing I See

Life on Stage series (2 standalone books)
Beat
Throb

MMA Fighter series (3 standalone books)
Worth the Fight
Worth the Chance
Worth Forgiving

The Cole Series (2 book serial)
Belong to You
Made for You

Made in the USA
Monee, IL
26 May 2020